Also available from Lauren Dane and Carina Press

Second Chances
Believe

Goddess with a Blade

Goddess with a Blade
Blade To the Keep
Blade on the Hunt
At Blade's Edge
Wrath of the Goddess
Blood and Blade

Diablo Lake

Moonstruck
Protected

Cascadia Wolves

Reluctant Mate (prequel)
Pack Enforcer
Wolves' Triad
Wolf Unbound
Alpha's Challenge
Bonded Pair
Twice Bitten

de La Vega Cats

Trinity
Revelation
Beneath the Skin

DIABLO LAKE: AWAKENED

LAUREN DANE

carina
press

carina
press®

Recycling programs
for this product may
not exist in your area.

ISBN-13: 978-1-335-21595-6

Diablo Lake: Awakened

Carina Press
22 Adelaide St. West, 41st Floor
Toronto, Ontario M5H 4E3, Canada
www.CarinaPress.com

Printed in U.S.A.

This one is for the people who kept showing up.

DIABLO LAKE: AWAKENED

Chapter One

Ruby pushed her buggy down the produce aisle. She'd been so smug about avoiding the one with the rickety front wheel, but the one she'd chosen instead would randomly lurch to the right and Ruby had only narrowly avoided colliding with an end cap of canned green beans.

She came to a stop at the display of oranges, piled high. They were so brilliantly orange they nearly glowed. How she'd missed the produce grown in Diablo Lake! Nothing like it anywhere else. The magic in the soil created something truly special.

Happiness spread through her as she grabbed several, bringing them to her nose to take in the gorgeous scent.

Home.

Being back in the place she'd been born and raised had filled Ruby with a sense of purpose and rightness. The magic embraced her, filled her with pleasure and comfort.

The woman at her side, chattering like a dingdong, was one of her oldest and dearest friends, Aimee. "That last time I was pretty sure you were going to take out the potato chip pyramid. Not gonna lie, I'd have pretended not to know you. But I'd have laughed about it with you later."

Ruby snorted a laugh as she tucked oranges into one of the produce bags she'd brought along. "True friendship."

"Obviously." Aimee pointed at the muslin bag Ruby had just filled. "Hey! Those are so cute! Where did you get them?"

"I made them. They're super easy. I can show you if you want."

"You did?" Aimee asked, one brow rising.

Ruby nodded, grinning at her friend's disbelief. "Right? I wasn't the craftiest growing up other than candles and my tinctures. But I got talked into a sewing class. I'd been away from Diablo Lake six months and I had a lot of school but I needed to do something else. Something more creative and there I was, absolutely in love with this craft I'd sort of only perfunctorily engaged in for most of my life."

"Oooh, *perfunctorily*. Lookit you all smart and stuff." Aimee bumped her hip to Ruby's. "What's the coolest is how as a grown-up, you're as amazing as you were when you were a kid and a teenager. I love that you're into sewing now and I'm totally up for learning how to make those little sacks. Easy is my speed. You can show me at the next Sip, Stitch and Bitch night. I bet Katie Faith would want to know how too."

Every other week, they had a standing date to hang out, drink, do some sort of craft—obviously one safe to do while drinking—and watch reality shows while talking terrible shit about all the casts. In the years she'd been gone, Ruby had been envious of the time they'd set aside so she was very much excited to be part of them at last.

Ruby leaned over to hug Aimee quickly because that made her happy. "Damn I missed your silly ass."

Aimee grinned. "My silly ass missed you too."

The small town grocery store was busy as she and her friend did their shopping. Ruby had to pause every few feet to say hello and accept welcome back wishes from friends and neighbors she'd known all her life—and keep her buggy from maiming anyone.

"When I was seventeen and dreaming of life as an adult I honestly never considered making a date with a friend over grocery shopping," Aimee said as they perused the jars of spaghetti sauce. "Yet here I am on a Wednesday night because you and I are so busy it was this or wait a few more days to hang out."

"Adulting involves far more time being awake and doing things I'd rather not like clean toilets and pay bills than I ever imagined," Ruby said.

"The only real consolation is the sex and the freedom to eat peach cobbler for breakfast if and when you might want."

"You're a sage." Ruby snickered, thinking of the cherry pie she'd had after finishing her eggs that morning. And that she'd shared that pie with her mom as they stood at the kitchen counter and watched through the window as the dogs played in the yard. "But that's totally true." She grabbed a few cans of chickpeas to make hummus and some Greek olives to add to the pasta sauce she and her mom planned to put up over the weekend. There were so many tomatoes waiting to be made into salsa and pasta sauce she probably wouldn't

need to buy any until near time to can more the following year.

"I totally am. Mac says I'm a *chatterbox stuck on
shuffle* but I'm sure he just misunderstands what the
words mean. Maybe he didn't pay attention in his
classes at the London School of Economics." Aimee
waved a hand airily. "Clearly I'm fucking brilliant."

"I probably wouldn't challenge him at figuring out
percentages or gross national product and what have
you. But you *are* the brilliantest," Ruby agreed as they
turned the corner and headed into the bakery section.
Her favorite. The scent of fresh bread and all the best
carbs greeted her.

"Right? God I love bread so much," Aimee said as
she picked up a pretty French loaf with a leaf pattern
cut into the crust. "Ever since Merilee took over the
bakery here, I've probably eaten my weight in baked
goods. All is right in the world."

Merilee was a witch in town whose skills with bread
and pastry were very well known. Her magic hands
made crusts perfectly chewy and crisp, the cinnamon
seductive, and her cherry thumbprint cookies were so
good, Ruby's mom used to send her a box wherever
in the world she was living. A little bit of magic from
home.

"I wish there was a way to bottle this smell," Ruby
said, beginning to think on how she might actually
make that happen. A candle that scented a room like
fresh baked goods would be pretty cool. She grabbed a
few loaves knowing that her parents' kitchen was nearly
always full of hungry family and sandwiches made an
excellent snack.

She paused to look over the selection of breakfast

bars to check the ingredients lists. "I'm working on a recipe for these. I can make them fresh for half the price and never come across a raisin unless I put it there myself. And I never would."

"Chocolate is good for you. Don't forget to put some in the recipe," Aimee added.

"You have good ideas. A great reason to keep you around. Walnuts for sure since my dad is allergic to hazelnuts. In case you're not following along, I've switched topics. I promised a bunch of baked goods in payment for help moving when I find a place. I got off pretty easy I think. I didn't even attempt to pay anyone with actual money. No one wants an offended Anita Thorne."

"Goodness no." Aimee shuddered at the thought. Ruby's mom, Anita, was, pretty much like Aimee's mom, a force of nature. She didn't get where she was in her life without a lot of kicking down doors and demanding her due. She was one of Ruby's idols. A compass in a chaotic world.

"As for your way of floating around on the wind of a conversation?" Aimee waved a hand. "Please. You and Katie Faith both have that stream of consciousness thing. So since she was here when you were gone, I never fell out of practice following your sentences into new and exciting topics at a moment's notice. Like a roller coaster and I don't even need to stand in line."

Ruby snickered. "One of the things that made it easier when Nichole and Greg moved back here was knowing she'd have you and Katie Faith to keep her company until I got here."

Aimee bumped her hip to Ruby's. "Well, as much as we love her and she's definitely fitting in just fine,

I missed you too. You were out in the world doing important stuff and I was here. Katie Faith was away for years too and it was just me and Lara. And now she's off in Scotland for however many years." Their friend had gone to England and Scotland to see some family and had found love when her car had broken down and the tow driver was now her husband. Life had its own plans.

"And now the three of us are living within two miles of one another for the first time in six years. You're *mayor*! And you're getting married in two months. Katie Faith is happy and married and at Jace's side to lead the Dooley wolves. These are hopeful, powerful days."

Aimee breathed out slowly and then quickly hugged Ruby. "Oh my god, I needed to hear all that. There's so much happening and we really do need to catch up but in private because everyone here is listening and watching everything we're doing."

"That part of small town life I didn't miss that much. Come on. I promised I'd grab a few gallons of milk for my mom. I'll be sure to keep the bread up here in the purse holder thing. Nobody ever wanted smushed bread," Ruby said.

"Says you. I'd still eat it that way. I mean if it was necessary like after the apocalypse or smushed by a can of soup. It's still bread. Some things are worth lowering your standards for, Ruby."

Before she could stop snickering and reply, Aimee came to a sudden halt and Ruby only barely managed to swerve the recalcitrant buggy at the last minute to save her friend's ankles from dreaded grocery buggy injury.

"Yikes! I nearly maimed you," she said but Aimee's

attention was on the woman coming their way, lodging her cart catawampus so that they couldn't get around her.

"Perfect," Aimee said under her breath.

"There you are. I need you to tell my son to return my calls." Scarlett Pembry attempted to loom over Aimee but Aimee was an alpha too and didn't show her throat.

"You need to leave a message when you call," Aimee told her soon-to-be mother-in-law with patience that frayed at the edges.

Scarlett Pembry was a striking woman. Not exceptionally tall, but she had a big presence. Light brown hair, cut well to flatter the slightly heart shaped face. Always made up and dressed well and that day was no exception. If she hadn't been such a spiteful, mean person, she'd be beautiful.

Regardless of the fact that she was no longer in charge of the Pembry pack, Scarlett would always be an alpha wolf. A dangerous predator with decades of political experience under her belt. Ruby knew a threat when she saw one. And Scarlett Pembry was a threat.

"I don't have to leave a message! He can see his mother has called. It says so on his phone. That's all he needs to understand he should call me back. He's a very smart boy but sometimes he misses the details. That's *your* job." Scarlett jabbed a long pink fingernail at Aimee for emphasis.

"My actual job is mayor of the Township of Diablo Lake. And I also have a stake in the town medical practice. Nowhere in the job description for either is being Macrae's personal assistant. First, he's a grown man. And he's already got a personal assistant as you well know. You can contact him if you like. But leave a message so he knows what you need."

Scarlett's mouth flattened and her eyes narrowed. "Don't play games with me. You know what I mean. I surely don't need to be calling in outsiders to get my child to return a phone call."

At that point Ruby knew her features showed her shock but Scarlett didn't deserve the effort to hide it.

"He's your nephew. Hardly an outsider. He's eaten pancakes at your table on Sunday mornings for years of his life," Aimee said quietly of Everett, Mac's cousin who Ruby figured was his personal assistant or whatever the packs called that person.

Scarlett had the dignity not to argue that point. Everett was more than just a guy who kept Mac's calendar. He grew up at Mac's side as a guard as well, Ruby knew that much. She was really proud of Aimee for keeping her composure but setting her boundaries. It was very badass.

"Your generation might be keen on airing your family business to all and sundry for the drama of it, but mine knows how to act. Everett is my nephew, but *you* are Mac's soon-to-be wife. You will lead the pack at his side once you're married. It is your *duty*. I know there are those who doubt your ability to lead with Mac. Because you're not one of us." Scarlett paused, looking Aimee up and down, grabbing the cart to hold her in place. "But I'm not one of them. I tell them you're a powerful witch who has already begun to bring Pembry strength. I know you can do a good job. But you have to let go of your modern ways and remember this is Pembry. We don't act out like Dooley does. The wolves look to you to lead by example. You must be worthy of this place in the world, Aimee."

Ruby slid her gaze over to Aimee, whose eyebrows had risen up her forehead. *Oh no.* This was not going the way Ms. Pembry thought it was. "Worthy?" Aimee asked, scorn in her tone.

"Ma'am. What the ever-loving heck are you talking about?" Ruby didn't say a curse word because her grandmother would have lectured her for three hours about how she needed to know how to *act in public.* But no one attacked her friend like that.

Scarlett looked around and finally noticed Ruby. "Oh. You." Scarlett's lip curled ever so slightly that Ruby hated her for it while also admiring the skill. "Why are you eavesdropping? This is not your business."

"*Eavesdropping?* You're in the grocery store at six thirty on a Wednesday night. Pretty much half the town is here listening to *you* air your business on aisle five," Ruby said. "If you don't want your private business aired out, you're in control of that."

"Be on your way," Scarlett hissed, waving her hand at Ruby.

At her side Aimee actually guffawed. "We're on a date so it's us who'll be on our way to the checkout line. Call your son, who is a *grown-up.* If he doesn't answer, leave him a message and tell him what you need after the beep. I'm not part of this in any way, nor will I be. I've made my stance clear about the Rule of Silence but the rest is up to the wolves. As you know." She pulled her cart free and they strolled past.

Ruby wasn't going to discuss any of what just happened with Aimee. Not while they were in the store with everyone watching. And they were watching and barely pretending not to. But there was clearly more to the story than she knew. So she'd make small talk until they could get out of there and speak in private.

"You should contact Damon. He and Major do most of the real estate stuff around here so he'd know what's available to rent and would have access. And you already know him so that's a plus." Aimee smirked but did not mention Ruby's knowledge included exactly four dates and some of the best kisses she'd ever shared in the short time they'd dated six years prior, right before she left Diablo Lake.

"Apparently you're still a shit stirrer," Ruby murmured.

Aimee laughed aloud at that and Ruby was glad she'd said it. She knew her friend had to be under an intense amount of pressure from all directions. Marrying the person you loved was wonderful. If you were fortunate enough to get good in-laws that was even better. But when you were getting some really bad ones, well that had to be a real damper on happiness.

It made Ruby even more protective of Aimee.

"I plan to give him a call to set up an appointment." It wasn't like they broke up and hated one another and as Aimee had said, Damon was the source of the service she needed and there was no reason not to contact him.

Chances were he'd still smell really good, look even better and that slow Southern drawl wouldn't fail to make her a little tingly. And she wasn't going to lie to herself. She wanted to show him what he'd been missing all those years.

Aimee said nothing but the smirk remained in place.

Once they got to the parking lot after checkout, Ruby paused at Aimee's car.

"Thank you for defending me like that. Oh god her face." Aimee hugged Ruby tight. "She's being a pest right now about wedding stuff. More than usual. And there's the Rule of Silence stuff that she's getting everyone worked up over." She looked down at her watch. "I can't talk more right now as I'm due to meet Mac in less than an hour for wedding stuff and I need to drop the groceries home first. I'll text you later. Love you."

"Love you too."

The news about that little scene in the market meant Ruby had to get home—her parents' house—to let them know what happened before the first phone call or text happened. There weren't many secrets in a town as isolated and small as Diablo Lake. Mainly because the gossip network was lightning fast.

Hell, the wolves had decided to claim it was part of being a wolf shifter to be bold and nosy as you please. It worked because they were generally harmless and tended to be charming too, which eased the nosiness. Usually.

As she drove away from town, she cranked the window down, her music up and let herself just be as the scents of her hometown flowed into the car.

Fall crept in through the bite in the air and the first burst of orange and gold had begun to dress the trees. Soon signs of the biggest holidays of the year would show up in town. First Halloween, then Samhain and Collins Hill Days. Which launched into Thanksgiving, and all the winter holidays. Her absolute favorite season and she was home for good, making the difference she'd spent years dreaming of and working toward.

She'd venture back out into the world again. Travel to get more training. Travel because she loved it. But not much could compete with the magic of Diablo Lake all dressed up for some shindig or other. No, this was home in a way she understood would not be true of any other place. She'd always return.

Nothing compared with the way she felt as she saw the lights burning inside the house she'd grown up in casting a glow on the spot Ruby parked her car. She faced the shed where her dad stored all the lawn junk in the shadow of a huge, gnarled oak that still held the swing she and countless other kids had played on.

Her dad had taught her how to ride a bike on the sidewalk out front. She'd learned to drive on their slow poke street. And now Nichole and Greg's car was there, parked in front of the garage their apartment was above. Her mom's youngest sister Ruby's aunt Rehema's Jeep was in front of the main house.

So many of her favorite people all in one place.

Before she went into the house though, she called Damon to leave a message about wanting his help, but he answered instead.

"Ruby Jean Thorne," he said. "What can I do for you?"

She couldn't help the smile at the sound of his voice and then naturally the tingles came right along. It was a great voice.

"Hey, Damon. I'm back in Diablo Lake now and I need a place to live. I hear you're the person to call. Do you have any time to show me what's available? House or apartment, though I prefer a house."

"I heard you were back. And I was glad to hear it. Yep, I've got some rentals available to look at. A few you'd have to wait a month or so to move into, most of them you'd be able to get within a few days at the longest. If you've got about ninety minutes I can show them all to you."

"That would be perfect. Thank you."

"How about tomorrow? Two or three? We get afternoon help at the Mercantile so I'll have the time then."

"Three works well. I'll be at the clinic. We're nearly ready to open up but there are last-minute details to finish. I can meet you at the Mercantile."

"I'll pick you up at the clinic. I'm nosy," he admitted. "I want to check it out."

Nosy, he most definitely was. She laughed and he joined her. That rhythm they'd had before seemed to *click* back into place. "Fine. I'll see you tomorrow at three."

Grinning, Damon updated his calendar before stepping back into what was three quarters of a laundry room. Pretty much every night after closing up the Mercantile, he headed up to the house he was building to work on it.

Winter was coming and he really wasn't relishing the idea of living in that trailer once it started snowing so he wanted to get enough finished that he could move in and complete the rest into the spring.

And then on to getting Major's house finished. Damon and his twin had bought the land over the summer and while Major was still working on his house plans, Damon had been ready to go first.

Major had been helping finish off the framing of the mudroom slash laundry room that would lead from the back of the house into the main living area. As dirty as he could get either working or running as wolf, he needed a place to dump his dirty stuff so he didn't bring it in.

"You sure took your time," Major groused without any real heat. He just wanted to complain.

"That's why it's my time. I do with it what I want."

His brother said some stuff their grandmother would have cut a peach tree switch over, but he just laughed and flipped Major off.

"I've got an appointment tomorrow afternoon at three. I'm showing Ruby Thorne some properties. She's looking to move out of her parents' house."

Major snorted. "I've seen her around town over the last two weeks. She's looking real good."

Damon had thought very much the same thing when he'd seen her across the street just a few days prior. But while it was okay when *he* thought so, Major didn't have those rights. When he came back to himself, Major stared at him, one brow raised.

"Interestin'. Just what are you up to?" Major didn't meet Damon's gaze straight on, instead focusing just to the left. Avoiding a fight.

How quickly had he shifted into that space where his wolf rose to a perceived challenge over Ruby? Damon shook his head and held up a hand, palm open. "That was unexpected. I apologize."

Major nodded and then rolled his eyes. "Apologize for what? Being a wolf shifter? Fuck off. You two had chemistry back then, seems only right you'd have it now." His brother went back to work without saying another thing.

Damon remembered having a very similar moment with his oldest brother, Jace, back when Jace and Katie Faith had first come together again. She'd been away from Diablo Lake for a few years and had returned home, all grown up. Just like Ruby had.

The similarities bore some thinking on, so he figured there was no harm in thinking while working.

Ruby heard laughter before she'd even reached the steps leading up to the back door. Her dogs, Kenneth the Magnificent and Biscuit, ran around in the large yard just outside the kitchen along with her parents' dog, Pipes—so named because she had no problem using hers to bark and yodel any time she felt a need.

"Hey there, babies," Ruby called out and they all three turned and galloped her way. Pipes was a leftover casserole of a rescue. Probably some Lab and maybe a German shepherd. A collie perhaps. Whatever she was, she was on the large side of a medium-sized dog with blue eyes and splotches of white and dark brown on her fur. She yodeled and crooned and barked and talked back and fit into their family just fine. She also kept an eye on the boys, busy, curious little Cairn terriers, like a responsible older sister.

After Ruby gave pets and compliments about general goodness and beauty, they all headed up into the house.

A chorus of hellos greeted her when she got into the kitchen. "There are some groceries in my backseat," she told her brother Greg. "Can you please bring them in?"

"Sure thing," he said, pausing to kiss her cheek on his way past.

Nichole rolled into the room with a big smile. "Hey there, gorgeous."

There were lots of hugs and smooches and the like once Ruby put her things in her old bedroom and changed into a far more comfortable outfit.

They ran things from the kitchen to the table, adding a few more settings as two more cousins showed up. But before long, they were all seated at the big, scarred wooden table in the dining room, passing around platters of food as a pleasant murmur of conversation settled in.

"Before the phone calls start, I need to tell y'all about what happened at the grocery store tonight," she said after the edge of hunger had been taken off.

Her mother put her fork down and clasped her hands, waiting.

"It's not a big deal," Ruby hastened to add before anyone got worried. She told them all about the scene at the grocery store and her mom rolled her eyes.

"That woman. She just can't help herself. It's like she's got a compulsion to embarrass her momma every chance she gets." Anita Thorne waved a hand. "I'm glad you spoke up and let her know you weren't the one. I'll be sure to underline that with a look if I see her around town." Her mother made a sound, like a hum, but with threat. Scarlett better run the other way if she caught sight of Anita.

Ruby hoped so because she didn't have the time or inclination to play clownish games with Scarlett Pembry. And if Scarlett started something with Anita, well, it'd be a whole different sort of problem.

"And I have an appointment tomorrow afternoon with Damon Dooley. He's gonna show me available rentals in town."

Her mother's dark look regarding Scarlett washed away, replaced with an arch smile at Ruby. "You make sure you like the feel of whatever place. You understand? You don't need to rush. It's important to feel right in your home. And I know you. You're going to need a big garden space. We're in no hurry to have you leave though. So don't choose some dark little place in a terrible neighborhood."

Ruby couldn't help but laugh at that. "Bad neighborhood? Oh that one with the house with the curtains drawn all the time?"

"I still say that's suspicious," her mom replied, setting off another wave of laughter. "What are they hiding?"

"Or, they're all freaked out by that witch in the thirty-year-old Buick who keeps driving by trying to peek in their front window," Ruby teased. "Ow!" She drew back the hand her mom had just whacked with the back of her spoon, trying not to laugh anymore. "Okay! I promise not to move into some dark little hovel in any bad neighborhood that may or may not exist. I can't live here forever, Mom. I do really appreciate being here until I find the right place though. And I'll most definitely use all the offers of help to move when it's time."

Her mom's mouth flattened into a line but it was really more a matter of her trying not to smile at being ribbed by her children.

"You didn't get all sad like this when I moved away," Greg said, grinning.

"Well. You brought back Nichole. So that saved me from being too sad about it."

Ruby snickered. "She likes me best," she told her brother in an exaggerated stage whisper. "But your wife is a close second."

Greg tapped the side of his nose, their childhood shorthand for a middle finger and wow, Ruby was simply joyous at having this back in her life regularly.

"Stop hogging the potatoes," she told her brother.

Chapter Two

"Pulsating pepperoni."

Peals of laughter rang through the air.

"Baloney pony."

"Oh! Pepperoni pony!"

"I'm not entirely sure where the relation to pony is and I'm a little wary about it."

Damon Dooley stood just outside the doorway of the soon to be opened Diablo Lake medical clinic and listened to his sister-in-law rattle off dirty names for dicks with her friends like that was what everyone did on a Tuesday afternoon.

And the second voice was Ruby's. The absolutely gorgeous witch he was about to show rental properties to. He shifted forward enough to see the room—and the women inside it—better.

"Pony, like you know, something you ride. You're a twisted hussy, Ruby. I always did admire that about you." That voice belonged to Aimee Benton, the new mayor.

They laughed again, their magic rising all around the room. A bar of autumn sunshine glinted around Ruby, her magic dancing in the air like dust motes. Damon—both man and wolf—was struck still at the sight.

"Snausage," Nichole, Ruby's sister-in-law, suggested.

Ruby's face screwed up. "Ew! No! My mom buys those for the dogs. Anyway, they're not very big and they make the boys fart really bad."

"Point taken," Aimee said. "I don't rightly recall if we decided on a meat theme, but I think it's always more festive to have a theme."

"You would. Because you're odd. I mean, the whole town knows it but just know I love you anyway." Katie Faith sighed exaggeratedly.

Ruby choked back a snicker. "Oh hush. *I* think a theme is wonderful. Like superheroes or puppies and whatnot. Only jauntier." More laughter. "What kind of person doesn't like jaunty things, Katie Faith?"

"A monster, that's what kind," Aimee said.

"Staff of love," Katie Faith offered after an eye roll at her friends.

"Weak."

"Was not! That was *old-school*. Vintage is very in fashion, you know." Katie Faith rolled her eyes when the other women just stared at her. "Fine. How about turgid torpedo?"

"Oh!" Ruby clapped. "Extra point for the use of turgid. Very traditional and old-school."

"If we're going back to old-school, how about tallywhacker?" Aimee asked. "That's one my Nan uses."

"Mine says pecker. Not very poetical or anything." Nichole sounded sad about that.

"There's something to be said for simplicity though," Ruby told her. "Maybe spice it up like. So purple-cloaked pecker."

In unison, the others made gagging sounds. "No.

That's just well, it conjures up some scary stuff," Katie Faith said.

"You know purple-helmeted love lance or what have you. Also, a cloak is very fashionable. I have several myself," Ruby said, one brow up.

Aimee put up a finger. "Peckers or capes?"

Ruby snickered. "Guess."

"Oh I know! Spear of destiny." Katie Faith nodded decisively.

"Isn't that something biblical? Because my mother will whip my ass if I'm over here making fun of penises with biblical references," Ruby said.

Though he was thoroughly enjoying sneaking a peek at the secret world of women, Damon couldn't stop the snicker of amusement from escaping his lips. Giving himself away. Ah well.

As a group, the four witches turned to catch sight of him standing there. That's when the *zing* rebounded between him and Ruby Thorne and he had to tighten his hand on the doorjamb to keep his knees from buckling.

One corner of her mouth rose and his watered because he *knew* what she tasted like. And until right then, he'd forgotten just how much he'd missed his lips on hers.

And now she was home and they were both six years older and wiser. He sure hoped he was because a woman like the one he currently stared at deserved that.

"Well, hey there, Damon Dooley," Ruby said, the smile taking over her entire face as she approached him.

She'd been pretty six years ago, but she was luminous now, her magic around her shoulders like a mantle. He wanted to roll around in her, coat himself in her.

Damon reined it in, assuring the wolf they'd get to that point but it was important to wait for the right time.

Rather than a handshake, Damon opened his arms, waiting a beat to be sure she had the chance to stop her trajectory. Thank the lord above, she came right into his hug, her body fitting just perfect against his.

Her magic washed over him. Roses and jasmine. Warm and lush and so fucking good he forced himself to step back before he buried his face in all those gorgeous dark curls and took a whiff.

His wolf stretched just beneath the skin, claws carefully unsheathed as if to say, *yes.* And the man agreed.

"Hey yourself, Ruby darlin'. You look great. I mean, the place looks great. Too," he said, blushing and wondering why he was so nervous. He was good at charming women! And he had a history with this one.

But she was just…*so much.* Ruby had always been confident but this woman before him had grown from confidence to magnificence in a deep red sweater and black pants that looked like leather but weren't. The sky-high heels on the boots completed the look and sent his pulse racing. Sexy. Gorgeous.

Katie Faith looked at him over Ruby's shoulder, a smirk on her face. Clearly he was telegraphing just how much she was affecting him all over his features. Damn it, he'd never hear the end of this.

He rubbed the back of his neck, ducking his head a moment but when he looked up once more, Ruby's smile brought his own in answer.

"It's really coming together, thanks," she said. "At this rate, we can start seeing patients here next week. I really appreciate you making time to show me places today."

You lived in a secret town in the middle of nowhere and you took as many jobs as you needed to pay the bills. Damon and his twin, Major, were the more or less official real estate agents for all of Diablo Lake so it fell to him to show vacancies for rent and for purchase on the several times a year the issue came up.

He sure as shit made sure to be available the soonest possible to help out an old friend. Ex-girlfriend. Both. Whatever.

Sometimes he was way smarter than he remembered.

"You ready to go or do you need a few more minutes?"

"Just let me grab my bag and jacket." She hurried off as he watched, Rubystruck.

"Wow."

Damon stifled back a growl of annoyance toward his sister-in-law at the remark.

"I heard that growl," Katie Faith said, laughter in her voice. "And before you say a word, remember how you tortured Jace when he and I were first dancing around one another."

He had to withhold an eye roll because she was right. He and Major messed with their older brother on a regular basis but especially when he'd been wooing Katie Faith.

"No matter what I say I'll get in trouble, so I just won't say a damned thing at all," he told her.

They just laughed at him. So pretty and talented and they laughed. Hmpf.

When Ruby came back, he forgot about his annoyance altogether. "Let me help you with that." He held out a hand for her jacket, which she allowed him to help her into. The backs of his fingers brushed against the skin of her neck, sending a shiver through them both.

"See y'all later," Ruby called out. "Tell Greg I'll bring him back those baking sheets later tonight or he can get them from Mom," she said to Nichole.

"Good luck. I hope you find the perfect place that's super close to me," Aimee said.

"I'm living with my parents right now. The perfect place is relative compared to that," Ruby muttered as he opened the passenger door of his truck for her.

"I bet."

As he walked back around to the driver's side, Damon thought about the time of day and the light and mentally rearranged the order of properties he was going to show her. He had one in mind, but he wanted to take her when the light was just perfect.

Ruby tried to fall back on the calming breathing she'd learned over the years. Damon Dooley set her all aquiver. Her entire system zinged as her magic reacted to his shifter magic, wanting to caress it, give it love and attention.

It wasn't like he was a stranger! Back six years ago when she'd been finishing up all the prerequisites she'd needed to go to nursing school they'd dated. Four times. Ruby had liked him a great deal and it'd felt mutual, but he'd broken things off. Said they both had growing up to do and she was leaving. It hadn't been fraught in any way. She'd moved away and when she'd come back for visits at the holidays, she'd waved a hello and they'd chatted here and there.

She'd grown up out there and gotten her education and in the end it had been absolutely the right thing to do. Even if it had been sad for a while after it first happened.

He'd gotten even more handsome as he'd aged, growing into a man's body. He'd reached six feet with broad shoulders. His hair was a little longer than it'd been the last time she'd taken notice of him, but she had no complaints about that. He looked *good* and smelled even better. There was something very sensual and sexy about a man who smelled good.

Of course, it was the way his forearms looked with his hands on the wheel that set more than her heart aflutter. Sun-kissed skin, taut over muscle. The right amount of hair too. She kept her happy sigh in her head because she had a task to take up his time with right then and that was real estate related instead of carnal.

Regardless, his presence had awakened something inside her in a different way than she'd ever experienced before. It was really fun. And a little scary.

"You said on the phone that you preferred a house, but you'd be okay looking at apartments. You still feel that way?" he asked.

"Well, how many places do you have to show me if you show me houses and apartments? Not like Diablo Lake has a huge inventory of empty housing."

He snorted as he pulled away from the curb and headed down Diablo Lake Ave. "That's surely true. You said two bedrooms and one bath at least, washer and dryer, good-sized kitchen and takes dogs." He frowned and she snorted a laugh. Shifters and their weird feelings about dogs as pets.

"Yep. I do most of my work in the kitchen. All my tonics, tinctures and other spellwork. I need a big sink, plenty of counter space. Light is good. And space to garden." As a green witch, a great deal of her talent came from the earth and the things that grew from it. She had more than just a green thumb. She had a natural gift with green things. Enough so that even in a family full of green witches, she was legendary already.

"There's a two-bedroom apartment above the Mercantile. Katie Faith says you should feel free to plant as big a garden as you want out back. Major is living up there in another unit so it's plenty safe." Damon snorted, Ruby figured at the very idea of anyone trying to break in with an alpha wolf shifter on the premises.

"It's also on Dooley land." She withheld an eye roll.

He chuckled as he pulled into a spot behind the Mercantile. "It sure is. You wanna see anything on Pembry land? There's a one-bedroom out on Poplar. The carriage house they call it. Has a yard shared with the main house. Scarlett Pembry'd be one of your neighbors."

Ruby didn't bother to stop her lip curl. "Ew. No thanks. I can't imagine how hard it's going to be for you to offload that one."

He chuckled as he got out and then led her to a big green space between the Mercantile and the Dooley pack house where Jace and Katie Faith lived. "That's where you could garden. Great light over here. You can also bring the dogs out this way to do their business."

She used to live in an upstairs apartment and having to take the boys out had been a pain on cold days or when she was tired. Plus the garden space was big but there wasn't a fence and so she'd have to be more watchful with them outside.

Ruby followed him up the stairs to a short hallway at the top and into the apartment he'd told her Katie Faith used to live in. It was bright and roomy enough. But having to take the dogs out down the steps at all hours and the relatively small kitchen had her asking to see the next place.

There were two other houses, both would have done fine. But none of them had really felt like home.

As they left the three-bedroom two-bath—it had no windows in the kitchen—and headed to his truck, Huston Pembry, one of Mac's right-hand wolves, waved from a few yards over.

"Hey, y'all. What's happening?" he called out.

"Huston! Looking good," Ruby replied with a wave of her own. "Damon's showing me some possible rentals. How's the neighborhood?"

At her side, Damon's sigh was annoyed and yet she was charmed. Wolves and all their posturing, good lord.

"Quiet. Always in need of a pretty green witch, just so you know."

"Aren't you the sweetest?" Ruby laughed.

"How often would she expect to see Scarlett trying to run one of y'all down to tell you her feelings about the sacred traditions of wolf packs and the Rule of Silence?" Damon grumbled.

Huston's surprised guffaw told Ruby Damon and the other wolf were easy with one another. Most likely friends.

"I can't rightly say. I pretend I'm not home if she knocks on my door," Huston teased but then got serious. "You and the rest of Dooley know Mac and the majority of Pembry leadership support ending those rules. She'll wear herself out flinging herself at folks and all the wolves can step into at least the last century."

"Can't she fling herself off a cliff or something instead? Or into another state? The ocean?" Damon winked and they all shared a laugh.

Once they'd left, Ruby said, "I like the way you underlined something about Scarlett but then joked. There was tension and then you eased it. Like a grown-up."

Damon grunted but kept his eyes on the road. "I've put a lot of time and effort into being a good leader. I want Dooley wolves to know they can rely on me and my brothers to get us through the rough times and into better days."

There was pride in his tone certainly. But a little bit of defensiveness. And that made her sad. Because she guessed at several of the reasons why. What she didn't hear though, was apology and that satisfied her deeply.

"Huston has sense," Damon continued. "He, Mac and Everett are a solid team. I like 'em more often than I want to hit them in the face." He shrugged.

She didn't bother stifling her snicker. "Y'all wolves have an entirely unique perspective on punching one another. But I get your point."

"Nice when your job is something you're good at and enjoy," he said, deadpan. "Sometimes it takes a joke. Sometimes it takes a pop to the nose. I'm working on knowing which is which."

"That's fair. Just wanted to say I noticed."

"You don't want to live there, do you? Next to Huston?" he asked, his opinion of that choice very clear in his tone.

That made her chuckle some more. "Well, I certainly can appreciate a neighborhood that loves a green witch. But the kitchen was small and dark. I spend so much time in there. It's my main work space inside a house. So probably not."

"One more place. I think you might like this one," was all he said.

And then, he drove around a curve on a little road with the trees not too far off and the scent of the river on the breeze. There it was, a little pale blue house on a nice plot of land, so fertile it seemed to lodge right in her belly.

When he pulled to a stop in the driveway, she was out the door before he'd even taken the keys from the ignition.

"Oh," she breathed out as she let the magic guide her through the yard. Fall had settled in, so the air had woodsmoke salting it, leaves on the trees in the forest nearby were already turning brilliant yellow, orange and red, and the ground beneath would be a carpet of color in a few weeks.

The little house sat surrounded by a generous front yard but the back leading to the trees and the river beyond was simply spectacular. The light was perfect for the gardens she was already busily planting in her imagination.

Roses would cover the sides of the house once she added trellises. There were already fruit trees, slumbering a little bit inside, Ruby felt their attention, as if they'd wake up quickly once a witch lived in that little house.

Her boys would love the yard. So much room for them to run and bark and play while she got her hands in the dirt. There were plenty of birds to chase and talk to.

And though the place was just at the edge of Dooley territory, that didn't matter to the heart of Diablo Lake's magic. Here it welcomed her, leaped eagerly, playfully. This would be a good place to work. Yes.

If the inside was anywhere as amazing as the yard, Ruby figured she'd found home.

* * *

Damon grinned to himself as he followed in her wake, terribly pleased with himself for holding this place until the time was just right to appeal to a pretty kitchen witch.

She walked through the yard behind the house and he swore it seemed as if all the flowers seemed to perk up, deepen in color and scent. He watched as the particular beauty of the place worked its own magic on her.

Damon understood that deeply. He too loved the whisper of the wind through the leaves, the birdsong, the scent of riverbanks and pine and clean mountain air.

Ruby turned back, a smile on her face he felt to his toes.

"This yard is perfect. I do worry that it's a little close to the tree line and hungry predators who'd make a snack of my boys. They don't remember that they're small. Do you think the landlord would be okay with me putting up a fence? Nothing huge. Just a boundary to keep them safe."

Boys? She probably meant her dogs. He'd have to give an order that all pack leave her canines alone. They wouldn't normally harm a pet anyway but it never hurt to underline that.

"It's safe to say yes, he'd be fine with that. Want to see the inside?"

"Yes!" She nearly clapped and Damon had to swallow back a laugh, so infectious was her joy.

He led her in through the back door, choosing it because it fed into the kitchen. Quiet, but with pleasure on her features, Ruby walked through the space, touching the counters, opening cabinet doors to peek inside.

Damon stood back as she wandered past him and into the living room. "A big couch and a few chairs will fit in here easy. TV hookup on that far wall. Fireplace works and there's already seasoned, split wood out on the covered rack next to the shed. Uh, lots of natural light too." He was very glad he'd spent the hours replacing the old windows.

Ruby looked out over the front and side yard. "Excellent view too. It's very quiet. How close is the nearest neighbor?" she asked as she headed down the short hall and to the right.

"Uh. Well that's me. I'm building a house but living in a trailer on-site. You won't be able to hear me mostly. Construction work, the loud stuff anyway, is over by nine thirty."

She turned, a grin on her mouth. "You're the landlord, aren't you?"

"Okay. So Major and I bought land a few years ago. We've each been saving to build houses since. This house and the half an acre it's on came up for sale a month ago so I snapped it up. I figured I'd rent it out. Help pay for construction costs and the like. It didn't take me that long to get it ready to go as it had been kept up well over the years. Paint. New windows. Floors are original. Is that…are you weirded out by that?" Aw fuck, if she was, he totally messed up.

"Huh? No. It's such a pretty piece of land. I love it. So much natural magic." Ruby tsked at the size of the closet but sighed happily as she checked the view.

Why he felt so…bashful and hopeful and proud was uncomfortable and sort of thrilling.

Ruby absolutely loved the house. The second bedroom was a little smaller but the closet was larger and it had a window seat so she knew she'd choose that one to make hers. There was just so much possibility ready to unfold.

The ground outside had awoken the moment she left the car. Her magic was exhilarated and the idea of this little piece of the world being a safe and healthy space to live and grow had dug roots into her heart.

It felt right. And important.

He told her what the rent was and she scowled. "No way. I know that's under market by at least two hundred bucks a month. It's really nice that you're giving me a break, but I don't want to take advantage of our friendship."

"Way I see it, Ruby darlin', having a witch on my property will bring flowers and bees and then honey and all sorts of good-smelling things that wolves like."

Ruby darlin'? Oooh, yeah, she liked that.

God. He was just so damned sexy and he owned this land that was like the sweetest treat she'd ever happened upon. It was…*he* was irresistible.

"Sure. And because of that, I'll happily accept a *modest* discount. But this isn't a modest discount. You're building a house. I know that costs money. Yes, I'm awesome. But let's come to a deal here that's fair."

They were friends and because Diablo Lake was a place where you traded on favors and goods as a healthy part of the economy, Ruby did know she added value simply by making a home on Dooley land. Because she was a green witch, things would grow. Also, her presence would strengthen Katie Faith who now ran Dooley along with her husband, Jace. Through her, the pack.

It wasn't that she didn't know her worth, it was that she knew the worth of what was fair.

He hemmed and hawed until she just gave him a

number she thought was closer to market value. "Come on. Wolves love money! I'll let you lug firewood into the house for me and you have to make sure the rest of the Dooleys can't eat my dogs, but I won't move in here unless the terms are just."

He laughed. "Okay. I think I can do that. I can also help with a fence when you're ready to put one up. Major and I just finished a fencing job a few weeks back, so we even have some leftover materials."

Maybe he'd build without a shirt on. That would be a nice thing. She'd have to invite Nichole over if that was the case.

"If you're not uncomfortable having some woman you dated a few times as your tenant, I don't want to look at anything else. This is a perfect option for me. My grandparents are about a mile to the west. I can walk there, which would be really nice." But not so close her Lovie would be popping in at all hours. Unless she wanted to. And in that case, Ruby would open the door, invite her in and make her a cup of tea.

"Stop it now, Ruby. If I was uncomfortable, I wouldn't have brought you here. And you're not *some woman*." He ducked his head and the late-afternoon sun glinted against the caramel strands in his dark brown hair.

She was glad they'd still had a connection because if nothing else, Ruby liked to keep her friends when they were worth keeping.

And so okay, he was super sexy and they had a zing. Zing was awesome and it had been a while since she'd had it with someone.

"When can I move in? I assume you'll want a deposit and all that and the extra for the fence."

Chapter Three

Ruby wasn't surprised at all to find her father sharing a peanut butter sandwich with the boys when she went home at the end of a very long day. Kenny the Magnificent, better known as K Mags, barked a hello and hopped down from his place in her dad's armchair, though Biscuit clearly planned to stick close until the sandwich was gone.

"Hey, Dad." She bent to kiss his cheek before hanging up her coat in the front closet.

"Hello there, sweetheart. Your momma was just in here wondering when you'd get home. How was your day?"

"I didn't forget you were there," Ruby crooned as she picked K Mags up for a snuggle and a kiss on the top of his head. "Today was a good day. Busy. Finished the install for the security system. They promised the phones will be working by tomorrow but we'll see about that."

By that point, Biscuit barked sharply to remind her he was *right there* waiting to be paid attention to and she'd already spent far too much time with his brother, thank you very much.

"Be patient," she said as she put K Mags down with one last smooch to his little noggin. "Were you a good boy for Grandpa today?" Ruby asked Biscuit as she picked him up, nestling his muscled little bulk in the crook of her arm.

"No, ma'am," her dad said. "That one right there," he pointed at Biscuit, "got Pipes all stirred up and there was a whole lot of howling and such."

"Sure. It was *Biscuit* who started that. Not the dog named Pipes because he never stops talking. He's saying you're a bad influence." Ruby snorted a laugh as she put the dog down.

Her mother came in with an armful of fresh produce and when she caught sight of Ruby, she smiled. "Hey there, baby. I've got some tomatoes and a cucumber to go with the salad."

Ruby took the produce and put it on the counter to wait while she went to her room to change out of work clothes.

Biscuit and K Mags had come with her and scampered up the ramp to her bed where they settled on the blanket she kept there or her mother would have whooped her for having dogs on the furniture.

"Found us a house today," she told them as she changed out of her work clothes. "You two are going to love the yard. In the summer you two can swim in the river and smell disgusting afterward."

Truth was, her childhood bedroom had been a nice place to softly land and get her bearings once more. Ruby adored her parents and her brother and cousins and their families all lived close. It had been made clear to her early on that she was welcome to stay as long as she wanted and she'd felt absolutely nothing to contradict that.

This was the beginning of her real, adult life in Diablo Lake. The future she'd been working toward had finally arrived.

It made her incredibly happy and finding a place to live that she could make her own was part of the journey she was on.

They barked at her a few times, tails wagging furiously so she scooped them both into her arms and gave them love before they all went out to help with dinner preparation.

"One of my favorite things about being back home," Ruby said to her mom right before she took a bite of smothered pork chop with just the right amount of smashed potatoes. "No one cooks like you."

Her mom laughed, clearly flattered.

"The favorite is back home again," Greg teased. "However I come by some smothered pork chops and mashed potatoes with coconut cake after, I'm glad to ride those coattails."

Greg and Nichole had just opened up a barbecue stand, a quick lunch spot with a few picnic tables. Nothing flashy but Ruby knew they each had a way with not only food, but people. In just a few months they'd already established a loyal customer base. They lived in the one-bedroom apartment above the garage while they got the lunch stand called You Want This Smoke up and running at a profit of some sort.

"Oh hush now." Their mother waved a hand their way.

"Stop crying because they love me best, dumbhead," Ruby whispered, which set her brother laughing.

She'd really missed this silly time with her family over a dinner table.

"How did house hunting go?" Nichole asked.

"Good! I was a little worried I'd have to pay more than I wanted to, or make concessions I didn't want to, but in the end, it was the last place we looked. A sweet little house about a ten-minute walk from the river at the curve near that patch of red elderberries. I just knew the moment I saw it. Huge yard. I'm already planning garden spaces. Figure I'll head over to Once and Again to see what sorts of furniture they have. At least to get me through until I can order something or go to Knoxville to shop. Nice to have a secondhand store in town now."

"Before you go spending any money, I think between us all, we can get your house furnished," her mother said. "Lovie and Pop have a garage full of not just their own things, but when your aunt passed and we sold her house, most of her stuff went in there and in storage too. If you want to take your bed and the other things in your room, go on. We just replaced that mattress last year when we knew you'd be coming back home."

Warmth spread through Ruby at how much her family loved and looked after her. "Thank you. I'll take you up on that offer. I signed the lease this afternoon and he said I could move in any time after tomorrow. I was thinking this upcoming weekend if that worked for everyone?"

Her brother shrugged. "Nichole and I can help in the morning before we go open up. I'll take a batch of blonde brownies by way of payment as per our agreement."

Frankly, if that's all he wanted in payment for lugging around a bunch of crap on her behalf, Ruby figured she was getting the far better end of the deal.

"So soon?" Her mom frowned a moment but then

sighed, resigned. "I guess. We raised you to be independent and don't you know you all moved out the first chance you got. Backfired on me, I guess."

Ruby snickered. "Stop that right now. I can see you already planning to make my old room your sewing room at long last. 'Specially now that I'll be taking the bed and dressers."

"Can't harm to think on some. All kinds of room in there. Great light. But you can still come to breakfast any old time you like." Her mom patted her hand before going back to her dinner. "I mean it. New craft room or not, there is always room for you under our roof. This isn't one of those families where you can just la di dah your way in and out whenever you please. You're a Thorne witch and that comes with responsibilities."

Her mother added a sniff to make it extra severe, but ruined it all with a wink in Ruby's direction.

She laughed, sure, but there was truth to what her mother had said. Thorne witches went all the way back to the origins of Diablo Lake. Their magic ran through the spell that kept them all safe.

"I know Sunday dinner is mandatory," Ruby said with a grin. Like she'd blow off a chance to eat meals cooked by her mom and aunts? Or miss all that time together, the group of them?

There was no denying that despite the fact that she'd enjoyed her last six years out in the wider world. She'd traveled and learned so much about not just her own magic, but magic in general. Healing methods from multiple disciplines had made her a better practitioner and a better asset to the town.

But Diablo Lake was *home*. It ran through her veins and coming back for good had only made that clearer.

"And?" Greg stirred the pot. Ruby gave him their secret signal for *fuck you* with a tap of her nose.

"And yes, I'll take Lovie and Pop to church like everyone else does." Her grandparents were deeply talented, powerful witches in their own right but they were elderly Southern people too, which meant they spent their Sundays at church. And their preacher never heard a voice he liked more than his own.

"Why y'all making it sound like a chore?" their mother demanded like everyone didn't know exactly what a chore it was.

"There's enough cousins you only have to do it once every two months or so," her dad said, making everyone laugh.

"Stop that now, Mel," their mom said to their father, trying to hold back a smile. "When the pastor shuts up, the music's always good. Plus afterward there's food. You have to stay anyway because if you think you can herd your grandparents anywhere they don't want to go, you're mistaken. May as well have cake while you wait."

"That and Lovie wants to show off how many of her grandchildren show up to take her to church. She's got to preen a little," her dad said with affection.

Pearl Thorne was a proud woman. Her reputation in the community meant a great deal to her. It was generally benevolent. But she had no problem showing off when the situation called for it. Her children and grandchildren gave her plenty of cause to show off a new scarf or a date to the women's luncheon. If it brought their grandmother pleasure and some social currency, why not?

"It's fine. I figure it'll give me the stamp of approval since I'm taking over most of Aimee's patients. I've been away awhile so if I'm at Lovie's side here and there, it gives me a chance to keep an eye on folks and they know I'm the real deal."

"Good idea. And that church does a sale of some sort every month too. May as well sell your tinctures and tea to them while they interrogate you about your love life." Her mother raised a shoulder.

That made Ruby guffaw. "Maybe I'll save that until I've been there with her a few Sundays."

"Wednesday nights too for her ladies' group. No wine in sight so I'm going to suggest you drink it before you go. You'll need it as your life flashes before your eyes and you realize all the stuff that's going to happen to your body when you're their age," Nichole said. "Believe me when I tell you, they hold nothing back. I'm doing Kegels multiple times a day."

Ruby guffawed again.

"When you go to pick her up, have a cup of coffee with Pop first. That's what I do. He'll slip some bourbon into it. You know that's how he's dealt with her all these years anyway," Greg teased.

After dinner and cleanup, Nichole and Greg gathered their things and made to go back to their apartment. Ruby hugged Nichole, who whispered, "We'll talk more later about how cute Damon Dooley is and how you had so much sexual chemistry going on it nearly scorched all that brand-new paint off the walls at the clinic."

Chapter Four

Damon looked down at his phone's screen and answered on a sigh. "She's not moving into your neighborhood so give that up right now," he told Huston by way of answering.

His counterpart for Pembry laughed. "You know I don't even like girls, dingbat. I'm calling to see if we can meet for a brief pack-related issue. Mac and I can make ourselves available any time today or tomorrow."

"What's up?" They'd been having inter-pack meetings all year long working on reforming their old laws that did more harm than good. Trying to make the relations between the wolf shifters in town better. And they had. But a few big issues remained, like the abolition of the Rule of Silence.

"It's easier to explain in person. It shouldn't take too long."

Damon groaned. "Fine. Salt & Pepper in an hour. The fries and cokes are on you."

"What did you just commit me to?" Jace asked after he tucked his phone away.

"God knows. Huston says he and Mac want to meet for a *brief pack-related issue*. I'm making them buy us refreshments."

"Katie Faith told me Scarlett made a scene the other day at the market. Again. Wonder if it's connected to whatever the hell that was about. I'll be back at ten 'til and we'll walk over to Salt & Pepper."

An hour later he and Jace sat across from Mac and Huston, a mound of fries and rings between them, four ice-cold cherry cokes their accompaniment.

"So? What's this little meeting about?" Jace asked Mac.

"I'm going to skip the official language and just say it. My mother has made an appeal to allow my father to return to Diablo Lake from Halloween to the day after my wedding. She says he wants to be part of the festivities from our engagement dinner on and it's easier if he's here instead of having to drive back and forth from Gatlinburg."

Jace's expression went flat and utterly blank. But the emotion leaked through and Damon knew his brother was pissed. As was he.

"And?" Jace asked.

"Obviously we won't make any decisions on this without input from Dooley." Mac shrugged. "We want to know what you think about it."

Jace's scoff was sharp enough to slice. "What the flying fuck does *Pembry* think about it? Dwayne got sent away for a *year* after breaking our most serious law. We were all there when he brought a human to this town without permission. He exposed us all to discovery by the outside world. He did it for pride. He did it for spite. He did it while he was the Patron of the Pembry pack. Everything about that act was selfish and aimed to cause the most harm. Here we are barely ten months later and he's got the nerve to ask to come back *for a month*. He doesn't even like Aimee, for god's sake."

Mac sighed deeply. "I understand that you're still angry over what happened. That's why we're here talking. To get your perspective."

Jace cocked his head. "Right now my perspective is that I want to punch your father in the face more than I did before I sat down. My dad, well I can't even mention his name because of pack punishment, but your dad wants to eat appetizers and drink champagne *for what*? He gets to come back early *for what*? What's so special about Dwayne Pembry that the rules don't apply to him?"

Mac raised his hands, open palms facing them. "Pembry is not inclined to grant that request for the reasons you outline. There's been enough special rules for certain people to last the pack a lifetime. I would like him to be allowed to come to the wedding itself. But he'd leave the day after and not be allowed back until after his sentence is up."

Jace's spine relaxed and Damon eased back a little as well.

"We don't object to him coming to your wedding. Him. Not your brother. His sentence stands." Jace referred to Darrell Pembry, Mac's brother and his dad's partner in the crime of bringing an outsider into Diablo Lake without permission. Not only had Darrell aided in bringing a human to town to attempt to smear Aimee during her mayoral campaign, he'd been tireless in stirring up trouble so severe it had created a schism between packs and the wolves and the rest of town. His crimes had been worse and his sentence had been a year longer than his father's. Damon doubted either of them had learned a damned thing.

Mac said, "On that we have news. Darrell and his wife have asked and received permission to move to Silver Falls. His children will still be Pembry should they ever wish to return, but Pembry gave our leave for them to go. And good riddance. My job is hard enough and he's a problem for someone else to solve now."

"Amen." It was a relief for Damon to hear. One less agitant in Diablo Lake made his life a lot easier. If only Scarlett and Dwayne would go as well.

"We good?" Mac asked. "I want to keep the air between us clear and not only because my fiancée and your wife are tight and will kick our butts if we don't get along. I feel the same way you do about special rules for my dad and not yours. You understand that, right? It's why we've been working on ending the Rule of Silence once and for all."

Jace tipped his chin. "We're good. Appreciate the heads-up and the transparency on this. And the efforts on the Rule of Silence. Oh and for the late-afternoon snack." Jace tapped his glass to Mac's.

"Silence helps no one." Mac shrugged. "Whatever the crime, it's not the denial of speaking of it or the criminal that prevents the next crime. It hurts families that had zero to do with the incident. Whatever your father did, not being able to say his name doesn't do any good. I'm sorry it's taking this long to get rid of it."

"I tell myself I should be comforted by all the rules in place to change our laws. These aren't changes we should ever make lightly. So I understand that part of the democratic process is that this all takes time. But when I watch your aunt Mary and your mother manipulate those rules to hold things up, it just pisses me off," Jace said of the administrative roadblocks thrown out to grind the whole process to a crawl.

"You're not the only one. But they don't have much left they can use. When it's all past, we'll hold a full pack vote and the rule will be ended. Progress takes time," Mac said.

"Fuck that. Progress is right there and your mother and her cronies are being assholes and it makes me wonder just exactly why," Major said.

Jace snorted a surprised laugh. Of the three Dooley brothers, Major was the least likely to say something like that in public.

"I hasten to point out how y'all have some older wolves who don't want any changes to our laws too," Huston told them as he dunked a ring into a pool of ranch dressing.

"Some are opposed to any change at all. Mostly the rest are cranky and spiteful and naturally contrary. They'll come along. More than enough to win a vote." Damon poked a finger in Mac's direction. "But the spiteful ones are getting stirred up by your spiteful ones."

That made everyone laugh because it was true. And because despite the grumbling, they were all stuck at a snail's pace together.

"I'm doing all I can on my end. I promise you." Mac meant it. Which was a good thing and why they weren't all brawling.

"Now, tell me why you and Ruby were in the neighborhood a few days ago," Mac told Damon.

"I'm absolutely sure your *special friend* the mayor already told you," Damon said with a snort.

"She said you took one look at Ruby and it was like you were struck stupid." Mac didn't bother to hide his smirk.

"You've seen Ruby Thorne, right? Who can look at her and not get struck stupid?" Damon tried to remain nonchalant but even he could hear the emotion in his words.

"True. Not that I look at anyone but Aimee or anything," Mac hastened to add.

Damon rolled his eyes. Looking—discreetly of course—wasn't a crime. And heaven knew just how much Mac loved Aimee.

"She was looking at rentals around town," he finally explained.

"Where'd she end up? Hopefully in our side of town since Pembry can always use another witch in our territory," Huston said just to poke at Damon. Which he had to admit, was masterfully done.

"Not on your side of town." Jace put money down for a tip and then flipped Mac off as the two of them grunted a laugh. "She's renting from Damon."

"On my land even." Damon stretched, looking smug because he had every reason to be smug. "She'll be moving into her place this weekend. I'll tell her you asked after her."

"Better make a claim quick if you're going to make one," Jace told him quietly as they walked back to the Mercantile.

"With Ruby?"

Jace nodded. "She's a power. From one of the original families. She's gorgeous and successful and works hard. Don't make the mistake of thinking you're the only one who notices and might want a bigger bite."

Damon saw red for a moment at the very fucking idea.

"Be mindful. Keep your control. The wolf has to co-operate or you'll be a mess. Handle that now so you'll be ready. Because shifters and witches alike notice she's back. And single."

And powerful. And beautiful and sexy.

"I get it." And Damon did. Wasn't he right there thinking about how the light seemed to flit off the magic floating all around her? Remembering the way she'd felt in his arms even all these years later?

"She's been in the outside world. Like Katie Faith had been," Jace said as they went back up the wide wooden front steps leading to the porch and beyond, the doors of the Mercantile. "Romantic stuff works different out there."

Damon shrugged. "Well, this last year has been about new ideas, so." They still had chemistry. His land had perked up just from the first visit, like it was preparing for her. "Anyway. It's early. I haven't even asked her on a date yet."

"Well why the hell not?" Jace demanded.

"I want to wait until she's moved in. It'd be weird if I made any romantic move first. What if she thought she had to say yes or what have you?"

Jace nodded. "Okay, you're probably right. Get back to it. I'll see you later. I'll leave it to you and Major to let whoever needs to know about Dwayne coming back for the wedding but not the whole rest of it."

"Got it."

Not that Ruby would have admitted it, but she didn't really need the supplies she currently had in her cart. Her father would have gotten snotty as heck if he'd have seen the bag of nails and the shiny new hammer when he'd pointed out the old coffee can full of nails just a few nights before and told her to use whatever she needed.

But Damon wouldn't be likely to hang out in the tool shed at her parents' house and he probably was somewhere in the building she currently stood in.

Another roller to replace the ones she had already would be good. She'd painted the bedroom and the living room and had a few spare rollers left for the bathroom, but a gal should always be prepared in case of a paint roller emergency.

It wasn't because she wanted to see Damon so badly she'd made up a reason to be in his vicinity. Except it was.

He was there. She felt it low in her belly. His magic, the green and brown shifter energy they carried with them, hung in the air. It did something to her magic. Made her magic sit up and notice in response.

She heard his voice before she caught sight of him. Explaining some sort of shipping schedule to someone. As Ruby made her way down the aisle of fabric and notions, she let herself be drawn to him until, at the end of the row when the view to the front of the store opened up, he looked up just as she stepped out.

A smile bloomed over his mouth and the customer— Noreen Painter, who'd been the town's librarian when Ruby was a kid—turned to see what he was looking at.

"We set on that schedule then, Mrs. Painter?" Damon asked.

Noreen looked Ruby over quickly and then back to Damon, a smile on her lips. "I think everything is just fine, Damon. You call me when it arrives." She reached out to pat his hand a few times and toddled toward Ruby. "Hey there, sweetheart. I bumped into your grandmother just a few days ago and she mentioned that you were back in Diablo Lake. Nice to see you making yourself at home again."

"Why thank you, Ms. Noreen. You look real pretty today. That pink suits you."

Ruby asked after Noreen's grandchildren and her husband, who'd been recovering after knee replacement, and ended up with some juicy gossip about possible cheating in a cake baking contest coming up.

After she'd left, Ruby turned her attention back to Damon.

"My day has just gotten three thousand percent better," he said as he came around the counter and toward her.

He moved with such powerful grace. The flex and play of what she could see only made her wonder what all that taut skin stretched over those muscles would look like as she rode him like a stallion.

After a peek in her basket, he grinned her way. "You need anything else?"

"Uh. I don't think so. I noticed the fence you put up at the house. Thank you. It takes the anxiety away."

"Not a problem. It didn't take that long. I noticed you coming and going this week."

He'd given her the keys and told her she could come in and paint, so she had a few evenings after work. "Nichole and I finished the living room and got all the prep work done to finish up the rest of the bathroom today." Ruby indicated the basket she'd set on the counter. "Figured it would be wise to have some extra rollers just in case."

"Smart. When you moving all your stuff in?"

"This weekend. Between my cousins and immediate family, it should be pretty quick. Nothing too heavy and that was a challenge. You know that old lady furniture everyone has extra of in the garage or whatever is all solid oak and weighs five hundred pounds. Most of my housewares I haven't even unpacked from when I returned so that's already in boxes and ready to go."

"Major and I will be around in the afternoon after we close here. Just pop over if you need anything, okay?"

"Appreciate it." Ruby planned to bake him cookies and brownies as a thank you anyway. And it was good to have a reason to see him again.

"Katie Faith says y'all opened the clinic earlier this week. I'm proud of you and Aimee."

That meant a lot and she told him so. "Folks are making appointments already. We're still figuring things out of course, but it's been a good learning experience so far."

He took her hand a moment and little arcs of electricity seemed to spark and then weave their energy together. "Just another reason to be glad you're back. Diablo Lake has been waiting for you."

Oh. That was wonderful. And what she'd needed to hear.

"Thank you again, Damon. I'll be seeing you around."

He'd moved to walk her out, but several people came in and she patted his arm. "Go deal with your customers."

"I'll definitely see you around," he said and watched her go.

Chapter Five

He'd watched, on and off all day as her family moved her into the little cottage. And didn't he need to be in different spots on his lot from time to time—because he had work to do which didn't include standing around staring at her—to see better around the big copse of trees that lay between the house site and her place.

Major poked him in the side hard enough to have Damon yelping and jumping away. "What the actual fuck is wrong with you?" he snarled.

"You have me out here on a fine Saturday afternoon to help you get the framing up in your master bedroom, you best pay attention. She's gonna be there all the time so you have lots of moments to gawp at her like a fuckin' weirdo." His younger brother—by a little more than a minute—wore what their grandpa JJ called a shit-eating grin.

"I'm working just fine," Damon said, planning on how to repay Major for that poke he couldn't rub away because then he'd be admitting it hurt. He'd die first. "And for your information I'm not gawping! She's my tenant and a friend. I just want to be sure she's moving in okay. If it was anyone else I'd do the same."

"You better not let Grandma hear you lie like that or she'll kick your ass."

Damon pointed a hammer Major's way. "She don't like tattlers neither. It'd be worth it to take a licking just so you got one first."

Both brothers snarled at one another and then burst into laughter that seemed to leap among the trees.

"Like you'd have spent hours building a fence for a fuckin' dog for anyone else but Ruby."

"I would!" he protested. "I'm a good landlord." Damon got to work once more as they pushed part of the beam framing the doorway into place. "Asshole," he muttered and then made a sound of victory as it fit perfectly.

Major's house would go up next. Sitting about three quarters of an acre away. Within view but with plenty of space for privacy.

Every Sunday afternoon after the Mercantile closed for the day, several of his friends and family came over for a few hours to help. Again, they'd all do the same for Major when it was his turn. And whoever else after that. Because pack was family and that's what you did for family.

Damon loved his pack. Was dedicated to their well-being. He'd bled for it more than once and figured he would again in the future. As Prime—a position he and Major shared—he was the claws and teeth as well as the shield. He enforced their laws. The wolves in the Dooley pack sought him out for help and advice and sometimes that help included application of pack justice like a pop in the face or a kick in the ass.

Over the last several years as the relationship between wolf packs began to deteriorate, it had taken a lot

of attention—a lot of hands-on, face-to-face attention—
to attempt to truly achieve reconciliation. A necessary
state of affairs so that Diablo Lake, and the magic that
kept the town safe and green, could grow and prosper.

The Mercantile had pretty much always been the
place Dooley wolves came to seek out leadership for one
reason or another. He and Major were there six days a
week as it was. And then the pack house was only right
out back. Even for a wolf like him who loved being
around other shifters, it was sometimes just too much.

So in the future, he'd bunk over the Mercantile or
in one of the spare rooms at Jace's when necessary, but
his home, *his den*, would be right where he stood. Even
ten minutes of privacy a day would be an improvement.
Space to truly let it all go for even a little while.

Naturally, Major spoke up and annoyed the shit out
of him. "You should have just offered to help her move
today instead of creeping on her."

"*Creeping?* I'm not doing anything even approaching creeping. We just so happened to be here because
of a power outage closing the Mercantile down. It's a
coincidence. Let's change the subject before I hit you
with this hammer," Damon said.

Major snickered. "Guess who I saw this morning."

Damon paused. "Who?"

"Scarlett running after Mac, trying to tell him something but he kept on going. I like that guy more every
day." Major snorted. "Guess he told her no on that request for dumbass Dwayne spending a month back
here for wedding stuff. Whatever it was, she seemed
pretty strident about it. She's fast and persistent. He
was nearly trotting and once he got to his car, I heard
him hit the locks. She may as well have shaken her fist

at him as he sped away. Looked like she was gonna explode into a thousand angry bees right there on the sidewalk. Fucker waved at his momma, all jaunty like as he drove past her."

By that point, both brothers were laughing at the visual.

"I surely do wish I'd have seen that," Damon said after he got over the last of the snickering.

Major shrugged one shoulder. "She's been pretty quiet through the spring and early summer but I've noticed her and Mary out in town more often stirring shit up over the last month or two."

"Quiet *adjacent* anyway. She and that sister of hers have been manipulating the process since it first started back in February. But yes, you're right." Damon tossed his gloves to the side and grabbed them both a canteen and some chocolate chip cookies nearly the size of their heads.

After fueling up, Damon stretched. "Not even a year has passed since her husband and one of her sons were sent away from the pack but she's getting her old lady mafia all stirred up. It's only a matter of time before *our* old lady mafia gets stirred up in response."

No one wanted stirred-up female wolves. No one. Especially ones of Scarlett's generation. They had no problem whatsoever just telling a body what they felt. No filters. None of that. Just flat-out truth. Damon shuddered at some of the stuff his grandmother said sometimes. It was wholly badass and admirable and utterly terrifying.

Scarlett Pembry was the seed of the problem, Damon had come to believe. Sure her husband and son had broken their laws and had been sent away from Diablo Lake in punishment. But their actions had been self-absorbed and about personal power. But Scarlett, well she'd remained in town and had slowly and deviously—along with her sister Mary—created a campaign of one procedural roadblock after the next to some of the sweeping changes the younger generation of shifters wanted to make. Most specifically ending the rule that said in the very worst of crimes, the perpetrator would not only be executed but all mention of their name and the crime would be stricken from the official record and never spoken of again.

Scarlett and Mary had managed to turn what should have been a simple and necessary rule change into a symbol of the old ways that had kept them safe from the attention of the outside world.

Scarlett's husband had played at silly cults of personality. Scarlett though, she managed to pull off true alpha wolf shit and even though Damon curled his lip every time he thought of her, he couldn't deny he admired her skill.

"She and Mary have certainly turned their behavior up to eleven these last two or three weeks. More than her usual bullshit about pack business, that's for sure. I don't know what she'll complain about next." And it was even nicer that Mac had come to Dooley with the request. Keeping things open between packs was a necessary change to how things had been.

Major shook his head. "I think she's on board with the marriage. Scarlett knows Mac is a good Patron, stronger than Dwayne even at his height. She may not like Aimee because of the friendship between her and Katie Faith, but she knows having Aimee as part of

Pembry will benefit everyone and close the power gap between them and Dooley."

Diablo Lake had been a melding of shifters and witches. Each coming together to live in relative peace and secrecy to protect what they had. Witches though, were the ones who'd created the magic that not only sustained their safety and privacy, but the very fertility of the earth that kept the rivers and lakes full of fish, the trees lush and heavy with fruit, the vines and bushes heavy with everything they'd need to prosper.

Dooley had Katie Faith and Pembry would be gaining Aimee when she and Mac married in late November. Scarlett wasn't a fool. Aimee made them stronger, and she supported that and the marriage. Regardless, she was for sure a meddlesome cow who seemed devoted to causing problems.

Damon said, "It's his son's wedding and Mac is the Patron and he's vouched for his dad's behavior for that day. Dwayne's presence in town before his sentence is up already says he's getting special treatment. But people will accept a one-day pass. Any more than that and wolves as well as witches are gonna get all worked up."

Major said, "Not to mention the fact that we know for sure Aimee's already under a lot of stress being the mayor and planning a wedding celebration around Collins Hill Days and Samhain and Halloween at the same time. Scarlett is turning up the heat and that's got to be getting back to Aimee, making her even more stressed. And that means Katie Faith is going to go off to defend her and if Dwayne just shows up at some dinner, it's going to be WrestleMania. Last thing we need is to piss them witches off even worse. *Their* old lady gang is the scariest because they all look so nice and sweet but will cut you to the quick if and when necessary. Anyway, I figure the aunties were keeping you updated on all the Scarlett gossip."

Speaking of female wolves of a *certain age*. The aunties were quite often the heart of the pack because they held the history of things. They remembered details and relationships. They kept an eye on the goings-on with the younger wolves, keeping them safe and attempting to teach them life lessons in the process. The aunties were your family even if you weren't blood. And many of them probably were your actual aunts too, as was the case with Damon and his brothers.

They were also better than any law enforcement when it came to intelligence gathering. They knew everything and everyone and he'd always been a favorite. Damon grinned to himself. He flattered them and took the time to check in. Partly his job, yes, but another factor was that he'd grown up without a mother and his grandmothers and aunts had always scooped him or Major into laps for snuggles. They checked in when he was sick or feeling down. They celebrated his victories and kicked his butt when he messed up. And they baked him stuff. All the time. And while they ate cake or pie or cookies together, they told him all the gossip in town.

Damon adored them.

Ruby opened up the pizza box and sighed happily as she grabbed two slices. "I don't know how we all lived here in Diablo Lake before we had pizza." Truth be told, the easy availability of a wide variety of take-out food was something she missed very much about the outside world.

She passed the box along to Greg. Not quite six hours with the help of her entire immediate family and five cousins, her house was moved into. Her dad and brother had hung up all her curtains and a set of blinds. Lovie had supervised the unpacking of linens and dishes and the like as Ruby's perfect little blue house began to settle into a home.

No one even batted an eye when she waved away offers of help unpacking and setting up the kitchen once they'd moved in the long oak table—her one big heavy piece liberated from Lovie's house. It had wonderful energy, much like the one in her parents' dining room but short enough that in the kitchen against a far wall, it became another workspace.

Ruby liked to listen to her gut whenever she could. And with a houseful of her family, it'd never quiet down long enough to hear anything, much less her magic. So over the next few days she'd arrange things as she went and figure out where they needed to go.

But at the moment, job done, they sat on her back porch on several different chairs and at tables she'd brought with her from her aunt's storage unit. There was a lovely sort of magic that seemed to hum deep within the furniture. Ruby and her aunt Charlene had been very close. Her loss had sent the whole family reeling and even a year later, they stumbled. Grief was like that. Tricksy and feral. But today as she leaned back in an Adirondack chair, Ruby chose to feel comforted by the familiar feel of her aunt's magic as it rose to join with everyone else's.

"I surely do like this place," Lovie told her as she settled on a nearby settee. "Your dogs like the yard. Big one. Even Pipes loves it here."

Ruby looked over the yard at the sight of her little guys running and playing hard with Pipes, who was easily twice their size. They kept running to the fence line to sniff up a storm before moving to the next spot to repeat. Every once in a while, they'd flop down on their bellies, noses up as they tried to rest up before the next round of activity.

"Big enough for them to get really tired I hope." Ruby snorted a laugh before taking a bite of pizza. "They're so excited about a new place. Happy to see everyone here. I imagine Pipes will do sleepovers from time to time." Her boys clearly considered her parents' dog their best friend and as she'd grown up with Pipes, it always made her happy to have her around.

"There's power here." Lovie tapped the rubber cap of her cane once on the porch to underline the point. "So close to shifters but this is our magic too. The land here likes you on it."

Ruby wasn't certain but it already seemed as if the greenery was waking up. Much more than even the day before. "I haven't done a lot of work here, but it does seem like my talent is pleased."

"I expect so. You've got plenty of power. Plenty of talent. Your passion...your compassion is the spark. I love to see it. You and your cousins going out into the world and coming back to make Diablo Lake better for her people." Lovie grinned a moment. "I had your grandpa drive us past the new medical clinic. We're so proud of you. Proud of all you've done and continue to do."

To hear it, to know her grandparents respected and were proud of her work meant so much. "Thank you, Lovie. Me too. Our schedule is already booked out two weeks solid. We'll still do home visits." Some residents weren't the joining type. They lived out in the woods, far away from town and they liked it that way. She and Aimee would continue to go to them. To keep that tie to town and other people and to make sure they understood their health and well-being was just as valuable as anyone else's. Aimee was very good with the super-cranky shifters. Ruby had been amazed at first but then she'd just doubled back and paid close attention to how her friend did it because learning new ways to connect with patients was important.

"Can't complain neither that you have shifters living so close by. Makes the neighborhood safer."

Safer again? It was adorable.

Ruby locked eyes with Nichole as they stifled a giggle.

"Damon and his brother are great neighbors to have. Not that I'd worry about any real danger in this town." Greg flashed a grin Ruby's way. "They'll treat Ruby like pack, so folks'll leave her alone."

"Not that you're biased," she said. Greg, Damon and Major were friends. They'd been in the same year at school and had bonded over baseball and football, season after season as they'd all grown up.

"Any fool can see that. Don't need to be pals with them to know Major and Damon are predators who'll keep our girl Ruby safe." Greg snagged another root beer. "Sure doesn't hurt you live so close to Lovie and Pops."

"Gotta keep an eye on 'em just in case they cause a ruckus and they need backup," Ruby teased.

On the way out, her mother pulled Ruby to the side. "Greg was right that Damon seeing you as pack will protect you. As for leaving you alone in other ways? Don't count on it. I've had more than one Pembry momma or aunt asking about you and if you were single. Never forget that wolves have their own way of doing things and that you're a witch who doesn't need anyone to make herself more powerful."

Ruby hugged her mother and kissed her cheek. "I love you."

"Love you too, baby."

After everyone had gone, Ruby wandered through the house awhile. She made her bed and put away her clothes in the dressers and closets.

In her kitchen, she cleaned carefully, according to a personal ritual she'd built over time. This was the space she did most of her magic and so her work surfaces needed to be cleaned and readied. Treated with respect, just like the healing mixtures she created.

She called the corners and set a working circle. One that would amplify and protect her as she Worked but that wouldn't keep the dogs out and she wouldn't have to set and reset it over and over.

A smooth stone, a candle and a crystal at each direction sat on the top of the cabinets. The energy of it buzzed over her skin until it seemed to seep into the very walls and settle into place. Solid and secure.

The drying racks for her herbs and flowers already hung on the far wall, near the back door. Her jars and bottles, some clear, some colored to protect the contents, were slid into place according to how often she needed to use them.

Every step was part of the spell, would be that foundation to every tincture and tisane she made.

The boys came in from time to time to check on her and to nose around and see whatever she'd done. K Mags paused at her feet and barked three times, staring up at her as if to say…something. "You already ate today. And don't even pretend you didn't get a bunch of sausage from Uncle Greg's pizza."

He sneezed and then snorted. And then barked again before running out of the room. With a sigh, she found him sitting in front of the dog ramp. "That's what you meant? You made me stop all my work to make sure you can get on my bed and supervise? Or maybe be sure I don't have any food, more likely."

Once she'd arranged it so the boys could easily access the bed—and she had another for the couch because Biscuit, despite his general roly-polyness, was a runner and a jumper. If he wanted somewhere he was going to get there and that led to vet visits and then the ramps. The dogs still ran and ran, though at least their hips and backs were safer from injury.

Biscuit wandered through to get a few scratches under his chin and to check on his brother. They were fiercely protective of one another. Got into a lot of trouble together too, but generally, they were very good boys who loved to run and dig and bark and nose around to see what they could see.

The light of late afternoon called to her. She wanted to be out among the plants, the earth at her feet. "Let's go outside. I want to garden a bit now that it warmed up some."

The way the house sat on the lot, there was some sort of green space out every door and window. The main street was partially screened by bushes that created a fence of greenery. She wanted to see how the dogs reacted and if she needed to keep them in the back, using the front only if she was with them. Ruby walked out front and the boys shot out at her heels, racing through the grass, sniffing and peeing and then peeing some more.

"What do y'all think? A trellis gate at the front where the mailbox is? I'll train some roses over. Yellow I think. Yellow and deep red." Her favorites and if she wasn't mistaken, that's what lay within the newly forming little buds on the rosebushes that dotted along the yard and had most likely served as a fence for whoever had lived here before. A brush of her fingertips over the leaves sent a warm wave of pleasure through her veins. Delight by all the green and living things in the soil that a witch was living there.

Her magic rose quickly and easily as she called it, sliding over the yard, uniting with the magic the earth at her feet gave off. Her magic, her talent would grow here, be nurtured. Soon this yard would be full of flowers and life. Bees and butterflies, birds of all types would find a haven there.

Ruby followed the boys around the side of the house into the backyard. There were two big bluebell bushes that she trimmed back. She'd take some plantings from the hollyhocks in her parents' yard and transplant them so the peaches and pinks of the blooms would fill the area. Dahlias maybe. She had a cousin who was just saying she had some rhizomes if Ruby wanted some. More Thorne magic in the soil would only strengthen her connection to the land there. There were already a few unkempt but perfectly happy hydrangeas around the yard. She couldn't wait to see what colors they'd be.

Because they'd always been sweet to her—and because their Lovie had given them a look—Ruby's cousins had dug out a nice-sized kitchen garden after she'd mentioned that part of the yard being perfect for it. Tomorrow, she'd start planting according to the seasons. Fresh ingredients for meals and for any sort of working she planned were necessary. Dried was acceptable for many things, but her tinctures, tisanes and balms were more powerful with fresh ingredients. Next fall she'd plant pumpkins and squash for soups. Until the weather warmed up, she'd keep her herbs on the many windowsills inside. She'd have the time to experiment now. Maybe even try lavender and some beekeeping for honey and wax for candles.

The future was wide open and full of so much promise. It filled her with a deep sense of comfort as well as excitement.

And just beyond, where Damon had worked all day long on the house, the land tugged at him too. Just a quick sort of *hello and did you know there was a witch living here now* thing. His wolf found it playful and bounded into the man to make him pay attention.

His wolf really liked Ruby. Loved the scent of her magic.

Major had left half an hour earlier. Heading over to Jace and Katie Faith's place for the evening. Alone, Damon had slowly put away the tools while making mental notes of what he'd need to do next. What needed to be ordered or if it could be accomplished in town.

Really, it was just his way of walking the perimeter of his den. The place he'd live and sleep and now, in the back of his mind, find that luscious witch who'd just moved in.

Perhaps because he'd been thinking of her so strongly, man and wolf were extra sensitive to the rush of magic that flowed over the woods all around where he stood.

Damon tipped his head back fully at the sensuous caress of it, but the wolf stretched just at the perimeter of becoming. Yearning to burst free to go to the source and roll in it. Make it partly his.

He let it go as long as possible, holding himself at that place where both sides of himself were aware and in control. A test of will. The man exhaled slowly, standing tall once more. After grabbing two ciders from his fridge, he took a leisurely walk down the way to visit with his new neighbor.

Night had fallen but white lights had been strung up in the backyard, along the posts of the porch, through the railings. It cast a pretty, golden glow over the space and—if he wasn't mistaken—the assorted plants in the yard that appeared to have gotten lusher in the last hours.

Even the peach and cherry trees in the yard had perked up.

In the fenced portion of the backyard, she'd already dug up rows for a garden and stood on the bottom step of the back porch, laughing as she watched something just beyond. Tiny balls of energy bounded up and down the fence line, pausing to mark every single tree and bush. They barked back and forth with one another, obviously sharing a familial bond.

Damon appreciated the way they included Ruby in their bond, frequently checking back with her verbally and with little drive-by runs as she talked to them.

But when the hefty little dude scented Damon their

joyful play changed. His buddy noticed and doubled up at his side as they charged in Damon's direction. Getting between him and Ruby.

Fierce. He'd eat them up in two bites, but the important part was the courage and loyalty they showed in Ruby's favor.

Still, it was important to establish the proper order of things. Damon was the alpha here. His wolf rose, shining through his eyes as he growled low and quick. Enough to bring them up to a stop as they tilted their heads.

"It's okay, boys. This is our landlord, Damon Dooley." Her smile his way warmed a path from his belly outward. "They're very protective, but really, they're total sweetie pies. Who like digging holes. I'm sorry about that. I should have mentioned that when I signed the lease."

The wolf liked digging too so Damon didn't judge.

They waited, staying between Ruby and the big bad predator. He put the cider bottles down before approaching them.

It wasn't often that Ruby found herself speechless. But the sight of Damon, all predator's grace and movement as he came toward them and knelt a little, letting the boys scent him, sent butterflies scattering through her belly.

It was strong and gentle at the same time. Her dogs were *so little* compared to him, but they were also loyal and very brave, so they kept between her and the big bad wolf. Protecting their human until they figured out if Damon was friend or foe. And Damon understood it and then went and honored it by letting them take a whiff, giving them his measure. Ruby caught the amusement and affection in Damon's eyes but he wasn't being mocking at all.

Both dogs eventually dropped their eyes and Damon's response was a satisfied grunt.

"Everything okay, guys?" Ruby asked at last.

Damon stood after he ran a hand over the top of each dog's head. "Yes. They're very good guards."

God. He was good with animals. Kind to smaller creatures. On top of the sexy and the sense of humor and the way he looked and how smart he was. She didn't stand a chance. "They are. Thank you for noticing and for reassuring them you aren't a threat. Let me formally introduce you three," she said once he'd gotten the bottles he'd set down earlier.

She knelt next to the dogs. "This is Biscuit. Biscuit, this is Damon. He's also a wolf but I guess you probably smell that."

Damon nodded his hello.

"And this is Kenny the Magnificent, or K Mags."

"Very nice to meet you."

"Okay, boys," Ruby said, accepting the hand Damon had extended to help her stand, "it's nearly bedtime so get that last run in." She grabbed the ball and tossed it, sending them off running to fight over it.

"I brought some cider to share," he told her.

"Well aren't you handy?" she said. "Come on inside. I was just about to have a snack and a glass of something."

He helped her put away all the tools she'd been using in the yard before they went inside. Before she could say anything, Damon gave a yip of sorts and the boys finished their business and came running inside, no backtalk.

Really handy.

They settled on the couch in her living room, a plate full of leftover pizza between them. "I can't believe they don't even try to give you the sad face to convince you how starved they are. I'm such a sucker for that face."

Damon had nearly leaned over to kiss the top of her head by the time he realized it and made himself stop.

Ruby turned, no fear or surprise on her features at finding him so close. "Hi."

"You smell good," he murmured before forcing himself upright.

"If you say so. I've been painting and moving and unpacking and working in the yard."

"You smell like roses and jasmine. That's your magic. And clean sweat. Laughter. A little bit of woodsmoke."

Her lips parted and she whispered, "Oh," and when he forced his gaze away from her mouth, it was to find her eyes, pupils so large, long dark lashes sweeping down a little.

"Um. Thank you. That was a lovely thing to say."

Damon cursed himself. Ruby Thorne tied up his tongue and fuzzed his brain with thoughts of kissing her until he couldn't kiss anymore. Memories of the handful of times he'd actually kissed her in real life were so much better than anything he could have dreamed up.

"You really did make it look good in here," Damon said, taking a sip of cider to do something with his hands and mouth.

"A little bit of this and that from various storage units, garages and spare rooms turned out pretty well.

There's a fair bit of stripping, sanding and painting in my future off time to tie it all in together and make it my own, but that's a fun sort of work. I'm told I can order things via the Mercantile, so I can get the fabric I want. The curtains in my bedroom right now are from my childhood room. I can sew exactly what I want easily enough. I guess I'm nesting."

When she laughed, the tiny bells on her earrings salted the sound and made it music that was hers alone.

"Winter's coming. You'll be glad you nested come December and January. Couple of years back, the Mercantile and Pembry Freight came to an agreement on who could handle what as far as goods being shipped to residents. Boring stuff really, but yes, we're the go-to for fabric. Or say you wanted a type or shade of paint or varnish, we can special order it if it's not on the shelves."

"Good to know." She settled back against the cushions, turning to the side enough to face him. "The last two times I was with you we talked a lot about rental stuff but not much about personal stuff. What have you been up to?"

"I think I told you I was building a house, right?"

She nodded. "I admit I saw you here and there through the trees. When I was in the driveway taking boxes from the truck, I mean. You're doing it all yourself?"

"What I can, yes. We've always done a lot of construction. Since we were kids. Fixed most everything mechanical when it broke. So luckily I'm able to do nearly all of it, at least helping in some way. Major is a whiz with wiring and that and I'm teaching myself plumbing."

"You're good at everything, apparently. That's really impressive. Doing it yourself, putting your energy and creativity into your house from the ground up sounds lovely. I'd like to see it sometime. The land here is special. Full of shifter magic. The green things are healthy and strong."

Damon ducked his head, blushing. *Blushing.* And glowing with pride at all she'd said.

"Yeah. Uh, thanks. I'm happy to show it to you anytime. I'm in a trailer but hope to have the entire first floor finished by the first of December so I can live in it and finish the second story and rest of the build over the spring and into the summer."

"I wouldn't say I was a carpenter or anything, but I'm good with landscaping and painting and the like and happy to help out a neighbor," Ruby managed to say as she wrenched her gaze away from his forearms where the hair there shone bronze and copper in the lamplight.

The dogs had belly crawled their way ever closer over the time they'd been in the living room and were now looking up at her with hopeful eyes. "Yes, you two can nap there awhile. But no more treats. You've had a lot today as it is and you ran a lot and had so much love and exercise you'll be sick if you eat another thing. And then you'll be so embarrassed that he saw you like that."

K Mags gave a furtive look in Damon's direction and with a sigh, he turned in a neat little circle and dropped, propping his chin on Ruby's slipper. Biscuit, well, he was far more food motivated and therefore more stubborn when it came to wheedling treats.

"He knows if he overrules me I'd kick him out of the house instantly," Ruby told Biscuit, who'd been giving starved eyes at Damon.

"Don't get me in trouble with her, little man," Damon

said in a surprisingly deep grumble. Biscuit held his gaze for about a quarter of a second before he plopped down, using his brother for a pillow.

"Don't think I didn't hear that little huff at the end," he told the dog and she was happy to be sitting because her knees went all rubbery. It was bossy, but also sort of cute and affectionate. Damon was most likely being their alpha too.

Biscuit opened one eye and wagged his tail hopefully before going back to sleep.

"I don't know how you do it without laughing. Or giving in," Damon said.

"I don't," Ruby admitted. "Not always. That one in particular," she pointed at Biscuit, "is very sassy. He tends to act out if he gets bored and he very much needs a firm hand and to know who's in charge of the family."

"Okay. That makes sense. Hierarchy and discipline are important when you have sharp teeth."

Ruby sucked in a breath at the very carnal response to the way his voice had gone low at the end of the sentence. Naturally, because he was a shifter, he noted it instantly and one corner of his mouth rose.

"Anyway." She only barely managed not to fan herself. "We didn't only call him Biscuit because he's perfectly golden. Even when he could just barely walk, he always showed up for any meal, ready to sop up any delicacies, sweet or savory. Like a biscuit. And obviously, you can see from his shape, he was just a dumpling from day one. Well, day two really."

"I'm afraid to ask about day one," Damon said.

"I was only supposed to be a foster home for them for a few weeks. A whole litter had been found after their mom got run over by a car. I took two because one of my friends was dating someone who ran a dog rescue. Day one was pretty much full of bathing. They were dirty and had fleas. I actually thought Biscuit was gray, but after the third bath most of the dirt and oil had been washed away and he was his golden brown self. They were a handful. So smart and so much energy. By the end of the first week I knew it was a case of a foster fail because there was no way I was giving them up."

Ruby bent to give them both a scratch under the chin before sitting up. "They're really good with kids and older people. They come with me when I visit some of the care homes. They're fearless and very empathetic so they'll hop up and be charming the grumpiest old lady in the place before I blink an eye. I've had them at two births and a number of different appointments. They're a natural soothing element. It's harder to be scared of a shot when K Mags is in your lap. When they were puppies I realized quickly that Cairns needed exercise and they loved brain challenges. I'd hide treats and let them search the house or the park or yard. That's when I started thinking about different ways of dealing with pain or fear in medical or healing procedures for witches and shifters. Medication surely, but for shifters, the dosage is high enough to be extra judicious and witches can have bad reactions to certain ingredients depending on what their magical talent is."

"I didn't know that," Damon said. "I knew that y'all needed specialized care with certain pills and whatnot. But not why. Fascinatin'."

He meant that and it filled her with pride. "It really is. Like shifters, we've made do with human medications and the variants our own doctors and scientists have come up with." She made herself stop there because having witches out in the world gaining the expertise needed to engineer medications and medical procedures that were tailored for the "Talented," as most witches and shifters generally referred to their group as a whole, was her great passion and she could talk about it for hours.

"But there are other things to try. Meditation. Music or other types of sound. And animals. Biscuit and K Mags bring sunshine and soft round bellies to rub and that lowers blood pressure. It gives the hands something to do while you're meeting with a therapist or when you're in the waiting room for the dentist. They're part of my practice in important ways."

"Sometimes, you don't plan your story, it just writes itself."

Ruby glanced up at Damon and he grinned at her in response.

"It's something one of my aunts says."

"She's right. I didn't plan on being a dog person. Especially not until after I'd come back to Diablo Lake. But I was meant to have them. And they were meant to be my family and to be part of the type of healing I practice."

K Mags's tail thumped against the floor as if he knew she was talking about them.

Not long after, Damon helped her clear away their snacks and the cider before taking his leave for the night.

He paused long enough on her back steps she wondered if he was going to close the gap and kiss her. But he hugged her, wrapping his arms around her. He smelled excellent, as he always had. No kiss though as he stepped back at last. "Be seeing you around. If you need anything, I'm just right up that hill there. Good night, Ruby darlin'."

Even after she'd closed and locked the door, she watched through the windows in her kitchen. Moonlight fell over him until he disappeared into the trees. She could still feel his presence, as if the earth at her feet connected them somehow.

Back at his trailer, he took his boots off before going inside but paused, the door still open, as he stared down toward the heart of town. Down toward where Ruby most likely puttered around her kitchen talking to those ridiculous dogs.

It wasn't—just—the connection they'd shared for years. It wasn't just her beauty and her magical talent. It wasn't just that she was funny and intelligent. Though all those things were a powerful lure. When she'd talked about the dogs and the way she'd been able to have them be part of her healing practice had convinced him utterly that Ruby Thorne was the one. The. One.

Compassion, passion, ferocity, beauty and intelligence all wrapped up into one delectable package. One he hadn't been ready or able to appreciate fully years ago. Neither of them was the same. Both had grown and learned their respective talents and place in the universe.

He knew enough to understand he had to be worthy of a woman like her at his side. Sure they had loads of chemistry and sexual attraction. That part wouldn't be hard. Well, okay, *that part was hard* but they'd burn up the sheets when the time came. She'd need wooing. And spoiling.

Damon grinned as he finally closed the door. Good thing he wasn't afraid of a little hard work.

Chapter Six

"Ruby, there's someone in the waiting area for you," Erica called out. "I'm leaving. See you tomorrow."

"No need to say who or anything. Girl should be glad she's my cousin," Ruby muttered as she locked the medication safe and then the room it was in. "Just a moment," she called out before securing the door leading back to the exam rooms.

"I'll give you as many moments as you need," Damon replied and Ruby heard that smile in his tone.

"I had to lock everything up since I'm the only one here," she told him as she went straight toward him for a hug whether he'd been intending to or not. He folded her into his chest a moment.

Her heart thundered so hard she could hear it in her voice.

He held her away from him, searching her face before a sly light came into his eyes. "I like the pattern. Dark blue and yellow. Makes your eyes even deeper brown."

Okay so maybe Ruby wouldn't be annoyed at Erica for not saying it was Damon waiting. She touched the scarf she'd used to wrap her hair that morning. "It was a graduation present from my cousin."

"Hard to believe Erica is already twenty-three and married. I always think of her as a seven-year-old. Played shortstop on my junior softball team. Never got tired of asking why. Ever. A good shortstop though. Leader."

Charmed, Ruby tipped her chin at the bag he held. "She still never shuts up. Good leader still too. What's up?"

"I've got two root beer floats. Do you have a few minutes to share them with me?"

She had home visits to make, but she didn't need to leave for at least half an hour.

"This beats the protein bar I was going to eat in my car on the way to my next appointment," Ruby told him.

They'd settled at the little bench just outside the clinic. Her face was tipped up to the sun, eyes closed, a smile marking her lips. At that moment he very much wished he was an artist because she should have been a painting.

She turned to him before sliding sunglasses into place. "I'm loving the sunny weather. I worked out in the yard and did some furniture painting in the carport most of yesterday but it got chilly fast once the sun set. Feels like this winter is going to be a cold one."

He'd driven by her place that morning on the way to work to see she'd been busy. The outside had been manicured a little. Trained into some order but still organic and a little wild. He couldn't wait to see what the place would look like come spring and summer next year.

"Let me know how the woodstove works. It's new so you'll need to use it a few times to figure out what you like best."

Ruby looked his way again and raised her nearly

empty root beer float. "Okay. I forgot to say thank you. Sure is nice when a friend brings ice cream by to enjoy in a spot of afternoon sun. How's your Monday so far?"

"Boring and annoying until now. Now it's really good. I think you should come out on a date. With me, I mean in case I wasn't clear on that point," he told her.

He'd meant to be more suave and charming and shit, but as usual, she befuddled him and got his wolf all goofy.

"All right."

"All right?"

"All right to the date. All right to the date with you," she said and smiled, revealing her dimple. God. That dimple.

"Excellent. This moment right here is my favorite part of today."

Her laugh brought his own. "Mine too."

"I was a little unsure if you'd say yes," he admitted.

"Because of the utter lack of chemistry between us?" she asked, deadpan.

That made him laugh again. "It's pitiful, really."

Ruby leaned in and slid her arm through his, squeezing him close. It had just been a quick thing but he still felt it though she'd moved away and was already talking about something else.

He took Ruby's glass and spoon back. He'd drop them at Katie Faith's on his way back to the Mercantile.

"I missed the simplicity of this. When I lived out there." Ruby pointed off to the distance, away from Diablo Lake. "A root beer float in a glass with a tall spoon is a simple pleasure. But a really wonderful one."

In a remote town like theirs, they couldn't afford some of the habits people who lived outside did. Trash needed to be dealt with. It took up space and resources. So they created as little as possible, especially in commercial settings. Take-out containers were nearly always reusable. Napkins as well. The Ruizes, one of the prominent big cat shifter families in town, handled the laundry and the Cuthberts, the other one, handled most of the washing of the dishes, silverware and glassware.

It would have been hard to adjust to, Damon realized. He knew people would move away from Diablo Lake, either for education or experience before returning or intending to never return. But the world out there didn't hold the same appeal for him that it had others. Here he was home. Wolf and man were safe. It was idyllic at times, but usually a pain in the ass because everyone knew your business.

But it was theirs. And it was safe.

He shook it off. They could talk about it on their date. Or not. "Friday night work for you for our date? Dinner?"

"Yes, that's good."

They agreed to check in with more details by midweek, though Damon knew he'd try to find a way to bump into her or stop by for a chat between now and then anyway.

"Thanks for the sweet treat and the flirting. I feel fortified for the rest of my appointments this afternoon."

He bent to hug her as she turned and he ended up grazing his lips across the corner of her mouth and cheek. She hummed her pleasure and he made himself pull away before he went in for a lot longer right there in broad daylight.

"All right then, Damon Dooley. I'll be seeing you." Ruby waved and then walked away to her car parked just to the rear of the clinic building. He stood there for a while, a silly smile on his face before spinning and heading back to work.

Later that night, Nichole showed up on Ruby's doorstep right about dinnertime. "She brings me food and a bottle of wine. How did I get the best friend on the planet?" Ruby hugged her and invited her inside.

"Pure luck, that's how. Let's eat. Greg's over at the high school playing soccer with all the other guys right around thirty. Really it's just a prelude to pitchers of beer. I think Damon is there too. He's in good shape. I mean I'd guess if the state of taut muscles is any indicator. Not that I noticed."

Ruby grabbed plates while Nichole unloaded the food at the table. "Super nonchalant way of bringing Damon up," she said as she sat.

"I thought so. I'm really sneaky. Like a spy. I could have gone to spy school or whatever," Nichole said.

Ruby snorted as she spooned up some macaroni salad. "Yeah, I can really see that. As for Damon being in shape, well, yeah. He's a total snack, as the kids say."

There was smoked turkey to go with the salad and Ruby added a quick pickle she'd tossed together just the day before and a loaf of bread.

"I've been experimenting with a cheesy rice bake that might be really tasty with barbecue. I'll save you some the next batch I make."

Nichole waved a hand with an annoyed growl. "Fuck your rice. We were talking about Damon *hot butt* Dooley."

"Fuck my rice? I would not ever. I am scandalized." Ruby put a hand to her throat, faking offense.

"You said you dated and then broke up before it got too serious and then you left town. Greg says Damon always asked after you over the years."

"Four dates. There'd been flirting for a while, but he's three years older and until I was out of high school he wouldn't have looked twice because that's just how he is. I liked him then, like I said. We never even got past some making out with a little dry humping. And then he said since I was leaving for so long we should break things off and remain friends. He respected my plans to get my education and all that. And so, I left town two or three months after that. We saw each other around town when I was back to visit. No drama or anything like that."

"You two were not looking at one another like two pals supporting one another's career path when I saw you and Damon sitting on the bench outside the clinic earlier today. You were sitting shoulder to shoulder and had your heads turned, nearly touching noses. Just lasted a moment but there's something between you."

"This town! Of course you saw it." Ruby had to laugh. "He brought cider to my house that day I moved in. Then he showed up at the clinic today. Brought me a root beer float and then asked me on a date. I obviously said yes. This time is different. We're both different. We've gone through stuff and it's made us better. I wouldn't have grown into who I am now if I hadn't left and gotten the education I needed. It was a good choice and I'm not mad about the original breakup. I'm pleased to see where this version of Damon and Ruby goes."

"Okay. I'm down with this plan. I like the way you think." Nichole tapped her glass to Ruby's. "And I want all the details afterward. Especially if they're dirty."

"Ha! I hope to have dirty details to share. It's been a while since I've had dirty details." Ruby had dated on and off over the years. She hadn't been chaste by any stretch. But none of it had been very serious. Because she was never going to stay out there and she couldn't bring an outsider back unless it was forever, like Nichole and Greg.

"I just realized Diablo Lake is probably crawling with women who've seen him naked." Ruby frowned.

"Whatever. Let them have those cherished memories because that's all over now. It comes with being with a person who oozes all that charisma and sensuality. Your brother does too and you know there's more than one person in this town who's seen him naked as well."

Ruby clapped her hands over her ears. "It's weird because that's my brother you're talking about," she said. "I'm glad you're happy and um compatible and all that."

"If I know about your little root beer date with Damon, you know your mom is going to hear about it. And the real date. You have to tell her about it too. Social currency is a big-ass deal in this town," Nichole said.

"Yeah, you're right. If she got called about the date and I hadn't told her she'd be so pissed. Good call. You're settling into Diablo Lake just fine."

"Everyone loves gossip."

"Especially when there are no nightclubs and a one-screen movie theater that doubles as the public meeting hall." Ruby picked her phone up to give her mother a heads-up.

"I'm going on a date. Friday night. With Damon. You already knew he and I were flirting and all that.

But once we go on a date, there'll be talk. I wanted you to know first."

Her mom made a noncommittal sound. "There's already talk about you two driving around town looking for a rental and then today you apparently got chummy with him in public on the Ave. But I'm glad to know before the date. I just want to ask you if you think he's worth it. You dated before and then you didn't. I assumed you broke up for a reason. I want you to be happy."

Ruby's mom was the best.

"We broke up but not because either of us had wronged the other. I liked him then. A lot. Breaking up wouldn't have been my idea, but we'd have had to at some point. I was going to leave for years. So, he didn't cheat or hurt me like that. If he had I wouldn't be dating him again. I don't know where this will go. But I also understand we're not nineteen. I'm open to something serious but also old enough to know I'll survive if things fizzle and it goes nowhere after all."

Her mom let out a breath. "Okay then. Keep me updated. I love you. Oh! I need to update you on some Lovie info. She got wind of that argument you had with Scarlett at the market. Your dad and I had to reassure her that you were fine and it wasn't like you got jumped or stabbed or what have you. Then she calmed down. For a while there I thought me and your Pops were going to have to duct tape her to her recliner to stop her from heading out to find Scarlett."

That would have been something to see. Lovie was petite, five feet tall on a good day. Hair always done if she went outside her house. She'd had a cute little pixie cut for the last decade or so, but before that, well the

pictures of her Lovie with big-ass hair gave Ruby life.
Beehives? Check. Giant afro? Check. Wigs of every
type imaginable showed Lovie's change over the years.
She was generally loved in Diablo Lake, having taught
a few generations piano over at the community center.
Those kids, now adults, also knew how lightning fast
and unflappable Pearl Thorne was. If you dared not take
your piano lesson seriously, you'd have found yourself
on your butt as she pushed you off the bench for lagging
or lollygagging. Two things she *did not abide.*

There was a list somewhere, Ruby was sure, of all
the things Lovie *didn't abide.* Gum chewing in church.
Cigar smoking. Being interrupted while watching *Family Feud.* Off-brand cereal and baked goods. "That had
better be Cheerios and Little Debbie. Last time you
brought me some other kinda health food Moon Pie
that tasted like sadness. I eat a Moon Pie because I'm
sad already!"

Lovie might be cute and feisty, but in defense of
those she loved? Scarlett might be a wolf shifter—an
alpha wolf shifter—but Pearl was absolutely not one
to mess with.

"Good thing for Scarlett that Lovie's walker will
slow her down when Scarlett makes a retreat," Ruby
said with a chuckle.

"Good Lord, Ruby! Do not even joke. You never
know with your grandmother," her mom chided through
laughter. "Tell Nichole I said hello. I'm going to see why
your father has been out back for forty-five minutes.
I bet he's out there with that brother of mine drinking
beer and playing dominoes."

Ruby's dad and her uncle Lamar had been best
friends since childhood. It was an adorable story that

her parents had been the older brother's best friend love match. Lamar was mellow like Ruby's grandfather. He and Ruby's dad were hilarious together, both of them having married fiery women but being more of the quiet type unless and until you pushed one of them too far. Then watch out.

Nichole stayed for another hour or so before heading home. Ruby, nice and tired, but also nice and satisfied with her life, sat on her back porch steps and watched the boys play and get their last bit of energy out before bedtime.

And just up the rise, she knew Damon breathed and worked and existed. That knowledge settled in her belly. Leaving a lovely warmth in its wake.

Chapter Seven

When Ruby had arrived home from work Friday, she was bone tired and if she hadn't already agreed to a date with Damon, she'd have showered and headed to bed early. But she had agreed and he was delicious and easy to look at and be with and she didn't have to cook at all so really, it was a total win for her to go out with him.

On her front doorstep there was a container of cuttings—the note said from bushes and flowers from his maternal grandmother's yard—and tulip bulbs. The end of the note told her he'd be by to pick her up at seven thirty and to dress warmly.

He gave her cuttings and bulbs. No suitor had ever given her anything like it before. She was utterly delighted and flattered that he'd put effort into a gift she'd enjoy. And if she planted them within a week, they'd be happy to return as flowers.

Ruby put them in her garden shed while the boys ran around the yard peeing, digging, barking, chasing birds and squirrels and then starting the whole cycle again. "Door's open for you to come inside when you're ready," she called out, leaving the sliding glass door open enough for them to come back in when they tired of peeing and barking.

The note said to dress warmly, but what for? Naturally this led to eleven wardrobe changes. What did that mean anyway? Dress warmly because they were walking along the Ave after dinner? Or because he was getting a pizza and they were eating it outside? What?

"Well we know your hair looks good," Nichole said as she came into the house ten minutes later after Ruby called her and asked for help getting ready.

"Thank you. It's nice to finally have a hair salon in Diablo Lake. I spent many a Saturday on the porch at Lovie's. She can't do it now because of her arthritis, but she used to be the best braider ever. Patterns and stuff. Our hair was always looking fantastic when we were growing up. But it sure is nice to be inside, out of the cold. I can have a coffee or whatever while sitting in a comfortable chair. Bonus is that Claudia doesn't whack me with the comb if I move too much like Lovie does."

They both laughed.

Yesterday, Claudia, her second cousin and hairdresser, had braided Ruby's hair away from her face but left her curls free at the back. It looked super cute, if she did say so herself.

"So the note said to dress warm. But does he mean formal warm or rugged warm?" Ruby asked, glancing at the clothes on her bed.

"Chances are he doesn't mean either. What formal events are there in Diablo Lake? Aside from Samhain and other holidays, it's not like there are fancy restaurants here, or anything fancy at all, for that matter. But he's not going to make you chop wood on a date either." Her sister-in-law began to look through the piles of clothing, pulling out a few things here and there. "We can definitely blow his socks off with a cute outfit you'll also be warm in when you're outside."

Nichole held out a bright yellow sweater. "This." And then pointed at a pair of black pants still on the bed. "With those."

Naturally her friend was right, and the combo was colorful and very flattering.

"You look like a sexy wasp," Nichole told her.

"Wasp? Not a bee?"

"Ma'am. A wasp keeps going even after they avenge whatever bullshit they had to suffer through. I love a bee, Rube. But you can sting and keep going." Her friend held out a pair of pretty dangle earrings.

"You look great. Sexy. You smell good. He's gonna be pleased as he should be." Nichole hugged her quickly. "Text me when you get home."

He knocked on her door not ten minutes later. "Hey," she said, opening up and coming face-to-face with Damon.

Damon Dooley on her doorstep. Ready to take her on a date. Things were looking up daily around Diablo Lake.

"Hey yourself." He grinned and then kissed her cheek quickly. "You look real pretty."

"Thank you. You look good too. That green is good with your eyes." He wore a fisherman's sweater of deep green that brought out the caramel of his hair and the hazel in his eyes.

God he was handsome. Especially when he blushed. He was big and tall and took up so much space and her lungs were full of him.

"You want to come in and see what I've done with

the place?" Ruby asked, amused. Wolves were so curious and nosy. She knew he'd want to come inside but the way his entire being lit up brought a laugh spilling from her belly.

She stepped aside to admit him and the dogs…where were the dogs? Ruby looked around until she saw them sitting side by side, tails wagging, gazes snagged on Damon.

Damon's grin transferred to the dogs and Ruby was grateful the looks were not the same. He made a sound deep in his throat and the boys came to attention. Biscuit's tail had slowed down to nearly a stop, though his joy at seeing Damon broke through every few seconds when it couldn't help itself but thump a few times.

It was so cute it took all Ruby's control not to fall to her knees and smooch his sweet little head. Also grab a few smooches from Damon because he was so adorable with the dogs her ovaries were having a dance party.

What a very good boy K Mags was sitting there so pretty and still! So handsome for Damon. He deserved an extra cookie before bed for that.

She really wanted little bow ties for each of them so her mom said she was going to make each of them one for Samhain. Her big old softhearted mom who tried to act like she'd never in a million years put a bow tie on a dog to make him look dapper but who already apparently had some sort of pattern ready.

Ruby bet Damon would find bow ties absolutely adorable.

When Damon looked back over his shoulder toward Ruby, he caught her, hands clutched against her heart, big-eyed with love for these darned little nuggets. She was normally beautiful, but just at that moment she was radiant and he swallowed against the lump of emotion.

"You've done a very good job patrolling the yard," he told them seriously. He could hear their chatty little vocalizations over the course of a day, but very rarely did he hear alert or danger barks or growling.

"Look at you two already part of the neighborhood watch," Ruby said at his back, making him laugh and give the dogs a quick scratch behind the ears.

"They're happier to see you than they are to see me," Ruby told him as he stood.

"How about you?" he murmured, getting closer. "*You* happy to see me?"

She squeaked what sounded like assent. A full two beats later she said, "I mean, yes. Yes, I'm happy to see you. I even made you treats."

The little intake of breath, the speed of her pulse was catnip. She swallowed and then chewed her bottom lip for a brief moment and hers wasn't the only pulse set to racing.

More. More. Damon wanted more of her.

"I like the way you smell, Ruby darlin'," he said leaning in to sniff deeply.

"It's probably the cookies. Half butterscotch and the other chocolate chips. That way you don't have to choose." Her gaze, those big gorgeous dark brown eyes held his. Met the challenge of the wolf by not looking away.

Her lips hitched into a sexy smile. Openly attracted. Flirtatious.

Damon liked this Ruby too. Bold and sexy. Confident.

"I'll have to taste all three. To be sure."

"Only two kinds of cookies. Not three. *Greedy.*"

Damon closed all but the barest of space between them and tipped her chin up with his finger. "I know. I meant *you* too. When it comes to you, I think I'm going to be very greedy."

"Oh, then we should be sure. For science," she said faintly, moving toward him as he did the same, meeting in the middle with a soft kiss, a sweet and sexy *hello there, it's been a while* feel.

He allowed himself to bury his consciousness in the experience. Glorying in the way she tasted and felt against him after so many years. Like yesterday and yet totally different. The heaviness of the moment hung between them warm and full of promise.

She tasted of honey and chocolate. Rich and decadent. The lush, heady aroma of roses with the sweet hint of jasmine rose and a growl of satisfaction rumbled in his chest. His hands rested at the swell of her hips.

He practically vibrated, a tuning fork that she had awakened that reacted only to her.

Damon needed to slow down or he'd gobble her up in one bite. She deserved savoring. Regretfully, he broke the kiss and stepped away.

She was all over him. Her taste, her scent, the way she'd felt against his chest, under his palms. The wolf retreated a little, satisfied to be marked like that.

It took a few moments for Ruby to get herself together after the kiss ended. He hadn't had a beard the last time she kissed him. "I like the bristles," she said, fingertips briefly brushing against her lips.

"Yeah?"

"Aside from being very handsome, it adds a nice texture to smooching you."

"No better reason to have it then." Damon tipped his chin in the direction of the dogs. "Figured, if you want to and all, that you could bring them along."

"You haven't said where we're going," she reminded him.

"I made dinner up at my place. Thought we could eat outside. Don't worry, you'll be warm."

"They might get into your construction or dig holes." Or run off into wherever. But Ruby figured he'd be able to catch them pretty quickly if they did. Hopefully before they got eaten by something bigger and tougher.

He laughed. "They won't."

Ruby thought anyone who thought they could tell a Cairn not to dig holes and have them listen and obey was bananas. But it was sweet of him to offer and the boys seemed to really love having him around.

"They'll be fine. Especially when they know you're fine." Damon gave them both a stern face. "They'll be safe and won't run off or use a nail gun on one another."

"That sounds pretty specific, Damon," Ruby said.

"I'm surprised Major never told you the story. He tells it all the time like it was some big tragic event and I was Freddy Krueger or whatever. Didn't even leave a scar though he had a little groove on his left cheek for a few years until it grew back in."

Not for the first time, Ruby winced even as she marveled at the relationship between the twin brothers. Tight. Even in the middle of a fight, they'd drop everything to save the other. They bickered constantly but even though their personalities were different, they were one another's biggest fan.

"Anyway, I just mean they'll be safe," Damon attempted to reassure her after that tale. "I drove over so you can bring their beds if you want."

"You're a big old softie," she said on her way past him. "Come let me show you the rest of the house and then we can go."

When he pulled in at the bottom of a slight rise she could see the house in progress and his trailer off to the side. Damon turned to the dogs, who sat excitedly in the jump seat where he'd installed them. "You can smell all you want. Lots of wolves around so be aware. Don't leave the clearing or I'll put you on a lead or never have you back."

He was very serious and the way the dogs so obviously wanted to please him was so cute she wanted to faint at the sweetness of it all.

When they got out, the dogs raced ahead, but not too far, and they kept checking in with Damon and Ruby, which admittedly eased Ruby's mind.

"It's going to be a lot for them," Damon said as he took her hand. "Half the pack was here last night helping get the final part of the roof in place."

Ruth lost the last bit of his sentence because once they'd gotten up the rise, she could see Damon had been busy preparing for their date.

He'd strung white lights up around the trailer he was living in and around the firepit where two chairs sat side by side, a table between them.

"I brought out blankets too. Once you're ready to sit, I'll tuck you in. Keep you warm."

"This is…wow." She turned in a circle to take it all in. "It feels like a fairy tale."

"I figured this would be nicer than a restaurant. Quieter for sure. We won't get interrupted. At least I hope not. Plus, I get you all to myself." He kissed her quickly, blushing, before getting about building the fire up.

Ruby gave him a little space, walking around the area, checking out the progress on the main house as well as she could by fire and fairy lights.

Biscuit followed her, dashing just slightly ahead of her and then waiting somewhat impatiently. He seemed rapturously happy to stop every few seconds to smell something else. "What do you think?" she asked the dog.

Biscuit barked sharply a few times, before sneezing and sitting down to stare up at her. Obviously he was happy. A new place to sniff and pee all around. Their superhero Damon to watch and learn from. Possible table scraps. Snuggles with mom. All big positives in their little canine world.

This was all so thoughtful. From the bulbs to making sure she'd be warm.

Outside Diablo Lake she'd wonder if a guy like Damon doing something like this was only trying to get into her panties. Though, lord knew someone with a face like his didn't need to work that hard to get into anyone's underpants.

But the truth she felt in her gut was that he wanted her to feel comfortable and taken care of. The way it made her feel was that she deserved a little taking care of. And wasn't that pretty wonderful?

Who didn't want someone who believed they were worth being spoiled? *It's a gift*, she thought as they ambled back to where Damon had already set out a mug for her and produced a platter of cheese and meat with a flourish.

"Biscuit and I were looking at the progress on the house. The view you're going to have from the kitchen sink is going to be staggering."

"I poured you some mulled cider. It's got bourbon in it. I also have nonalcoholic. I've got the usual suspects as well. Beer. I can make you hot tea. There's wine and bourbon as I mentioned."

"I love mulled cider, especially when it's also got bourbon. Thanks." Ruby settled into the chair and he showed up with a blanket lined in shearling that he tucked around her legs.

"I figure we can have a snack while we wait. I made chicken. Country captain chicken, my grandmother calls it. It's her recipe. It's got about twenty minutes left."

Smooth-talking cool kid Damon Dooley was flustered and nervous. What a thrill!

"Sounds really good. Perfect for a chilly night." Ruby sipped her drink and then patted her knees. "The blankets are a very nice touch. Thoughtful."

"I want you to be comfortable."

It was a simple thing but integral.

Ruby reached out to squeeze his hand briefly before she helped herself to some of the cheese and crackers and stuff he'd laid out. "This would have been a fine dinner in and of itself," she told him as she added a little bit more of the strawberry jam to the pile on her cracker.

His grumble of outrage told her what he thought about that. "How was your week?" he asked, settling back, his long, powerful legs stretched out.

"Weird. But mostly not too bad. We're getting into a rhythm at work. Partly because we haven't had long enough to get into fights, but also because we seem to work well together. I learn things from them all every day. I'm doing what I love to do and I'm back in my community. It feels absolutely like where I'm supposed to be right now. What about you? How was your week?"

He clinked his mug to hers. "It's been a busy week at the Mercantile. With Samhain, Collins Hill Days and Halloween all coming up we've been slammed with mail orders and all sorts of housewares. Everyone wants to get the last of their outdoor home improvement done before the middle of next month so we always stock up on paint and nails and new drills. Weatherizing and all that too. Jace works over at the mechanic shop when he's not working on Dooley business."

"I imagine getting ready for the Halloween dinner is taking up all sorts of energy and time."

Every year, the shifters in Diablo Lake held a huge dinner after the little ones finished trick-or-treating. Some of them showed up the day before to start whatever meat they were presenting to the community. They had their specialties and guarded recipes zealously. Everyone brought something. It was an undertaking that took up a huge amount of work hours just to coordinate who was doing what and when. And to do it all without offending anyone. There were a lot of moving parts and a lot of them had sharp teeth.

Damon snorted. "You could say that. My grandma Patty's in charge of the organizing committee so I know things'll be handled well. It's a load off my mind to know she can handle it and then Katie Faith can learn on the job, which is good too."

"Helps everyone see she's learning to be part of Dooley even if she's a witch and not a shifter. Plus your grandmother is like mine, cunning. And Ms. Patty is good at politics too. Katie Faith knows how fortunate she is to be learning from someone like her."

"Thank you. That means a lot. People underestimate her. They don't think she's smart when in reality, she can run circles around most folks. When I say that to her, she just laughs all evil-like and says it's even more satisfying to kick their asses when they thought she was a dumb hick instead of an alpha wolf."

"I sure do love your grandparents," Ruby said, laughing.

The dogs went right to the edge they'd agreed upon—somehow—with Damon, but not one nose farther. There was much snuffling and barking and peeing and running back to check on Ruby.

"This plot, lot, whatever you call it where a house goes," Ruby waved a hand at the area they sat in, "is perfect. The light at my house is lovely at sunrise and sunset, but up here you've got enough elevation that there's not much to get in the way."

"You guessed that the kitchen would have an excellent view of sunrise light. And I definitely think it will. The master takes up a corner that'll have a wrap-around balcony to take advantage of both. Shifters get up early so the eastern exposure will help me wake up but also since I'm up, why not have the house built in such a way that I get the most out of it?"

"Absolutely. I didn't take the largest bedroom in my house because the smaller one had a better view and feel to it. Your house should make you happy. There's very good magic here," she told him. "So many shades of green. Browns, some deep blues. The water is very clean. I've never lived anywhere in Diablo Lake that wasn't surrounded by other witches, so this is new to me. But my magic seems to love it."

He nodded. "Your presence, even in just the week or so that you've lived in the house, has changed the land. There are apple trees just over there." Damon pointed. "They're fruiting now. Won't be long before the branches will be heavy with ripe apples."

"Excellent! I'm making spiced apple cake for the Samhain bonfire. I'll pay you in baked goods if you let me pick them."

He just looked at her for long moments and then shook his head. "Ruby darlin', you're welcome to the apples on my trees and whatever else that suits your fancy and grows on my land. I'll even help you harvest it all."

Ruby knew she gulped like a cartoon character, but he managed to make an offer to help her pick apples into something sexy and mysterious.

That moment, naturally, was interrupted by the approaching gallop of the dogs. Ruby managed to sternly order K Mags *drop it* before she got a lapful of warm and bloody dead rodent.

K Mags sat next to the treasure though, proud, and Ruby sucked up her dread and apologized. "Yikes. I'm sorry, Damon. Let me get that cleaned up."

Damon just rolled his eyes, but stayed her progress with a wave of his hand. "I did some reading about Cairn terriers," Damon said, surprising her. "They dig and hunt rats and the like. It's what they were bred to do."

"Maybe. But last week he dropped a still-twitching mole on my bare foot." Ruby shuddered.

Damon tossed a piece of salami to K Mags. "We can

work on that. But I promise I'm not offended with the little brothers doing their jobs."

"Little brothers?"

"I've gone back and forth about dogs and what they are in relation to what I am. But Biscuit and K Mags are part of your pack, and in some way also part of mine. They're curious and brave. That's a combo that means it's helpful to have a big brother or sister. Essentially an older shifter who can relate and help guide the younger ones through hard times. When they're here, I think on them as little brothers."

"Well. That's just." She looked up at him, struck by the depth of sweetness in him. "What lucky dogs they are. Their mom too," she settled on.

He ducked his head again and busied himself dealing with whatever type of deceased rodent K Mags had brought and cleaning up the evidence well enough that within a few minutes, it had been forgotten.

At last, a timer dinged and he popped into the trailer and five minutes later he'd come out again, carrying a tray with steaming plates of chicken and rice and a little basket overflowing with bread.

"Here we go. I hope you're hungry."

"I even get tableside service? This date is really good so far, Damon. I'll leave a positive review online."

He snorted.

The food smelled really tasty and after the first bite neither of them said much for a few minutes, just eating and enjoying the night.

"This is really good," Ruby told him.

"It's one of my *company* recipes. I have four or so that I'm good enough at I make them for special occasions. My grandma's is better, I think. But this is close."

"I've had this lots of times, but I can say without lying that this is my favorite so far. The tomatoes are what takes it over the top."

"Last jar of tomatoes I had. Aimee's mom brought me all sorts of stuff at the end of summer last year. I only realized recently that the tomatoes would be perfect. She puts a little hot pepper in hers. Makes the sauce a little extra zesty."

Who'd have thought he'd appreciate home-canned ingredients and perfecting recipes? It only made him more attractive.

"Maybe next time I'm canning I'll give you a call so you can come help," she told him, thinking about how a second helping would be a compliment to his skills in the kitchen so it was a nice thing to do.

It certainly made him look happy as he popped up and took her plate off to get her some more.

And then, after they'd finished dinner, Damon pulled out marshmallows, chocolate bars and graham crackers. "Figured s'mores for dessert would be a good thing," he said. "If grown-up Ruby is anything like twelve-year-old on a campout Ruby, that is."

"Sure isn't a bad thing," she agreed. Also not bad that he'd remembered something she'd loved as a kid.

"That was probably the most fun I've ever had on a camping trip," Ruby told him honestly. Then again, it had been before she'd known the real difference of camping in places that had community showers and toilets at the very least. "Even though I was the only girl and you and my brother just pretended I wasn't there. Gathering around the campfire at night for s'mores made up for it though."

He laughed, taking her hand in his and kissing her

fingertips. "I like having you around," he said quietly. "You were gone for years but now that you're back, it's like, well, I don't like to think about you being anywhere else."

In the yellowy gold light from the string lights, Damon looked even sexier as he leaned close enough for her to meet him halfway for a kiss. She hummed, delighted, as he licked over her bottom lip before he nibbled it.

He just meandered around her mouth, tasting and teasing in little licks and nips. It left her caught between breathless anticipation at what he'd do next and pleasure from whatever he'd just done.

But then he pulled away, the cad, and set about impaling fluffy marshmallows on the end of a stick before handing it over. "You get those all gooey and hot and I'll stack the chocolate."

If she hadn't heard the slightest tremble in his voice, she would have been annoyed he'd been so unaffected by that kiss.

And it wasn't even just the kiss—though ten of ten, would kiss again—it was also that whispered confession that he liked her around. And the date as a whole.

It was wonderful. And thoughtful. It wasn't as if Damon was a bad guy at all. He was funny and flirty and good at all sorts of stuff. But this…she'd never experienced a date like this. She was probably spoiled for life now. How else could anyone compete with this?

Just shy of totally blackened outsides, Ruby left two marshmallows on each bed of cookie and chocolate while Damon held the top—more cookie and chocolate—on. Smooshed together, it was a melty, gooey, sweet and sticky mess that tasted a little of woodsmoke and fresh air.

The best dessert she'd ever had, hands down.

It didn't hurt at all that it was eaten while she sat next to the most beautiful individual she'd ever met in person who also kissed her like she was the tastiest thing in the universe.

When Damon rose, Ruby helped him clean up the remains of their dessert but before she tried to wash the dishes, he pulled her close.

"I think we should dance awhile."

"That so?" The attempt at super-confident sexy bravado was undercut a bit by the way her pulse thundered in her ears. She knew without a doubt he heard it too.

"Don't move," he murmured after kissing her quickly. A few beats later, music began to play. "In Case You Didn't Know" by Brett Young. "Dance with me," he said and she took the hand he held her way and in a few steps, she rested her body against his. His arm banded her waist, holding her close and her cheek rested on his chest, over his heart.

Damon had danced his share. Had always loved the dance floor because that's always where the girls and the fun were. But this was different. This was different even from the times he'd held Ruby against his body before.

The stars wheeled overhead as the fire in the firepit crackled. He buried his face in the curve of her neck and breathed in deep with a groan of pleasure he hoped didn't scare her. She snuggled closer and he smiled against her skin.

By that time, her scent had burrowed into him, snagging his attention. Teasing. Sensual. Delightful.

Anticipation rode his spine as the few seconds it took for Ruby to turn her face up to his for a kiss stretched and heated. It was no time at all while also feeling like hours.

His gaze flicked from her lips, parting on a sigh, to her eyes and the way her lashes had swept down.

Damon bent his knees and met her lips with his. A soft, warm brush as she opened on a gasp. A good gasp, that had a little teeth at the end as she grazed his bottom lip. When he returned the nip of teeth, she gasped again and he knew he'd never, ever tire of that sound.

She grabbed a fistful of his shirt and pulled him along with her to the footstool she stood on to bring herself closer to his height.

Fuck. Yes.

With a snarl, he stepped closer and banded her waist as she slid her arms around his neck and pulled him impossibly nearer. His heart beat so hard Damon was sure she heard it too.

And then they were kissing. Lips, teeth and tongues a tangle of need and pleasure.

It went on, an endless loop of kissing that seemed to spin a web that bound them together.

She was fire in his arms, her body against his, every brush of contact sending sparks of desire through him. Damon wanted to strip her down slowly and worship every inch of skin he revealed.

He would.

Not that night though.

As much as he ached for her, the first time they

slept together wasn't going to be in the lumpy bed of the trailer.

When they moved back, both dazed, mouths kiss swollen, Damon picked her up and put her safely back on the ground.

"Thanks for dinner. And dessert. And the s'mores." Her grin brought one of his own in answer.

"You're welcome. When I say it was my pleasure I really do mean it."

He had to be at the Mercantile at seven thirty to get it ready to open at eight and it was already after one in the morning so he loaded the dogs and their gear up and then helped Ruby into the passenger side and drove them back to her place.

"What are you doing Sunday?" he asked once he'd carried the dog beds back inside. "I'm at the Mercantile until six tomorrow night and then there's Dooley business I need to attend to."

"I'm taking my grandparents to church. But they go to the first service so I'll be free by noon or so."

"Want to go for a hike? Not strenuous or far. But up to the ridge and back? It's easy enough you could bring the dogs too."

"All right. Yes, that sounds fun."

"I'll pick you up here at twelve fifteen or so. Just text me if you're running behind."

"I'll be here."

"Yeah. Liking that more and more every day," he told her as he gave her a quick kiss and then headed off into the night. He needed a run before he went to sleep.

Ruby watched his taillights as they faded from view and then closed the curtains.

"So, that happened," she told the dogs.

In the mirror after she'd taken off her makeup and was getting ready to brush her teeth, she noted how swollen her lips were even still.

The last few minutes before she left weren't full of sweet kisses. Or even brief kisses. No, Damon's kisses were a claim. It didn't matter that her lips would be fine in a few minutes. She'd feel the weight of those kisses long after that night.

Chapter Eight

"If you don't tell me about that date right now I'm going to get mad," Nichole said as she cruised into the clinic the following afternoon. "A text that says, *ohmigod it was an amazing date, ttyl*, isn't enough. Oh and I brought you a sandwich." Her sister-in-law held up a tote bag. "Coleslaw too. Take a break. I know it's your break time. I called ahead to see."

"You're so bossy," Ruby said with a snicker. "It was a really good night," Ruby admitted after they got themselves seated in the little break room. "He made me dinner. And we had s'mores for dessert. We danced under the stars. The dogs were there, by invitation. There was a goodly amount of kissing. All of which I'd give a ten of ten."

Ruby described how he'd decorated the whole area and had a fire going and all the accessories she'd need to stay warm.

"That's so romantic! He's really going for it, huh?"

"It's familiar and very different at the same time. Being with him is easy. I like him. I've always liked him. But as a man, he's grown into someone I'd like to know better. When I talk, he *listens*, you know? All his attention is on me, even if he's in the middle of something. It's flattering and sexy and overwhelming."

"This is all very promising, I must say. Your brother is like that. As if there's nothing in the world but me when I'm speaking or doing something. The men in your family were raised right."

"Hello? Certainly they're all fine, yeah. But as the only daughter, it's not just them."

Nichole snickered. "I know. Without you I never would have met Greg so I know you were raised right. It's not weird because he broke it off before?" Nichole asked.

"I wondered if it would be but it really isn't. Maybe if it had been a dramatic breakup or if he'd been awful I'd feel differently. But it sort of felt like that was training wheels for this grown-up thing we started again last night."

They laughed some more while Ruby finished her sandwich and then she got back to work, happy to have a sister-in-law who was also a very dear friend.

A few hours later, she came in through her parents' kitchen door. The dogs headed off to say hello to everyone while Ruby paused to hug her mother, grandmother and two of her cousins.

"A full house tonight," Ruby said after hanging her coat and bag up.

"Rita and Bill drove up here for the Consort meeting tomorrow so we figured we'd make a nice dinner to take advantage of seeing them."

Rita was her mom's youngest sister Erica's mother. Her husband, Bill, was a chemist and they lived in Knoxville but visited Diablo Lake at least once a month.

Their daughter was a part-time receptionist at the clinic and their son Joel was a farrier and took care of the large animals in town so it wasn't like Rita and Bill didn't have a place to stay when they did visit. But Ruby's mom loved her sisters fiercely and there was always laughter and excellent food when they were all together.

Naturally once everyone was seated and the food began the slow, clockwise turn around the table, her aunt Rita gave Ruby a careful look. "Your grandmother says Scarlett tried it the other day in the middle of the grocery store."

Ruby laughed as she scooped herself some potatoes. "It wasn't about me really. She was poking at Aimee and it made me mad. She only turned it my way because I spoke up. Now she knows and that's that. She's not important in my life." Ruby didn't want to waste a second in some silly fight with Scarlett. She'd rather move about her life and not give Scarlett another thought unless or until the other woman gave Ruby a reason.

Ruby's mom gave her an approving look. She'd raised Ruby to be no one's fool but not to let her time get wrapped up in someone else's issues. She was all about Ruby being confident and ambitious. Though she'd also taught Ruby how to take someone down if they came for you.

Ruby waggled her eyebrows at her mom and they both grinned a moment.

There was talk of Ruby's new house and some hilarious stories about a horse that managed to get into Joel's lunch cooler that he kept in the bed of his truck and had eaten most of it by the time he'd caught it in the act.

The lightness of it, the deep bonds they all shared never failed to make Ruby happy. It was raucous and silly, affectionate. Definitely passionate! Though they all tended toward magical talents around healing of some type, opinions about things were never scarce and rarely ever boring.

"I brought over some ice cream. Fudge ripple, Dad," Greg told their father who was up like a shot to get spoons and bowls.

"Did they start carrying it again at the market?" her dad asked a few minutes later. "I knew my letters would work." Mel Barker was pretty much the most easygoing person Ruby had ever known. He was slow to anger and quick to forgive. Confident in his strength as a person, as a man and a father. Married to a woman who was his equal and he'd be the first to correct that and say she was his superior in character and magic. He could make a friend of most anyone. No one was a stranger when Mel was in the room.

But he had his lines in the sand and things he would not tolerate. Like Lovie, he did not tolerate gum in his classroom. All that easygoing would fade away and leave behind an expression that told any fourteen-year-old to spit that gum into a napkin and throw it away, apologize and never do it again. You didn't read the newspaper first. He had a paper subscription to several state and national newspapers and magazines that arrived three days a week. There was a process. He had a definite order of sections. He'd eat most anything but liver was not allowed in the house.

And his favorite ice cream was Yellow Daisy fudge ripple. They were some brand from his youth and over the years, their geographic reach had gotten smaller and smaller. When the local grocery store was out of stock a few months ago, he'd begun a letter writing campaign to get it back in the freezer section.

"I spoke with the grocery manager and though he was appreciative of your letters, he's sorry but they buy through some third-party service and that service doesn't deal with Yellow Daisy anymore. He says they can special order it for you, but it'll be at about quadruple the price because of whatever process it is. Turns out, Katie Faith has an ice cream connection due to the soda fountain and she was able to order it for me at the wholesale price," Greg said. "I put in a weekly order for it for you."

Their dad beamed at Greg. "Thank you, son. I appreciate your doing all that. Don't tell anyone I said this, but you always were my favorite."

That started a whole bunch of hooting and laughter as teasing insults were tossed back and forth.

Ruby stayed until nine or so but as she was heading to her car, her aunt Rita ran out to catch her. "Bill and I are taking Lovie and Pops to church tomorrow so you don't need to."

"Oh. Okay. Thanks. I'll still see you at the Consort meeting though, right?"

Her aunt rolled her eyes. "All this early-morning stuff. I like to sleep in, but you know your grandmother. She's excited about that seven a.m. meeting. Thank goodness Miz Rose always has coffee. I'll need it." She hugged Ruby. "So good to have you back, baby. See you tomorrow."

And yes, she took the long way home so she could drive by and see the lights on up at the building site where Damon was most likely working. She knew his time off was spent on house stuff, which meant that stolen afternoon they had planned for the following day felt like a gift.

While she wanted to go on up there with a thermos of hot chocolate to maybe get a smooch as thanks, Ruby went home instead, leaving him to his work though he was certainly not far from her thoughts.

The next morning Ruby was up by six. Though she loved to sleep, mornings were often her best time for magical work. Her magic seemed to like it best so that's why she'd originally started out with early work sessions.

And by that point, decades later, it was habit.

She liked the quiet before dawn. The sense of the day inhaling slow and easy. And by mid-October, it was dark for a while yet so she put on a kettle for tea and fed the dogs while she waited for the water to boil.

There was a Consort meeting at seven but as Miz Rose's was only a short drive, Ruby watered her plants and let her magic rise and fill her kitchen.

When she'd been barely old enough to walk, the other witches in her life had begun to let her watch them work magic. Each witch had their own voice. Their own rites and rituals when it came to the practice of magic.

Over time, Ruby had incorporated bits and pieces she picked up along the way and had tweaked them as she'd grown in age and maturity, and in power. Everything she made she put her magic into in some way or other. As part of that then, she made sure to honor what she was doing and had her own ritual.

The kitchen was her favorite place to work in the house. Soon enough the morning light would come in, catching the stained glass on her wind chimes and casting blues and yellows across the walls and the smooth wood of the floors.

While the dogs were outside, Ruby packaged up the lemon ginger tisane she'd created for one of her patients who was suffering with terrible first trimester nausea. Each step of the process she'd imbued with protective and healing magics. Then, as she sealed the little jar, Ruby reached out for her magic as she tied the spell together.

The heart of Diablo Lake protected her citizens. That magic that coursed through the town was eager to help as she knit together the layers of her own magic to weave one larger working.

Some hot water in a mug with the mixture with honey, and as she drank, she'd warm up and the ginger—and magic—would alleviate the nausea. Bethany, the patient, was also a witch in town and Ruby would see her at the meeting and give it to her then.

And since she didn't need to take her grandparents to church, Ruby had some time now after the Consort meeting and the hike. If she didn't nap, she'd work on a new formula for a joint pain tincture. Ruby was going to try it on some of her sweeter patients and if it worked, she'd set about figuring out ways to get her most suspicious folks with arthritis and the like to use it as well.

Working her magic had always felt like a conversation with it. She thought about her needs and wants and then saw ways to weave her skill together, marrying intention with her power, and sealed it together.

And when it was all done, Ruby blew out her candles and opened her circle. The feel of her magic dissipating back into the earth was a warm, comfortable caress. She thanked the earth and her magic before she cleaned up her workspace.

With a quick look at the clock, she got moving. If she was late, Lovie would never let her hear the end of it.

Lovie and Miz Rose Collins were of the same generation. The two were friends and sometimes competitors, but always dedicated to the health and well-being of the witches and the magic of Diablo Lake.

The Consort—called that because Rose hadn't liked the term *coven* nearly as much—met at all the major sabbats as well as twice a month for full moon and dark moon days. That day they were all discussing the upcoming Samhain bonfire and dinner while eating a delightful breakfast and enjoying the garden at Miz Rose's place.

Ruby absolutely loved walking into any space filled by witches. All sorts of different flavors of magical talent seemed to float in the air. There was a shared bond, all these people who kept the town's magic safe and thriving.

She loved it that when she walked through the doors, all the faces turned her way wore smiles, clearly pleased to see her. That welcome warmed her. Filled her with fierce gratitude.

They divvied up tasks and Ruby gave her update when it was time. She'd been assigned the dessert table and she'd been busily collecting donations for it. She and a few others would decorate it appropriately, which meant she needed to finish her blueprint. It would be the map to follow with ingredients spelled out from the food to the greenery and table arrangement. She hated last-minute rushes to get things done in a half-assed way and found keeping lists was the best method to keep herself on track and get projects done.

At her side, Aimee took some notes while both of them gave Katie Faith the space to finish her second cup of coffee before they said hello. Ruby was a morning person. Katie Faith was…not. But after a cup of coffee she was much less murderous and after two, she was actually friendly and nearly a hundred percent less murdery.

Still, when it was their turn, Aimee spoke on behalf of both witches. "For the first time, the wolf shifter packs will be officially represented at the bonfire and buffet. Katie Faith and I talked and then we brought in Jace and Mac. We wanted to take a step to bridge the gap between the wolves and the rest of town after how fractured everything and everyone was by the end of last year. We'll coordinate with the food committees on what to bring."

Everyone thought this was a good idea and then the next item was heard.

Humans would be surprised to learn meetings were the same pretty much all over the country. Witches or humans, there were agendas and chairpersons and reports. They did learn new spellwork regularly, but mainly they got together, ate food and told each other stuff about what they did when they weren't at the meeting.

Once all the agenda items were finally done and they were about to adjourn, Miz Rose cleared her throat to get everyone's attention. "Before y'all leave, I just wanted to take a moment and tell you how proud I am. There've been struggles over the last few years. But there have been so many more blessings. Weddings.

Babies on the way." Miz Rose smiled over at a witch who'd announced her pregnancy in the *What's New* portion of the meeting. "We've lost dear ones." Everyone was quiet as they remembered Ruby's aunt, uncle and cousins who'd died in a car crash. "But here I am looking out over a sea of faces I've watched grow up. Faces of generations now that have learned magic here in this very garden. You're all the beating heart of this town. The reason why magic flourishes here the way it does. Even when things were very dark, we stuck by one another and kept the promise we made and together, we've made a difference. I love each and every one of you and I'm truly looking forward to the bonfire this year more than I have in a very long time."

There were several audible sniffles and Miz Rose waved a hand to tell them they could leave. Ruby hugged her and then after checking in to be sure Lovie was going with her aunt and uncle, she headed back home to get ready for her hiking date.

Damon knocked on her door promptly at twelve fifteen. It had been a little foggy and drizzly that morning, but by noon, the rain had eased off and the sun played peekaboo through the clouds.

All his anticipation and impatience to see her again flitted away when the door swung open, revealing her smiling face.

"Hey there," she told him. "Come in a second. I need to grab my backpack and their leads."

"Wait." He paused before her and bent to kiss those lips he'd been thinking about since he'd driven away from her door the night prior. A slow, sweet kiss hello. "That's so much better. Thank you." Damon grinned her way and she grinned back. "You look real pretty today. The puffs are perfect." He indicated the two little puffs she'd pulled the loose curls into, one low on each side of her head.

She looked like a flower in a bright red long-sleeved shirt and jeans that hugged all her curves perfectly. She mimed fluffing her hair, smiling as she did. "One does try." With a flutter of her lashes, she dashed over to grab her things and they got on their way.

"I'm saving all the good conversation for the hike," she told him.

"Do you only have two hours' worth of things to talk about with me, Ruby darlin'? 'Cause I'm pretty sure I could listen to you talk about paint drying and love it. Not that I'm encouraging anything of the like," Damon teased. "There's lots to catch up on. How was the DLWA meetin'?"

"The what?"

"Diablo Lake Witches Association. Like the PTA only with witches."

Her laugh filled the car and danced over his skin.

"It was fine. Lots of agenda items. Lots of reports and updates. More than one tearful speech, which was charming instead of grating. I like belonging. No. I think it's more like I like feeling like I belong. I like it when I sit around a big table with people I've known all my life. Several of them have had a major part in who I am today, you understand?"

Damon nodded. "I do understand. Wolf shifters are pack creatures much like our wild, one-natured brethren are. Belonging is part of my DNA."

Her dogs barked as if to remind him they were pack

animals as well. And all of them wanted Ruby's love and attention.

"So anyway. It was a good meeting. And my aunt and uncle took Lovie and Pops to church so I came home and baked, worked in the garden some and then began a new batch of tinctures. Made us all lunch. Overall, very productive."

He parked not too far from the trailhead and helped her out. Damon admired her ease in the quick way she snapped the leads to each dog's harness and their excited but disciplined presence at her side.

"They're very clever," Ruby said in reply to his unspoken comment.

They were, he had to admit.

"In the warmer weather you'll need to watch for snakes. Not today though," he said as they began the lazy curve up and around the northern end of town, leading to a ridge that looked out over one of his favorite vantage points on the planet.

It was a good walk and one he took at least weekly. Sometimes as a man, sometimes on four legs. Ten minutes through the edge of the forest and around the first corner where it opened up to a wider avenue, the town and paved roads forgotten because all that was replaced by the immensity of life. Birds and wildlife, trees of several types, most in some measure of colored glory.

There was no one else out but the four of them so they had what felt like the whole world to themselves.

Though he'd told her he was a pack animal, he most definitely considered her part of that pack and having her all to himself given how busy both their lives were felt like a gift.

"How goes the build?" she asked him.

"Not bad. Kitchen and two downstairs bathrooms are plumbed now."

"Fast work!"

"I wish it could go faster. I'm impatient to live in the house now. Each day that trailer seems smaller and smaller," he said with a half laugh. He could easily sleep in his old apartment, but Ruby was now just right down the way from him. The scent of her magic on the breeze. What was going to compare to that?

"I have a spare room if you get cold or sick of sleeping in the trailer," she said over her shoulder.

If he spent the night at her house, he hoped to hell it was with her, in her bed with her body next to his. But he appreciated the offer nonetheless and said so.

"Just working to get it to a point where I can move in. I can do all the finishing stuff that helps to have good weather for."

She bent to unhook the leads. "Don't leave my sight," Ruby told the dogs seriously.

"I'd hear if something bad was coming for them," Damon reassured her.

"Once they rolled in bear shit while we were out on a hike. Disgusting. I was gagging so hard when I was bathing them."

That made him laugh, just imagining her face.

Biscuit trotted back carrying a stick roughly twice his size, not that it stopped him.

"Look at how proud you are," Ruby said to him, kneeling to give him a scratch behind his ears. "This is an amazing stick. You're one of two best boys in the whole world."

Good lord above, Damon was struck absolutely smitten by the sheer joy she seemed to breathe out like oxygen.

K Mags trotted up with a stick of his own, with a far better sense of proportion.

"Look at that! Kenneth, you're a star too. My goodness! Look at you both. So good and handsome and clever."

Within moments there was so much jumping and barking and rushing to love up all over her until she fell back onto her backside on the trail, her laughter drawing him closer to them so he could get a little love too.

"You're turning me into a dog person," he told her like she hadn't just witnessed him telling her boys what fine hunters they were like ten minutes before.

"Some might argue you're *already* a dog person, but okay. I mean, obviously the boys are totally irresistible. Plus they sort of adore you, so there's that."

"I see what you did there," he said, amusement in his tone.

They'd stopped at the turn-around point and spread out the blanket she'd packed. The dogs lay on their sides, soaking in the rays of sun as clouds surfed the breeze.

Ruby watched him as he ate, his face slightly turned up to the sky. In profile, he was even more arrestingly handsome.

"I know you're aware of this fact, but Damon Dooley, you're a pleasure to look at."

He turned, blushing, his grin a sweet version of the flirty one he gave all the time.

"Feel free to look your fill."

"Well, that's good. Since I do already. It's also nice that under those looks you're also a bighearted pleasure to know."

"Ruby Thorne, you trying to butter me up to get me to let you into my underpants?"

That made her laugh. "Would it work?"

"I will tell you honestly that pretty much anything you got would work for that."

"That's handy." She said that because in reality she wanted to climb on and take him out for a spin right that moment. There'd only been kisses before. A hand up the shirt. But this time would be different. Ruby knew it to her toes.

There'd be plenty of sexytimes with him. They had wild chemistry and while his hedonistic streak was more obvious, she had one too. Oh yeah, they'd tear it up.

This slow burn worked for her just fine. It felt like he was courting her. An old-fashioned term, sure, but there was something very charming and definitely sexy about it.

"I don't think I've ever tasted better brownies," Damon told her earnestly, wresting her mind away from sex.

"Thank you. I don't know if it's the magic in the air or the altitude or what, but my recipes of all sorts simply work better here. From banana bread to relaxation spells. It's pretty cool."

"I have noticed that the plants and trees all around your house practically glow with health as well as the apple trees on my lot just exploding with fruit. You find that your cooking is also a sort of spell then?"

"Sometimes, yes, I do. If I'm making soup for someone who is feeling poorly, it's imbued with my concern and a general wish for healing as well as the ingredients I choose, a little ginger if there's a stomach issue, vegetables that are bountiful with the vitamins needed for healing. Whatever little touch I can add. A tincture or tisane might have more herbs or ingredients used in healing, but chicken broth with ginger and turmeric can help someone warm up and will help with immune defense."

"What's a tisane? It sounds like something an old lady drinks."

Ruby snickered. "Tea is the drink containing tea leaves. A tisane is an herbal mix served hot or cold. So if you hear *chamomile tea*, but there's just chamomile and mint, that's a tisane, not a tea. And a tincture is a product of soaking something in alcohol to extract its properties."

"Like the dropper with a few drops under the tongue or in orange juice?"

"Yes. Like a super immune booster with echinacea, or a nausea aid like ginger. Valerian to sleep. I learned the chemistry of it and over the years I've been strengthening the magical elements, boosting the natural properties of the ingredients. Obviously it changes patient to patient depending on what each needs and has to be careful of."

"Fascinating. And that has gotten stronger since you've been home?" he asked.

"Yep. Exactly that. Miz Rose says she thinks it's because Thorne magic is such a powerful part of the existence of Diablo Lake that when I'm here, I'm able to tap into it more than I can anywhere else. I'm growing some of my own herbs for tinctures now. We'll see in a few months if that makes things more powerful and effective as well."

On the walk back, Damon thought a lot about what Ruby had said. There was something special about the way she'd returned home to the open arms of whatever magic that held Diablo Lake together.

And certainly as they hiked, he'd noticed how much the nature all around them had seemed to turn its attention to her. The leaves on the trees, falling as autumn took hold, seemed to go out of their way to shower her gently. Fucking birds all over the place, all singing to her. The dogs went a little nuts over that though.

"You two need a break?" Ruby stopped to ask Biscuit and K Mags.

He'd noticed they'd been flagging a little. Those tiny little legs had run and played for a few hours. Their energy seemed boundless but hell, Damon was tired and he was a full-grown alpha wolf shifter.

"I get it. It's been a big day," Damon said and then bent to scoop up a dog to carry under each arm. "I got you."

"You don't have to do that," Ruby said.

She had the sweetest, most open smile on her face. Pure pleasure and delight and it filled him to nearly overflowing with pride and a sense of rightness.

"Sure I don't have to. We could slow down and take more breaks. But this way they can rest up and you won't worry and it's truly not much effort on my part."

"You're a really special person, Damon," Ruby said to him, making him even more glad he'd done it. And the dogs were just so pleased to be with him they behaved perfectly.

Back at the Mercantile, he headed straight for his truck but Katie Faith came bounding out of the building, already in mid-sentence by the time she stopped hugging Ruby.

"What are you two up to?" Katie Faith asked him, blocking their path to his truck.

"Just finished a hike. In an hour or so I'm meeting up with everyone at my house to start some drywalling. Why are you lurking?" he asked.

"I do not lurk!"

She absolutely did lurk.

"I'll have you know I stopped Major and Jace from going out on that hike to mess with you like you did back when Jace and I were out there. You should be grateful. Oh my god, you have the dogs with you!" Katie Faith leaned in to talk to the dogs Damon still held and after a few long moments, turned her attention back to Damon. "You're holding them. Are they okay? Are you okay?"

"Rein it in there, ma'am," Ruby said with laughter in her voice. "They're very tired after the hike so Damon was letting them hitchhike back to the truck."

"I do appreciate you dissuading my brothers from pestering the shit out of me while I was out on a date with Ruby. See you later." Damon kissed her cheek. "It's not like Ruby isn't going to fill you in on everything later anyway, so stop pouting."

Ruby snickered as she unsnapped the leads from the dogs and then after accepting a thousand kisses, she loaded them into the truck where they got into the clever little doggie car seats she had brought along.

He'd probably just need to accept it and buy some to keep in his truck so she didn't have to move them back and forth. Damon knew her enough to understand that she came with the dogs. Period. It didn't hurt that they were so fiercely loyal and affectionate and clever.

"I'll talk to you later. You and Aimee are still on for

Tuesday night, right? I'm making four types of dips and will provide bread and chips and that sort of thing. You and your girl are tasked with the liquid portion of the night's menu. Nichole is bringing something sweet. We have a lot to catch up with for sure!" Ruby hugged Katie Faith one last time before jumping up into the truck.

"You're really good at getting away from her," Damon said once they were on the way back to her place.

Ruby snorted. "There's something so refreshing about how blunt wolves can be. I mean, you're gorgeous and charming and you have that accent all sexy and stuff so it softens the blow."

He opened his mouth to apologize but she said, "Oh don't you dare apologize. I said I find it refreshing."

Grinning, Damon grabbed her hand, kissing her knuckles quickly.

Ruby continued. "The key with Katie Faith is to always know she's full of love and excitement she wants to share. Also, she's like a magpie. Just let her talk awhile and then shake something sparkly and she moves on. And I mean that with utter love for her. She and Aimee are the sisters I don't share parents with. Now I'd add Nichole to that group, though I suppose she's my sister-in-law now, which is close enough."

"I'm regretting the fact that five people are due at my house in about forty-five minutes. I'd surely like to hang out with you more. I realize I don't know the story of how you and Nichole met. How about you tell me on Wednesday? When do you have a lunch break?"

"I respect that you're building this house and that it takes time to do it. On top of the two full-time jobs you already have. Wednesday I'm not back in town until two."

"You made a beautiful lunch today so let me take care of lunch this time. I'll meet you at the clinic at two."

She smiled, so fucking pretty and luscious. "All right. Thanks for the hike today. And for carrying my little nuggets the last bit. They adored you before, I'm sure they'll set up a shrine to you in the backyard now. Hopefully that's where they can put all the dead marmots or whatever."

Damon helped her get the dogs and seats unloaded and regretfully headed back to the truck. But before he left the yard he came to a stop where she stood, face tipped up, her fingertips trailing over a pale green leaf bud on one of the plants already climbing through the lattice on her front gate.

Damon approached, but when she turned her head and met his gaze, the shock of it, of deep and electric connection, had both holding a breath a few moments.

"Wow," he murmured, reaching out to brush the flesh of his thumb over her bottom lip. "You're everything."

And then his lips were on hers, the softness of his skin, the prickle of his beard and mustache. The way he held her firmly, but also gently, made her weak. It was delicious and scarily intimate.

Heat flushed through her as his tongue did something to hers and stroked along it. It was rawly sexual and sent shivers over her skin. Her back arched as she sucked in air but it was full of him. She drowned in the way he bared his teeth on her lips, ears, neck, even her chin.

A deep, slow need throbbed in her lower belly and he hummed, the vibrations echoing through her.

A car honking several times would have sent Ruby three feet high if Damon hadn't somehow put himself in front of her. Between her and the car.

"Asshole! You scared her," Damon growled at his brother, who'd been laughing but then turned to her.

"I'm sorry, Ruby. I didn't mean to scare you." Major's remorse was genuine.

"You startled me. I wasn't actually scared," Ruby called back. "Hey, Major. Damon has some brownies and banana bread to share with you."

"Score! Thank you. See you in a few. Don't dick around. I'm not doing all that work while you're over here making out with your girlfriend. Bye, Ruby."

Damon growled but it only made Ruby laugh. "You two are so cute together. Go on and get to work. Just know it was pretty sexy how you went all commando to protect me just now. We'll need to explore that in the future."

He growled again, kissed her one last time and got moving. "I'll see you soon, Ruby darlin'."

"You bet you will," she said.

A few hours later, Damon's phone rang and when he noted it was his aunt Carmen, he answered immediately.

"Evenin', Aunt Carmen. What can I do for you?" he said.

"Thought you might want to know there's a group of teens over at the school. Looked like they were worked up."

"How many we talking?" he asked her.

"Six or so. All Dooleys that I saw."

"I'm on it. Thanks."

"You check back in when things are handled or I'll worry," she told him.

And though he was more than capable of handling a group of hormonal teenaged wolf shifters, he reassured her he'd do that very thing.

"Everything okay?" Major asked.

"Yeah. Sounds like some sort of criminal mischief might be about to happen so I'm gonna run over to the school and kick some asses," Damon tossed back over his shoulder as he headed to his truck.

The young of any group of wolf shifters needed a lot more discipline as well as more physical freedom. Often one came before the other, Damon thought with a chuckle. They had strength and speed and the instincts of a predator but without the control older shifters had.

It made them fun as hell to be around one day and miserable as little assholes the next. It was his responsibility not just as second and enforcer of the pack to keep them from hurting themselves and others, but as an older alpha wolf.

He didn't bother to hide his approach. He parked in the small lot next to the elementary building and headed toward the football field that separated the high school from the rest.

There were six and Damon knew them all. One was a problem because there was a lot going on at home and not enough of it was parenting. There were a few more who were problems because they were easily led. The remaining teens were barely out of high school. All hormones and no fucking sense.

There was hooting and the like. Dick-measuring

bullshit but he certainly wasn't innocent of the same at their age.

Youthful dumbassery was one thing. Acting like wild animals and destroying property in town was another. So he was very much not pleased to note the path of destruction, including the empty brown glass bottles that held the shifter homebrew that'd have them questioning their life choices come morning.

He surely didn't like the two trash cans that'd been tossed—along with their contents—onto the playing field.

Damon snarled as he saw they'd carved into the wooden stand that usually held the cans.

At that sound, half the boys turned to face him, fear immediate on their features. Good. They should be scared. One made a run for it, but Damon was faster and had him hauled back by the hair within a few seconds.

"I didn't say you could go." Damon looked around, taking in the mess. "You messed up the field in a few places. I'll let Major handle the punishment for that." His brother coached on that field mostly year-round and would make them do some sort of terrible physical labor to set it to rights.

First thing though was to handle these boys who needed to remember just who and what they were. And who and what *he* was.

"We'll talk more after y'all pick up all this trash and put things back the way they were," he said. Damon didn't yell. Because he didn't need to.

"We didn't do that," one of them said, sullen. Another stood at his side, not quite throwing his lot in with the rebellious one but not submitting like the others were.

Damon shifted his weight, gladdened at the way the others flinched slightly, keeping their eyes down. "That so? Y'all just out for a stroll and came upon this destruction." He bent to look at the names carved into the wood on the can holder. "Ladd. Huh." He stood straight again. "I recall that's your name too. Quite a coincidence."

Damon just stared at Ladd.

Until Ladd sneered and said, "What's it to you? You're not the cops." And he found himself on his ass.

"The rest of you clean this mess up. Now." Damon didn't take his gaze from Ladd as he spoke.

The sound of feet moving quickly to do as he commanded pleased Damon as he kept his gaze on the shithead before him.

Ladd appeared to have gotten over his surprise. "You can't do that!"

"I just did." Damon had the time it would take to educate this fool.

Ladd shoved to his feet only to find his ass in the dirt once more.

"Stay there," Damon told him after he'd planted Ladd's ass another time. Stubborn. "I *am* the cops as far as you're concerned. I'm the law. Pack law. I don't get too worked up over stupid vandalism." He shrugged. "Messes can—and will—be cleaned up. Growing pains and all that. Y'all aren't so special that you're not just repeating the same things generations have done before you. What I won't tolerate is a liar. What I will not accept is disrespect."

"I don't owe you anything."

It happened that Damon knew of the problems Ladd's parents were having. He also knew Ladd's grandmomma, a very solid—and calming—presence in his life was terminally ill. A generally steady family but currently under a great deal of strain. Here was a situation where the pack would close ranks and be there to help.

"That's where you're wrong. This town relies on everyone who lives here to mind it. Take care of it. We can't just run out and buy a new Diablo Lake. The little kids use these fields, so do the middle and high schoolers. You think they like having to deal with broken glass and trash everywhere? You out here playing at being an adult but you're acting like a toddler. How can anyone around you trust you when you behave this way? You can learn from your mistakes and be better or I can kick your ass until I break you and you comply. One is better in just about every way. Don't waste my time. I'd rather be doing pretty much anything else than kicking your ass, but I've got all night to do it and I won't even be tired. But I will be so annoyed. And I'd have to take you home at dawn and wake your family up and tell them what happened here. I think y'all have enough going on just now, don't you?"

Ladd groaned, putting his hands over his face a few moments as he got himself back under control. Damon felt for the kid. He'd had his butt kicked a time or five by his grandfather's Prime back when he'd been a little younger than Ladd.

Damon made a mental note to find some ways to keep the boy busy. Burn off that energy in healthy ways to build the young shifter's control and confidence.

He held a hand to Ladd. "Get to cleaning this mess."

"I apologize, sir." Ladd kept his gaze down as he spoke.

"Get."

He stayed there, monitoring their cleanup and the rest of their laps and then he drove each one home. Damon didn't talk to their parents. He'd hold that in reserve for later.

Chapter Nine

Jace loped into the Mercantile the following Tuesday night. "Need any help?"

"Katie Faith left for Ruby's?" Damon teased.

"You'll see. Once you get used to them, it's weird when they're not around." Jace, a notoriously grumpy man, exuded satisfaction. He was where he was supposed to be, and the pack was better for his leadership during a really unstable time. Katie Faith was an anchor. She held him down and gave him the perspective he needed.

It also gave Damon an inside view of a working marriage and one he appreciated. Especially as he courted his very own witch.

"Whatever the cause, I'll take your help. We're restocking." Damon pointed toward the cart.

Their great-grandfather had opened the Mercantile back when their grandpa was just a baby. It'd been a way to serve those who lived in town so they didn't have to leave the safety of Diablo Lake to get basic goods. In the generations since, there'd been a grocery store added. The feed store around the same time. But the wood floors, worn to a shine by the footsteps of thousands over the years, were a reminder to Damon that their blood was part of the foundation of Diablo Lake too.

"So. How are things with Ruby anyway?" Jace asked. Major snorted, but kept working.

"We've gone out a few times. Dinner once up at my house lot and over the weekend we went on a hike. We're having lunch tomorrow."

"Why?"

Surprised, Damon glanced Jace's way. "Why? Why am I seeing her? Why are we having lunch? Why what?"

Jace rolled his fucking eyes and Damon really wanted to pop him one. Smug dick.

"You broke up with her six years ago and went about your life, bold as you please. Why now? Why her now and not then?"

It was, Damon figured, a fair line of questioning. He'd asked himself that too.

"We had the raw ingredients then. But we were too young. She had a path to leave and get her education. If I'd have pursued it then, what would have happened? Would I have slowed her down? Derailed her path? And I had my own damned journey to go on. I had to grow up and mature. Put the pack before anything else because now I know I have the room to have her and still lead Dooley with you.

"I didn't dump her. It didn't end badly. It just sort of went on hold for a while. She's always been there in the background. I can't speak for her, but every time I'm with her and I learn something else about her, it only makes me surer that right now with this witch is the exact thing for me."

Jace nodded a few times. "Okay. I just wanted to know what to say because people are already asking me about you two. We had a brief moment the other day, but I get it now."

"She's also an excellent source of healthcare and brownies," Major added.

"Welcome to the family," Jace said with a snort.

"So, Mac told his mother no to their request for Dwayne coming back to town for an entire month," Aimee told them.

"I bet that went well," Ruby said. "Did Mac ask what you thought?"

The four of them, as Nichole had joined their sip and bitch session, were snuggled up in Ruby's living room. A fire crackled merrily in her fireplace and the television was on, but they'd lost interest in reality TV because the gossip had started.

"He did," Aimee said. "And I first said it was his job to run the pack so I'd stand behind whatever choice he made for the good of the wolves. And then I said, *why the fuck does he want to come back here? He hates me and the feeling is entirely mutual. It's not like he's raring to celebrate our love.*"

The other women raised their glasses in agreement with that.

"Dwayne says he wants to come back, attend Halloween dinner and other town events during Collins Hill Days as well as the engagement dinner and wedding events. Like a vacation. On my back. Halloween has nothing to do with my wedding. That fucknut can drive his ass back up here in November for the wedding because he can't just come back for funsies and say it's about our wedding stuff. And that's what made Mac the angriest. His mom, well she's a handful, but she's generally supportive of our relationship. But his dad doesn't give a fuck about me and maybe a half a fuck about Mac. He just wanted to come eat free food and see what sort of trouble he can cause."

"Dwayne Pembry and his wife have some nerve!" Katie Faith made a little growl that sounded a lot like Jace's.

"He was exiled from town for a year, right?" Nichole asked. As a newcomer to Diablo Lake, she didn't always have the background details. "For bringing a human here?"

"Yes. Long story, but Dwayne is Mac's dad of course. And before me, he was mayor. But things in town were getting really unhealthy. Pembry and Dooley were fighting all the time. The magic here was weakening. But Dwayne was useless and disinterested in attempting to solve the problems. So I ran against him. That disgusting dirty dog pulled all sorts of shady shenanigans and when it looked like he was going to lose he brought a human up here to try to embarrass me. There was a tussle at a town hall meeting of all places. It was a huge mess and it was complicated by Darrell, Mac's brother, who was also on a tear through town, causing violence and mayhem. And I still won the mayoral race by a landslide so he can sit on an anthill."

More laughter while everyone topped up drinks and snacks.

"Technically, he isn't allowed back until near the end of January," Aimee said and then sipped her sangria. "I'm not claiming I like my soon-to-be father-in-law. I don't. He's a pissant with delusions of grandeur who treated his best and smartest son like a redheaded stepchild in favor of the second biggest dipshit in town,

Darrell, who was exiled for *two* years. The good news is that some shifter town up in Minnesota has agreed to let him and his family move in and join that pack. Good riddance. I don't even want Dwayne here. I think he needs to fulfil his sentence like any other wolf would have to. He never shuts his face about pack law and discipline, blah blah blah, but he wants special treatment when it's about him." Aimee made a rude hand gesture and rolled her eyes.

"Drunk Aimee is my favorite," Ruby said with a snicker.

Aimee laughed, unable to deny it. Few people saw this side of her friend, who in her day-to-day life was very much in charge. She used that power to make things better, which meant a lot of diplomacy and the like. But with them, with these few friends, she got to let that burden go for a little while and just be a friend hanging out with her besties.

"I allowed him to be at the wedding. Which given how he acted and the things he tried to do *to* me is pretty fuckin' amazing on my part. Right?" Aimee asked.

Everyone nodded.

"And now he wants to be here for a whole month. In the middle of this situation between the packs to end the Rule of Silence. Scarlett and her dumbass sister Mary are stirring up all the older wolves and playing *the younger generation are trying to get rid of all our discipline* game. And some of them are of the 'all change is bad' camp so it just gets them upset. He doesn't even like me so there's zero reason he needs to be here the whole time."

"What does Mac think?" Ruby asked.

Aimee's anger faded into amused affection. "He

wants peace. He wants stability. Despite the fact that Mac is worth a hundred Dwayne Pembrys, there's no way there's not at least some part of him that wants the respect and attention of his parents. Even if they are total asshats."

"Word," Katie Faith agreed.

"They don't deserve him. But Mac deserves to have proud parents at his wedding. He's the Patron. I want him to have all the events possible to cement that and to celebrate him. He works sixteen-hour days most days of the week. He's all in to serve his wolves."

"Aw, you love him so much," Ruby said.

"I do. And he's just so good to me and my family. He lets my mom have her way on so much it's out of control. But she adores him and that counts for a whole lot. Anyway, that's what's going on."

"There's something about Mary that always has my guard up," Nichole said. "I don't have the history you all do with either of them. But I'll say the handful of times I've come across her, I've always walked away uncomfortable and anxious. She wears a mask when she's out in public."

Nichole had been born and raised in the outside world and that's where they'd first met and become friends via Nichole's mom, who'd been one of Ruby's midwifery instructors. Ruby and Nichole had clicked immediately and had ended up sharing an apartment for two years.

Greg had come out to visit and within six months of their first meeting, he'd already asked Nichole to marry him and six months after that they'd gotten married and planned to move to Diablo Lake to open their lunch counter.

Ruby had gained a best friend, a sister-in-law and someone else to make faces at during family dinners. Ruby's sweet, heart on his sleeve brother found a true partner for life and their family had gained another witch full of love and a commitment to make the town a better and happier place.

"I think *mask* is a perfect word for it." Aimee refilled her glass. "Scarlett and her sister are tight. Always a united front. On one hand, that's nice, you know? Sometimes though it seems like Scarlett is a controlling parent and Mary the errant child. Still, I think she's closer with her sister than she is with Dwayne. And I think Nichole is picking up something important. I don't know but it seems to me Mary hasn't said or done much to call attention to herself. Not for years. Now though? Odd. But that whole family is odd. Fortunately for me, Mac's weird is the good kind."

"Ugh. Enough about all these terrible people who make my day longer," Katie Faith said. "It's time for us to talk about Damon and Ruby. Y'all should have seen Damon on Sunday. I bumped into them after they'd taken a hike and he had a dog under each arm. Plus, he kept looking at Ruby like he wanted to rub all over her."

Ruby's skin heated. "We had a picnic and he got to be outdoors. He *shines* outside. I found a patch of mountain mint and the witch hazel is plentiful. I also caught sight of some wood nettle on the way back but I didn't have gloves so I made a note and I'll go back later when I'm prepared. Anyway, he was patient while I foraged and half the time I'd look up to see him climbing up some tree or rocks or whatever. He's appreciative of baked goods. He's really nice to my dogs. He's a seriously excellent kisser. I like him. He's nice to smaller and weaker creatures. He strung up Christmas lights at his trailer for our dinner date. We danced under the stars. He had blankets so I wouldn't be cold. I'm really having a very nice time living my life just now."

"Have you gone to bonetown?" Katie Faith asked, sending everyone else into faux outraged gasps and then raucous laughter.

Ruby snorted one last time. "Not yet. But. We will."

Aimee asked, "But you didn't before, right? I mean, don't give me that look! You know I'm only saying what everyone else was thinking."

"We didn't. I mean, he could have. I'm not going to lie to you at this point. I'd have given it up! But there was just a lot of kissing and hand holding and the like. No sex. I think, in retrospect, I'm glad. It might have been harder to move away, or to have been broken up with, if we'd have slept together. We've got chemistry. Off the charts zing. But it's a slow seduction he's after and I'm good with that."

"Slow seduction like a year or slow seduction a few weeks? One is okay and the other I would not be okay with. I like sex too much to go without," Katie Faith said.

"It's just right there. The sex is about to happen, I mean. We both know that. I think that's why we're both so chill about it and letting ourselves get to know one another again as adults before we end up in bed. Given the way he kisses, I'm pretty sure I may not want to let him leave my bed afterward."

"I can speak to the sexual prowess of shifters. As can Aimee." Katie Faith waggled her eyebrows and then nearly fell off the couch because she was trying to look up at them as she did it.

"It's a good thing she's got a pretty face," Ruby said in a dramatic stage whisper to Nichole.

That sent everyone into giggles again.

"After Samhain, Jace and I are going to stop trying not to get pregnant," Katie Faith said. "That's a secret. We're not saying anything yet. Obviously he'll tell his brothers and he knows I'll tell you. But I don't plan to tell my parents until I'm actually knocked up."

"Wow!"

"We'd been waiting awhile. I wanted to be with him without any of that pressure for the first year or two. There's so much politics and power play bullshit involved with wolves that he and I needed to strengthen our family of two before we went beyond that. And to be utterly honest with you, before Ruby came back to town, I'd have had to go down to Knoxville to see a doctor for all the pregnancy stuff and that's a whole other level of commitment. And another thing to be anxious about."

Ruby hugged her. "I'm right here now and we've got the basics at the clinic now so I can handle most of your prenatal care." Depending on what sort of pregnancy she had, of course, but Ruby knew it wasn't necessary to say any of that. This was why she'd gone away, and this was why she'd returned home to a place without sushi and hot chicken. To usher new life into the world and be a comfort to those already here.

"So I've weaned way back on the booze but figured it was a night for celebration," Katie Faith explained of her sangria-addled state.

"Make an appointment to come in if you like. I can get you started with the foundations and then once you're pregnant, we'll adjust. Vitamins and the like to start. We'll talk about birthing options and things as well. Oh my lands this is so exciting."

"I think Jace is torn between wanting to just have sex all the time and hoping I get pregnant and wanting to have sex all the time and hoping I don't get pregnant right away so we can have sex all the time," Katie Faith explained.

"I'm sensing a theme here. It could be, and just hear me out, it could be that he likes sex with you," Ruby said through laughter.

Katie Faith nodded. "You're not hearing me complain at all. That man knows how to make everything all better. But I do think he'll be a great dad. And I think I'll be a good mom. You're all going to be excellent aunts. And my parents and his grandparents will all be great. I can trust Major and Damon to make sure our kid has a sense of humor and isn't deadly serious all the time like Jace. Anyway. It's early yet. But I wanted to say it to you because you all matter to me so much. And I know you'll keep it to yourselves. Once Patty and JJ hear it'll be relentless. He already sniffs at me and then says to Jace how I'm fertile and that he should get to work on the next generation of Dooleys instead of farting around wasting time."

"Scarlett told Mac not to get me pregnant until after the wedding so people won't think he had to marry me out of pity for my whorish ways and such. That last was only slightly dramatized, by the way," Aimee said.

"You really do win for worst in-laws," Katie Faith told Aimee.

"I guess we can't all be Nichole, who gets Mel and Anita for in-laws," Aimee said of Ruby's parents.

"I am really lucky. Every time I hear a story like Aimee's I know even more just how lucky I am," Nichole admitted. "Even my mom, who wasn't a fan of me moving all the way to Tennessee, was far happier about it once she met Mel and Anita. She and my mom are really tight and of course my mom loves Ruby to death."

"She's coming to visit during Samhain so you'll get to meet her then," Ruby said of Nichole's mother, Harmony.

Nichole said, "My brother and his husband live in Atlanta and they have two kids. My mom goes to visit at least every two months. Enough that they have a little tiny house-type thing in their backyard for her now. My brother-in-law is an architect so he drew up the plans himself as a gift to her. I'm fairly sure she'll end up in Atlanta sooner rather than later. She can just as easily take students there as she could in San Pedro. And it's a heck of a lot closer to Diablo Lake that after the weather warms up, we'll see her here more often as well."

The dogs came in and out, got their fill of snuggles and snacks everyone thought they were sneaking past her. They sat in her living room. Her friends, these sisters of her heart, mattered to her more than she could have ever managed to articulate.

They were her home too.

Chapter Ten

Ruby sat on a blanket in the middle of her yard as the sun rose. Her eyes were closed, her hands loosely open, palm up, resting on her knees. All around her life pulsed. The seasons were changing. Some trees would sleep for the winter and others would manage another round of fruiting.

In the background, she heard birdsong and the whisper of the breeze through the tall grass ringing the meadow next to her house. Beneath her, the earth fed her magic in a steady stream.

It sprang to attention, flowing through her body. This connection made her so happy. It was a universe away from what it had felt like when she'd been in her late teens.

Using her gifts in all parts of her job was a pleasure. She continued to find new ways to open up all the connections she could, intuition and magic were closely linked, and used that to make individual treatment decisions for her different patients.

She wasn't a doctor and they sorely needed one full-time. But she could take care of most of the ailments shifter or witch might deal with and get the traveling doctor up regularly to address treatment beyond her or Aimee. And in a few years when his residency was done, her cousin Xavier would eradicate the need for a traveling doctor when he moved back to Diablo Lake and took the office awaiting him at the clinic.

Using her magical talent to heal hurting living things? There was such *rightness* in her heart and gut.

Passion and a path.

And maybe something more with the wolf down the way.

No maybes about it, she told herself as she felt the tug of his shifter magic and opened her eyes. Damon as wolf stood at the top of the rise looking down from his house lot. The dogs had been quietly and patiently patrolling the backyard fence line but they'd frozen, all their attention on Damon.

She couldn't blame them. Hell, Ruby found herself stunned into stillness as she took him in, so massive, and even at a distance, intelligent.

His fur in the early-morning light was dark honey, burned sugar. A little lighter than the hair the man had. There was a splash of darker browns across his nose and cheek.

The wolf gave a half bark half yip and the dogs howled before running back to the blanket, still keeping themselves between their mom and the wolf.

"It's okay," she murmured. "Isn't Damon beautiful in that skin?"

K Mags wagged his tail end so hard he kept having to move himself back into place as he rattled off to the side like an old washing machine.

Ruby raised a hand to wave before she blew a kiss.

She could have sworn he grinned at her before trotting away, back into the trees.

"Well now and doesn't that make for a nice wake-up?" she asked the dogs as they ran back to the fence to double-check the perimeter.

"Y'all get your exercise in before breakfast. You're coming with me first thing for a few hours. We're going visiting."

She shook out and then folded up the blanket before taking it back inside. The boys would be in shortly, after running out their excitement and anxiety at seeing Damon's wolf.

When at work, Ruby always tried to project a bright, soothing presence. There'd always be green elements of what she did and her magic but since she'd been back home, that earthy, green element of her magic had deepened to a sun-dappled forest with loads of tropical flowers like colorful secrets scattered through.

That morning Ruby and the dogs were going to two of the places shifters and witches ended up when their health needs were beyond what could be provided in Diablo Lake. A nursing and rehab home and a more recent addition, a memory care facility for those suffering from dementia. The visits were more like social work and less nursing. They got those services already. But if you're stuck in rehab for three months after surgery or a car accident or a fall, it's isolating. Aimee had started the check-ins a few years prior and Ruby was pleased to take those duties on. It was precisely the sort of outreach and care she wanted to provide.

She chose a wine-colored blouse and a pair of navy blue wide-legged trousers. Confident, professional but soft rather than hard. Approachable, she hoped, as she grabbed warm boots with good soles. Comfortable shoes were super important but that didn't mean they didn't have to be cute as well.

The tippity tap of nails on the back porch and then into the kitchen signaled breakfast time for everyone so she finished up her makeup and hair and then went out to meet the boys.

"Lordy she's just so pretty," Damon said to Major. He was ready to take his lunch break and the two brothers stood on the long porch that wrapped around the front and sides of the Mercantile.

Ruby darlin', his gorgeous witch, looked smart and lush and so beautiful he was struck a little stupid with it. Just looking at her made him smile.

As if he'd said her name, she looked his way and waved before pointing to an open picnic table nearer to the Mercantile and he nodded, indicating he'd meet her there.

"You're having lunch right there on the Ave?" Major snickered and then clapped Damon's shoulder. "Okay then."

Damon grabbed the cooler he'd brought their lunch and drinks in, and headed her way.

"Hey there," she said, tipping her face up to look him in the eye.

"Hey yourself," he replied before hugging her. "You smell good," he said before brushing a quick kiss over her mouth. Though he'd certainly love to smooch up all over her, it wasn't the place or the time.

"Thank you. I'm trying my hand at perfume oils and making the mixes myself. I made us some pumpkin chocolate chip bread for dessert."

"You're my dream woman," he told her, kissing her

again. "I brought chips and some pasta salad to go with everything. Ice tea, naturally."

She whipped out a pretty tablecloth and he then piled the sandwiches he'd made on the plates. Four sandwiches for him and one for her.

"Figured you'd need the calories after that run this morning," she said as she sat. "The dogs were so excited they ran in the yard for another twenty minutes after you left."

"I didn't expect to see you up so early."

"I'm a morning person. It's a curse and a gift. But it means I get a lot done before others are even awake, which is a nice exchange."

The afternoon was busy enough and a steady stream of car and foot traffic made its way up and down the Ave and Damon knew that within the next few hours, the whole damned town was going to know who was having lunch together.

That was fine with him.

"I like being up early when it's quiet and still. Not as much traffic so if I'm on a run as wolf, I don't worry about cars as much. And my new tenant likes to meditate in her backyard all bathed in morning light. You got the land all happy. Me too." And she'd made him something thinking about his metabolism. It was nice being thought of like that. "This visit with you and that pumpkin bread are gonna get me through the rest of my day."

She rustled in a tote and pulled out another container, sliding it his way. "The pumpkin bread is a dessert. But these are for later. Protein bites. They're honey, peanut butter and oats. There's chocolate in there too. They get high marks from my beta testers. I know the shift takes energy and burns a lot of calories."

"You made me protein snacks?" That hit him hard. Like being taken care of by someone who didn't have any reason other than kindness.

Her grin was so sweet, slightly bashful. "Well. Yeah. I mean, it's not like you're skin and bones or anything. A bit of magic but in a boost of rejuvenation not so much a spell that would change your behavior. But you know, I just want you to be healthy."

She totally did. And wasn't that sort of miraculous?

He snuck one, expecting it to be a health food–type thing but they were really good and he had to force himself not to eat them all at once.

"They're really tasty. Hard to believe something that tastes so good is actually healthy. And I like the healing magic in them and appreciate you taking care of me. What have you been up to today? I really do like the color of your lipstick. Makes me want to kiss you even more."

Her laugh sent a wave of pleasure through him.

"Thank you." She sent him an air kiss. "The boys and I did some visiting. One of the ladies at the rehab center had hip replacement surgery so the boys were there to give her encouragement as she does PT to help her walk again. They visited with a few folks there and then over at the memory care place they just do a lot of snuggling."

Damon heard the sadness in her tone.

"Hard huh?"

She shrugged. "Well, I'm not the one dealing with Alzheimer's or some other sort of dementia. I care for them all, of course. But my sadness and my challenge are nothing compared to theirs and their loved ones. It's heartbreaking to see, even as there are moments where the sun clears. They remember music they loved in their youth. They know how to love dogs. I got to meet some new people and hopefully brought some happiness with my visit. My magic is pleased to do what it should be so that's been hugely positive."

She sipped her drink. "Anyway, enough about that. How is your day?"

"Pretty good. Started out with a gorgeous witch, lunch with the same gorgeous witch. Excellent business in the Mercantile. Everyone wants to finish up those home and garden projects before winter sets in. Samhain and Halloween coming. Collins Hill Days prep. You witches keep us selling all sorts of stuff for your sabbats."

"We like a party, that's for sure. Do you and Major still do backcountry guiding?"

He brightened. She remembered that? "We do. Had an excellent summer. Thank goodness for hikers. They paid for most of the windows in the house. I say most because holy crap good windows are expensive. We sell 'em so it's not like I never noticed they were costly. But it's different when it's your money."

Ruby snickered. "You know it. Everything is more expensive than you think it should be when you need to buy it with your own money. I was like, *mattresses cost how much?*"

She told him about meeting Nichole and the friendship that'd developed since. Damon liked Nichole. Certainly liked the food she made with Greg at their lunch counter. To know what sort of friend she'd been to Ruby made him like her even more.

"I missed her like mad when they moved here. But now that I'm here and I can see how much she and

Greg are in love and making their own sort of magic at 'Smoke, I'm good. She's got a way with Lovie. My parents adore her. It's nice. Makes me happy."

He took her hand because he wanted to touch her. The warmth of her skin against his eased his heart. He loved it even more when she smiled back his way.

"I like it when you're happy. Happy is good. I'm already friends with Greg so I'd love to get to know Nichole better."

"Like a double date?"

If anyone else had said something similar he might have gotten a little uncomfortable. Wanting to make sure no one caught feelings for him. He never wanted anyone to feel like he'd led them on. His father had done that. More than once. And it had wrecked more than one life.

"Yeah." Because he *wanted* Ruby to catch feelings. Damon most certainly already had.

"All right. I'll talk to her and see what their schedule is like." Ruby paused a moment before saying, "You give me butterflies."

He sucked in a breath, pleased and surprised. "Well now. I guess my plan is working."

"Your plan?"

"Sure. Listen, I'm a smart guy. You think I'd be able to woo a woman like you without a plan like some amateur? You're a goddess. I gotta bring my A game."

Her delighted laugh was almost as good as the look of unguarded appreciation and affection on her features.

"What time are we having lunch tomorrow?" he asked, taking a chance.

"Is two too late?"

"Nah, it's perfect." Though he'd have said that about

whatever time she'd have suggested. Any opportunity to be around her was all right with him. "And Friday night. Are you busy?"

"Come over to my house. I'll make *you* dinner this time."

Being taken care of by Ruby seemed like the best thing he could possibly imagine. "I'll bring something to drink."

"You've got a deal." Ruby glanced down at her phone. "I need to get back to the clinic. My next patient is due in fifteen minutes. Thanks for the company and the excellent array of food. I'm fortified for the rest of my day."

They tidied up the area and he tried not to drag his feet as their time together dwindled. He hugged her and gave her another kiss before burying his face in her neck for one last sniff. "I'll talk to you later, beauty."

"You better," she said over her shoulder as she headed back to work.

Damn right. Grinning, he turned to head back to his own job and caught sight of Scarlett staring at him from across the Ave. Damon, so happy even Scarlett glowering at him wasn't going to ruin it, tipped his chin in greeting before jogging the last half block.

When he got back to work, he found himself thinking about her constantly. The way her voice sounded with the birds singing in the background. The kindness and compassion in her eyes when she spoke about her work. The fire of her passion over things she believed in.

The way she felt against him when he kissed those luscious lips.

Katie Faith and Aimee strolled in an hour or so later.

Damon didn't complain one bit because his sister-in-law brought him and Major milkshakes.

"I'm headed over the clinic in a bit. Anything you want me to say to Ruby?" Aimee asked.

"She and I had lunch an hour ago, but you can always send her my hello." Damon grinned.

"Ah! This was in public, obviously. And that's why Scarlett asked about Ruby not even an hour past."

"Well, good. Now she knows," Damon said, trying not to be snippy. It wasn't about anyone within earshot, and his beef with Scarlett Pembry shouldn't cause any strife for anyone else.

"She's been told. What she does now? She's unpredictable. And she's not the only Pembry who's asked me about Ruby. Gorgeous witch, single, great job, talented, you have to know you're not the only one who likes her peaches and wants to shake her tree."

Damon laughed as Major began singing the Steve Miller Band's "The Joker" in the background.

"I'm not worried about competition. She and I are meant to be." No one, leastwise Scarlett Pembry, could threaten that. At all.

"Well, okay then." Katie Faith's smile went up a notch.

"That smile scares me," he told her.

Katie Faith shrugged but it was slightly menacing and his respect for her rose. "I just think you and Ruby should come to dinner on Friday at our house. Aimee and Mac can come. Major, naturally because his biscuits are better than mine."

"Not a metaphor," Major said.

"Ruby and I have a date on Friday. At her place. She's cooking for me. So that's a no on the dinner. However, I don't mind it on another night. I'll check with her on

her availability. She likes you people. God knows why."
He snorted and then laughed.

In truth, it pleased him greatly to grow his relationship as part of a larger one with his pack. Part of his makeup was to crave time with other shifters to reassure himself they were all right and happy. He tended to enjoy being around others socially, especially now that he'd have his house away from the chaos of the pack house.

Ruby was already part of town. Already close friends with his close friends. It made the meshing of their worlds easier and hopefully more vital and strong.

"I'll call her myself," Katie Faith said. "You'll forget."

"I won't forget. You'll make her feel obligated."

Aimee laughed really hard at that because they all knew it was true.

"I would not!"

Even Jace lost his composure at that and kissed the top of his wife's head. "Not to harm her, no. You're not mean."

"Not unless someone deserves it," Katie Faith admitted. "It's not a bad thing. We all like each other. We're all friends or related. She's our friend and she's been gone for six years. We want to be around her too."

Damon nodded her way. Of course she just wanted to be around her friends. And Damon just wanted to keep Ruby to himself for these first foundational dates and because he liked her undivided attention. And, if he was to admit it to himself, he liked it that these were the early, quiet days before everyone in town would begin to offer opinions and perspectives. Like a secret.

Though it was a small town where everyone was

in everyone's business and naturally no secrets stayed that way forever.

"I promise I'll talk to her about it at lunch tomorrow," he told his sister-in-law, which perked her up. Damon figured she'd call Ruby anyway because Katie Faith was gonna Katie Faith.

The following afternoon, Ruby stopped by the market to grab chips to go with the sandwiches she'd brought for their lunch date. He said he'd handle the drinks so she only needed the last ingredients.

Two different wolf shifters gave her long slow looks. Though to their credit, it was generally surreptitious and not gross. She waved at them as she hustled past. She had a hot shifter of her own to meet up with.

"How're you liking being back in Diablo Lake?" Cheryl Johnson was at the checkout. Cheryl taught gymnastics at the grange hall for years. Ruby had been one of countless Diablo Lake kids who'd satisfied her physical education credits with a class with Mrs. Johnson.

And like other wolves, she was nosy as heck and Ruby was a gold mine of new material.

"I like it fine, thanks for asking. Got the clinic up and running. I get to see my friends and family regularly. My magic loves it here."

"You dating anyone?" Cheryl asked. "I mean, I've heard the talk about Damon Dooley, but not if you were seeing other people too. You're young still. Got plenty of oats to sow if you know what I mean. My nephew, Lou, I think you and he are roughly the same age. Anyway, he's doing roofing with Mr. Johnson. Stable. Earns a good, solid living. Handsome. Single."

"I remember Lou. He's a nice guy and I appreciate you thinking of me. But as you mentioned, I'm with Damon so I'm not dating anyone else." Ruby handed over the money and grabbed the chips. "I've got to run. Have a good day, Mrs. Johnson."

Damon waited at the table they'd sat at the day before but got up to help her unpack the food.

He raised one brow when she pulled off the top piece of bread to spread a layer of barbecue chips and then smooshed it slightly to hear the crunch.

"Don't worry," she told him before taking a bite, "it's not mandatory. But it's recommended."

"Okay. I trust you. I haven't done this since I was a kid. You have a good influence on me." He copied her actions and took a bite. After a bit he nodded. "Yeah, this adds just a little something special to the whole package."

"Right? It's a little salty and crunchy, perfect."

"Just like you," he said and made her smile. She was totally going to let him touch her boobs.

"Is it just me, or are there way more people out on this sidewalk than there were yesterday?" Ruby asked after several groups had walked past them.

Damon growled, sending two dudes who'd been hanging around scattering.

"That wasn't nice," she said through laughter.

"They're lucky all I did was snarl. Here we are sitting together and they try to catch your eye hoping to say hey? The fuck outta here with that."

"They're nosy parkers. Not like that's unusual in Diablo Lake," Ruby told him, thinking of Cheryl in the checkout line and deciding not to share it. He'd just get annoyed and it didn't matter anyway. "Far as I'm concerned, the quicker people pick up that we're together, they'll back off."

His harrumph said he didn't agree, but she smiled at him brightly. "You look so handsome today."

That grumpy face melted away and that sexy grin of his made an appearance. "Have to keep up with you. I'm supposed to ask you to have dinner at Katie Faith and Jace's on Saturday. She roped in Aimee and Mac too. If you don't want to, you can say no to me and I'll find a nice way around it."

She tipped her head back to laugh at that.

"Christ almighty," Damon muttered. "You're like a shot of sunshine straight to the heart."

His compliments weren't like anything anyone had ever said to her and she told him so.

"I can't remember ever blushing as much as I do around you," he said as he blushed.

"I love your blushes." And she did. "Thank you for your offer to deal with Katie Faith. Do you want to go to dinner there? Don't you work on your house Saturday night and Sundays?"

"You can't really dissuade Katie Faith once she puts her mind to something."

"That's for sure," Ruby said. "And she's one of my oldest friends. She's fun. You agreed to a double date with Nichole and Greg so it's only fair. But also, I want to get to know Jace and Mac better because my closest friends love these guys and I want to love them too. Or, in a you're good enough for my friends way. You know what I mean."

He snorted. "Well I do, thank goodness."

"And how about the house stuff? I know you're trying to finish it so you can move in around Thanksgiving or thereabouts. Things like dinner with friends take away from that."

"I'll still work on it before and after dinner and on Sunday too. Body's got to eat to keep going so it may as well be over at their house where I'm not responsible for it. I'm selfish with you." He winked. "But I can share."

"And you're really social. Don't think I haven't noticed."

"One of the things that comes with a wolf." He grinned easily and sent a shiver through her. "Tomorrow night we'll talk details."

They both had to get back to work and cleaned up their mess before pausing, facing one another. "I'll see you later," she said, stretching up as he bent down, meeting in the middle for a kiss that left her knees rubbery.

"You sure will. Have a good rest of your day, Ruby darlin'," he called out, walking backward toward the Mercantile with effortless grace.

She blew him a kiss and hustled so she'd have time to prep for her next appointment.

Chapter Eleven

Though Ruby had seen Damon pretty much daily and had smooched up on him plenty over the last few weeks, the sight of him on her doorstep, arms full, brought butterflies to her belly.

"Why hello there. Come on in." She stood aside, holding the door open so he could enter.

"I brought some wine and beer and also some garden gloves that came in yesterday and I thought you might like them."

He handed over the blue and yellow gloves she knew for sure the Mercantile didn't carry because she'd looked through their garden section multiple times. They had brown. Denim blue. Army green.

"I love them. Thank you." And she did. They were pretty and thick enough to handle tough jobs but thin enough to remain pliable and easy to work in.

"I hope you're hungry. We're having brisket enchiladas and salad. Double chocolate brownies for dessert and hot chocolate," she said.

"Really? Damn. You're my own personal miracle. Clearly I need to keep up with you. Spoil you like you do me or someone else will."

Ruby snorted. "You literally just showed up on my

doorstep with garden gloves and dog treats you're pretending probably just fell into your basket so you bought them. I see you, Damon. Right to your very big heart. You're spoiling me just fine."

"Darlin'." He shook his head at her. "I've only just started spoiling you."

"Yeah?" She smiled up at him and he didn't miss the opportunity to steal a kiss.

"Yeah. I'm going to be the best at spoiling you."

The smile he gave her brought a shiver up her spine. Sexy and sweet, laced with mischief.

"That's a very bold claim, Damon Dooley," she told him, mock seriously.

"I like bold claims, darlin'. But I deliver." He waggled his eyebrows, which made her giggle. She hadn't even giggled like that when she was a schoolgirl.

"I'm all aquiver with anticipation."

"Oh, Ruby darlin', making you aquiver is my lifetime dream. And look at that. I'm delivering already."

A shiver rode down her spine. If he only knew just exactly what he was giving her. Then again, given the look on his face, he knew. And liked it.

"Can I help?" he asked, and it took her a few seconds to remember what words meant.

Ruby drew in a breath and talked herself into releasing the hold she had on his waist even though he was warm and firm and smelled really good. What she really wanted to do was pull that shirt off what she knew was a stellar upper body and kiss every last bit of skin.

"Sure. I'd love a glass of wine, and give the boys one of those treats they know you have."

He bent to kiss her again before following her into

the kitchen to grab glasses from the cabinet and pouring them both a glass of red wine.

"To second chances," he murmured before they drank.

And he was back, his body against hers, mouth sliding down her jaw to the spot where her neck met her shoulder and she couldn't stop the gasp of pleasure as he grazed the edge of his teeth against that oh so sensitive skin there.

He hummed a little before he moved away from her, that sexy smile on his mouth.

Ruby pretended to casually work in her kitchen but really she spied on him with the dogs, who sat, rapt as he brought out treats. He was just so good to them. And to her.

Damon knelt facing Biscuit and K Mags. Little brothers indeed. Both dogs looked up at him, wide eyed, trying to stay still but they were too excited by his presence and Biscuit's rear practically vibrated with the pent-up tail wagging.

He brought out two of the little bone-shaped cookies he'd special ordered for them and a delighted whimper sounded from one—Biscuit, Damon thought—at the sight.

"Y'all have been doing a great job keeping an eye on your momma and the property." Major had trotted over to check things out and told him later that the dogs had instantly gone alert and got in between him and the house where Ruby must have been. Major told them both he wasn't a threat to their human and they'd yipped and howled once or twice and waited on the back steps until Major had gone from sight.

"I hear you boys like peanut butter. Major, that's my

brother, you met his wolf a few days ago and I'm sure you'll meet his human at some point too since we're all neighbors. But you already know I'm the best twin."

In the background, Ruby's laughter rang through the air, making him grin.

"Anyway, I digress. Your mother is very diverting. Major and I saw these cookies and decided to order some on spec. You know, see if any other dog lovers in town might like to give their very good boys a treat."

Damon absolutely drew the line at making them perform for their food so he gently held one cookie in each hand and each dog—though unsurprisingly Biscuit moved first—took their treat quickly and carefully.

"Let me know your verdict," he murmured, nearly laughing as Biscuit had to cough up a piece he'd inhaled. "I guess that's a thumbs-up. Keep up the good work protecting the rest of the pack and there'll be more where that came from." Damon wouldn't make them do a trick for food, but he definitely considered it as payment for the job they did as Ruby's danger early alarm system. They liked to be busy. They were courageous and curious and so far, several Dooley wolves had come by to introduce themselves to the two furry dynamos Ruby lived with. Ruby's boys had charmed them all.

When he stood—after giving each dog a scritch behind the ears—she didn't bother to hide her expression and it set him back on his heels. Metaphorically of course.

"Thank you for being so sweet with them. And with me."

"I'm the one who's getting dinner and lots of chocolate created by a witch who cares about what I like. Seems to me I'm the one *you're* being sweet to."

Her house was absolutely full of magic, but there in the kitchen, it seemed to glow the brightest. Since she'd moved in and begun working there regularly, the trees all over the property hung heavy with apples and a blueberry patch he and Major had secretly enjoyed for the last months exploded to the extent he and his brother had to freeze and donate them to the food pantry in town.

Ruby's presence in town had brightened pretty much every aspect of not just Damon's life, but the life of everyone in town.

"You should come over and pick apples tomorrow," he told her as they began to ferry food to the little table in the alcove next to the kitchen. She even poured each of them a glass of tea to go along with the wine.

"Okay! I'm starting a lot of my Samhain prep this coming week so that would be wonderful." She looked up at him, smiling so pretty he was helpless to do anything but keep falling in love with her.

"I don't know enough about Samhain," Damon admitted. "I mean, I like the food part and I know you do a bonfire and banquet thing but it's like the Halloween dinner I guess. Each group doing their own thing. You should come to Halloween dinner with me. See it from my side."

That had flown from his lips without even a how do you do. She made him happy in a silly, vulnerable way. A way that he'd never really given over to in the past. Being vulnerable made him less effective at Jace's right hand. Being vulnerable with a partner, well, he'd never felt any strong urge to lay himself that bare with anyone else.

But anything less than that with Ruby would have felt lazy. And frankly beneath them both.

Still scared the hell out of him from time to time. But more often it invigorated him. It was…addictive to be that open with her. Each step he took to trust her she'd met with the same level of trust. Mutually assured destruction, he'd have called it before her.

But now there she was. In his heart and life and her magic weaving its way back through town again. He wanted her at his side. Wanted to be worthy of her. *Before* Ruby seemed to pale in comparison.

"Who is this?" he asked of the song playing in the background.

"H.E.R. The song is 'Damage.'"

"I like it," he told her.

"Me too." She hummed and then piled enchiladas on his plate and handed it back to him. "I can't take credit for the chicken. I'm super lucky to be related to someone who'll rotisserie several whole chickens for a little sister trying to impress her beau."

"I'm your beau?"

"You aren't?"

"Ruby darlin', I think what we are, what I am to you and so forth, is way way beyond words like *beau.* You lived here your whole life so you know how wolf shifters work. I'm not interested in being your boyfriend. I'm interested in being your everything."

Ruby went hot all over. In a good way. Adrenaline spiked and her magic sort of bloomed all around them both.

"All right. We agree that before was just an appetizer. But this now, well, it's a chef's table. We have so many courses ahead."

"I'm glad we can see eye to eye on this point." He didn't really look like he'd worried about it. Which was sexy and sweet and just a smidge smug. "Not that I plan to start slacking off in the spoiling Ruby department."

"I've never been to the Halloween shifter dinner. Aimee and Katie Faith say it's really fun." And also that there were all sorts of longstanding hierarchical grudge matches and that it really mattered what you were asked to bring.

Ruby had been to enough cookouts in her time that she understood that very well.

Damon ate at a steady pace, his delight with the food clear in his responses. He groaned and she pushed his glass of tea a little closer. The boys kept a respectable distance but remained close enough to jump on any scraps that might fall from on high.

"Damn. These are fantastic," he told her.

"I can't take most of the credit. That rotisserie did the real work. All I had to do was shred the meat, stuff it into the tortilla with cheese, roll them and then pour the leftover sauce on the enchiladas and cover with more cheese."

"Yeah that doesn't sound like you did anything at all." He rolled his eyes. "These are fantastic. And it's your magic that makes them that way even if someone else cooked the meat. So hush."

She rolled her eyes but the heat of her blush brought a wholly different look to his face. Still, she was made of sterner stuff and found her words. "Thank you." Ruby did feel that her magic laced through the food she made as much as it did her tisanes, balms and tinctures so it was lovely that he'd noticed.

It *mattered* that he'd noticed.

"I love to cook. Spells are just recipes, after all."

"I think it's far more complicated because magic is about all sorts of stuff and you're downplaying your talent. As for loving to cook in general, it seems to me it's how you take care of your people."

She tilted her head, a little breathless that he'd understood her so well.

He added, "That's a nice thing because I find I like it a lot that you take care of me. I like it even more that you consider me one of your people."

How could it be any other way? It just all felt…right. Scary. Terrifying to find herself falling for this person the way she was. But exhilarating too.

"I don't know if you were this," Ruby flapped a hand in his direction, "back six years ago. You were a lot. It was intoxicating. But who you are now, how you treat me now is still intoxicating." Ruby broke off to laugh a little. "But it's more now. And somehow you plus me equals something that leads me to believe yes, you are one of my people."

Their gazes remained locked for long moments. She knew she should look away. He was a predator and there she was all bold. But…it sent a thrill through her because he wouldn't hurt her. She knew that to her toes. It was a safe sort of danger.

Physically anyway. Ruby was certain he could do her emotional damage. She already felt deeply for him and it only strengthened by the day. If he was careless with her heart, it would hurt. But wasn't that the way regardless?

Ruby didn't consider herself a coward. They liked one another and she'd been a little startled to realize it was far more than just like by that point.

"You're having an entire conversation in your head," he murmured. "Wanna share?"

"I was just confirming, internally, that I was good with this deepening of our relationship."

"Ah. Okay then. I have similar internal conversations about you."

"There's more. An entire second pan is on the counter," she waved toward the kitchen and he was up before she'd even completed the sentence.

"You see, Ruby Jean, if you feed me, I'm not going anywhere," he told her as he refilled his plate.

It filled her with pleasure that he enjoyed what she'd made. Feeding people was, as Nichole told her, Ruby's love language. It was impossible to argue that point.

He returned to the table and scooted the chair so he was next to her. The look he gave her was intense. "I surely do want you, Ruby darlin'. I want you to be mine."

A shiver passed through her at the intensity of his tone. "I am no bird; and no net ensnares me," she quoted Charlotte Brontë. "But I'll gladly stay of my own accord."

He tipped his chin, taking her point. "All right then."

"We've established several important things which all boil down to you and me being into one another in a long-term way. Can you share about wolf stuff? I love Katie Faith and Aimee like sisters, you know? So while I'm always happy to hear whatever they tell me—'cause I love gossip too—I try not to get too nosy about pack stuff because I don't know what they can tell me and I don't want to make them feel weird. You? You'll tell me you can't share and we'll move on."

Damon took her hand and kissed her knuckles. The

heat of his mouth stole through her, rendering her silly, witless and super horny.

Naturally he knew all this, especially the latter which he'd scent on the air. The slow, lazy smile he sent her only confirmed that.

"I like it that you want to know more. I'll tell you what I can and when I can't, I'll say so."

"So, I know y'all had decided between packs that it was a no to Dwayne coming back for a whole month. But when he comes back after his sentence is over, I mean, will they be living right here in town where Katie Faith does? And oh my god, Aimee has to deal with them and given what her soon-to-be father-in-law did to her is bad enough, but obviously can she really have personal feelings because she'll be a sort of wolf when she marries Mac and is Patron too?"

"I approve of how protective you are of your friends. Understand of course that Dooley will not tolerate any more of Scarlett or Dwayne Pembry's foolishness. That's been made very clear. And to be fair, Mac is absolutely behind that as well. He's been working hard to eradicate the rot out of Pembry. As for the rest? We've been negotiating and meeting and yelling and negotiating some more since early this year. I imagine Aimee will let Mac know how she feels about things. But you're right. She'll be Patron once they're married. Her responsibilities will be different. Allegiances will change and she'll have to think about her wolves and what's best for them."

That bothered her. She hated that Aimee would have to put up with mess from anyone who wished her ill like Dwayne had done. At the same time, they were grown up and had responsibilities bigger than personal feelings.

"Being an adult really sucks sometimes," Ruby muttered, bringing a bark of laughter from Damon. "Obviously Aimee will do the best thing for everyone else because I know she takes all this very seriously. And, also, because she's no one's doormat and there will be an opportunity for her to underline that with her soon-to-be in-laws and she'll take it."

"Y'all three are scary." Damon winced at her tone.

"Whatever. You know as well as anyone, I'd wager, about having to underline a lesson every once in a while or people try to run you over. All you laid-back people have that other side to balance you out."

Damon snorted. "Everyone knows I'm scary. But they underestimate witches and I don't know why. It's not like we haven't seen what y'all can do. I kinda like it that you're so beautiful and full of joy but also scary in defense of people you care about. Sexy."

With a giggle, Ruby waved a hand and then started to clear away the dishes. He joined her in the kitchen, helping her load the dishwasher and get the leftovers packed up.

"You sometimes mention being scary or whatever in relation to your place in the pack. And maybe there are moments when it feels like you might wonder if I might feel a way about it."

"Do you?" he asked.

Ruby leaned against the counter to face him fully. "It's part of your job as next in line to be Patron and run the pack. Sometimes you're a diplomat and sometimes you're a soldier. You aren't violent. You use violence to teach wolf shifters lessons. That's not the same thing."

Damon scratched his chin through his beard. "You're just...well you're the opposite of all that."

"Sure I am! I'm a healing witch. A green witch. My job, my talents and what my community needs from me are totally different. Even at that, I want to knock a wolf shifter out on a regular basis. I don't know how you manage to get through any day without having to kick someone's butt for being out of line."

He snorted, amusement in the sound.

"Damon, I know wolf shifters crave discipline and hierarchy. I also know y'all have ways to teach control. I admire the job you do and I understand and expect you to continue to do it with integrity. If I perceive it differently at some point in the future, we can talk things through."

He sucked in a breath, held it and then said, "Okay. Okay that's fair. I worry that you'll come to believe I'm a bad guy. Or that you'll be disgusted by what I do. I don't want that. I don't want to be that guy."

She spent several long seconds as she thought it over because she had some things to say and she wanted to say them correctly. Ruby knew this was some deep stuff they were beginning to talk about honestly. He was exposing his heart to her and she wanted to protect it the best she could. "You're not your father. Is that what you mean?"

"Maybe? No. Partly. It's ridiculous. He's been gone pretty much my whole life. It's not even like anyone can talk about him or what he did."

"It isn't ridiculous though." Ruby reached out to touch his chest briefly, wanting to soothe and reassure. "Sometimes what isn't said speaks volumes. This is exactly why your packs have to change. How can we all be better and cast off generations of broken-ass bullshit if we don't get rid of the traditions that shore that up? This Rule of Silence crap just perpetuates more brokenness."

His posture had been taut, his arms crossed but after several breaths he eased back and relaxed his spine. "Yes. All that. I hope you won't mind if I use those words to describe it to others. Mainly with the older shifters. Younger wolves get it. We've grown up in different worlds and so there are different obstacles when talking about changing laws. Especially our oldest ones."

"You want them to know you're gaining things, not losing them. And don't worry that I'll take anything you say outside this place."

"Appreciate you saying that. Not that I thought otherwise. Older wolves didn't grow up in a world with the internet. Or video on cell phones. They were taught to believe silence was safe."

"Scarlett's manipulating that, I wager."

He snorted again. "Maybe she truly believes the things she's saying. Regardless, it gets shifters extra worked up when they start thinking about being exposed to a hostile world. She's meaner than a wet cat, but smart."

Ruby had noticed the way Scarlett seemed to use the silence about Josiah Dooley and his punishment as a way to keep people feeling negatively regarding anything to do with him. Even rules that applied to him. It was really devious.

"I trust you," Ruby told him. "I don't judge you negatively about your job. I'm not afraid of you." She took his hands and got close again. "I know you're sort of hemmed in about what you can share regarding all this pack law change stuff and I won't push. I just wanted you to know I understand the nature of your place in the Dooley pack and respect you. Any time you want to talk and have me be a sounding board or just an ear to vent, I'm here."

He bent to kiss her. "Thank you, Ruby darlin', for thinking about me the way you do. I needed to hear all that. Lots of meetings with more to come and honestly I'd like it all handled before Dwayne comes back to Diablo Lake for good."

"Let me know if you need me to kick anyone's shin for you," she teased, easing back and getting to cleaning up their mess.

There in her kitchen, her laughter in the air between them, Damon just let his feelings for her sweep him along. *This* was utter happiness and contentment. Real intimacy.

Dinner at her table, eating food she'd created for him, being spoiled by his witch suited him perfectly. He'd eaten date-type meals with lots of women and he'd felt nothing that even approached what he did then.

But then, she went and doubled down by being so honest and open with him. Assuring him how much she understood his world and damn if he didn't believe she meant it.

"Dear sweet jesus, but you're perfect," he murmured as she turned his way. He reached out to brush a fingertip over the swell of her cheek and down into the dip of the dimple to the left of her mouth. "Tomorrow is Saturday."

"Yeah?" she asked, a little breathless.

"Mercantile doesn't open until eight but I don't have to be anywhere until ten."

"What a coincidence. I don't have to be anywhere until nine thirty." Her voice had gone lower just a bit. Coated in something soft and delicious that seemed to swirl around his body, caressing him with the sound.

"What I was thinking, and you know, stop me if I'm moving too fast."

Ruby grabbed the front of his shirt and tugged him to her body. "Yes, I want you naked and in my bed right this very moment," she said. "You're also welcome to sleep over if you like. That way we can do it again before we head off to our respective days."

"Remember I said I was good with breakfast. I'll cook for you. After." Damon paused, breathing deep, her magic rushing into his lungs. "Jesus. Is this really happening or am I just fantasizing about you yet again? All the blood has rushed from my head so I don't rightly know for sure."

Heat flashed through her as desire left her a little dizzy. "Damn, you're a lot of fun, Damon," she said as she pulled him toward her bedroom. He made her *so* happy. Filled her with a sense that it was not only okay to be herself around him, but that he got off on who she was and what she did.

"Just trying to earn my keep," he said, slowing his words down like he tasted them. This big, muscled man who was the prettiest thing she'd ever seen in her entire life was all in. For her. With her.

And underneath that slow Southern sex drawl, he was surprisingly playful.

He was irresistible.

The dogs had stayed out from under her feet, which Ruby figured was a byproduct of Damon being around. They'd run if he called, but behave until then because they craved his approval.

Huh. Ruby *really* got that craving.

At her bedroom door he paused, bringing her to a halt and letting her know he was *allowing* himself to be tugged into her bedroom, but no one made this shifter do anything he didn't want to.

And just then he tipped his head back and breathed in deep. He did it several times until a low growl trickled from his lips and he met her gaze.

"Your magic is so heavy in here. It's like a mist of pleasure against my skin."

"Really?" She smiled, pleased he'd found it as alluring as he so clearly did. Pleased that this moment had finally come. Beyond pleased that it was a billion times better in reality than it had been in her fantasies.

Her breathing slowed as she took him in, standing on her bedroom rug just half a foot from her bed. The room was cozy rather than small, but with him in it, he nearly overwhelmed. But she rode that until the panic ebbed and all that remained was heady. Desire. Greed to see more. A deep satisfaction that yes, she would be seeing more. Lots more.

And that was all before he reached down, one-handed, grabbed the hem of his shirt and pulled it over his head in one liquid movement. The beauty of it left her struck still. It was all she could do to stare at him and all that exposed, muscled skin, still tawny from the summer sun.

When he'd tossed his shirt over a nearby chair and turned his attention back to her face he started, and then he took the three steps separating them and laid a long, hot, openmouthed kiss on her, making her head spin.

"Makes me pretty hard to see you look at me like that," he said, voice rough as he rested his forehead against hers.

"There's literally no other way to look at you shirt-less. I mean. You're exceptionally genetically gifted. You hit the lottery. Or rather, I guess I should say *I* hit the lottery. I really can't wait to see what else you've got going on under the rest of these clothes."

Ruby's fingers had just grabbed his zipper pull when her phone rang. Her mother's tone. "I'm sorry, I have to take this," she said, wrenching herself away to rush to answer.

It was after midnight. Any call from her mother after nine at night would be urgent.

"What's wrong?" she said, answering.

"Is Lovie there with you?" her mother asked.

"No. What's going on?" Ruby headed to the door and Damon appeared, going out into the yard with her.

"She's missing and no one knows where she is."

Damon indicated he'd head off to the left so she took the right, calling her grandmother's name.

"How long has she been gone?" Ruby asked.

"Your grandfather called about ten minutes ago. He'd fallen asleep on the couch and woke up to find the front door and the screen door wide open and Lovie nowhere to be found. Daddy went over there to help keep your grandpa calm. Greg is looking out on our land." Her mother's voice trailed off, the worry in it painfully obvious.

Her grandmother was getting older and sometimes her thoughts wandered away and Ruby fervently hoped it wasn't a step into dementia. Her mother was the one who needed calm and comfort just then so she sucked it up.

"We're going to find her. It's Diablo Lake. If anyone comes across her they'll bring her home." And they would. They all took care of their own. Lovie was an elder in the community. Most people loved her and nearly all respected her.

Not two minutes later, she heard Damon call out, "Over here!"

Ruby rushed around the side of the house and into the backyard before catching sight of him walking quickly, holding Lovie in his arms, cradling her against his chest.

Lovie had a big smile on her face and she kept patting his biceps and Ruby was so relieved she wanted to cry. Instead, she turned her attention to her mother and the phone still against her ear.

"Damon found her. We'll bring her home shortly and I'll explain whatever I find out," she told her mother. "It's okay, Momma."

She hung up and cleared the way for him to bring Lovie into the house and settle her on the couch.

"Hi there, sweetheart," her grandmother said.

"Hey yourself, Lovie. Mom is worried about you. No one knew where you were." Ruby checked her over quickly and efficiently, sending her magic out in a warm wave to soothe and comfort. Nothing broken that she could sense or feel. No blood or wounds of any sort.

"I wanted to go for a walk. I must have gotten turnt around. Thought..." she paused and a hand of fear squeezed around Ruby's heart as she watched Lovie struggle to remember. "Thought I remembered you saying you lived down this way. I wanted to say hello. I had things to say. Can't recall now."

"Well, you were right. I do live here and if you ever want to say hello, call me and I'll come get you. You can stay over and we'll have a slumber party like the old days. It'll be my turn to make you cheese toast. For now, we should get you home," Ruby managed to say, hoping she kept it light.

"Not even gonna offer me a cup of tea? Some toast? You were raised better than that, Ruby," Lovie said as she watched Damon.

"Want a cup of tea, Lovie? I have chamomile mint." It'd calm her down and hopefully make her sleepy.

"That sounds good. It's chilly out there. Add a little something sweet to go with," Lovie ordered.

Damon tried not to smile but he was losing the battle and Ruby snorted as she got up to start the water boiling.

She called her mother to let her know they were having tea and a snack and would be back soon. Her mom understood Lovie had demanded that and seemed to agree it was best to have the tea and then bring her back. She was relieved everything was okay and though Ruby told her to go to bed, she knew her mother wouldn't do that until Lovie was settled safely once more.

When Ruby brought the steeped tea and a brownie over to both her grandmother and her very sweet wolf, she settled in the chair across from them.

"He came out of the dark like a gentleman," her Lovie said of Damon. "So strong! Just swept me up into his arms because I was down in that gulley and the moon hid behind the clouds so I couldn't see well enough to find the steps. He did ask first. *Ms. Lovie,*

*how about I give you a ride over to Ruby's? I'm going
to pick you up, all right?* That's why I said he was a
gentleman."

"He's very well versed on asking first. Especially for
a wolf," Ruby said and then winked at him.

"I guess things are going well if he's over here so
late at night. Hope I didn't interrupt anything," Lovie
said with a cackle of glee.

Ruby knew her Lovie wouldn't see the flush rise
to her cheeks, but Damon would scent the heating of
her skin.

"He made me country captain chicken for our first
official date. I had to keep him around after that."

Lovie thought that was hilarious. "Why, that's a bold
choice! Maybe he wanted to see the state of your manners and if you could eat without getting sauce everywhere."

"It's one of my specialties," Damon said. "And Ruby
has excellent manners from all I've ever seen."

Lovie laughed again as she shook her head at him
and looked to Ruby. "He's handsome as the dickens.
Usually a handsome man isn't worth the hassle." She
turned to Damon a moment. "Present company ex-
cepted."

He smiled at her, all flirty charm. "I surely do thank
you, Ms. Thorne."

"You can call me Lovie if you're going to fall for my
granddaughter."

"Well thank you very much, Lovie." Damon took
her hand and kissed her knuckles all courtly-like and
Ruby's heart melted.

"As I was saying, Ruby." Her grandmother nibbled
the brownie. "Usually a handsome man is not worth the

trouble they bring. They can't do a damned thing because everyone else has served them just to get a little
attention." Lovie snorted. "Gotta wade through all the
women they attract, or men I suppose depending on the
handsome man. They never want to take responsibility for what they do wrong and think a kiss is enough."
She shook her head. "Your grandfather is a handsome
man. A lot of trouble." Then Lovie's expression softened. "*Usually* worth it. 'Specially when he puts on a
suit and takes me down to town and out to dinner. With
flowers and a bit of candy. He knows my weakness for
pralines. And handsome men," she added with a waggle
of her brows and Ruby couldn't hold back her laughter.

"And a handsome man who'd jump into a gulley in
one bound to sweep an old lady up off her feet and drop
her gently at her granddaughter's? One who looks at you
the way he does? You better keep him."

Damon was blushing by that point and Ruby watched
them both and realized the truth of her grandmother's
story. Damon Dooley was a total keeper.

"I came looking for you because I had a dream. Not
a bad one," Lovie reassured Ruby quickly. "Big things
going on. I guess I just got caught up and didn't think
long and hard enough before I left. I just wanted to see
your pretty face. And I got two pretty faces and something sweet for my trouble."

After half an hour Lovie had gotten sleepy and the
excitement and fear from her adventure had worn off.
Damon had picked her up, again easily and had carried her to the car, settling her on the passenger's side.

"Call me tomorrow," he told Ruby as she headed
around to the driver's-side door. "You need to focus on

getting her settled back in and on making your mom feel better. She's got to be on edge." He touched her cheek.

"I'm sorry about all this," she said.

"Nothing to be sorry about. I'm not going anywhere other than home to get some sleep. I'll be back around, sniffing all over you, rubbing up on you, tomorrow. Don't forget we have dinner with Katie Faith." He kissed the tip of her nose and then her lips before bending to say good-night to Lovie. Ruby might have watched his butt a little longer than was strictly necessary as he ambled off to his car.

"He's very pretty," Lovie said once they started the short drive to her grandparents' house.

"He is. He's so nice to me. He gets me. And more than that, he *likes* me."

"And he should. Look at you, power shining around you like a halo. Big beautiful black girl full up with talent and potential. He'd better not only like it but be grateful he even gets close to you. You're a queen, sweetheart."

Ruby grinned in the dark.

When she pulled to a stop at the front porch, her mother and father both came out and down to meet them.

Ruby saw the lines of worry around her father's eyes and same in the set of her mom's mouth.

Her grandpa strolled over, giving Lovie a careful but casual once-over. "Pearl, I know we had an agreement about letting someone know when you leave. Especially late at night. You gave me quite a fright only a big pan of biscuits smothered in gravy will soothe."

Lovie laughed and patted his arm. "I'm sorry. I had a dream and wanted to see Ruby. But when I saw her,

I forgot the dream, but I think it's all right. I'll remember. I'm tired though."

Her grandpa wrapped an arm around Lovie's shoulders along with a shawl. "Let's get you all tucked up into bed for the night so you can get your beauty sleep. Biscuits and gravy are hard work and I want you rested."

Lovie laughed, looking up at Ruby's grandfather with open affection before turning back to Ruby. "Remember what I said about handsome men, baby. Thank you for the company and the sweets. You should bring some of those over so your grandpa won't feel left out."

"We wouldn't want that. I'll bring you some tomorrow after I get off work. I love you both."

Her grandfather left Lovie's side for a moment. Long enough to kiss Ruby's cheek and squeeze her hands. "Love you," he said before returning to his wife to take her inside.

Once they'd gone from sight, Ruby hugged her mom tight. "She's okay. When Damon brought her to my house, she wasn't hurt. Thought to put on her rain boots, she said, to avoid any snakes. I worried. At first. I worried she'd be confused or forgetful but I think it was more like she was in the grip of her dream. She knew she was trying to get to my house. She remembered where my house was from me describing it to her a few weeks ago." She wanted to reassure her mother of that because the older her grandparents got, the worries grew.

Still, the situation as it was concerned Ruby too.

"Maybe we could set up an alarm of some sort to trigger when she leaves the house. Pops could have gone off looking for her and ended up getting hurt too. We sure don't want that or him feeling guilty when she goes off on one of her walks without saying anything and gets hurt."

Her mom leaned her head against Ruby's dad's shoulder a moment. "Seems harder for her to shake off her dreams. Least that's what I think. We talked about an alarm yesterday, as a matter of fact. But she likes to be on her porch and in her yard. And during the day the house is busy. People coming and going all the time."

Ruby's aunts, all her cousins and various folks in town knew how much Lovie liked a visit and she was fun to be around so she remained a social butterfly. That meant they had to think about a spell that could be active but not at all times.

"The longer she stays active and involved, the sharper her brain will be so obviously we don't want to impede her daily life."

"If we treat it like a ward of protection that might do the trick. Activate it after dinner or when *NCIS* is over. Have it coupled with the ward at your house so if she leaves it'll alert you," Ruby said. "Then you can check in with Pops first to see if everything is okay. And if it isn't and she's missing, I learned a tracker spell that should help locate her."

"We're going to chip your grandmother like we chipped Pipes," her dad joked to break the tension. Which it did.

"I'll talk with Rita and Rehema tomorrow. It's a good time to perform the working when everyone is here in town." Her mom took a deep breath, calmer now. "Thanks for dropping everything to find her and bring her home."

"You're welcome. That's what you do when you love someone. Anyway, I think she'll be fine. She was more enamored of Damon than scared. He was so good to her tonight." Ruby flattened her hand over her heart a moment.

"He was at your house at one in the morning?" Her mother's right eyebrow rose imperiously.

"He was. Now he's back at his place. I'll see him again soon. Tomorrow. Or I guess later today. We have a dinner thing with Katie Faith and Jace. I'll tell him you said hey," Ruby teased before she got serious again. "There are enough of us to work this out. And do what we need to do to keep Lovie safe."

Her mom nodded and hugged Ruby once more before sending her home.

Chapter Twelve

Ruby got into work that Saturday morning to find two flower arrangements on the counter where the receptionist sat.

Aimee popped her head around the corner. "Hey. Those are for you." She pointed at the flowers.

Had Damon sent her flowers? Ruby pulled the card free of the roses and lavender. "Why is Craig Pembry sending me roses?" The note said he wanted to take her out for pizza. "Shoulda sent a pizza instead of roses," she muttered.

Aimee grabbed the other card. "This is from Reese Dickinson. Also a Pembry wolf. He says you're real pretty and wants to call on you."

"I barely know either one of them. Craig was in one or two of my classes back in school. Reese and Greg hung out sometimes but I don't think I've said a word to him in years. Why are they doing this?"

Aimee rolled her eyes. "Duh. Look at you. Plus you're powerful and from a well-connected family. You're single and on track to be successful here in Diablo Lake. I'm surprised it took this long, if I'm honest. The only reason there aren't any Dooleys sniffing around is because Damon scares the hell out of them."

"This might explain a few things."

Ruby told Aimee about the looks she'd been getting and the inquiries into her romantic status coupled with suggestions of nephews and the like.

Aimee's mouth flattened into a frown and she shook it off, telling Ruby, "Scarlett showed up at the house day before yesterday. She invited herself to a breakfast my mom and I were having with my grandmother to talk about wedding stuff. She did offer her wedding dress, which I have to admit is really pretty. But unless I could exorcise all the bitter, terrible harpy out of it, I don't want to drag that energy down the aisle with me. Then she started talking about you and how pretty you were—even though you'd be prettier if you lost some weight—and how she'd been telling all her friends about the clinic so they could get any of their healthcare seen to. Like I was invisible! Anyway, the point is, she's interested in you so I'm not surprised one bit the single wolf shifters are taking a look. She's behind most of it I wager. And, to be up front with you, she's going to be insufferable when it becomes clear to all and sundry that you're with Damon and off the market. Even though I told her that very thing. Underlined it. *Ruby and Damon are together, don't bother or it'll just agitate everyone and it won't change the outcome anyway.*"

"That shit is medieval. Like I'm part of a war chest or something to be traded for power. Even if I'm fatty mcfat."

Aimee snickered. "Bless your heart." And set them both laughing so hard Ruby got the hiccups.

Aimee continued, "I mean, yes, it's sexist as hell. But you're powerful in your own right. Whoever you end up with will benefit. If you don't think the wolves in this town aren't keeping a tally of who marries who and what they bring to the pack as a whole, you're sorely mistaken. I'm surprised JJ hasn't been crowing about how you and Damon are together from the top step of city hall."

Aimee and Ruby chuckled at that.

"That's coming. It's only a matter of time," Aimee admitted. "Brace yourself."

"So far, all the interaction I've had with his family has been good. But I've known Major and Jace my whole life practically anyway. I've been around Patty and JJ before, multiple times. But. Well it's different now. I want them to approve of me. I want to make Damon proud. Which sounds weird, I know. But there it is."

Aimee hugged her quickly. "That doesn't sound weird at all. Of course you want him to be happy. And if his grandparents are happy, he'll be happy. That's normal. It's why I do my best to remember there are so many great Pembrys who aren't Scarlett. Mac's aunt and uncle are really close with him and they've gone out of their way to accept me and make me feel comfortable."

"Does it make you mad when people judge all of Pembry by what Scarlett does? I know I'd be hot over it in your place. Hell, I'm hot about it anyway," Ruby said.

"At first it was worse. In the weeks after Dwayne and Darrell were punished and sent away, there was so much upheaval. People had to call out stuff that was wrong when their friends had done it. By now, a lot of fences have been mended. A lot of relationships that were fractured have healed or are on the way."

"I'm so impressed with you," Ruby confessed to Aimee. "You're mayor. *Mayor.* And you're a partner in this clinic. And you're going to be Patron of Pembry after you and Mac get married. People respect you. They trust you. Good job."

Aimee's bottom lip trembled just a moment before she got herself under control. "You have no idea how much I needed to hear that. Thank you. I love you."

Just a few minutes later, Ruby's next appointment came in and her workday started. She called out that she'd see Aimee that night at dinner and got to it.

The streetlamps along Diablo Lake Avenue cast a golden light as they walked, hand in hand. They didn't need to be at dinner for another hour and so he'd lured her away from his truck and toward the pub for a beer.

"Just a little while longer where it's me and you only," he whispered against her ear and got her all revved up again.

"You're going to get me in trouble," Ruby said with a laugh while she kept her hand in his and they continued their stroll toward the pub.

"I'm fun that way."

"Indeed."

"How's your Lovie?"

"I checked in on her first thing and she was already up and making those victory biscuits and gravy. All my aunts and my mom are working on a spell that sets off an alarm if anyone leaves the house after bedtime. Once we get all that up and working right, I learned a tracking spell two or three years back that I'll customize to her. In the meantime, Greg and my dad installed a door alarm that my parents can turn on remotely if my grandparents forget. But I think my mom and the aunts are all feeling better that they're doing all these things to keep Lovie safe. She asked about you at least four times. I think my grandmother has a crush on you, so watch out. Thanks again for helping and being so good with her."

He chuckled and squeezed her hand, flattered and pleased. He liked Pearl Thorne a lot, though it was tempered by a healthy fear. She might have been barely five feet tall and light in his arms, but she wasn't weak or fragile. Her strength was one the predator in Damon respected.

"I'm glad she's okay today. What's this about biscuits and gravy?"

Ruby laughed. "I totally forgot you weren't there last night when we brought her back to her house." She explained her grandfather's demand for the breakfast for Lovie scaring him so. "We Thorne women are *a lot*. So when we get old we're even more." She shrugged one shoulder. "Lovie is the matriarch. I find myself learning from her every day and I know she's got plenty more to pass on. That we can keep her safer makes everyone feel better and then Lovie doesn't get annoyed that everyone fusses over her and pesters her about where she's going and where she's been."

"A lot is worth it when it's a Thorne witch, I've been discovering," he told her truthfully. Unique. Powerful. Priceless for myriad reasons.

Her pupils seemed to swallow her irises and her lips parted on a soft intake of breath. An invitation and one he had no plans to decline as he lowered his head for a kiss.

She smelled so nice and felt so good, tasted even better. All his.

"I was going to ask you last night but then we had a

Lovie-shaped emergency. Would you like to do some Samhain stuff with me? The bonfire is always fun, but there's other stuff too. I make an ancestor's altar every year and I was thinking of including something for your mother. Katie Faith said she'd included her before in her altar in the past and I just thought it sounded wonderful."

That knocked the breath from him for a few beats. "Wow." He took her face in his hands and kissed her once more. "I'd love that. I don't know as much as I should so I hope you don't mind if I ask you lots of questions. But I want to learn and I'm really touched that you'd trust me enough to include me."

"You're important to me and Samhain is important to me so why not mix them up like a stir fry?"

"Lucky me." He kissed her because he wanted to. "An ancestor's altar is a way to celebrate their lives?"

"Yes, just that. I'll include my aunt, uncle and cousins this year. A way to celebrate the lives of loved ones who came before. People, like energy, are never truly all the way gone. You keep their lives at the forefront. Celebrate their place in the cycle of creation. It helps with grief. For me anyway. A positive way to get in touch with memories of the ones whose metaphorical shoulders we stand on."

"That makes sense. I like it a lot. Thank you again."

Ruby rested her head on his upper arm a moment.

Maybe he could charm her over to her house until closer to dinner. That way they could smooch and snuggle. Ask her all about Samhain and being a witch so her voice could tease and ease his wolf.

But before he could suggest that to Ruby...

"There you are!"

Damon froze up on a snarled curse.

Ruby waved at Katie Faith, who stood in the yard between the Mercantile and the pack house. Jace stood behind her trying to make hand signs to Damon that he had nothing to do with his wife's interrupting their date.

"Hey, Katie Faith," Ruby said, far too friendly in Damon's opinion. You couldn't give Katie Faith one tiny inch or she'd take seven thousand miles.

"Aimee is here with Mac. Damon, you get on over and bring Ruby. You promised." She pointed and gave puppy dog eyes at the same time. Jace just looked on like, *hey, you know what she's like*. Damon glared at his brother anyway.

"I am utterly sure I made clear Ruby and I were going to be at your place *in an hour.* We'll eat dinner with y'all. Until then, we're going to have a beer. We'll be back on time." Damon sent her a smile that told her there'd be hell to pay if she kept pushing.

"Well, but you're here *now*! Major is too. Do it for Aimee. She's mayor and getting married in a month and her soon-to-be in-laws are *terrible* people. She's in a sad state and needs the support." Katie Faith sent them a sunny smile.

"Were you just here *lying in wait* until we walked past? Were you listening for my truck?" Damon asked.

"No!" Katie Faith shook her head vehemently but her smile belied the denial.

Behind her, Jace nodded enthusiastically.

"I don't need to be looking at you to know you're back there making an ass of yourself, Jace Dooley," Katie Faith said.

Damon groaned and turned to face Ruby. "She'll only find fifteen reasons to interrupt our beer."

Laughter spilled from her lips as she lifted a hand to slide her fingers through his hair. "You're right," she said and kissed him quickly. "I'll make you boozy hot chocolate after we're done working on your house later tonight instead."

"Remember what I told you about how we'll never leave once you feed us or give us chocolate?" he murmured to her and delighted in her smile.

"Why do you think I offered?"

Damon kissed her quick. "Perfection."

"She tried to make you sound all pathetic and lonely, Aimee," Damon tattled as they got dragged into the pack house where Jace and Katie Faith lived. "*Oh Aimee is so sad and depressed and needs you to put off alone time with your woman to soothe her.*"

"She's a liarpants!" Aimee replied as she poured a glass of wine and handed it to Ruby. "Did you participate in this assassination of my character?" she asked Ruby while laughing.

"No. But I would have in different circumstances, obviously." Ruby clinked her glass to Aimee's before she let Damon guide her to a love seat the size of which would mean they needed to cuddle to sit comfortably in. A thing she had literally no complaints about as he held her against his chest.

This was so fun and normal that while she was bummed to miss a beer with Damon, it was fine. Because being with these people she really enjoyed so much was a total delight.

Across from where she and Damon sat, Mac lounged while he kept an eye on Aimee. Ruby loved the way he looked at her friend. Like Aimee was the best thing in the world.

He sensed Ruby's attention and turned his gaze on her. "Hey, Mac." Ruby waved, pleased to see he was at ease in this group of mainly Dooley wolves.

"Evenin', Ruby." He tipped his chin her way and then to Damon. "Nice to see you got sucked into this too. I'd be pissed if I was the only one robbed of alone time with my soon-to-be wife."

Major came in, caught sight of everyone and snickered. He paused to kiss Katie Faith and Aimee's cheeks and then did the same to Ruby.

Damon's growl seemed to echo through his chest and into Ruby's body and she snorted, patting his knee to calm him down.

He huffed hard enough to make the baby hairs at her ear tickle a little.

"You're looking beautiful tonight, Ruby, Aimee and Katie Faith," Major said with a bow. "How lucky am I to be having dinner with such gorgeous witches?"

Jace groaned in the background.

"So very lucky," Aimee said.

"He made the biscuits to go with dinner, so we're lucky too," Katie Faith called out. "And speaking of dinner, y'all come on to the table."

Everyone else got up but Damon held Ruby in place with an arm around her waist. "I just wanted a quick cuddle before we have to head in there."

He just held her close for several long moments until he sighed and in one easy move, he was on his feet and helping her to do the same. He was so strong but it didn't make her feel weak in any way.

"I want to thank you again for inviting me into your Samhain celebrations." He kissed her forehead.

Ruby was doubly glad she had. It pleased her to underline that he was truly wanted in her life. Pleased her even more that he clearly enjoyed it as well.

"Move your behinds or we're going to start without you," Jace bellowed.

"That fuckin' guy," Damon grumbled as he spun Ruby neatly and they joined everyone else at the table.

"Everyone getting ready for Samhain?" Katie Faith asked as the platters and bowls of food began to make a circuit.

Ruby's friend had grown up. More than just the amazing food, enough to easily feed seven people, four of them shifters, Katie Faith had a confidence and an ease with herself that served her well as Patron of the Dooley wolves. An air of competence. Like whatever came up, she'd handle it.

Ruby knew for certain that if her friend had ended up with a human in the outside world, or with her ex, this blossoming into the alpha, powerful witch and Patron she was wouldn't have happened. And it would have been a shame.

"I'm learning more about it every day. Does that count?" Damon asked with a wink Ruby's way.

"It does, as it happens," Ruby assured him. "He'll be at the bonfire and I'm using the apples from the trees on his house lot to make apple hand pies for the dinner."

"She's coming to the Halloween dinner with me," Damon told everyone, the pride so clear in his voice she wanted to throw her arms around him.

Katie Faith beamed at him like she'd done it herself and Ruby adored her friend for it.

"Don't fret too much. Patty'll be who assigns you a dish to bring. Whatever she says, do it because she always has a big-picture plan of some type that'll make you look good in the end," Katie Faith said.

"That's what Damon told me. I do feel better knowing that. And that you'll all be there so I won't be totally alone."

"It really is fun," Aimee reassured her. "I hope this year we can leave all the drama behind and celebrate all the good. I really don't want any crap coming into the engagement dinner and the dance a few days later."

Collins Hill Days was named in the honor of two of the founding families in Diablo Lake. It was the town's Founder's Day celebration and included Halloween when the shifters had their big celebration dinner and the four days of Samhain the witches in town observed. It was a usually busy and slightly hectic time of year before winter settled in. Add to it that Mac and Aimee were having a big pre-wedding/engagement party and dance for the entire town as an official close to the festivities. Ruby was frankly astonished Aimee hadn't fallen over by that point.

"I just want to repeat to you that I know how busy you are and how many things you have to finish before the dinner, much less the wedding. I'm here. Can I pick things up for you? Show up early to set up? Clean after an event? Cook or bake?" Ruby asked. Between the engagement dinner at the end of Collins Hill Days to their wedding just two days after Thanksgiving, there was plenty to do so Ruby wanted Aimee to know she was down for whatever needed handling.

"Thank you," Aimee said. "Things are on track at this point. You and Katie Faith are handling the bridal shower. Mac's aunt is planning something pack-wise. At this point it's pretty much all my mother and Miz Rose and the rest of her friends who are handling all the last-minute stuff so I don't have to."

Aimee and Mac were having a very simple wedding ceremony in Miz Rose's garden. Aimee's father was going to officiate—after he walked her down the aisle with her mother. She chose to have no attendants or anything like that, as did Mac. Aimee wanted to share that very intimate moment with less than twenty people.

After that though, they were shutting down Diablo Lake Avenue from city hall all the way down to the brew pub and had invited the entire community for cake, pie and other sweets, live music, dancing and apple cider.

She and Mac wanted to unify not just their lives, but to hold everyone in town close and share food and drink with them. It was a really good idea, not that Ruby was surprised. Aimee and Mac both were natural leaders. Together, they'd be unstoppable.

"Listen, Mac Pembry," Katie Faith said and Damon and Jace both groaned.

Mac managed not to smile but it was clear he worked very hard not to. "Yes, ma'am?" he asked.

"I know your dad won't be at the party, but Scarlett's coming to both. How will she be muzzled?"

Jace's sigh was so deep it made Ruby laugh.

"You're a dick," Aimee told Katie Faith while she delivered a pinch to her arm.

"Ow!" Katie Faith slapped Aimee's hand away. "What? *Me?* Why? I'm over here trying to protect you."

"Because that's Mac's *mom* and he had to send his

dad and brother away and take pack leadership from his father who is a jerk who loves one of his kids pretty much to the exclusion of the others," Aimee said.

"Fucking ouch!" Mac exclaimed.

"Well it's true and I'm sorry. Both that it's true and that it got brought up." Aimee smiled at Mac, patting his arm.

Damon's groan brought Ruby's attention to her wolf, who rolled his eyes and shook his head.

"I'm happy to be your assistant if you need one," Damon told Ruby, ignoring the bickering. "I know how to peel and slice apples."

Ruby imagined him in an apron and it was hotter than the sun.

"The Mercantile is open six days a week," she told him. "You're building a house and running a pack. You're busier than I am."

"I'd rather be busy because I'm with you than have a bunch of free time without you. And you help me too. Just looking at you helps."

That made Ruby smile. Who wouldn't smile when someone said things like that and meant them? What a gift he was.

Ruby turned back as Katie Faith apologized for being a dick, and Mac waved it away because most likely he'd accepted that if he was with Aimee, Katie Faith was part of the package and she had *opinions* about things.

"Yes, Scarlett is coming to pretty much all the wedding and wedding-related events," Aimee said, putting her hand in Mac's. "She's Mac's mother. His dad can't come because of the punishment. Scarlett wasn't sent up, and in her own way, she's pro Aimee and Mac."

Everyone just stared at her and then Mac.

"She's promised to behave herself. If she doesn't, she'll be removed. I know she has been truly awful to you and Jace and I apologize for that," Mac said.

Aimee made a cutting motion through the air. "We don't need their permission to have your mother at our wedding and that's that."

Speaking of ouch. That hit home, Ruby realized. Defensiveness rose and then eased back because wasn't it nice that Aimee just told them to back off as she defended her new family with Mac?

And maybe it was shady to keep talking about it once the point had been made.

"You're absolutely right," Ruby told Aimee and Mac. "I'm excited for this wedding. I can't wait to get dressed up to dance, eat cake and drink to celebrate *you*."

Katie Faith reached forward and squeezed Aimee's hand. "Me too. I love you both."

As the moment passed, Aimee buttered a biscuit and then asked after Ruby's family.

"My Lovie got a little turned around on her way to my house and my mom called, worried because they couldn't find her. Damon not only tracked her down, but leaped into a gully, swept her up into his arms and carried her all the way to my front door. It's a good thing I'm faster than she is or I might have some competition. She positively swooned over him."

"She told us how she has a weakness for handsome men and meant me too," Damon said, a little smug.

"Well, for heaven's sake, obviously she meant you. Acting like you've never looked in the mirror, Damon Dooley, when we all know you have," Katie Faith told him with a roll of her eyes.

"But it's always nice to hear it from someone else," Ruby said, her hand still in Damon's.

"She's okay now though?" Aimee asked.

"Yes. I don't think it's cognitive decline as much as it's age. Still, it's hard on her when she has her dreams." Ruby looked over at Jace, Mac and Major. "One of my grandmother's gifts is foresight. Usually through dreams or little spells she might have. But it takes a physical toll and we don't want her to get hurt when she's under the influence of her gift." She explained the spells the family was working on to keep Lovie safe.

While Aimee's magic had been soothing and warm, Damon's was something else entirely. Ruby knew it was his wolf she sensed when the heat spiked and the scent of loam rose.

At her side he was solid. Big and protective. Damon leaned into her then, his weight an anchor in the storm; all that electric shifter magic had risen *for her*. It fascinated and flattered both the witch and her magic.

As she more fully leaned back into him, accepting the comfort he offered, Aimee smiled as she took the scene in. She squeezed Ruby's left hand and sat back, slightly against Mac.

Ruby loved watching the two of them together. They were clearly in love and very much in synch.

A wash of tenderness rushed through Damon as Ruby spoke of her grandmother. The concern and affection in her tone was a physical thing, prodding the wolf to urge the man to comfort and spoil her.

His gaze flicked up to Jace's and they shared a look. His brother had no pity on his features, rather he stared at Damon. Taking his measure in that supercharged moment.

The wolf and the brother understood it then. Yes, he'd had a few conversations about Ruby with his brothers. Enough that both knew things were serious. But that moment was a turning point. A forever moment. Patron and brother asking if this person was evoking emotional responses in Damon that were far more than any sort of concern for a girlfriend.

If so, Damon would need to acknowledge that and insert himself more firmly in her life because once he gave over to his wolf, all those hyper-protective instincts would settle into place. It was a choice that once made, would change everything.

Damon took a deep breath, drawing her magic and that essential part of her into his lungs and then nodded—a barely perceptible tip of his chin—at his brother.

After they'd finished eating, Major, Damon, Jace and Mac headed to the kitchen to clean up.

"I'm sorry about Katie Faith," Jace said as he snickered. "I did try to stop her multiple times. She's missed Ruby too and when she heard your truck and realized you were already here, she ran like a gazelle."

"What's her excuse with Aimee?" Mac asked.

"I can't even be mad at you for that," Jace told him. "Those two have their own set of rules and it's best for me to stay out of the way when it comes to that."

Mac growled as he packed the leftovers up and put them in the fridge.

"Now that Ruby is back, I expect it'll be Damon who gets to come home to find eight witches watching reality television and drinking too much vodka in the living room," Jace added helpfully.

Damon never had minded the rhythm Katie Faith and Aimee had. He loved the way their magic drifted on the breeze all around the property and he couldn't get mad at a group of tipsy, pretty witches jeering at the television while swearing like sailors.

But when he said so, both Mac and Jace started to laugh.

"I should take pity on you for that terrible misunderstanding," Mac said. "But I'm going to laugh at your pain because you'd laugh at mine."

He and Jace laughed some more while Damon finished loading the dishwasher.

"We'll see how adorable you think it is when they show up, pounding on your door, or sending a thousand texts with this or that problem when you're trying to have a little quality alone time with your woman," Mac said.

"Or when you realize how much detail they share with one another. Aimee threw a muffin at my head the other day because of some stupid argument Katie Faith and I had," Jace said.

"To be fair, I want to toss a muffin at your head pretty much constantly," Damon told his brother.

"Yeah. I gotta agree with that," Mac said.

Jace flipped them both off and then sobered a little.

Mac returned the gesture. "I thought you should know I overheard a group talking about the rule changes and overwhelmingly it was positive. But there were a few wolves who got heated. The usual suspects on both sides."

"I think the PR campaign we've been running to get the votes we need has been really effective. There are family lines, of course, and I'm not sure we can change all those minds. But the more we can manage, the better."

* * *

"You're an asshole for manipulating Damon and Ruby over here early," Aimee said, voice lazy.

They'd ended up in Katie Faith's very comfortable living room, tucked up on the couch.

"She needs to get used to it now. It's how wolves are," Katie Faith said, trying to sound virtuous instead of meddlesome.

"You just wanted to get a look at them together," Aimee said.

"They're really cute though, right? Plus Jace was all nosy because he's Patron but also Damon's brother. He can't blame this all on me."

Ruby laughed. "Sure he can."

"Totally cute," Aimee agreed. "But you're still devious and just know we see you."

They talked more about the wedding and the party details but it seemed pretty much like Aimee's mom and Mac's aunt had most things handled.

"Mac's been living in my house for nearly a year now. I already feel like we're married so I don't think that'll be any different. But what will be different is that I'll be part of a wolf pack and won't that be interesting?" Aimee said. "Huston has been giving me all sorts of etiquette lessons. History about Pembry's line and the like. I'm grateful to be learning from him. I wondered if the shifters would be upset because a witch was marrying their Patron but that hasn't been the case. Even the old-school wolves who support Dwayne and Scarlett have been welcoming."

Ruby snorted. "Of course they have! You're powerful and smart and you're going to make Pembry more powerful. Katie Faith has brought that to Dooley and they want some of that too. Plus, you're remarkable and you clearly love and care about Mac. You've been caring for Pembry wolves your whole life."

Aimee's alarm seemed to ease back a little as Ruby and Katie Faith reassured her she was making the right choices. "They're really very nice. I hate that a few Pembrys have destroyed the public perception of the rest of the pack. But I love Mac and want nothing but the best for him and his…our wolves."

"Well you'll be Patron after the wedding. So if they do act up, handle it. It'll be your job at that point," Katie Faith told her. "Mac isn't just marrying you for the sexytimes and all the healing mojo you've got. Take it from me because I'm married to a Patron too. Once you marry and you're accepted into the pack by whatever ceremony they do, you'll outrank her and even if people want her back, if you want her gone, they'll follow you. Pembry is yours. You have got this, Aimee Benton."

"That was such an excellent pep talk," Ruby told Katie Faith, who smiled, warmed by the compliment. "You're both amazing and I just love you so much."

There was some crying and a lot of laughing when Damon cleared his throat as he came into the room. "Everything okay?" he asked warily.

"It's perfect," Aimee said as she stood. "Come on, Macrae. Take a gal home." She held a hand out and Mac took it.

"I'd be happy to." He pulled her close and tucked her against his side as he turned to Katie Faith and Jace. "Thanks for dinner and company."

Chapter Thirteen

Damon strolled over and got all up in her space, sending her heartbeat skittering. "Hi."

"Hey," she said, her mouth suddenly dry at the intensity in his gaze.

"Ready to go back to your place because my trailer is too small for all the things I want to do to you?" he asked quietly.

Beyond words, she nodded.

"Katie Faith and Jace, good night. I'd say thanks for the meal, but you railroaded me over here in a move more wolf shifter than any actual wolf shifter I know. So nicely played but you know what they say about turnabout being fair play. I guarantee I can be nosier than you can imagine."

He turned Ruby and they headed to the door. She waved and called out her goodbyes as he did.

He didn't rush them, though she was aware of his barely reined impatience and she understood it to her toes. She knew he was holding himself in control because of her. For her.

At her place, they paused at the top of her front steps and looked up at the sky. "I never knew how brilliant a sky full of stars could be until I lived in a city and left this behind," she said. "I missed this a lot."

"I guide the same group every November for a back-country hike. This is remote, but the places we go there are no electric lights for miles and miles. There's no sound but nature. It's a completely different world," he said quietly. "It's like the magic from Diablo Lake seeks me out when I'm there. Just checking in on me."

Ruby turned to him. "Really? That's wonderful."

"We should go. To my favorite spot. Camp awhile. Look at the stars."

"Just how backcountry is backcountry? I don't mind a nice day hike but if I recall correctly you and your brothers love shit like hiking straight up mountains and sleeping on leaves."

"Major is part mountain goat, no lie. But I'd love to have you all to myself out in the middle of the forest. The river nearby. I bet you'd be extra witchy surrounded by all that nature. Half a day's hike. Not up a mountain. I'll pack in the tent. There are hot springs too."

"I could probably be talked into that. Come inside. I need to let the dogs out, give them treats and then it's you and me."

"I'll handle the dogs," he told her, brushing a kiss over her brow. "You handle the rest. Make sure all the lights outside are off so no one thinks tonight is a good time to visit."

Though the dogs adored Damon, they saved most of their love for her so after a check-in and some treats, they settled in one of their favorite spots in the living room. Ruby put some *Blue Planet* on the television—their favorite—before turning to Damon.

Neither moved as the tension stretched between

them, warm and slow. He stared at her, into her it seemed, every bit of his attention *on her* and her senses sort of ran wild and flopped to their backs with their knees open. The green in his eyes bled into amber and as had happened all the other times his wolf surfaced that way, Ruby froze at his presence.

"Don't be afraid," he said, voice rough as he stepped back.

She followed in his wake, not accepting his retreat before raising her hands to cup his cheeks. Ruby could see he worried she'd reject that aspect of him or be afraid. She didn't want him blunting such an integral part of who he was for worry she'd turn away. Especially not when she found him—all parts of him—so sexy and powerful and fascinating. As she went to her toes, she tugged him down so she could kiss him before resting her forehead against his a moment.

"I'm not afraid. Get that out of your head right now. When the wolf rises the way he does, often in reaction to me, my own magic reacts in turn. It's not fear, it's just that I'm sort of…stunned because he's so powerful I get caught in the wash of the energy. It's all new so I don't have the right words at the moment. But there are times when your persona changes depending on which aspect of your nature is more in control. Some of the changes are small, but I notice. My magic notices. In a good way. But it's still a little startling how intense it is."

He nodded and she was pleased to see that worry wisp from his eyes.

The man was so damned gorgeous she had to kiss him as senseless as he managed to make her.

But naturally as she sank into his mouth, he turned the tables with a nip of her bottom lip and then a long lick over the curve there. He wasn't even really taking over as much as she just sort of lost herself any time he put his hands or mouth on her.

As cliché as it sounded, she had never in her life experienced anything as thoroughly mind-blowing as one of his kisses. It wasn't as if kisses hadn't been perfectly nice with other men. A few had been expert-level kissers. But it was more than that. It was the exact right combination of Ruby and Damon, their magic mixing and flirting.

The overwhelming *rightness* shook her to her core. It was tremendous.

Before he lost his mind entirely to how good she smelled, looked and felt, he wanted to get a few things out of the way. "Sometimes we're going to get interrupted when we're out. Or in. And I'll have to go. Even when I *really* don't want to."

They'd only bother him in an emergency. Those happened. Frequently. Because a pack needed constant tending. Adjusting between lenience and discipline. It was Damon's job to mete out discipline, which ranged from having younger wolves do physical labor to benefit someone in the pack—Damon loved to knock some pup down a few pegs by having him build a fence or some other heavy job an elder needed doing—to a beating.

"It's your job. More than that. It's part of who you are. And as you've already seen, sometimes it'll be me who gets interrupted. You and I have responsibilities and obligations outside this." She waved a hand back and forth between them.

Damon nodded, pleased by her acceptance of his responsibilities. "But only in case of an emergency this late at night when the door is closed and locked." He'd kill anyone otherwise.

"I'm not even sure I could get that sort of promise out of my family, so you win in that category," she told him as he led her to the couch. She looked back to the hall where her bedroom was and then to him again, a question in her eyes.

"Oh yes. But let's not rush," he said.

There was only the light in the hallway and the television in the background and it broke around her like a halo. Damon threaded their fingers together and tugged a little, needing to be closer to her. Wanting to touch.

In an easy move, he picked her up and brought her into his lap. It was heaven when she wrapped her arms around his neck and squeezed as her happy energy soaked into him.

All that softness, warmth, the solid, sexy weight of her against him as her magic swirled up and around them both, nearly shocked him with how immense and good it was.

It had been that moment between him and Jace when Damon had fully accepted his want of this beautiful witch, that his wolf had dug itself in even deeper. On a primal level he had claimed her. He'd given himself over to pleasing and protecting her.

"You're roses and jasmine. Sultry and sensual." He'd heard a rumor that the scent of a witch's magic changed during sex and hoped he'd be able to verify it very soon.

"I bet it's the wolf recognizing a magical signature in his own way." She nodded and then because she was leaning back against the arm of the couch with her legs over his thighs, he had very easy access to the hollow of her throat where he'd been entranced by the beat of her pulse.

He brushed his lips over it as he tasted her skin, laced with the same magic that hung in the air. She hummed low in her throat and everything in him seemed to throb.

To be extra sure and to have a reason to take a sniff of her, he sucked in a deep breath of her. Just there at her throat, her pulse racing, skin heating—*fuck*, she smelled so damned good—before answering. "The dominant scent is roses. The kind that race up the sides of your cottage, a little wild, heavy with blossoms and perfume. Just beneath that is jasmine. Like the kind you've got growing with those roses up the trellises." He smiled as he straightened enough to look at her. "On purpose, I realize at this moment."

He bent his head to drop kisses from her ear down to her shoulder, growling a little when she slid her fingers through his hair and tugged to keep him in a spot she liked.

"I've had an easy hand with roses and jasmine for as long as I can remember. Some green witches have magical signatures that align with a gift at growing those things. Not all. Some witches smell like raindrops or wood campfires. You're making it very difficult to concentrate. Not that I'm complaining. I'm a fan of what you're bringing to the table but as you can see the result of your very talented mouth is me wandering around topics like a bee in the garden."

He laughed before stealing a kiss.

"I think that's quite enough chitchat. It's getting in the way of smooching."

He had no plans whatsoever to argue with that invitation, so he got back to work, his lips tracing over her cheekbones and the sweet swell of her cheeks. He wanted to throw his head back and howl at how fucking fantastic it was to kiss Ruby Thorne.

He took his time though he wanted to binge and binge himself of her. With each sip, every tiny taste he took of her delicious mouth he discovered what made her sigh, what brought that low, sexy grunt, what made her nails dig into his shoulders.

Gradually, little by little he sank into her. Made himself at home as he drowned in every curve, in the heady sensuality of her scent, man and wolf preferred every part of her to all others.

In his arms she bloomed, opening up to his kiss, to this deeper connection between them. It was the way she chose to be there. This was about Ruby and Damon. No politics.

The pride made him a little dizzy, but not enough to stop him.

Ruby practically reeled from the near overpowering charisma and sexual appeal flowing from Damon. Somewhere at the back of her mind she knew she should be scared of just how big this moment was. Everything was changing and the man in whose arms she rested as he kissed her absolutely witless was the reason for most of it.

His skin vibrated as he kept himself in check and never had anything been hotter. Each and every step of the way he'd waited, held back until he was certain she was as into it as he was. Caution was one thing, but she wanted him to accept that she wasn't going to break or run away when she saw his strength. Rough wasn't bad when done right.

"I'm not fragile," she murmured into his mouth.

He cursed under his breath and she squirmed a little to get closer and also to rub all over him.

Again with the cursing.

But his kiss remained slow and deep and Ruby finally understood what it meant to have aching loins.

Finally she scrambled to straddle his lap facing him. When she ground herself against his cock the cursing made a return but it sounded less fervent and a little more pleading.

She grabbed his hair and yanked harder than she normally would have and when his head tipped back, she leaned down to kiss him. His hands were at her hips, palms spread open, the heat, even through her clothes, was a brand. A memory burned into her skin.

"I'm." She dipped down to take his lips and this time she remained in control. Or more likely he allowed it, but whatever. "Not." Another kiss. "Fragile."

Ruby caressed her palms down his shoulders to his biceps and stopped to shackle his wrists in her hands a moment. "I can feel your control. The fine tremble of muscle as you ruthlessly tamp down your—what I surely do hope are—filthy urges."

His mulish mood softened into amusement at that last bit. "I'm a werewolf. My filthy urges could seriously hurt you."

"Well sure if you *wanted* them to. But you don't. And you don't do things you don't want to. It's a thing I noticed." She smiled.

"All this time I was assuming I'd be the handful in the relationship," he said. "I've been so wrong, haven't I?"

"You're obviously a handful, Damon. Don't get it

twisted." Because she wanted to, she kissed the tip of his nose and he wrapped his arms around her to keep her close. "But you're also obviously a shifter. And I'm not. So you can't go all supercharged on me. But you're not going to. Because you have finely honed control. That's why you hold the position you do in the pack. It's part of who you are. So I'm not worried you're going to hurt me because you won't."

"That doesn't even make sense."

"Of course it does," she said. "Stop thinking I'd compare what you do in the pack to other shifters who break your laws to getting a little animated in bed. We already talked about this."

"I could injure you by accident."

"*Accident.* You don't make accidents or have them when it comes to your strength."

He smirked and she pressed an openmouthed kiss to the left corner of his mouth.

"If I didn't know you better, I'd be worried you were looking for a way out of a relationship with me," she told him, one brow raised.

He snarled and stood in an easy movement. She had to wrap her legs around his waist to keep her balance but he just grabbed a handful of her ass and kept walking toward her bedroom.

All a very good direction.

"But you *do* know me better. It's not easy to be with a shifter, Ruby." He kissed her.

"Again with the trying to scare me off," she teased when he stopped kissing her.

He tossed her to the bed and for a few delightful moments, she was airborne before bouncing once and then twice onto the mattress.

"I was raised right," he said very seriously. "I only want you here if you want to be. And it's only fair that I iterate the drawbacks first. Then once you're in, you're in."

She lay on her bed, arms above her head, pleased she'd dressed up after work into cute underpants beneath the flattering tangerine-colored pants and shirt.

Still, he looked at her as if she were in a couture gown wearing half a million dollars' worth of diamonds. Which, she supposed, was better.

"Drawbacks. We're nosy," he said with the ill grace to interrupt her fantasy, but he was really cute so Ruby figured she'd let it go that one time.

"Tell it to someone who didn't grow up in Diablo Lake," she said. *Obviously* he was nosy, all shifters were nosy.

"Once we take this step it's probably going to be…" Damon cleared his throat. "Okay well I promised Katie Faith I'd let you know that once we've gotten all imprinted on a person we get even nosier. And we need a lot of physical affection."

Very interested, she got to her elbows to lean up a little more. "Sex-wise or just every-day-holding-hands-wise?" She was down for either. Or both.

The way he had to concentrate a little not to laugh and stay on track was adorable but she managed not to comment on it.

"I was just going to say the latter though I do like sex. But that'd make me a liar. Because, Ruby darlin', I want to roll in you. I want to rub up all over your skin and mark you with my scent so everyone in town knows you're mine. I want to fuck you so hard and so thoroughly you won't want to leave my bed. Aside from that, shifters like to be petted and you do a very good job at that already."

A flush heated from her toes up to her scalp. Lord have mercy, but this man was delicious. "I'm not hearing any of these drawbacks you keep talking about," she said. "And I'm over here on the bed and you, for some reason, are not."

Damon frowned a moment but soldiered on. "My grandfather is probably the nosiest and most interfering wolf shifter in the country. When he finds out about us, and he will if he hasn't yet, he's going to be all over you. Paying you little visits to pester you for details about our relationship. He's going to offer to carve our first baby's cradle. He's a master manipulator. JJ does absolutely nothing without a reason."

"A cradle? Aww! But he's just trying to lead me by the ovaries? I mean, no offense to your grandpa or anything but you already have control over my ovaries," Ruby said.

"Your extreme honesty should disturb me. I mean, no. Let me rephrase that. Your extreme honesty *does* disturb me."

Ruby kept her smile sunny as she looked him over. All the damned way over there. Still standing while she was on the bed. She wasn't even certain how one person could be so ridiculously sexy and funny and dorky and smart and fierce and gorgeous all at once.

"Has anyone ever told you that looking at you was something like looking at the sun?" She pointed at him, aggrieved a moment.

"So yeah, it's got to be a witch thing. All the flitting around from topic to topic and the whole just-blurt-it-out-type communication. Which," he added quickly, "is my all-time favorite type of communication so how fun is that?"

Her cheeks were going to hurt from all the smiling and laughing she did with him.

"I can think of some other fun things we can do with one another," Ruby told him.

"We're still talking drawbacks," he said.

"Your charm is going to wear thin if that's your attitude."

He burst out laughing a moment. "In addition to JJ, there'll be my grandmother. She's a master-level manipulator. You don't even know she manipulated you until years later. Some of which I'm sure I'll never realize. She's the best mother I could have asked for. I'm a little afraid that you'll join forces and take over the world."

"I'll name you my consort so we can still get it on the regular though."

Damon nodded once. "Good idea. All the aunties of the pack are going to start poking around too."

"Does that mean they'll bake me stuff? If so, I'm doubly interested." Ruby sent him a sunny smile. If he was trying to scare her off he really had to do better than an offer of a lot of sex with a dude who thought she was sexy and awesome and maybe some nosy older female shifters who wanted to be sure she wasn't some twat who'd screw him over.

"Probably. If they like you. And they will."

Her laugh seemed to skip down his spine, drawing a smile in response. "Of course they will. I'll bake for them first. I'll get everyone's specialty from Katie Faith so I never ever make that but otherwise, I'll lead with sugar and fat. I know how easy you all are for something sweet."

He loved that she'd think to charm the aunties with baked goods but was nearly overwhelmed by how sexy it was that she knew to never do anything to threaten what the aunties were known for baking.

"They'll also ask you totally rude questions. I apologize for that in advance."

She snickered. "My grandmother sort of propositioned you, so there's that."

"Your Lovie has excellent taste in men, Ruby. What can I say?"

She giggled a little, her mouth curved up, demanding a kiss. Damon had certainly enjoyed a number of hot and heavy relationships but he'd never been so drawn to someone that he saw their lips and felt such a deep desire to kiss them that everything else sort of dimmed in comparison.

"The aunties will possibly also tell you stories about me when I was a kid."

"I knew you when you were a kid. And I still want to have sex with you. If that doesn't indicate my level of interest in you and a relationship I don't know what does."

The expression on his face shifted from patient explanation to slight annoyance. Ruby realized it was sort of fun to make that happen.

"What do you mean by that? I've been handsome from a very early age," he said.

"I certainly don't argue that you've been handsome for as long as I've known you. But you were a pest for a long time. You and Greg used to get my mom so annoyed she'd have an eye tic for a few hours after you went home. And you had a funk, so did Greg, and I don't mean funk in a good way. Fortunately, you both discovered girls liked you more when you bathed."

She gave him the once-over and then with a raised eyebrow she asked, "Are we done with the warnings yet or do you want to still stand all the way over there and not be here with me in this bed?"

Unable to keep a straight face any longer, Damon whipped his shirt off and dove to the bed beside Ruby, pulling her close so he could get her against his bare skin.

Ruby ran her hands all over his upper body. "You're so warm and you smell really good. I don't care about your nosy family. As long as they don't try to break us up I'm fine. You want to rub on me? Go ahead. I'm amenable. You want to sniff me? Okay then. If I'm not? I'll let you know."

He buried his face in all those curls and breathed deep. Coconut, most likely from the coconut oil she used to keep her hair soft. Her roses and jasmine—and he couldn't help but wonder if *he* was the reason why she smelled different—all scents he'd come to associate with her. With this beautiful, curvy, powerful witch.

But he was totally sure, as he flicked his tongue over her collarbone, what she was now. His. As certainly as he was hers.

She moved up a little and he backed off but it was only so that she could pull her shirt over her head and when she turned her face to his and their gazes met, the carnal delight in her expression melted him to his toes.

Ruby was not just beautiful, she was ethereally beautiful. Luminous. The magic seemed to glow around her.

The best part was that she knew it. She wasn't one of those people some might say didn't know the depth of their appeal. No. Ruby Thorne knew she was gorgeous. Knew she had a devastating appeal to him. That confidence was sexy as fuck.

He tried not to dive back to her and hoped he managed not to scare her with the nearly frenzied need he had to get skin to skin.

When he pulled her tight against him and her arms wrapped around his shoulders, they both hissed at the intensity when the bare skin of their upper bodies met except for the whisper-thin material of her bra, which didn't disguise her very hard nipples.

Damon closed his eyes, seeking control as he let himself gulp every bit of her that he could.

Ruby hummed deep and a little ragged and then squirmed to get closer. She kissed over his cheekbones and then found her way to his mouth.

"Never gonna get tired of this mouth," she murmured.

"Same," he managed to reply.

And how fucking wonderful was it that he'd waited, knowing that someday there'd be *this* with someone and here she was? This girl he'd kissed before, when they'd been too young to really understand just what it was their potential would create. There all along. Just waiting for them both to get their acts together enough that when they next came into contact there was room for what they had become to one another.

What they'd continue to be as they grew both as individuals and a couple.

Damon kissed her, never wanting to release her from his arms, but that also meant he couldn't get far enough back to get her bra undone. Or to see her expression when he did it.

What finally got him moving was her hand sliding

down his spine so she could then grab his butt and haul him even closer. His cock hurt by that point it was so damned hard and yet he didn't stop. That pain rode the line between pleasure and hurt.

He rolled them over so that she was on top and when she reared up he saw stars.

Ruby popped the hooks on the back of her bra and tossed it over her shoulder. She'd worry about where it landed later. Right then she was all about the look on Damon's face when he caught sight of her boobs.

Pleasure. A sense of mystery and maybe a little found treasure. It was sexy and sweet and boyish and very, very manly all at once.

He brought his hands up to take the weight of her breasts, brushing his thumbs back and forth over her nipples until she arched into his touch.

"That sound, make it again," he urged, pinching her already aching nipples between his thumb and forefinger.

It should have been outrageous but it wasn't. It was hot. So. Very. Hot. Pretty much by that point she was a big puddle of goo under his hands. She was probably going to explode when she climaxed.

She bent to kiss him slowly and realized kissing him would never get old. How cool was that?

He groaned and she swallowed the sound eagerly. The tables were turned and it was Ruby who wanted more of that sound from Damon. Wanted all the evidence of how much she affected him. Every gasp, every arch and twitch of his muscles—she wanted everything.

And she wanted it right then.

"I've waited for this way longer than I should have," she told him when she pulled away from him. "We were nearly there just a few days ago until my grandmother went on a little holiday. Now? Well, this is pretty much all I imagined it would be. And more. Let's see what you've got going on."

His grin made the muscles in her belly twitch. She wasn't even sure that was possible but it happened anyway.

"I'm shy," he said.

That made her laugh again. Ruby had never laughed the way she did with him. It made everything so much better. Sexier.

She undulated her hips, grinding herself against his prodigious hard-on and his gaze glazed over a little bit. "I hope you're not too shy to kill anyone who interrupts this time. I mean. It's only fair."

Laughing, he shifted his upper body and in some shifter wrestling move she was on her back and he loomed over her. His shoulders, so broad and muscled, blocked the light behind him, outlining that span of hard, toned skin.

"Honest to god, Damon. I mean how can you even exist? You're just so big and brawny and damn," she said with feeling.

His cocky expression shifted to pride and no small amount of vulnerability. Ruby swallowed hard.

"Yeah?" he asked and her ovaries probably exploded.

She nodded. It couldn't be that he never heard compliments like that. He was genetic perfection combined with a great deal of charisma and charm. Hell, back in the day when they'd been out together, women approached him to tell him how handsome he was all the time.

"Thank you. Here I was just thinking something

similar. Looking at you, all those dips and curves that demand to be worshipped."

To underline that, he bent to feast on her throat and everything in her heated. Ruby shifted, squeezing her thighs a little to ease the ache he'd ignited. His palms, large, strong, work rough, slid over her arms and then down her sides, over her hips where he dug in and she stuttered a breath that sounded an awful lot like begging.

Damon shifted, sliding down her body until he got to her boobs.

"Don't forget to breathe," he said right before he licked over her left nipple.

Ruby couldn't even be annoyed because she'd been holding her breath while watching him.

He ran the edge of his teeth over that tightened, aching point after he'd licked and sent bolts of pleasure through her system.

Her magic had risen to his presence hours ago, but at that point it simply poured from her like a warm wave.

Damon sucked in a breath and arched back. "Holy shit," he muttered. "Your magic feels so fucking good."

She managed to wrench her hands away from his frankly incredible biceps to work her pants free and decided to toss the underpants too because she was too grown to act like he wasn't going to be inside her very soon.

By the time she turned back to Damon he was also naked and she just sort of froze, her mouth paused on an *oh*.

The man was big. Probably near six five or so. She'd seen him shirtless and in shorts countless times every summer as they'd grown up and it had always been a delight. But *this* sprawled out naked and ready to sex her up? Ruby unstuck herself and shook her head, speechless.

She'd already been entranced by the width of his shoulders and now she could see the entirety of Damon Dooley and it was nearly too much. Powerful thighs, hard, toned calves. Just the right amount of hair. And then there was the matter of his cock. Ruby had never considered herself a size queen, certainly she'd believed that there'd be a *whoa way too much* dick out there. What he was sporting at full mast was startling and proportioned to the rest of him. "My brain is struggling to accept this entire situation," she said. "You're going to challenge all my skills with what you've got there. Fortunately, I like a challenge. I'm competitive that way."

He'd begun to feel a little worried the longer she hadn't spoken but that made him laugh and then filled him with that feral pride he'd discovered only Ruby was able to stoke within him.

Damon knew he wasn't alone in his reaction to this growing thing between them. Knew she was as off balance and yet excited as he was. It made it all right that for the first time in his life a compliment on his looks had sent a thrill down to his very core. He wasn't used to feeling exposed like this. Wasn't used to having it matter so damned much what another person thought of him. Not outside his immediate family anyway.

He reached out quick to grab her and bring her to him entirely naked. A groan ripped from his belly as he held her tight.

Her scent, lush and heady, fully aroused, reached his senses, teasing. Damon wanted to be in her right that moment, but he *needed* her to come first.

He kissed and licked his way over her skin, deep bronze and glittering with magic before he rolled off the bed and hauled her butt to the edge of the mattress.

Before she said a word, he dropped to his knees and all he heard was her audible gulp.

He hitched her thighs up on his shoulders to get her pussy at the angle he wanted and then took a long, slow lick.

Here at the center of her, she was rich and a little sweet. Salty and already very wet. Damon breathed her in deep, his entire body tightening in response. His approval rumbled in his chest as he hauled her even closer until there was only Ruby.

Her clit, swollen and waiting, was sensitive, he learned as she responded to the ways he touched her. Damon tickled his tongue across it and was rewarded with a trembly moan that seemed to echo through him.

Gripping her ass firmly—so firmly he realized he might leave a mark—Damon held her to his mouth, served himself this gorgeous witch.

The light in the hallway flickered and the hair on his arms lifted slightly. He seemed to throb in time with his pulse, his human skin a little tight as her magic soaked into him along with her taste.

Her pussy heated and her taste bloomed wide open on his tongue. Roses. Summer sunshine and roses.

The sound of his name on her lips as she climaxed rated up there with his all-time best experiences, along with the way her scent had deepened and changed. Just for him.

Her taste on his lips, he stood and stared down at her. Her lips swollen from their kisses, gaze still a little glassy from orgasm.

One corner of her mouth rose as she lifted both arms and gave him two thumbs up.

"I need you," he murmured.

All that lazy, hypnotic post-orgasm haze reshaped into something that dug its claws deep at the sound of the words and the tone in them. She'd give him anything he asked; and let him see that in her eyes.

Things had started out hot and heavy, but their first time had been that and something deeper than she'd expected. It had left her exhilarated, terrified, turned on and deeply satisfied.

He cursed at her look. "I'm trying to have some finesse here, but I can't if you do that," he said when she reached for his cock.

"Fuck me and show me your moves. That's when I want your finesse. In case I'm not totally clear, I totally and utterly want you to put your dick in me. Right now," she added.

Damon bent, taking her hips and twisting, rolling her to her belly. "When I tossed you on the bed earlier I noticed the height might be perfect for bending you over," he said into her ear as he walked his fingertips down her sides, over her hips and then lower to widen her legs. With a grunt he leaned over to grab a pillow to tuck under her hips.

Two of his fingers slid into her pussy for several long moments. Damon froze and Ruby closed her eyes as she listened to him breathe. He seemed to get himself back under control shortly as he got the pillow in place.

The pad of his thumb rubbed over her clit with just the right amount of pressure. That finesse he'd been talking about. When she sighed softly he pressed the head of his cock into her in one slow, delicious thrust.

At the edges of the pleasure there was a little pain as she had to stretch around him but he'd gotten her so wet and had taken it slow enough those first few thrusts that the pain had gone, replaced with a sort of pleasure that at first glance seemed calm but shortly changed into something else entirely.

Ruby, grateful she could keep her eyes closed and simply trust, let go of her fears.

Then, as he set a deep, hypnotic rhythm, he fucked her while petting down her back, over her arms, hands and fingers. Riding the curve of each of her butt cheeks until goose pimples rose.

He thrust into her body until she was little more than fuckdrunk. All the while keeping deep, adding a little leftward swivel and then sliding a hand around her, his fingertips finding her clit, brushing over it with each flex of his hips that sent him deep.

Each time she saw sparks of color against her eyelids as her orgasm built from her toes up until there was nothing to do but cry out as she came, twisting to thrust herself back at him.

Damon snarled a low curse and then her name that sounded like a prayer and he came, burying himself and falling down over her, half off the mattress, still. Managing to hold her as her body still tightened around his cock.

Finally he rolled to the side and pulled out gently. Without even a grunt, he picked her up and carried her into his bathroom where he let her clean up as he did the same.

Five minutes later they were back in his bed.

"So that was pretty okay," she said before bursting into laughter.

Chapter Fourteen

Ruby knew there was a bounce in her step after she'd
locked the front doors of the clinic and hugged her
cousin goodbye. She had plans to take dinner over to
Damon's house site. She wouldn't keep him long but
she wanted to see him and reassure herself he was taking care of himself.

She stopped by the market to grab more milk for hot
chocolate. Having a wolf shifter who loved chocolate
in her life had resulted in the need to stock up on supplies more often. With that in mind, she also picked up
some strawberries to dip in the chocolate she'd just put
in her basket.

Everyone needed to get their daily servings of fruit
and vegetables and there wasn't even anything saying
she shouldn't eat a strawberry after she smeared the
chocolate part all over Damon's belly.

It was a stellar belly after all.

So she was smiling and in a very good mood indeed when she turned a corner and came cart to cart
with Scarlett.

What the actual fuck? Had she been cursed or something?

Given the surprise on Scarlett's features at the sight

of Ruby, at least she could let go of her suspicion that she'd been followed.

Ruby nodded once and continued on her way, but Scarlett angled her cart to impede her progress.

"Hey, Ruby. Fancy seeing you here again. How are you?" Scarlett asked.

So close!

"Oh you know, places to go and people to see. I've got to run."

Scarlett and her cart—what the hell kind of ninja was that woman with her cart skills anyway—edged forward enough to continue to block Ruby's way.

And now Ruby was just annoyed. She'd been all caught up in some sex thoughts about Damon and this ding-dong was trying to ruin that.

Ruby sighed. "What?"

"I don't know what you mean." Scarlett tried to look innocent and Ruby was having none of it.

Ruby shook her head. "No. As I said, I have things to do. You're impeding those things. All my politeness is used up and I'm not playing games with you. Tell me whatever it is that's on your mind so I can be done."

"There's no need to be rude," Scarlett said.

"You're right. But you're the one who decided to escalate the situation when I was civil in passing and you're now penning me in next to the peas for some reason. Spit it out."

Scarlett's mouth firmed and her eyes narrowed. Ruby knew she was having some sort of internal argument with herself. Knowing Aimee would hear about whatever she got up to. Wondering if whatever she was stirring up was worth the price.

As far as Ruby was concerned, Aimee had enough

on her plate and she wasn't going to give Scarlett a reason to add to her friend's troubles if she could avoid it.

So instead of ramming the buggy at Scarlett's ankles and making a dash for the door, Ruby waited for her to get to the point.

"I know you recently moved back home and have started your clinic with Aimee. Now, I don't know what your romantic situation is, but I imagine you'll be looking for someone to date and possibly settle down with. You come from an excellent family with deep ties in town. Powerful witch. Pretty. Girl like you is a real catch. 'Specially if you lost some weight. Regardless, Pembry would love to have you as part of the family along with your dear friend Aimee."

"I'm seeing someone. But thank you for the offer," Ruby said.

"There are plenty of eligible men in Diablo Lake. *Pembrys* with good jobs, who come from good families. No stench of scandal. Stable. They'd show you a fine quality of life. I'm happy to introduce you to any of them."

"I'm *happily* in a relationship with Damon Dooley," Ruby clarified, keeping her tone civil even though the other woman didn't deserve it.

Naturally, Scarlett took not making a scene as permission to press her position.

She pretended to lower her voice but really she whispered loudly, calling even more attention to what was going on. "Now, I know for sure your family wouldn't want you to ruin your life with a choice like that. Look at what and who those boys came from." Scarlett sniffed. "Think about it. I can't even tell you what sort of terrible thing his father did, it was that bad. But

I'm warning you, Damon's father was a philandering cheat and the apple doesn't fall far from the tree. Hell, his mother was a sickly weakling. You don't need to go mixing your genes with that mess. You could do a lot better and your family deserves more than you dragging their reputation down to the Dooley level. I've seen him beat other shifters bloody when they broke even minor rules. Would you trust your sweet, elderly grandmother with a body like that?"

Ruby tucked her basket more securely on her arm before she pushed Scarlett's cart to the side. "I'm going to go ahead and fill you in on a few things. That way, after today you'll know and can behave accordingly." Ruby stood with her feet slightly apart and cocked her head. She held a finger—though not the one she *really* wanted to use. "The most important thing is for you to believe in your heart that I am not the one to be played with. Or interrupted," she added when Scarlett opened her mouth.

Once Scarlett's lips met once more, Ruby nodded.

"Good. You know who raised me and believe me when I tell you I learned very well. Let's just get to the bottom line here because I have better things to do than stand here trading insults with you. You are not entitled to my time and attention. I am certainly not interested in what *you* have to say about other people's scandals when everyone in this town knows about you and your husband and your son."

"Getting sent away isn't the same as what happened to those boys' father," Scarlett said in the same fierce whisper that carried perfectly fine. "Think of the shame you'll bring your family. What if he does to you what his father did to his mother? Damon is the Dooley enforcer. You think he could hold that position if he was anything less than vicious?"

Generally, Ruby thought violence was a lazy way to get back at someone who wronged you. Not that she was above petty revenge. Just that she considered being petty an art and what was worth doing, was worth doing well.

Any person could be a bitch. It took dedication to scorch the entire fucking earth to teach a basic bitch she messed with an empress of bitchology. Didn't mean there wasn't a small part of her that wanted to slap Scarlett's face.

"Ma'am. Hold up." Ruby put a hand up to get herself together. "Just because I wasn't living here at the time it doesn't mean I don't know what damage y'all did. Your husband and one of your sons brought a *human* here without permission. She had to have her memories altered before she could return home to her children! They violated our most inviolable law because he got his feelings hurt that people liked Aimee better than him. Your son was involved in all sorts of chicanery that got him tossed out of town even longer than your husband. You so embarrassed by your own family dirt you think it's cute to make fun of what happened to Damon's mother? You really are a monster. Mind your own yard, Scarlett Pembry. Because right now you're in mine and I don't take kindly to trespassers. Don't make an enemy of me or you might choke biting off more than you can chew."

Ruby didn't use her magic to move Scarlett, but she did create enough of an electric buzz around her body that Scarlett needed to move back or get zapped. It wasn't hard at all, because she was mad. Big mad.

* * *

Damon and his brothers and three or four others finally finished up all the drywall not just on the first floor, but the second as well. Probably given another wind after Ruby showed up with enough food for everyone and multiple containers of chocolate double chunk cookies. She'd even brought two big containers of tea.

"Your girlfriend is awesome," Major said as he shoved another cookie into his face.

"Right? And she told me if I wasn't too tired I was welcome to come to her house for a nightcap of hot chocolate after we finished up. I mean, am I dreaming or what?"

"She's a keeper," Jace agreed. "Katie Faith loves that girl like a sister so I hope you understand how much talk there is about you and Ruby and your future babies and whatever. Can't really complain about that though because since we're not trying not to get pregnant anymore, every time she gets a reason to start thinking about having a baby usually ends up well for me because then we get to practice."

"And then Ruby will be the midwife. I gotta admit the symbolism of that is pretty cool. Plus when you knock her up, JJ and Patty will be focused on you and Katie Faith instead of me. I need Ruby to be all in before she starts dealing with the grandparents," Damon said. "She's making an ancestor's altar for Samhain and there's a part of it for Mom. Said Katie Faith had done the same thing last year and the year before. I had no idea, but I think it's really cool. We're going out later on this week to gather some of the things for it. I like that she's sharing this part of herself with me. All this witch stuff we've taken for granted for so long is more fascinating than I figured it would be. And, not gonna lie, I can't wait to show her off at the Halloween dinner."

Ever since he'd slept over at her place over the weekend, he found himself really craving the sound of things when he was at her side. The hum of the fridge. The sounds of the boys depending on the time of day.

"God almighty, y'all should hear her place at sunrise. It's as if all the birds in the country journey to sing outside her window."

"Should we now?" Jace asked.

"Well, no *you* shouldn't at all. But I'll let you know what a fucking miracle she is."

"All right. I've been asked about you and her multiple times. I'll say what I see in your eyes when you talk about her." Jace tipped his chin. "That'll handle most inquiries and I suspect you and her being seen together around town will do the rest. Well, we all know after that dinner at our place that you and Ruby are *together* together, so things will progress and we don't need to hide anything. Katie Faith will be sure to always invite her to pack stuff from now on too."

Damon liked the sound of that.

"You're bringing her to the Halloween dinner, which will be sort of an official debut of your relationship. That'll be a hoot, right?" Major's sarcasm made Damon chuckle.

"It sounds weird as hell, but most everything I do with her is a hoot. And I don't mean sex—though that's even better than a hoot. I mean she has a way of making things fun and interesting. Plus, she's sweet and soft and beautiful, but also can be fierce and sharp when necessary. It's sexy as hell and obviously a trait that'll serve her well when dealing with any bullshit."

* * *

Ruby knew she'd have to tell everyone about that stupid bullshit with Scarlett but she wanted to be free of her anger before that. So, knowing Damon had a crowd up the hill working on his house, she set to work making sandwiches with extra-thick slices of bread. Cleaning and tearing lettuce, cutting fat, juicy tomatoes, red onion, some white cheddar with flecks of sea salt began to unbunch the muscles in her shoulders. She let the rhythm of the assembly soothe as she laid each component on top of mayo, tangy yellow mustard and turkey meat loaf she'd experimented with and discovered made excellent sandwiches.

She took a wagon full of food and two dogs on leash up the road and over to his house site. The wheels were supposed to be able to handle rugged terrain and she was pleased to see they did a fine job of it.

He walked out of the house like he knew she was coming and the smile on his face washed the last bit of bitterness from her.

It was at that moment when the land truly greeted her, washing over her with pleasure at her presence. A playful little *why hello there* that underlined her instincts to let go of all the negativity of that exchange.

She had so much more to look forward to and experience than the ignorance and small-mindedness that underlay most of the things Scarlett had said. She was absolutely in love. She had this beautiful core to her life.

That didn't mean she wasn't going to protect him. Because Damon and his brothers were hers now and Scarlett wore a mask for a reason. For what reason Ruby didn't know. But she understood that it meant the other woman was hiding something. Something she was worried about.

Once Ruby figured that out there'd be no further need for any more tedious bullshit with Scarlett's name all over it. Because she'd have whatever it took to get the former Patron out of Ruby and Damon's life.

And because she was an empress of bitchology and knew the deliciousness of excellent comeuppances, Ruby would simply wait until she figured it out and then she'd handle things.

It was about time someone stepped in to protect Damon, Major and Jace from whatever the hell it was that made Scarlett so determined to be a miserable bitch.

"Hey there! The boys and I thought you all might need a meal break."

It hadn't occurred to Ruby that the dogs were used to the scents of these shifters because they frequently roamed the land all around Damon's lot but as several very large wolf shifters poured from the house at the sound of the word *food*, she was very glad.

They jumped between Ruby and the house but didn't growl. They did bark a few times but Damon approached before the others.

"Everything's fine, boys. Easy now. They're friends and you're part of the pack." He bent and gave each dog a touch to the head before all that considerable attention landed on Ruby and stole her breath. "Well look here. Hey there, Ruby darlin'."

She went into his arms and breathed in deep. Another anchor settling her into Diablo Lake. More roots. It fit her just perfectly. "Hey. I don't want to keep you long. I know you have things to get done tonight. But I made meat loaf sandwiches and cookies. Oh and some apple cake. Tell me what y'all think of it because I'm trying to decide on a recipe for Samhain."

Everyone came forward to help unload the food, ferrying it to the sawhorse where they'd made a work table. And began to eat, calling out compliments as they did.

"I'm headed home. I know you're busy so don't argue. When you finish up if you feel like coming to me, do that. I'll make you hot chocolate after you use my shower. You can sleep over." She brushed her thumb over his beard a moment. Petting him because she wanted to and she could.

The thought cheered her further. Seeking him out the way she had turned out to be just the perfect thing.

She said her goodbyes and after the boys howled along with Damon and his crew, they headed off.

Chapter Fifteen

"I invited Ruby to Halloween dinner," Damon told his grandparents. He and Major had stopped by their retirement cabin to work on some improvements that would keep their grandparents safer but not so obvious they'd get offended.

They sat at the little table just off the kitchen and their grandmother had made coffee to warm them up after their job was done.

"I was wondering when you were going to tell us," their grandmother said calmly. "You have no idea what a trial it's been keeping your grandpa in line while we waited. He wanted to invite her over under the guise of needing medical care so he could grill her but I managed to stop him."

Major thought that was way funnier than it actually was and Damon curled his lip at his brother.

"Thank you, Grandma, for encouraging him to behave. Though, y'all should know Ruby would show up and all the while you think you're grilling her and she's really just watching your blood pressure and telling you what she wants you to know."

"Devious? She'll fit in fine then," Patty said. "Let

me look over the list to see what she should bring. Can she cook?"

Both brothers nodded enthusiastically. "She's magic, I mean, metaphorically as well as literally, in the kitchen."

"Even back when she was younger she was a competent person. Levelheaded and goodness knows that's the kind of match you need. But this one has sharp claws, which is also what you need. I'll call her directly to let her know."

And though Damon wanted to argue, he didn't. Damon was a wolf shifter and there were ways things got done. The higher up in the pack, the more meddling happened. Ruby could take it and he'd help as much as he could.

Ruby and his grandmother had to create their own relationship. When they'd dated before, Patty had seen Ruby as a pretty, talented witch who dated her grandson but was leaving town. Now was a whole different thing. Patty would be hugely instrumental in Ruby's acceptance within Dooley. Katie Faith too, but Patty was an old-school wolf. She'd seen most of the people in their pack through something, be it big or small, and she had so much to teach. Damon was pretty sure his grandmother was going to connect with just how much Ruby was committed to the health and well-being of the residents of Diablo Lake. They shared that sense of responsibility and purpose.

"So this is permanent then?" JJ looked over to Major. "What do you think?"

"Of Ruby or of Ruby and Damon?" Major asked.

"Both."

He shrugged one shoulder. "I've always liked Ruby.

But you can see she's pretty and powerful so I don't need to tell you that. What you really want to know is if she's right for him."

Patty and JJ both nodded.

"She's one of those people who brightens a room when she enters it. I think she's already excellent at Damon's side and that'll only be more true the longer they're together. She does for others. She's nice to small animals and big shifters."

Damon said, "She sees me. Bumps and bruises, dark spots and all. And she accepts me. I want to be better and do better when I'm around her. I already know her family because Greg and I have been friends so long. It's more than love. More than infatuation. More than lust. I've experienced those. She's my center. I don't know if that makes sense or not. But she is."

"That mean what I think it means?" JJ asked.

Major groaned. "Why can't we just ask straight up. Hey, Damon, do you think you're imprinting on Ruby? If yes, do you plan on the binding ceremony? If no, that's fine, we just needed to know."

Wolf shifters didn't have fated mates. Not of the one sniff and you're gone variety. Mostly they met and dated and got married like lots of others did. Sometimes they divorced like lots of others did. And sometimes shifters and their romantic partners had a deeper connection. Unique, ancient magic that created a union that was a pact. A bond that was a deep and eternal connection. It was the most sacred sort of relationship to wolves even though most of them didn't have marriages like that.

"I think she feels the same. It'll happen the way it's supposed to. When it's supposed to. I'm in love with Ruby Thorne and miracle though it might be, she loves me back. But I don't need any assistance in the match-making department." Damon looked over at his grand-father. "Let us handle it at our own pace."

His grandfather waved a hand. "Sure, sure. You act like it's the only thing on my schedule to get into your business all day. I have other priorities. You're a man grown and mostly make good choices. And when you don't, I'm happy to kick your behind into shape."

When he approached her front door, it pleased him to see she'd gotten the place all gussied up for Samhain and Halloween. Pumpkins of all sizes made little piles and patterns on her porch with bits and pieces of other types of greenery tucked in.

A big cornucopia stuffed with gourds, pomegran-ates, apples and clove-studded citrus dominated the table and he could scent the rosemary in the wreath hanging on her door.

When she opened up, she greeted him, her hair wrapped in a scarf, glasses perched on her nose. "Hey. Come in."

He did, breathing deep like he always did so he could fill his lungs with her.

"I just wanted to stop by to let you know the pack and I are going out on a hunt tonight to bring down the rest of the meat for the Halloween dinner. Jace and I will also be contributing meat to the Samhain banquet."

Her sunny smile made him happy to his toes. "Lovie is in raptures over that, by the way. She thought it was nice the way Jace did for Katie Faith last year. But now she gets to brag on you. That's the best part. Thank you."

Suddenly he would far rather kick off his shoes and hang out with his pretty witch and the little brothers.

They'd listen to music. Ruby would pause to let him smooch up on her as she did her thing.

"There are three shifters approaching," she told him, a palm on his chest as he'd been talking himself into not going.

"How did you know that?" he asked. He had shifter hearing, but she didn't.

"When my mom, cousins and aunts worked on a spell to alarm my grandparents' house, I also created better wards for my house. Including a little ping when anyone steps into the main yard. It could be two, or four. But definitely wolf. Your magic is very unique."

He heard Major call his name and that made Ruby laugh. "Go on now. Have fun. Don't get hurt. I'm doing a Working tonight so when you return I might be out doing that."

"Can I follow my nose to find you?" He nuzzled her neck.

"I will always want to be found by you."

"You kill me with the stuff you say."

He kissed her, full of happiness. Then he tossed two dog cookies to the boys and headed out. "I'll see you later, Ruby darlin'."

The veil was thin, Ruby knew. Thinnest time of year. The moon hung above as she walked along the bank of the river, gathering various ingredients for her spells. She'd dry some, but most of the things she'd use within the next few days, knowing their potency would help more when used quickly.

The natural world was different at night. It scared some folks, but to Ruby, it was magnificent. Lush and secretive and a little coy. But full of magic.

The dogs had remained home, napping, but that was all right with her. Sometimes her best thinking came from alone time. Samhain, after all, was a time of contemplation. Of shifts from seasons, of light to dark, warm to cool. For her, the center was that things were connected. Life and death. Sun and moon.

Harvest season had come and gone and the world was shifting. Preparing to leap back to life in the spring. Between now and then, she knew things beneath the soil would rest all while getting stronger.

Each time she clipped an herb or pinched off a flower head she gave thanks to the earth for providing such bounty. Ruby didn't take more than she needed or could use. That was her place in the scheme of things. To give more than she took.

And at that moment, her life burgeoned with blessings.

She spread out a blanket and stepped from her shoes, loving the coolness against her skin as the grass poked her gently. At each corner, she said a brief blessing and asked protection from any force that wished her ill.

The energy of that magic eased over her as the circle set into place. Seated, crisscross applesauce style, Ruby lay out another square of fabric and spread out the various things she'd collected that evening.

Each witch's magic worked a little differently. For Ruby, ritual was part of any spellcraft. It helped her keep focus as she amplified her energy. She ran her palms over the plants and cuttings, listening to what each could do, what each had to offer and teased it up. It was an intimate sort of dance between her magic and the green things.

Each bundle was handled differently. Some things

she placed in muslin bags. Some she tied at the base so they'd be easier to hang and dry. And the elderberries, not something she'd expected to find so late in the year, were a happy discovery she'd have to clean up when she got home.

At the end, Ruby murmured, *"I will see to the heart of things. My actions will promote healing and well-being. I will know who and when to use these gifts from Mother Earth. I will use my gifts to comfort."* She sliced a place on the side of her leg, near the ankle that would heal easily but bled fine.

Her offering sealed the spell to amp up the positive effects of her ingredients and when she broke her circle the stored-up magic wisped free, swirling around her lovingly before riding the breeze.

That's when she allowed herself to focus more on the big caramel-colored wolf, Damon, who'd lain down nearby, head on his paws as he'd watched.

"Hello there, Damon," she said quietly as she packed her things up. "You coming home with me or do you have more work to do?"

He got up and stretched before trotting her way and butting her with his enormous head. Wolf shifters weren't anywhere near nonshifter-sized and when he leaned in a moment, he could rest his head on her shoulder. While she stood and he didn't.

They walked the short distance across the nearby meadow and to the back part of her yard. It was well past midnight and the moon had begun to set but her basket teemed with life and a giant man who could change into a wolf stood at her side.

"You're a very handsome wolf," she said when they reached her back porch. She put her things down and turned back to him. "May I?" She indicated touching him and he got closer, giving her all the access she could want, tipping his chin up so she could hug him, burying her face in the fur at his neck.

He didn't smell like a wild animal. The wolf part of Damon smelled a lot like the human part did. Pine and loam. The tang of the river. Moss and sun-warmed bark. Ruby wanted to ask him if all wolves smelled like that or if it was unique to him. It wasn't like she sniffed up on any other wolf shifters other than this one.

The muscles of his shoulders were powerful as she slid her hands over them. Like the man, the wolf was under control. Not a threat to her in any way. "I'm not afraid," she told him.

"Come on inside. There's a spare set of clothes on top of the dryer," she told him after kissing the top of his head. "I expect by the time you're done, the hot chocolate will be ready. I'll keep the dogs inside until you're wearing a human skin again."

Chapter Sixteen

"What do you think?" Ruby asked when she came out to the living room. "I'll stop back here to change for the walk at midnight."

Nichole was there, handling any trick-or-treaters coming to the door while Ruby got ready. She was handy with suggestions and pep talks.

Ruby had decided on a cap-sleeved black dress with golden accents. The high boots she wore had gold threaded at the outer seams, the only color against matte black. The night before, Ruby's cousin had done her hair in a long braid with a fauxhawk and Nichole had tucked little jeweled pins in along the scalp line, accentuating the rise of hair twisted into the rope of braid that fell down her back. Damon hadn't even seen it yet because he'd spent the night before doing wolf shifter stuff to get preparations for Halloween finished.

It made her feel like a queen and she hoped he liked it too. Hoped his family did as well. This dinner was sort of an official debut for them. Her presence at his side a banner that a new union of witch and wolf had taken place.

"I hate being nervous. I am amazing!" she told Nichole, who nodded.

"Obviously you're amazing. And obviously you're nervous because this is the real deal and you're telling everyone that. I was anxious as hell when Greg first brought me here and as we both know, I'm amazing too."

They grinned at one another. "I'm so grateful for you," Ruby told her sister-in-law.

"Back atcha. I expect to hear all about it when I see you at midnight and if there's any leftovers from your funeral potatoes, you know I want some."

"I made you and Greg extra."

Nichole hugged her again. "You're the best."

"Says the woman who supplies all my smoked meat needs. Which sounds oddly sexual, but you know what I mean," Ruby teased.

"Did you tell him about that whole scene with Scarlett in the grocery store?"

"Not yet. Turns out, Scarlett has a long history of creating scenes at the grocery store and Mr. Hawkins is considering banning her." That last was from Lovie, who'd been on the lookout for Scarlett and fortunately hadn't found her yet.

"I'll tell him soon enough. But it's not really a thing and I don't want it encroaching into any of stuff we've got coming up. What's he going to do? Accompany me every minute of the day and glare at her when she acts up? It's her general setting. She came for me and got smacked down. Which was fun, I admit. So if she keeps to herself, there won't be any issues. Tonight that is."

And truth be told, Ruby knew of the importance of the upcoming shifter meetings when the issue of getting rid of the Rule of Silence would finally, after months of going back and forth over, come up for a final vote.

* * *

Just outside the grange hall where the dinner would take place, he stopped her, kissing her softly. "Everything is going to be fine. No one in there, or anywhere for that matter, means what you do to me. I love you, Ruby." He nuzzled her neck again quickly before they got to the front doors.

"I love you too. I'm as ready as I can be. Let's do this." Ruby smiled up at him.

Patty saw them enter and waved, heading their way. She scooped Ruby up in a hug that probably squeezed a breath out of her. "Hello there, sweetheart. My goodness, don't you look ever so pretty."

The most important women in his life stood there chatting and he loved them both impossibly more for the way they were with one another. His grandmother so welcoming and warm, Ruby so good at drawing other people out and making them feel listened to.

Damon knew his grandfather would be at the head tables dealing with the elk sausage he'd made fresh, so they'd need to seek him out, and officially present Ruby to the former Patron of the Dooley wolves.

He'd assumed his grandmother would grab hold of Ruby and take her off to meet people, but instead she took the potatoes they'd brought and gave him a pointed look before tipping her chin slightly. Ah, they'd head to their part of the Dooley table as a couple. Openly.

He smiled his understanding and thanks his grandmother's way.

"You okay?" he asked Ruby as they started on the way through the already crowded room.

All these shifters could be totally overwhelming on

the best of days and this was her first big event with them.

Ruby looked up at him and gave him a brilliant smile that he felt to his toes. He was smiling back before he'd even thought about it. "Yep. Lots of good energy here."

Ruby felt the weight of all that attention as she and Damon made their way through the crowded space. Several of her friends were there already so it was nice to have many of those faces be familiar ones.

Scarlett stood off near what was probably the Pembry section and when Ruby's attention landed on her, it was clear the older woman had been watching her already.

Ruby channeled her mother and squared her shoulders and looked right the fuck back. And her expression told Scarlett to mind her own damned business and keep away. Scarlett's gaze narrowed but Ruby just raised one eyebrow ever so slowly.

Someone stepped between them and Damon continued to steer them to where his mother waited. "Want to explain what that was about?" he asked her.

"I'll tell you later. It's not important." Ruby wanted a good night as her introduction into his shifter life. Since they were going to gossip about her anyway, she preferred it was about how great a catch she was.

He made that little huffy harrumph sound that never failed to make her smile.

"Leave your things here at your seat," Patty said as they finally caught up with her at the table. "We'll go say hi to your grandfather. He's been on the lookout for you both."

"And then it'll be fine for other people to talk to us. It's a hierarchy thing," Damon explained.

Ruby nodded, tucking away that information. She knew she had a lot to learn about his world.

She'd always liked JJ Dooley. He was a hale, barrel-chested know-it-all with a great laugh. When she was growing up and he and Patty ran the Mercantile, he always wore cowboy boots and those shirts with the pearly snaps down the front.

JJ looked up from barking orders at someone regarding how to carve turkeys to smile at her and head their way. That day, because it was a holiday celebration, his boots were covered in skulls and roses.

He wore a bolo tie with his pearly snap shirt and she wanted to *aww* but she didn't because that would have been bad. But he was really stinkin' cute.

JJ took her hands and squeezed them. There was a sense of ritual to his motions so she went with it, trusting Damon to steer her back if she made a mistake.

"Happy Halloween, JJ. I love the boots."

Laughing, JJ kissed each of her cheeks and stepped back. "Ruby! It sure is good to see you here tonight. With Damon. You two suit one another. I've got to go supervise these knuckleheads or lord knows what those turkeys will end up like and the sausages will be like leather. You're seated across from me and Patty so we can catch up."

With that, the volume of the room rose again after everyone who had been eavesdropping began to talk once more.

"Go mix and mingle, Damon." Patty waved at them both.

"Your wolves want your attention," Ruby said quietly. She'd noticed the way they sought him out when he entered any room. How they liked to approach the table during their now daily lunches and say hello and pass along some information of the *how's your momma* variety.

But Ruby could see their energies and how they connected to Damon's. Little check-ins. After that their auras were brighter and calmer. Damon's as well. This was his life and with her in it now, something she needed to accept and nourish in her own way.

"I assume there's a process of some sort so you lead the way and I'll follow," she told him.

There had been a process of course. A specific order of who they had to meet and talk to. Most of them Ruby knew already anyway and none of it felt fake or forced. The entire time she was just in awe of what a leader he was. Yes, she was well aware he was the enforcer of the pack and sometimes he had to mete out physical discipline and keep the wolves in line. But there was no fear in the way these shifters looked at Damon. Respect. Loyalty. Affection.

A group of female Dooley wolves headed their way. The aunties Katie Faith and Aimee had told her about. They ranged in age from midforties to Esther Shuttlesworth at a spry eighty-eight.

"Damon! You brought Ruby. Finally. She's so busy we haven't been able to meet her yet." First they all hugged up on him until he blushed furiously but he was so pleased it radiated from him in warm waves.

"Y'all probably know her anyway," he said with a grin. "Ruby Thorne, let me introduce you to these wonderful ladies. The heart of Dooley."

These women so obviously loved Damon and cared for his well-being and his future. They touched him from time to time, reassuring themselves and most likely Damon. It wasn't romantic in any sense. It was maternal most definitely and Ruby rejoiced that he had these ladies when he hadn't had his mother.

"Sure we do. But that's before."

"Yes, ma'am. This is Esther Shuttlesworth. She's the pack genealogist. She knows everything about everyone."

"That's why everyone's scared of me," Esther said with a smile that had Ruby smiling back.

"Pleased to meet you, Ms. Esther."

"This is Alice Dooley," Damon said of the woman who'd just spoken. "She's my great-aunt even though we look like siblings."

Ruby didn't have to fake the warmth she showed Alice.

"It's very nice to meet you," Ruby told her.

"And this is Carmen. She's my second cousin and makes the best meatballs I've ever eaten."

"You're such a flatterer. Even though that's totally true," Carmen said as she stepped up to hug Ruby.

"And this is Deidre and she's my honorary aunt. She used to babysit me and make me and my brothers graham crackers with frosting," Damon said.

"His mother and I were best friends," Deidre explained of their connection. "She loved her boys even though she never got to hold the twins. It has never been hard for me to love those three Dooley brothers either."

Ruby fiercely loved each and every one of these women who clearly considered themselves mother figures to Damon.

"Can you walk me back to my seat, Damon?" Esther asked.

Damon looked over to Ruby and she shrugged. He

obviously wanted to help but also wanted to stay at her side. But she didn't need protecting and the aunties clearly wanted to speak with her without him around.

"I'll be right back," he told Ruby.

"I'm fine," she said. "Go on."

"Like anything's gonna happen to this girl when we're standing with her? Really, Damon?" Alice said and he ducked his head but still kept his gaze on Ruby, assuring them both that all she had to do was squeak and he'd be there.

But truthfully she felt no threat at all. Yes, shifters could rip a person apart, but the fact was, it rarely happened and the penalty for such a loss of control was severe. And Ruby could protect herself. Green witch or not.

Once he'd moved away with Esther the remaining three smiled at Ruby and it was genuine. "We just wanted to check in with you to see how you were feeling," Carmen told her.

"I'm good. Happy to be back home at last. Happy to have found something real with my favorite wolf shifter."

They all positively beamed at her for that.

"He is?" Carmen asked.

"He absolutely is. Y'all making sure I'm not going to sully his reputation?" Ruby teased with a laugh.

"Pfft. He's already got a reputation. But you're here anyway," Alice told her with a question on her face.

"I am in love with Damon," Ruby admitted to them. "I know the difference between everyone who came before and this. Now. With him."

Deidre grinned at the others, who returned the expression.

"Earlier this week my oldest daughter was at the market grabbing milk and eggs for a birthday cake we made for my grandson. When she came home, she told me what she'd overheard and as you might imagine, I was pretty angry," Deidre said.

"I take it she overheard me and a certain shifter?"

Carmen laughed. "Is this like Voldemort? If we say her name she'll show up? I wish it was that easy."

"She's not that scary," Ruby said. "She's afraid and I don't know of what or why. Most ignorance of her type is like a bunch of lies stacked up under a coat trying to be a person."

Alice laughed heartily. "Like in the cartoons when three kids do that to get into an R-rated movie? Love it." She sobered up though. "I don't like the things she said. And I heard enough from two other people who saw the throw down to know the reports are true. I don't like that she went after Damon through you. I hear you gave her back twice what she gave you and I am proud of you for defending Damon. Lord above knows that child needs more fierce defenders. Still, I don't like her trying to scare anyone, much less Damon's lady love." She touched Ruby's shoulder.

Wolves loved touch. They constantly touched one another. A caress. A pat on the shoulder or the back. Hand holding and nuzzling. Lots of reassuring and connecting with the tip of a finger or a tuck of hair behind an ear.

For Alice to touch Ruby that way, in fact for all of them to have touched Ruby the way they had was a public declaration that she was one of theirs and took any ill treatment her way as an attack against the whole.

"And I really didn't like that look on her face when

you two walked in here tonight," Deidre said. "No more than I've liked her comments about Annie."

"I was wondering. I'm making photo books for my family for Christmas and I wanted to make one for Damon, Major and Jace as well. Do you have pictures of Annie? I'll have copies made and get them back to you."

Deidre pulled Ruby into a hug that had her face deep in cleavage and the scent of White Diamonds. She had a number of great-aunts who hugged the same way. It was an older Southern lady bosom hug and in most cases was meant to be nurturing and maternal. This hug certainly was.

She put her hands on Ruby's shoulders moments later and looked her over. "I'll look through my photo albums tomorrow when I get up. She's been on my mind, especially at this time of year so it'll be a happy few hours."

"Very much appreciated." Ruby figured she'd make an extra for Deidre too as a thank-you.

Carmen's expression was satisfied and Ruby felt as if she'd passed a test. "Now, as for Scarlett and that business earlier this week. I surely do know that witches can protect themselves. I've seen it my own self. But I also know there are rules. And they should apply to everyone."

"What rules? Who we talking about?" Damon put an arm around Ruby's shoulder.

Ruby had been so intent on what Carmen had been saying she hadn't even noticed Damon approach.

But now that Damon had joined the group, Dooley wolves approached, wanting to say hello. Wanting to meet Ruby officially.

"You reach out to any one of us if you need anything," Alice said quietly before they drifted away.

Ruby met shifter after shifter. Said hello to babies and toddlers. Connected with three different pregnant women she'd see the following week at the clinic.

"You're so good at working a room I hadn't even noticed you moving us across the entire hall," Ruby told him quietly.

"Darlin', it's all you. You're like a porch light and they're moths. I thought I was going to have to beat them off with a stick." But Damon's tone was light, so happy. He was in his element. A leader people sought out. Trusted.

Aimee saw them as she stood hand in hand with Mac near the Pembry area. A grin broke over her features and she tugged on Mac and they headed across the room.

"You're here!" Aimee hugged Ruby tight. "You look ethereally gorgeous. Like a goddess. This entire ensemble from head to toe, damn."

Ruby returned the compliments as Damon and Mac chatted.

"So, uh, just so you know a sticky note saying you'd had yet another encounter in the grocery with our favorite villain is only to be used as a temporary stopgap until you can explain to me in detail about the whole thing. And here we are days later and I still don't know all the details and the ones I've learned today didn't come from you."

"I had to work through some stuff while I worked and baked pretty much nonstop from the moment I woke up until I dropped into bed. I'll talk to you about it later," Ruby promised. "But this, wow. You weren't kidding about this dinner. So many people and so much food. I'm astonished and super jealous I've missed out all these years."

A dinner bell rang loudly but joyously. "Y'all get to your seats please," Patty said over the PA system.

"And you haven't had a bite yet. Just wait. So good. Well, most of it. Just remember what I told you about that stew of Randy Dooley's," Aimee whispered in Ruby's ear. "I'll touch base with you again after dinner."

Jace kissed Ruby's cheek as they passed by and after a hug from Katie Faith, he held out her chair and Damon did the same for Ruby.

And then the food. Wave after wave of it. "It's a good thing we're going on a walk at midnight. I'll need the exercise after this."

"Don't think I'm going to forget about whatever it was you and the aunties were talking about," Damon told her in an undertone.

"It's not a thing," she attempted to reassure him, but her wolf just gave her a look that said he'd be back to the topic when things calmed down.

JJ, true to his word, sat across from her and pelted Ruby with questions and suggestions the whole meal long while Damon attempted to interfere when he thought his grandfather had gone too far or was too nosy.

Damon was full to bursting with happiness. Ruby shone like the bright, beautiful light she was. She attracted people to her like bees to flowers. She complimented the kids on their costumes and he watched her convert several older shifters who were averse to medical attention to letting her come by and visit.

His grandfather was in raptures as he flirted with

Katie Faith and Ruby at the same time. Thought no one noticed him interrogating Ruby in and around the flirting.

Ruby answered all his questions patiently though. Even when Damon attempted to get JJ to ease back, Ruby just kept her calm and continued to charm everyone.

"I'll be right back," he said quietly before getting up.

Near the restroom doors, Damon bumped into a woman he'd dallied with a time or three a few years before. Nothing serious. "I see congratulations are in order," she told him.

"Thank you, Stacy."

"Though I do wonder why."

"Huh?" Damon had been distracted, looking down the hall to where he caught a glimpse of the table where she sat with the rest of his family.

"You dumped her back years ago and now you're sniffing around her again but this time she's the one?"

"Well, now. I guess I'd assumed everyone grew over time but maybe not." He shrugged. "We had some seasoning to acquire first. Things are bland without seasoning." He smiled as he said it, thinking of the dizzying array of spices in Ruby's kitchen.

"I get that she's powerful and all, and this is for the good of the pack. But you and I both know there're skinny, *white* witches. Most of them, in fact. You got some sort of fetish? You hate your own kind? Trying to get points?"

Damon was sure he'd misheard so he ran it back through his head three more times until he realized, nope, he'd heard correctly.

The wolf most assuredly considered this other shifter

to be a threat to their witch. Damon let that show in his eyes as he spoke clearly. "You started off right with congratulations and had to go and ruin it with all that bigoted bullshit you vomited out after that. Frankly, I won't bother with any stuff like how I'm sure you don't mean it that way, because you do. I won't say you're better than that, because obviously you aren't."

"I don't have a racist bone in my body. There's nothing racist about staying with your own kind." Stacy practically hissed it out. Mad that he'd called out her racism but not ashamed that she was racist to start with.

"Both of us know the truth of that statement. I'm too fucking satisfied with my life to continue this conversation with you. Stay the hell away from me and Ruby and get yourself right with your ignorance."

Damon turned his back on her and walked across the crowded room toward the rest of his life.

Ruby had one of his baby third cousins on her lap, eating off her plate by the time he got back to the table.

"You trying to steal my girl, little dude?" Damon asked before dropping a kiss first on the baby's head and then on Ruby's.

"Just her food I think," his grandma said.

"Sometimes a momma just needs half an hour to herself to eat. It's not a chore to have this sweet little muffin on my lap and heaven knows there's plenty of food," Ruby managed to say around a suddenly squirming baby.

"Hi there, boo." Damon's cousin Joelle held her arms out toward the child whose drooly smile revealed four shiny new teeth.

Ruby made the handover expertly.

"I really appreciate the break, Ruby. Hey, Damon."

He greeted his cousin before turning back to Ruby. "We're in the sweet spot right before all the desserts. Want to go outside for some fresh air?"

"Yes, that'd be very nice." When she stood, Damon helped her into her coat and they snuck out a side door.

"You having fun?" he asked her as they stood looking at the lights running down the Ave.

"I really am. I was nervous but I know a lot of people. Your brothers kept checking in on me, making sure I was okay. Everyone's been very welcoming."

"'Specially the aunties, huh?" he teased.

"They love you and wanted to be sure I was good enough for you."

"Well and isn't that a nice thing? As it goes, I love them all right back. They've been really good to me and my brothers my whole life. They bake me things and give me good gossip. And they came to you tonight to check on you because something has happened. Go on and tell me now."

"It's absolutely nothing serious. A certain terrible bitch tried it on and she learned I wasn't one to be messed with." Ruby brushed her palms together as if getting rid of dirt.

"If it's not serious, you can tell me the details."

Ruby heard the hurt in his tone that she hadn't told him. "She came at me all nice trying to hook me up with some lovelorn relatives of hers. I said no thanks, that we were in a relationship and she went bananas talking about how special and holy all her people are in contrast to you and yours being Satan's minions and all."

Damon snorted but lost some of the rigidity that'd been in his spine. "I've seen you several times since that night. You never said anything. And when I heard talk about some set to in the grocery store, I thought it was the first one. That woman is a fuckin' public menace."

Ruby laughed. "Well Lovie says the grocery store is considering banning her outright because she's caused so many scenes in there for one thing or another. I guess I should be glad I'm not alone. Anyway." She took his face in her palms a moment, tugging him down to kiss her.

She continued. "At first I didn't tell you because I got home from the market and I was still mad. I was mad for hours and I didn't trust myself to be able to relay any of the information. I had to process it. Not what she said, which was all her usual bullshit. But my response because I've never wanted to use my power to hurt anyone before and lordamighty that night I really did. I couldn't bring that to you, or anyone else. I had to process it first.

"As for the rest, I let her know what she'd get if she didn't back off. With the exception of a dirty look or two tonight, she backed off." Ruby shrugged. "From what everyone keeps telling me, I have to push back against aggressive shifters sometimes. I did. Problem solved."

"I won't have any of this shit aimed at you. All the stuff she pulled on Katie Faith was difficult enough to watch but you're mine."

Ruby laughed. "You deal with real violations of pack law and stuff. Being a garbage person isn't illegal."

"I don't like her upsetting you," Damon said after a long silence. "I want you to trust me to protect you."

"Well for heaven's sake, Damon. Who said I don't trust you? I explained why I didn't tell you that night. If she'd done something that scared me or was a violation of whatever of your laws I know of, I'd tell you. You're a shifter. You're second-highest rank in your pack and I'm with you. I have to make my own way with your wolves. Within reason obviously."

"I hate that I can't argue with that last point," he grumbled.

That made her laugh and pull him down to kiss her again.

"After all that—the aunties, Scarlett—you still with me?" he asked when the kiss broke.

Ruby rolled her eyes at him and then grinned. "Of course I am. If not, do you think I'd have told them I loved you?"

He started to reply as the words sank in and then stopped.

"I love you too, Ruby darlin'," he murmured, face still so close to hers she could see the pulse at his neck.

Reluctantly, they headed back inside even though after that emotional breakthrough outside, Damon really wanted to be alone with her. Naked.

He tried to be a good person. Tried to take care of his wolves and keep them in line. But whatever he'd done to deserve a woman like Ruby loving him he truly couldn't guess. He was thankful nonetheless.

Aimee and Katie Faith drew her away the moment they'd gotten through the doors so he found Major talking to Jace and joined them, checking in with Ruby every few minutes to assure himself she was okay.

Of course she was. Aimee had one of her arms and Katie Faith the other as they chatted animatedly with several other folks around their age. They were young, vibrant and oh so pretty. Magic hung all around them and from all appearances, the shifters near them loved it as much as he did. All that magic was like candy.

He also noted they were—all three of them—talking about the upcoming vote to abolish the Rule of Silence with those same young shifters. Overheard Aimee giving some talking points to a Pembry who was trying to talk his great-aunt into voting to abolish.

Yes, each of these witches brought something special to each pack. Perspective and different approaches to old problems.

"Did you notice Katie Faith's scent changing once you and she got together?" Damon asked Jace, still watching Ruby.

"Her magical scent you mean? Yeah. So subtle I didn't notice it at first. But when she joined the pack she acquired just a hint of pine. Right after the buds break open."

Damon nodded. He'd begun to notice the slight addition of loam to her scent. As if just by living nearby and doing her magic on his land, she'd begun to take it into her power as well. Shifter magic in her veins too, now.

Part of him lived in her. Made her stronger and faster. It was…more than he'd ever even imagined. Massive and important and so fucking wonderful. Damon wasn't even sure if he deserved to feel this…enormous thing.

It wasn't that he'd felt alone. He'd always had Major and Jace. But this was something he hadn't expected. Hell, he hadn't even known this was something he'd ever be lucky enough to experience.

Joy cascaded through him, filling him with light and pleasure and a sense of absolute, unshakable surety that he was Ruby's wolf and would forever be that way. As she was most assuredly his witch.

That cascading joy was his love of her. Of their love as its own force that forged their connection into an unshakable, unbreakable foundation.

Ruby had turned her attention to Damon as he'd stood with his brothers. He was so beautiful. He had hidden depths most people probably never imagined. Not fragile but he let himself be vulnerable with her.

When they'd been outside earlier and she'd told him about the fight with Scarlett, it could have been a fight. He'd been hurt. But he'd *listened* to her. And he'd understood and accepted her explanation. So many people she knew got into stupid arguments all the time because they never just talked stuff out. But there he was all emotionally available and honest. Knocking her on her ass.

But also bolstering her. Shoring her up.

Damon Dooley had been there all along but *this* love? This love that left her breathless, grateful and at the same time calm and satisfied. She found herself thinking of him all day long and not just sex stuff. The way he was so gentle with her dogs. His laugh. That look he got when he was in official mode and was listening to one of his wolves who needed him.

The totality of Damon Dooley was something she'd happily spend the rest of her life learning but she doubted she'd ever see all his kindnesses because he did them so regularly and without any expectation of thanks.

Oh but he deserved thanks. And all the pets and compliments for his deeds as well as his looks. For his brain and his heart.

He was her brilliant love. Her strong, sexy wolf who

brought her bulbs and garden gloves and expensive chocolate for the cocoa she made for the end of each day they spent together.

To her left Katie Faith said something but a surge of tawny, golden shifter energy slammed into her with enough force to take her breath. At the center of the gold were blues, greens, browns.

It filled her up, washed over and through her, clung to her skin and eyelashes. Shifter magic, most assuredly. But more specifically, Damon's shifter magic. Made into something else. Something *more*.

Ruby's magic swirled all around this new center in her until it grew roots. Together.

And when she blinked, Damon was just a few steps away and there was no sound but her pounding pulse and the sizzle of energy when they made physical contact. All of it, everything between them threaded together when he put his arms around her waist.

"So, that happened," he said as he bent to kiss her. A soft, sweet brush of those talented lips and she sighed happily into him.

"Yeah. But what is that?"

He chuckled. "We just sort of performed a binding. At Halloween dinner in front of several dozen people."

By accident?

But magic didn't work that way. What had happened was a spell of intent. From them both. And because the veil was so thin and because they were surrounded by all his folk. All those elements had clicked together at the very instant they were supposed to and had made their own unique connection spell.

"Well look at that. We sure did. You good?" she asked as quietly as she could.

He laughed, the delight of the sound dropping over her like rain and she realized part of it was that she had picked up his pleasure via their new connection. Which brought a smile to her mouth in answer.

When they broke apart, she realized pretty much the whole room watched them both.

Chapter Seventeen

"Well that was quite the capper to the evening," Patty said to Ruby just seconds later. Things had gone back to normal. Or. Normal adjacent anyway. At least the whole room wasn't staring at them and while she knew everyone was talking about them, at least it wasn't in her face.

This felt happy. For the most part. She noted the dark look from Scarlett but who cared about that when her magic had up and claimed the man in front of half the town like it just wasn't content to wait around any longer?

"I'm so pleased to welcome you to the pack, Ruby." Patty hugged her—also a Southern woman bosom hug but instead of White Diamonds, Patty smelled of Shalimar.

"Thank you. I'm…well this is quite a surprise."

"A happy one I hope." Patty looked to Damon, who was deep in conversation with Major but still held Ruby's hand.

"Oh my goodness, yes. Damon is the kind of person I've always dreamed of ending up with. But he's his own package. There's no one like him. I'm so thrilled. But it's sudden. I mean one minute we're walking in and now we're like bound. I hope people don't think it's rushed."

"Who gives a shit what anyone else thinks?" Patty said in an undertone. "But we're shifters. We have different rules and what do you call 'em, cultural norms. This is far from rushing for us."

And for her too. Her magic took things into its own hands and Ruby chose to see that as a very good beginning for them.

"We need to have a ceremony. To welcome you to the pack. A wedding of sorts as well," Patty said. "Between me and some of the other elders, we can work with you to give you lessons. A sort of Dooley 101."

"You're so good to me. I'd love that. I know there's so much I need to learn." What had they called Jace, his brothers and Mac back in the day? The Princes of Diablo Lake. Ruby supposed being with him was rather like marrying into royalty and she'd need lessons.

Major swept Ruby from Damon's arms and danced her down the walkway between the long tables. "I am so fuckin' happy for you two. Truly. You're a catch, Ruby. And Damon knows it. He'll do you right. He's so gone for you and this means you're just as gone for him. Damn. This is the best." He hugged her and kissed her cheeks.

Katie Faith and Aimee hugged them both, crying about how happy they were and soon enough, Damon was there at Ruby's back.

"I do need to go. There's the midnight Consort event and I need to tell my family before they hear this from anyone else," she told him. "I know there's probably stuff you have to do here, especially after that whole… whatever."

He spun her out of Major's arms and into his, kissing the tip of her nose. "Where you go, I go. That's how it is and I'm entirely good with that. I don't want your family to be mad that they heard about this secondhand. I know what they mean to you."

They said their goodbyes as quickly as they could given how many people wanted to congratulate them.

"I'll see you all in a bit. I need to change my clothes first and then I'll head my family off at Miz Rose's," she told Aimee and Katie Faith as she hugged them one more time.

"We'll go over now to attempt rumor control," Katie Faith said.

In the truck, Ruby scooted over to the middle so she could put her head on his shoulder. Needing that touch after the events of the evening.

"Are you really all right with this?" Ruby asked as they headed into her house. She changed out of her dress and into the gown and cape that went over it. Her Samhain celebratory gown was red with yellow piping and the cloak was deep black lined with red. "Like hello you're married!"

"Ruby darlin', I wanted to marry you weeks ago. The wolf knew and the man knew. But we understood some time needed to pass for you to understand what we had this time out. And that binding tonight? Baby, that doesn't just happen. Imprinted couples who choose the binding aren't even a majority in our community. And what happened tonight? That simultaneous whatever it was that made our own unique magical binding? So very rare. We showed every single shifter in town that you and I are it. People can talk until the sun burns out and try to make trouble but the truth is, they all saw the magic of what you and I are. I love you and everyone knows it."

She let that soothe and center her. "All right then. I have no reason to think they won't be happy for us. But they're going to demand an actual wedding for my family to attend and all that. I know you're building a house and you have a business to run and a pack and we'll fit it in the best we can."

She put on thick-soled boots because they'd be walking and she wanted to stay warm and comfortable. No one would see them anyway because the gown and cloak were long.

"I'm nearly finished with what will be our house. *Ours*. And a wedding is part of my to-do list if that's what you and your family want. As far as I'm concerned, we're already married. Whatever we need to do to make your family feel included and satisfied, whatever *you* need to be happy and satisfied, is what I'm happy doing." He took her hand and kissed her knuckles. "I just need to get you a ring."

Ruby sent a quick text to the family group chat to let them know she needed to speak with them all ASAP and would meet them in five minutes at Miz Rose's to explain everything.

"You better just spit it out up front," Ruby's dad said when they arrived. "You've got us worried. If you're pregnant, that's okay. We're pleased as punch."

Ruby laughed. "Good to know. But I'm not pregnant."

Lovie snorted. "Good. That boy best marry you first."

"About that," Ruby said.

Ruby explained the whole thing. The way Damon's feelings and energy had combined with hers and how it had created a binding spell of sorts leaving them married in the eyes of pack law.

"And me," Damon added. "I mean, this is more than a rules situation. Just to be clear."

Ruby squeezed his hand.

Her mother swept them both into hugs and it went down a row of her family until she and Nichole hugged, both crying happy tears.

"Your energy feels different. Just a little. But there's a bit of pack magic in you now," Nichole said.

"I understand and respect that you're officially considered married as far as the shifters are concerned. But just know we expect a wedding ceremony as well," her mother said and Lovie nodded.

"Sooner rather than later if you'll be living together," Lovie said and Ruby didn't have the heart to tell her grandmother they already were pretty much half the week at least.

"We can talk about it tomorrow. Everyone is gathering near the gate," Ruby said, pointing to the rest of the consort.

The town cemetery was only half a mile away so they walked, solemn, holding lanterns, candles and torches down the quiet little lane it lay on.

Damon wasn't nervous at all, just fascinated as they entered the cemetery and fanned out, heading to the markers where friends and loved ones were buried.

"Now we leave offerings and tokens," Ruby told him quietly. "A way to memorialize that exchange between the living and those who've passed on."

She explained that Samhain was a time to celebrate the lives of those who'd passed. To make offerings and recognize that life and death are on a continuum. One made way for the other. Over and over again.

At the time of year when the veil between worlds was so thin, it was thought to be possible to connect with the dead and departed from this plane of existence to the next.

At her aunt's grave, she left a fabric-wrapped bundle propped against the stone. Her lips moved, eyes closed as she held a smooth river rock in her hand she placed atop the marker.

She repeated the process at several graves until they reached his mother's and they both went to their knees. Ruby pulled out a small bunch of apple blossoms tied with a red ribbon and placed it on the ground while again she gave her prayer/observance.

Her magic was elegant and yet very simple and Damon loved to watch her at work.

Damon pulled out the offering he'd brought for his mother. Ruby had explained it didn't need to be expensive or rare or anything like that, but a token that would mean something to him or his mother. Just a moment of thanks. He'd brought a little porcelain fairy he'd picked up a few years before at a secondhand shop in Nashville. Now he knew why it had called to him.

"You don't have to say anything out loud," Ruby explained. "Keep it in your head if you want. Or feel without words. My point is, however you want and need to manifest this is absolutely fine."

"Thanks." Damon meant it. All this was new and could have been overwhelming or worse, made him feel inadequate or ignorant. Instead, Ruby made sure it was warm and welcoming.

The whole cemetery was full of scenes just like the

one he and Ruby made. Some people had brought beach chairs and had set them up at gravesites to celebrate that way.

"This is the solemn part. Tomorrow we burn shit and eat all the food," Ruby had told him earlier. But what he saw then was full of joy. Solemn yes. It hurt to lose those you love. But instead of ache, these witches chose to use these moments for joy. For love and happiness.

That lightened his heart as he placed his palm on his mother's headstone and closed his eyes. He'd never get to know her in person. She'd never hold the babies he and Ruby would go on to have. But she'd be there anyway. In the shape of his future son or daughter's eyes. In his own when he looked back in the mirror.

That's all Damon could have and it sucked. But. For the first time in years, this felt like enough. She was gone and that wasn't going to change. But she could still be in his life. She was his mother after all and her love would always be there.

On the way home, Ruby took their route to a three-way stop not so very far from where the truck was parked.

"This is a crossroads. I'm going to leave an offering for Hecate," she explained to Damon.

She pulled several things from her basket and placed them in the center where other offerings already had been placed. That made her happy. This celebration that countless others had celebrated and observed over generations of witches like herself. She was part of something larger.

A loaf of apple cake and a bottle of mulled wine offered to appease the hungry ghosts.

Hecate, please take this token of food and libation in

*your name at Samhain. I request that you watch over
and protect the people of Diablo Lake against anything
malevolent.*

Ruby poked her thumb in a place she knew would
heal quickly and let several drops of blood hit the dirt
next to her offering.

Magic rode the air. Metallic and sharp, like the scent
of her blood. The goddess was pleased.

She stood and turned, her gaze finding Damon. "We
don't look back," she said as he took her hand and they
walked the other way, back toward where they'd parked
earlier.

"Ready to go home?" she asked him.

"Sure am, wifey."

That made her smile as she put her head against his
shoulder a moment as they walked on, toward home
and bed. Sleep would come after a bit of celebration.

Damon had never once in his life been nervous about
sexing a beautiful woman up. Especially if they'd already been together before as he and Ruby had. But
everything was different.

More. Better.

At her front door he felt so damned shy. She turned
and when he noted she had some nervousness too, everything felt easier.

He pulled her close as the dogs ran into the living
room, beyond happy they were home.

Damon smiled at the sound of the dogs' nails tippy
tapping against the floors as they pranced and danced
and jumped with joy at their feet.

Ruby went to her tiptoes, stretching up to kiss him
before she knelt to give the dogs attention. "Guess what?

Damon is your daddy now. Forever. If he tries to run we'll find him so get a good sniff for reference."

That made him laugh as he joined her. "You can't get rid of me now."

"As if we want that anyway."

She stood and let them outside, where they barked and ran and played happily, pausing to do their business before getting back to the house.

Ruby threw the locks on the doors once the boys came in from outside. The enormity of everything that had happened over the last several hours could crash outside all it wanted. But for the next hours she and Damon would be together. Alone. To celebrate what had just happened.

He went to be sure there was fresh water for the dogs and after giving them one last burst of love and scratches behind the ear, Damon stood and looked at Ruby with so much intensity it left her weak in the knees.

So she held out her hand and he took it, leading him to the bedroom where she closed the door or the dogs would come in for company at the exact wrong moment.

"I need you," she told him simply. Honestly.

"I'm yours. Always."

And he gave himself to her. Going to his knees and bowing his head, as if seeking benediction. The simple devotion of it was so pure it nearly hurt. She vowed to be worthy of the heart this man had just given her.

He helped her out of her boots and stood, taking her cloak and laying it over the back of a nearby chair.

He slowly unbuttoned the front of her gown and parted it, baring her body to his gaze. His hands that slowly caressed her shoulders and her neck as he pulled the gown free.

"You're my beautiful goddess. The finest gift I've ever been given. You're more than anything I've ever imagined."

Tears pricked the back of her eyes.

She took his hands in hers and kissed his palms.

"We're the best gift. Damon, you and I will move mountains together. We are magic."

Though they tried to keep it slow, the remainder of their clothes lay in a pile on the floor and they stumbled back to the bed in a tangle of limbs, their mouths together in a flurry of passionate kisses.

Pleasure arced up her spine as his mouth skated down her neck and over her collarbone. He murmured that she was beautiful. That she was precious and talented. That she was kind and compassionate, sexy, smart.

Sweat beaded on their skin as she kissed his chest over his heart, felt the vibration and knew it beat for her. That he was hers in every way and that she would die before she purposely hurt or misused him.

His very talented tongue circled her left nipple, then over to the right. But what really got her attention was the edge of his teeth. She gasped and he lifted his head to look into her face. "More. I want more of that sound."

Which he proved by licking a trail down her belly, around her belly button and then farther, parting her thighs—already primed and ready to go—and spread her pussy wide to his gaze and the attentions of his mouth.

She was really glad she had strength in her thighs as she arched up off the bed as he stroked the tip of his tongue against the underside of her clit.

Over and over as the pressure built, her orgasm like a storm building.

The bright, brand-new binds between them filled her with not just everything she felt, but the brilliant edges of what he felt as well.

She knew the depth and beauty of his love for her. The words he'd given her before now flowed out as feeling that she understood to her bones.

Pleasure drowned her as climax seemed to fill up every single cell in her body to bursting.

And then he was sliding into her. Wet as she was, ready for him as she was, it was still a snug fit that echoed up her spine.

Damon had never needed anything more than he needed the woman beneath him. Never craved anything more than her thighs wrapped around his waist as he took agonizingly slow strokes into her. Over and over. As deep as he could get.

There was good sex. Great sex. Excellent sex and this. Ruby sex, he supposed.

Her taste lived in him. Her scent was all over his skin and he was nearly senseless with how good it felt.

She was his. Forever.

He saw in her gaze how much she understood that fact and loved it as much as he did. Saw in her eyes that she trusted him. Believed in all his best qualities and loved him despite the worst.

"I love you, Ruby," he said before he leaned down to kiss her.

"I love you, Damon," she told him between kisses. "I'm so glad you're in good physical shape. I mean, not just because your abs are ripply which is…" she couldn't finish because he got extra deep, eliciting a grunt or two from her. "Your stamina. That's it," she wheezed out.

Stamina or not, he wasn't Superman and he couldn't hold back the orgasm that'd been building for hours. Since before the binding. But certainly that kicked his need for her into high gear.

"Come again," he urged.

She slid a hand between their bodies and when she touched her clit her pussy clamped around his cock so tight his vision grayed a little.

There was something so ridiculously sexy about the way she so unashamedly took her pleasure. Demanded it of him.

"Yes," she whispered as he sped up and got even deeper. He made sure to add pressure where her hand was, pressing it into her clit.

He knew when she came and had a few seconds before he could no longer hold back his own climax that seemed to pull his entire spine out and then put it back. Waves of pleasure so deep they nearly hurt buffeted them until at last he fell to the mattress at her side as they both caught their breath.

"Once I'm able to move again, we're hitting round two," he said.

She laughed. "I've already had round two. You go first."

Chapter Eighteen

Damon woke up to find himself in his witch's bed and stretched muscles he'd worked so hard just hours before.

He knew she was nearby. Could hear the rustle of her movements in the kitchen and the scent of coffee hung in the air. But more than the sounds and scents, her presence seemed to live in him now.

What a fucking awesome thing this imprint deal was. He picked up on her emotions. She was pleased, which brought a smile to his face.

It wasn't the first time he'd slept over but everything was different that morning. He rolled from bed and found some boxers to throw on. He had to go to work but not for a while yet.

And he wanted to spend as much time as he could with Ruby before he left.

She was out on her back porch, hair still in her bonnet, a blanket wrapped around herself as she sipped coffee and watched the dogs run around.

"There's coffee in the pot," she called out.

"You're the best," he said, bending to kiss her. "You need a refill?"

"Yes. But I'll come with you. I've got biscuits in the oven and I'll make us eggs and bacon to go with."

"Damn. How did I merit all this bounty?" He pulled her to her feet and into his arms. His wife. Wolf and man burned for her, settled into the way she felt, tasted and smelled.

She hummed and hugged him back. "Don't get used to it. It won't be every day. But I'm feeling particularly celebratory today. By the way, a few wolves trotted by the yard this morning. I waved at them all and said you were still sleeping."

Why he found it so fucking cute that she would just yell out a howdy do to a werewolf come to check her out now that she was his, he didn't know. But he accepted it.

"I expect we'll both need the fortification today. I'll get us both more coffee and set the table. Have the boys eaten?"

Ruby saw the love bite she'd left on his neck and embarrassment rose in her belly. Along with a sense of satisfaction that everyone would know she left it and that he was hers.

"You keep looking at me like that and we'll both be late for whatever we're supposed to do today."

"You're saying it like that's a bad thing. You'd think we got a day or two to ourselves to celebrate but no."

He laughed. "Ruby darlin', it's like you never met my family. Plus, it's witch high holy days and stuff so I know you'll be in high demand. I'm surprised we haven't had a bunch of calls already."

"I haven't turned my phone on for that reason. I wanted to have this time, these last few minutes."

"I love how sneaky you are."

"I'm greedy for you," she confessed. "I like this simple, sweet time with you when neither of us has any other responsibility but our relationship."

He took her hand, threading their fingers together. "You and I both know our lives will always be full of competing responsibilities. We have lives full of people who need us. Depend on us and our actions and judgment. It's one of the reasons you and I were drawn together. A shared passion for community and family. So I'm in total agreement on these stolen moments. I don't even know where my phone is to turn it on or off anyway."

Ruby went all gooey inside at how adorable he was. "It's on the dresser in the bedroom. Speaking of bedroom dressers, you should move your things into one of them. I'll make room in my closet too. Our closet. That's going to take a while. The shift from me to we."

"Easier ways to get out of paying rent," he teased, "than taking on an entire pack of wolf shifters."

"I took you on. They come with you. That's how it goes. You get two dogs, a super-nosy family of witches and all my goofy friends. I think I got off easy."

"I get *everything*. Everything I've ever dreamed of and more. Here I am, with you in a time of chaos. I just know you and I have a lifetime ahead of us full of joy. And excellent sex."

She really accepted it. The purest joy that was this connection she shared with Damon. There was work ahead, she knew. Relationships took attention and work to keep them healthy. Which had seemed like wise words before and now she understood them so much better.

A magic tie wasn't a substitute for being a good partner. They'd have to put in the time and effort needed, but when they did, Ruby had a very certain feeling they'd be strong and brilliant and capable of changing the world.

And no lie, the sex was utterly spectacular.

She busied herself tidying up after breakfast. Damon handled loading the dishwasher.

"Hey, Ruby darlin'? I want you to think hard about what you need in our house. I can still customize quite a bit at this stage. And what I can't, we can create. I expect to be able to move in by Thanksgiving."

"Thank you. For being you, Damon. For thinking of me the way you do. You're a gift."

"Well. Now, I don't think I'd go that far. It's not hard to love you."

"You duck your head and rub the back of your neck when you're feeling bashful. It's adorable and it makes me want to kiss you for hours."

"There you go again, begging me to get you on your back and without your panties."

She laughed, grabbing a kiss. "You can shower first. I need to pull together my outfit but before I go to work I need to be sure the dinner stuff is moving like it's supposed to."

He wanted her to take one with him but he knew for sure he'd never make it out of the house if they were naked in the same place. So he got himself together, pleased he'd already had his shaving stuff in the bathroom, and gathered his things to head out.

"I'll call to check in with you later. I've got a bunch of stuff to deal with this morning but I'll be clear by five so we can go to the bonfire together."

"Okay. Be careful today. I love you."

Damon took the few steps back to her to capture her face in his hands. "I love you."

* * *

When Damon parked his vehicle at work, he noted how many shifters milled around the space. Probably looking for him.

He wasn't ready to be found just yet. He had to deal with his family, who'd respectfully given him and Ruby the space they needed on their own the night before.

He knew they'd probably be over at Jace's place eating breakfast and although he'd had a very nice breakfast before, he could always use some coffee to bolster him as he handled family.

"There you are!" JJ called out as Damon entered Katie Faith and Jace's kitchen.

His grandparents were seated at the big table, finishing breakfast. His brothers were there already, along with Katie Faith.

"Where's Ruby?" Patty asked.

"I just left her place ten minutes ago. She's got witch stuff today. Work stuff too."

"I imagine she's got a lot of family stuff as well after last night," Jace said before he walked over to Damon and gave him a hug. "Congratulations to you both. Katie Faith and I are just waiting for you to let us know when we can do a pack ceremony. Everyone is going to want to welcome her in person and the sooner we put a public seal of approval on your relationship, the safer she'll be and the less hassle she'll get from any upset parties."

"Scarlett probably wept into her pillow last night," Patty said. "I sure hope she did."

"Let me tell you about what she pulled on Ruby," Damon said and gave them all the details about the latest Scarlett crap.

Damon saw the looks on faces and knew Katie Faith

had already heard some of it. But to a one, there was outrage. He held up a hand to forestall any speaking. "Listen, before you all start in, let me say Ruby has urged me to let it go because as she puts it so succinctly, *being a bitch isn't against the law.* And she's right. Yes, we need to keep an eye on her as usual. But I'd rather we keep pushing on the Rule of Silence and use all our juice for that."

Katie Faith harrumphed but didn't argue.

"Fine. But that means we need an official pack ceremony to induct Ruby sooner rather than later. It extends our protection to her and hers to us. And it means we have the ability to step in if necessary to intercede on Ruby's behalf if this keeps up and gets worse," Patty said.

"*Agree*d."

Major said, "Ruby is right. We keep our attention on the abolition of the Rule of Silence and ignore all Scarlett's grandstanding."

"So your grandma was right. Gonna repeat her wisdom and say we need to schedule a pack ceremony," JJ told them. "Before the next big inter-pack meeting so it's not an issue hanging out there to be exploited."

"Y'all don't get me into a fight with my witch. Let me talk to her about it. We already know it's coming up. We're trying to accommodate her people too. If you want to take on her Lovie, go on ahead, but I'll pass," Damon said.

Katie Faith sighed. "Damon is right. He knows what needs to be done and why. Let him and Ruby handle it. I'm going to drop by the clinic today to see what I can do to help with the dinner tonight because I'm sure there are three dozen new tasks on her to-do list today. Aside from all this technicality stuff, we're just so happy for you both. She's one of my favorite people on earth and you're, well, you're one of the few people who truly deserve her. You two are so good together. Your magic just clicks like a lock and key. It's really just wonderful."

Damon grinned. "It really is. I'm a dog owner now, God help me, but they're really cute. And good little protectors. Brave. I'll be moving into the house with her until construction on the new place is done and we'll settle there."

Major rubbed his hands together with glee. "Excellent. More apples, peaches and roses for me since I live next door."

"She's a great cook too. I really did luck out," Damon said. "I'll head over to the Mercantile to open up. There's already a crowd milling around so I'll be sure to sell them an item or two while I've got 'em in the store."

There were hugs and hair rubs and kisses all around before Major and Damon got out the door and over to the Mercantile.

Ruby met Damon at their usual spot at two that afternoon. When he saw her waiting there, a huge grin broke over his face. Damn he was pretty.

"My mother made us both lunch. Turkey sandwiches, three for you, along with her famous potato salad and some baked beans." She'd done it while they negotiated next steps for Ruby and Damon. "She even made you deviled eggs and said I couldn't have any because they were for you. She's mean but darn she's sure sweet on you."

Damon pulled her close and they stood there for long moments, just together, reconnecting. "Ruby darlin', I've missed you. And I'm relieved she's sweet on me instead of wanting to dig my grave."

"The conversation was a journey, I can't lie. But it was never anything but positive. They see how happy I am. They see that I love you and that what we have together made its own unique binding spell. They're just focused on a church wedding. I didn't agree to anything. I told her we'd be talking about all this stuff and would let them know what we decided." She was married now. Their relationship was her priority and she'd back him up because that's what was necessary and frankly, it was up to them to make these choices anyway.

"Gosh you're pretty," she told him as they sat and began to eat.

"Says you. Gorgeous." He ate awhile before he chuckled. "These sandwiches are really awesome."

"She picked the tomatoes while I was there. Said you should have fresh. Of course she also asked if I was pregnant, so take that as you will."

That made him laugh. "Plenty of time for that. My grandparents were at Jace's place this morning. They're very happy and supportive too. They love you and see what you mean to me. How you do for me. They want a pack welcoming ceremony. For very good reasons, chief of which is extending the protection and safety of the pack to you. And also, I'm…"

"Don't get shy now, Mr. Prince of Diablo Lake. You're at the top of pack hierarchy. A ruling family member. That means if you don't have a shindig as soon as possible, people might doubt our commitment or be insulted in some way."

"I can't believe you remembered that," he said of the old nickname for him and his brothers, blushing. "But yes for all the reasons you pointed out. And also, you deserve a party."

"Here's part two of that conversation with my mom," Ruby began. "Tonight before the bonfire and dinner, the Consort will host light appetizers at Miz Rose's home to celebrate our union. This is nonnegotiable on my family's part. They want to publicly recognize that we're married. Lovie showed up while I was there and played all the big guilt cards, even though I didn't refuse. I just said I wanted to talk with you first."

"I'm touched and honored that the Consort wants to honor us in that way. It's nice enough to be included in all the festivities. It's really nice that they want to have a little party for us," Damon said.

"There will be so much food tonight. I can't emphasize that enough. Sure we start off with *light appetizers* but then we go to the bonfire and then have cake and ale before the feast. Then the actual feast that includes a cake and dessert table I've been planning and creating for weeks now. Not that you ever seem to get full. I just wanted you to know that."

"If we do this tonight, and the pack ceremony say, next week, then when do we do this church wedding?"

"I don't want to step in the middle of Aimee and Mac's wedding stuff. That all starts in two days and will run through to right after Thanksgiving when they have the wedding itself. My family wants a big reception afterward with as many family members as possible. They'll all be back for Christmas and Yule. So in late December sometime. I'll coordinate with your grandmother and the aunties as well to get a date that works

for everyone. I mean, we're already married in here."
She pressed a hand over her heart. "As it is though, all
sorts of mommas and grandmas would not be pleased
if we chose not to let them celebrate with us. So what
do you think? I know it's less than two months out, but
I think we can pull something wonderful together that
makes pack and witch feel welcome."

"I love all this. I'll handle things on my end with the
ceremony next week and let them know about the wedding plans. I trust everyone will connect but I'll also be
sure to get contact information to all parties involved."

"Yesterday at this time everything was different and
yet, the same. Life comes at you fast. Lucky me." Ruby
waved at two shifters who'd been lurking, pretending
they weren't trying to get Damon's attention, which led
to several more rounds of congratulations once they approached and let the others who'd been watching know
it was okay.

Ruby escaped to get back to work and blew Damon
a kiss, telling him she'd see him later on and he called
back that he loved her.

The man made her all gooey inside. Like a marsh-
mallow.

Chapter Nineteen

"All I'm saying is that you could count it a victory and we can move on. Why are you fighting this one little safeguard?" Mac's aunt Mary asked him.

Damon remained where he'd been, standing right around the corner from where Mac and Mary stood, in front of his car. Mac had to have known Damon was there. Or maybe he didn't. But Damon didn't give a shit because something was going on and he wanted to know what it was.

"You propose changing the rule but only in a way that wouldn't address families now living with the results of the Rule of Silence. There are only four instances of the rule being applied and only one was in the last thirty years. Yes, we want a better future, but that won't come from changing the law in such a way that the living victims can't actually reap the benefits of that change. That's empty justice.

"And let's be real here, Mary, every one of the wolves whose lives have been impacted by that disciplinary action thirty years ago are all in favor of the repeal applying retroactively which is really what should count here. There's no *moving on* until we've laid the past to rest. And we can't until we do the right thing. The overwhelming majority of both packs want this and that has only become more clear in the months since these negotiations have started. So the real question, I guess, is what's it to you that some nearly thirty-year-old case gets unsealed?" Mac asked.

Damon wondered the same thing. What was it to her indeed? Just being a bitch because her sister was and they hated for anyone to have something good?

"It's the principle of the thing, Macrae," Mary said. "We live in chaotic times. The outside world is out of control and what keeps us safe, what keeps us well and prospering are our rules. Our traditions. The world may try to tear them down, but they're the only thing holding the dark at bay."

Damon thought that was a bit dramatic, but he did understand the fear that giving up old rules meant a loss of discipline. But there was something darker in Mary's tone. Bigots used words like the ones Mary had to try to excuse their closed-mindedness. *The way it's always been* surely didn't mean the same for different groups of people.

"Stop fighting me on this, Mary. You and my mother need to back off on this point. It looks suspicious. It's stirring up a divide between older and younger pack members. The Rule of Silence does nothing more than any other sort of punishment for those crimes. We just created a culture of secrecy and shame by making it an equal crime to even mention someone's name or what they did. It doesn't make that crime disappear just because truth does. We've only used it four times so it's not as if it's had a big impact. You're trying to scare people that Armageddon will happen if a man's family is allowed to say his name in public." Mac's tone was of patience stretching thin.

"If you don't stand up for your people what good are you?" Mary demanded, dodging the questions Mac had asked her.

"I *am* standing up for my people!" Mac said. "Leadership is a lot more than sitting in the back of the room scaring old people. Times change. Rules change with them. At one point we needed the Rule of Silence, I guess. But that moment has long passed. This town has gained a lot of ground as both packs have done major work to improve the relationship between us. The witches are beginning to trust us again. Your little crusade is a waste of my time and energy at a critical juncture. Knock it off. We both know I'll win."

"Eventually. Maybe. But you could win right now if you made the proposal we've been suggesting. End the rule from this day forward. Don't stir up the past. The man wasn't anything to get worked up over anyway," Mary said. Of Josiah Dooley. Damon's father.

Mac snarled. "He was someone's son. Someone's father. And those others involved have had to suffer as well. For what? The price you're going to extract, all to end up losing anyway, is your own fault. Remember I tried to warn you. Now if you'll excuse me, I have a date with my fiancée."

"That's another thing. Why are you mixing with the witches?"

"I'm a rebel I guess. Plus the one I mix with smells really good and makes me food. She's pretty and I love her. All excellent reasons to my mind. Evening, Aunt Mary."

Damon heard the car start up and drive off and he backtracked to walk through the alley behind the businesses on the Ave.

* * *

Ruby had spent several hours setting up the cake and dessert table. This after she'd spent time gathering all the elements to create the organic feel she wanted and the season often embraced. The bows she'd created with cotton and linen glistened with the little amber and gold tone beads she'd used. All down the table she'd created clusters of pumpkins, gourds, apples and apple blossoms and had tucked the cakes, brownies, pies, cookies, bars and quick breads around them.

Flameless candles flickered all through the space, just as pretty as the real thing and far less prone to getting knocked over in the wind and setting something on fire while everyone looked at other stuff.

Lit torches led from the main entrance to the field they'd transformed for the celebration. Those torches would then be used to start the bonfire. And for the first time they'd have the feast outside after that.

"Y'all, we really did turn this place into something magical," Aimee said.

"We really did." Ruby turned in a circle to take everything in. "This is just so pretty and surreal and I am so happy to be back here and part of this with y'all."

There was a reception area for the first part of the evening—cake and ale. Libations and bite-sized snacks as a social hour to mark the coming feast. And in the banquet space, long tables lined up in neat rows with one at the head. That ceremonial table held the goblet full of libations that Miz Rose would consecrate as an offering.

"Have any of you seen Damon?" Ruby asked, looking around. They'd come together after the reception at Miz Rose's house where everyone had toasted Ruby and Damon as well as Aimee and Mac. She felt bad about taking the spotlight away from Mac and Aimee, but her friend wouldn't hear of anything else.

"Love is magic, Rube. We'll all celebrate together. This is wonderful and I'm really happy to share. I promise," Aimee had told her. One of myriad reasons she simply adored Aimee.

Nichole said, "I saw him with Jace earlier. They were moving something for your grandfather."

Ruby's Pops had taken a liking to Damon, which was very much a relief to her. Ruby wanted Damon to be loved and accepted and so far her family had done exactly that.

She found him sitting with Lovie and Pops near where the bonfire would be in less than an hour, listening to one of her grandfather's stories about Diablo Lake in the old days.

"Your man was just making sure we were warm and feeling all right," Lovie told her as Ruby bent to kiss her grandmother's cheek.

"He's adorable that way, no?"

Lovie laughed and laughed.

Damon took Ruby's hand and squeezed. Everything inside her stilled and soothed.

"Handy," she murmured.

"Glad to hear it," Damon said with that grin of his. "Do you need me to help with anything?"

"Nah. We're good at this point. Bonfire starts soon enough. I just wanted to check on you. Make sure everything was all right."

Naturally she shouldn't have worried because Damon knew—and charmed—most everyone. The mood at Miz Rose's earlier that night had been delighted. Happy to celebrate their union. Pleased for one of their own to have found something so special.

Damon stood next to Ruby, his arm around her shoulders, hers around his waist. Firelight flickered over her features as Miz Rose spoke to the witches of the Consort.

"Tonight we celebrate the changes of the year. The harvest has come and the earth will quiet as she sleeps, readying for spring. When light slowly dies, ceding to longer nights, the fire will light the way. We will remember the miracles of the seasons before, those lost who we've loved. That love ensures your connection to them will not end, even after death. The leaves will return. The light will return. Until then, we make our own."

At each one of the tables for the feast there were empty seats to remember those loved ones no longer alive. Or to hear Rose Collins tell it, the ones no longer on this plane of existence. And really, it wasn't like he wanted to argue with that idea. It was a comforting one to imagine his mom there in some way.

Ruby hadn't lied when she'd said that night was for burning things and eating a lot. Kids ran around with sparklers, their laughter carrying on the breeze.

"I guess I hadn't figured this would be so much like our dinner on Halloween," Damon told her. "I hope you won't mind if I talk to my grandmother about a cake table at our next dinner. Y'all have some great ideas here."

"Nope, I don't mind at all. In fact, I'm happy to help if she needs it. I expect she won't given how well the dinner went off last night, but the offer is there if she needs me."

Just a few days before, Damon had a girlfriend he was in love with. They'd started to talk about the future here and there, enough that they both had confidence they'd build a life together. And then, well, fate was fine with their love, but wanted to go on and shove them forward several steps. That should have scared him, or even given him pause. But…it hadn't. Maybe it would later, but he didn't think so. It felt absolutely natural and right to be there with her. And to know the following year he'd be there at her side for these events too.

"What time is your meeting tomorrow?" Ruby asked Damon as they readied for bed later that evening.

He looked up from a lapful of happy-to-see-him dogs to catch the pleased surprise on her face at the sight. "I need to open the Mercantile so I usually get there about eight. The inter-pack meeting isn't until next week but there's a meeting with Jace and Major and a few others at ten. We still on for lunch at two? How about we go somewhere this time? There are tables at You Want This Smoke and they're open until three. How does that work for you? I'll pick you up from the clinic and we'll walk over together." Damon liked the idea of walking hand in hand with his sweetheart so the whole town knew about them.

"Sounds good. It's taco Tuesday menu tomorrow so I'm all about it. I know you need to keep working on the house so don't feel bad about being away for that. I'll help with whatever I can too."

"We'd never turn away an offer of food and drink. It's nice when you show up with your wagon of treats. There'll be some painting stuff that you can definitely help with. But the big stuff is nearly all finished so that's us shifters who can lift that sort of weight without a problem. I don't want you to get hurt and I know you're busy with a million other things. But I do appreciate the offer, Ruby darlin'," Damon told her as he stood, placing both dogs on the floor.

She stole a kiss and said she was heading to bed to do a little reading and he told her he'd join her shortly after letting the boys out one last time.

He let the dogs out and stood on the porch, breathing in the late-night air while Biscuit and K Mags ran around, peed and sniffed. They'd let him know if anything was amiss if his own nose failed him.

A yip from beyond the fence line sounded and Damon recognized pack. Not immediate family but one of his lieutenants, Charlie. Damon sent a yip back, letting Charlie know things were fine and that he appreciated being checked in on.

The dogs ran to him when he made a little sound and they trooped into the house. Damon smiled at the sounds of water being gulped down and then the tappy tap as they made their way down the hall.

They yodeled their hellos to Ruby and then settled into their beds.

Ruby talked to them a bit, getting out of bed to go give each dog some love and told them good-night with kisses to the tops of their noggins.

She was going to be such a wonderful mother someday. "Come to bed, wife."

Ruby gave him an amused look and then slid into the bed at his side. For absolutely sure they were getting a much bigger bed once they moved into the new house. It wasn't a chore really to snuggle up to Ruby, but a full bed wasn't something he could really stretch out in. Not without his feet hanging over the edge.

Still, the warmth of his witch soaked into him, settling wolf and man as she backed into his body and he
put his arms around her. Nothing in his life had been a
better sleep aid than this. He took a deep breath, taking her in, her scent now laced with loam.

"Night, darlin'," he murmured. "Love you."

She hummed sleepily. "Love you."

Chapter Twenty

Ruby had chosen an eggplant-toned jumpsuit with a cowl at the neck and pockets. Real actual pockets. The clips in her hair matched the bracelet she wore. Gold apple blossoms.

Her lipstick was dark purple with a nice smoky eye and a new set of lashes she'd been dying to try out. She smelled good and looked good and was damned excited to see Damon's reaction.

Still, she'd deliberately decided on each item in the outfit to appeal to her wolf and also to be pretty, but not do anything that could be construed as trying to overshadow Aimee.

Every year, Collins Hill Days ended two days after Samhain with a big party. The dance was held down at the grange hall with live music, food and nonalcoholic beverages. They also had a cash bar or you could bring your own for the table. The whole town showed up, sang, dance, visited and generally partied to mark the transition of the seasons and the year.

And this year, Aimee and Mac were hosting the dance as a celebration of their engagement and upcoming wedding. It'd bring folks together socially and continue to strengthen relationships. Hard to be mad at your neighbor when they give you some food and a party to go to.

Ruby drove over to her parents' place to drop the dogs with Pipes for a sleepover. They wouldn't be lonely with Ruby and Damon out late because they adored Pipes and being spoiled by Ruby's parents.

"You two wanna hang out with Pipes at Gramma's house?" she said as they pulled up. The dogs started barking excitedly, their little butts moving from side to side as they wagged their tails so hard.

They ran straight up to the back door where Ruby's dad let them in. "Hey, you two. Pipes is in the television room," he said as they tore past. He smiled when he saw Ruby. "Now, don't you look regal. Elegant. Where's your man?"

Ruby paused to hug him on her way into the house. "He's getting ready at Jace's house and meeting me at the grange. It's big business at the Mercantile today so he's working late. I'll meet him there."

"I dropped a present off at city hall today for Aimee and Mac. I'm making them a quilt for their wedding, but everyone needs towels so I got a set to celebrate the engagement," Ruby's mom said. Before she too asked where Damon was.

"Now you know how I feel," Greg said as she came into the television room where he and Nichole sat. "Every time I come over here it's all, where's Nichole? How is Nichole? Greg who?"

"It's nice they love our spouses though," Ruby said with a snort.

They rode over to the grange together but Ruby parted ways there and headed down the way over to the Mercantile. She got held up half a dozen times by different Dooleys asking for medical assistance or advice, which was worth the delay. Real interactions with patients came when they could trust you and if marrying Damon gave them a reason to trust her, she'd gladly take the opportunity.

Damon decided to walk toward the grange to perhaps meet her halfway since she was running behind and he was already dressed. He hated the idea of her being out there alone after dark. Even though it was Diablo Lake and dance night so there were people everywhere and his witch could absolutely take care of herself. He was already an overprotective shifter, but now that he had Ruby all those instincts had kicked into overdrive.

Really though, at the heart of it, he wanted to see her. It had been hours since lunch where he'd shared her with half the pack who'd seen them eating and stopped by to congratulate them. He'd still have to share her with the town at the dance, but neither of them would be working and he could be at her side all night long.

A few blocks up he caught sight of her. She looked sexy and regal and beautiful and elegant in a purple pants thing as she leaned toward Etta Dooley, who'd already been old when he was a kid so heaven knew her age now and he sure as hell wasn't going to ask because ancient as she might have been, she was still fast enough to twist an ear if necessary.

He caught Ruby telling Etta she'd drop by next week to check in on her. Then Ruby walked slowly beside the older shifter until she reached her grandson, who'd jogged over to meet them and escort Etta to the dance.

"Ruby darlin', you look good enough to eat," he told her and then nibbled on her ear.

"I'm all about that," she told him and then grabbed his butt while they were still relatively alone. "Sorry I'm running a little late. I kept bumping into people and then having to make notes about appointments for the next few weeks. Looks like marrying you has convinced more than one person I won't chop them up and bury them in the woods."

"Okay then." They began to walk in the same direction as a steady stream of others. Toward the lights and the music.

"Nichole and Greg went ahead and are saving us seats. Did I tell you how handsome you look?" Ruby pulled them to a halt and looked him up and down before she smoothed her palm down his chest.

"Look here, missy. You and I have had a discussion about this," he teased, ridiculously flattered that she'd found him attractive. It was just a button-down shirt tucked into black pants. Nothing that fancy but suddenly he was doubly glad he'd chosen the deep green shirt she'd said brought out his eyes.

"We look good, you know that, right?" she said, her dimple showing as she smiled.

"We absolutely do." She was totally correct. His witch was lush and beautiful and she smelled really good and her laugh was like music. Together, side by side they complemented the best qualities of the other.

When they entered the hall things were already humming. A bluegrass band was on the stage and folks stood in groups just listening, some danced already.

"Y'all did a bang-up job decorating," Damon told her as they headed to the other side of the event space where the tables were set up. After the cocktail and food portion was over, most of the tables would be cleared away to extend the dance floor. Which was a good thing because even the most antisocial of the shifters liked to come in for at least a few turns around the room to say hello and get something to eat. In some years, the dancing overflowed to outside where there were community barbecues in the summer.

That night fairy lights hung from the rafters. Amber hurricane glass lanterns held flickering lights inside and were strung along the walls. There were pumpkins and the like. Lots of flowers and fruit as well.

Ruby looked around, happy everything looked so nice. When the main lights went down it'd look even better.

"Is there a table for presents?" Damon asked her after a few people holding packages seemed to be looking for one.

"Aimee didn't want to do that because she told everyone not to give them presents because they had a wedding just next month. And we told her that of course people were going to bring presents, for goodness' sake. This is Diablo Lake. My mother gave them towels. That's just what you do. Which is a long way of saying there's a small table over there in the corner that we decorated. I see presents on it already."

"Did we get them a present?" Damon asked.

"I donated money to the community health service in their name. I signed your name to the card though."

He smiled and it was so vulnerable and open she got a little choked up.

"You did?" he asked.

"Sure I did. We're Damon and Ruby now."

"I don't think I ever imagined being in a relationship with someone who signs my name to cards. I like it a lot." He stole a quick kiss.

She liked it too.

"Let's go find Aimee and Mac to say our congratulations before it gets really crowded," Ruby said.

And when they walked around a large group of people, Ruby saw Aimee facing Scarlett and looking annoyed.

"Well I don't know why you don't set up a head table," Scarlett was saying to Aimee.

"Because we don't want a head table," Aimee replied.

"Why not? It's your party even if your supposed friends are trying to steal your spotlight. Some friend she is."

Ruby rolled her eyes and Damon echoed that as they continued to eavesdrop.

"No one is stealing anything. There's a limitless amount of joy in the universe. More isn't going to spoil this party. She is my friend and I love her dearly and I'm warning you now not to make a big deal out of this or attempt to make her feel bad," Aimee said, putting her hands on her hips.

Mac strolled up and put an arm around Aimee so she relaxed the fists at her hips. "Werewolves love a party, Mom. There's plenty of good time to be had. Plenty of celebration to share."

"It's just like a Dooley to cheap out and try to step on your celebrations to take it for themselves," Scarlett said loud enough that several people turned to look at her. Abashed, she shut her mouth.

Aimee put her hand up in Scarlett's face. "Enough! This is my night, as you keep reminding me. And I'm telling you to stop this right now. No one is having a bad time but you. And you can't just enjoy your bad time on

your own, now you're trying to make everyone else mad
and I'm not having it. Get yourself together and celebrate like you promised you would, or get the hell out."

Mac gave a quick sideways glance at Aimee and then
backed her up. "You made a commitment to behave so
you could attend. And so that Dad could come to the
wedding when you kept your promises to behave. And
here you are not doing that. Don't make me change my
mind. You're making Aimee upset and you're pissing
me off. Please, for the love of God, Mom, go and have
a nice time without ruining anyone else's night."

Scarlett started to argue but Aimee's gaze narrowed
dangerously and suddenly, TeeFay, Aimee's mom and
most absolutely not a member of the Scarlett Pembry
fan club, materialized at Aimee's side.

"There a problem here, Scarlett?"

Ruby adored TeeFay and because she and Aimee
had been close, Aimee's mom was like another mother
to her.

"No problem at all," Mac interjected smoothly. And
since at one of these town events TeeFay had actually
punched Scarlett square in the nose, he had reason to
want to keep things calm.

"Good. I'd hate for there to be any issues at my
daughter's engagement party." TeeFay smiled but
showed all her teeth, which meant she'd gotten some
good shifter lessons.

"She's scary," Damon said once Scarlett huffed and
walked away to a group of her friends.

TeeFay leaned in close to speak to Aimee and Mac
and Ruby figured they'd say hello after all the emotions
from that scene had blown over.

"Which one? TeeFay or Scarlett?"

"Well, both to be honest. But I meant TeeFay. She's got momma bear all over her. You can't reason with that. Makes a body do all sorts of things they never would otherwise like lift burning cars and sucker punching an alpha wolf shifter."

"You got that right. Come on. I'd like a beer and I see Greg brought the cooler we packed at the house." She hooked her arm through his and they went off to meet everyone else.

Werewolves were terrible at karaoke. And they loved it anyway. The cats were far better and the witches often had special effects. Wolves couldn't keep the beat or a tune but what they lacked in talent they made up for in sheer joy.

Damon, Jace and Major were deep into "Bye Bye Bye" except they weren't reading the prompter and didn't know all the words and they were also three sheets to the wind on whatever rotgut managed to get shifters drunk for longer than half an hour.

"It's a good thing we don't have to depend on their music career to pay the bills," Katie Faith said.

"No shit. But they're so cute and having so much fun. Plus Damon can find the rhythm in bed and that's really all I care about."

Mac and Huston joined and were trying to do the choreography and they all looked like toddlers who'd refused naps. Adorable and utterly uncoordinated but also slightly chaotic like someone might cry at any given minute.

After that, a group of witches did "Macarena" and no one knew the words to that either, but the whole room sang "hey, Macarena" at the chorus so that was fun.

Aimee slid into the group, giving everyone kisses.

"Someone's a little tipsy," Katie Faith sang.

"You?" Ruby asked.

That made them all laugh and then she let them talk her into "Girls Just Wanna Have Fun" before she headed over to Damon and he put his arms around her.

"Hey, Ruby darlin'. Y'all did great up there. I especially liked all the parts where you bounced enough for me to ogle all my favorite parts."

"Hey there, Damon Dooley. I'm tired and my feet hurt."

"Let's go pick up the boys and head home then."

She drove as he was still a little buzzed. "We don't need to get the dogs tonight. It's late anyway."

"What will they sleep on though?"

He worried about that? When he'd tried to be so gruff at first about dogs as pets? Awww.

"They have their own beds at my parents' house. Believe me when I tell you they get even more spoiled over there than at home. Plus they get to play with Pipes. It's like a trip to grandma's to play with your cousins for them."

"Okay. Gonna be so quiet without them."

"We can make our own noise."

"Oh. Suddenly I feel a lot more awake." He straightened and took several deep breaths.

"I love that the promise of sex wakes you right up."

"Listen, Ruby darlin', the promise of sex with you could wake me from the dead. Just for future reference."

"You keep showing me how handy you are every single day and we're going to have a long, successful marriage."

"What a fuckin' lucky guy I am."

Chapter Twenty-One

Ruby finished with her tinctures and after placing stoppers in all the little amber-colored bottles, she broke the circle. In the other room she heard Damon sigh happily.

"Don't you have to be at a meeting in a few minutes?" she asked as she walked past where he'd set up on the couch, the boys at his side.

"Forty-five minutes. It'll take four minutes to get there. I'd rather be here with you three." He held up the mug of hot cocoa she'd made him when they'd gotten up.

"Okay then. We like you around too. But there are three shifters on the front lawn so maybe go say hello before they start looking in the windows. We don't want a repeat of *that*."

Damon laughed with glee at that memory. "Well, now they know why I adore you so much."

She snorted on her way past to get dressed for work. Living together, even in their snug little house, was working surprisingly well. He did his own thing. She did her own thing and at the end of the day they came back together. He picked up after himself, brought home groceries and put out so much body heat she was sure they'd save money on wood to heat the place at night.

However, there were always shifters around. They patrolled around the land, which was nice, though an alpha werewolf shared her bed so it wasn't like she had many safety worries. Still, they were social. And they needed the contact and connection with Damon and now her.

The new house would be three times the size and had a lot more space outside to accommodate all the wolves who liked to cruise by just to say hey.

And the master suite would have better window coverings so the shifters who just wanted to pop by and say hey wouldn't catch Ruby and Damon naked and working hard to make one another climax.

She got ready for work quickly and was out the door with the dogs within half an hour though it was hard to leave a still-sleep-sweet werewolf who looked so damned sexy behind.

Damon rolled into the meeting and grabbed the pot of coffee for a top-up. Not as good as the brew Ruby made for him every morning, but if he had to spend hours with these numb nuts, he needed to stay awake.

He should have brought the boys along. They'd love all the attention after they got past the fear of a room full of shifters. And they would. They were small but tenacious and fairly easygoing once they knew they were safe.

But his missus took them to work so he'd save it for another day.

"Morning, all," he said to the group assembled. That day was just the top leadership from each pack. Jace, Major, Damon, Mac, Huston and Everett so at least it wasn't a crowd of shifters he'd have to try not to punch.

Between the six of them, they could be honest because they all shared the same goals to modernize the
laws and move the packs into the current era.

"Morning," Major called back.

Mac looked pretty good for a man who had a bunch
of trouble on his hands. Then again, as a guy who also
probably looked good because of the love of a pretty
witch, Damon got why.

"Let's get straight to the point because I have a very
full day," Jace said as Damon took his seat and Everett
came in to join them all.

Jace said, "We've handed issues of territory and re-
source usage and fees to be paid into the unified fund
to take care of our folks. The last issue remaining is the
eradication of the Rule of Silence."

"We're taking a pack vote on it next week," Mac
told them.

"And what? You can fuck around and waste more
time?" Damon asked.

"There's a process. You know that as well as I do,"
Mac said. "We've done everything the way we needed
to. Step by step."

"And step by step your mother and aunt and their old
lady mafia have used the rules to hold you up. Hold everyone up with their rule manipulation. They're using
the process to shut you up and shut you down."

"This obsession with the old ways is just a front anyway," Major said. "What? You really think that's their
true motivation? Come on. Scarlett is a lot of things, but
scared? She's never been against change of pack rules
and yet suddenly this is an issue? To this extent after
all the discussion?"

"I've talked to these older wolves and it's a real worry for them," Huston said.

Damon rolled his eyes. "No denying it's effective to manipulate the older, most suspicious wolves. They're afraid of the outside world and change and Mary is playing that tune. She's even better than your mother at using people's fear to get them to do what she wants. For years we barely hear a peep from Mary and now all of a sudden she's what? A warrior for tradition? Bullshit. But it can't just be spite because of whatever boner they have for the Dooleys."

"I don't give a fart in a high wind what she is at this point other than the fact that she's manipulating this process to slow it down because she doesn't have the support she needs if the full pack votes," Everett said, surprising everyone at the table. "Y'all think it's rough for Dooleys? This shit is dividing Pembry families."

In order to finally abolish the Rule of Silence, *both* packs had to vote to do so. Pack power structure was based on laws. It's what kept them safe and undiscovered while witches were being drowned and burned. But their governmental process came in steps. Each with myriad rules and customs.

Each time the Rule of Silence came up for a vote, a small group of Pembry wolves found an administrative way to slow things down, demanding yet another layer of voting and hearings. They'd dragged what should have been a sixty-day process into nearly ten months. If it wasn't such an outrageous pain in the ass, Damon would admire the skill they showed.

"I don't like your mother yanking my chain for her personal kicks," Jace said to Mac.

His brother was normally more patient, especially

since in truth it wasn't about Mac but werewolves being assholes for whatever reason other than the fact that they all loved to fuck with one another for fun.

"I don't like it either. And it's not just her. But I've done all I can at this point given the way the rules are set up. They've got one more meeting to fuck up. That's the one next week. Then we'll finally be able to schedule an all-pack meeting. We'll do a roll call vote for the entire body and then they'll lose. And then we'll do what needs doing. And they'll whine, but every last rule was obeyed and the change cannot be challenged. We win in the end and there won't be any more kids growing up like you three did." Mac ran his hands through his hair, as frustrated as everyone else.

"That why you let me overhear that conversation you had with your aunt Mary the other day?" Damon asked him.

Mac allowed a ghost of a smile before he shrugged. "Don't know what you mean. Did you listen in on a private conversation?"

"If you wanted it to be private you don't have it on the middle of the sidewalk in broad daylight," Damon said with a smirk. "In any case, we appreciate your efforts on this. And we have our own small group of wolves very resistant to change. Thankfully smaller than yours and they're afraid of my grandparents so that helps. Your grandma Rebecca is fucking scary as hell, why haven't you had her putting your mother and her sister down?"

"They already hate one another so there's no real leverage. Plus, to be honest, my grandmother has been pretty effective chipping away at their base quietly and ferociously."

They dealt with the remaining few small issues and

within an hour, they were breaking free to get to their own workdays.

Mac called out to Damon on the street outside. "Congratulations once again. I didn't get much of a chance to visit with you at the party the other night. You two are good. You can see it."

"Thank you. You too, man."

"And thank you for understanding this isn't about me personally, or even Pembry."

"If anyone on earth understands you can't blame the actions of the father or mother on the sons or daughters, it's me. I get it. I see you and the work you've done. I know your heart and it's in the right place."

Mac clapped his shoulder. "I needed to hear that today."

"Say hey to Aimee for me," Damon said with a wave as he headed toward work.

The dogs were tuckered out from all the hugs, snuggles and games of fetch they'd played on and off for hours. They'd been little loaves of sleeping fur when she'd pulled up outside her grandparents' place but once she turned the car off and opened the door they'd scented Lovie and perked up.

"Yes, yes, she's right inside. Let's go in and deliver our treats and you can give her kisses."

By the time Ruby got them and the pink bakery box out of the car, Lovie and Pops had come out.

"I had to make a run down to Gatlinburg so I stopped by a bakery and picked you both up some maple bars. Pecan sticky buns too." Ruby wanted to keep an eye on them both. They were precious to her and getting older and she knew her Pops had a serious love for pecan sticky buns. Plus, though Lovie hadn't repeated her late-night adventures, it didn't hurt to give a quick look at the warding and other protective spells to be sure they were all still working fine.

"Aw, you sure do spoil us," Lovie said as they went into the house.

"You deserve it. I didn't get much of a chance to visit with you the other night at the dance so the boys and I thought we'd stop by to get some love and drop off sugar and fat."

"We're always pleased to see you. Especially when something tasty to eat is involved," her grandfather said.

She made them all a pot of tea while her grandmother set out a few plates for the sweets. As she did, Ruby told them about her day and the people she'd visited with and how the dogs were so good and full of love for her patients.

They sat together in that cozy, beautifully familiar kitchen and had a sweet treat while they talked about wedding details, which made Ruby gladder that she'd stopped by and that she'd agreed to the wedding her family had desired for her and for them.

"It's not about a church. Or that we don't consider you and Damon married without it. It's about generations of Thorne witches who've married in that very place. There will be handkerchiefs my grandmother embroidered tucked into your sleeve and bouquet. Same as I did. And your mom and aunts. Tradition and ritual are important. Old magic. Strong. Now more than ever, we need magic like this. It's our shield."

"And a way to reinforce our family ties. Losing your aunt, uncle and cousins was hard. Broke our hearts. But you returned to us and now you have Damon and you're building a future. You and he will make Diablo Lake better for your kids and their kids too," Pops told Ruby.

Ruby explained the pack induction they were having for her that week to her grandparents.

"As far as their law is concerned, Damon and I are married. But this induction ceremony will bring me into the pack, protected by them. It's a pretty good deal for me. There are rules I'll have to obey and all, but not as exhaustive as what applies to Damon. Our kids will be considered pack whether they're witches or shifters. It's nice that they've got that birthright protected."

"Kids? Are you in a family way?" Lovie asked.

Ruby struggled not to laugh. "No. It'll happen in due time. But we've both got things to get done first."

"Don't wait too long. I want to be around for my great-grandbabies."

"Lovie, don't talk that way. You're going to be around a long time more. Long enough to hold lots more babies on your lap."

Her grandmother waved a hand. "I'm just saying."

Ruby visited awhile longer as she surreptitiously gauged both her grandparents' health. Satisfied they were doing fine and full emotionally from a lovely time, she headed out.

Katie Faith had texted to ask if she and a few others could come over so Ruby figured she'd meet them all at the house. Thinking it'd be her friends come over to gossip and hang out, she whipped up some snacks and brewed fresh iced tea. It was still too early for wine, though she could probably be convinced it was five somewhere because Katie Faith was the best kind of bad influence.

But when her friend showed up, it was with Patty,

Alice, Deidre and Carmen. Not the crew she'd been expecting at all.

Still, she quite liked them all so she opened the door and invited them in.

"Hello, sweetheart," Deidre said. "Thanks so much for having us." She handed Ruby a thick manila envelope. "Pictures of Annie. When I started looking I found lots of great ones I think the boys will like."

"Thank you so much." Ruby placed the envelope in her desk so Damon wouldn't wander across the photos and ruin her surprise.

They settled in her living room with refreshments.

"We thought you might like it if we gave a quick rundown of what to expect tomorrow at the pack induction ceremony," Katie Faith said.

"The first time Dooley inducted someone from outside the pack was two generations ago. Before that, if a shifter married a nonshifter they were considered an associate member. Which led later on to a perception that associate members weren't as good as the rest. And the children who came from those unions had an uncertain place. The purpose of pack is unity. That is not unity," Patty explained. "So we decided on an induction ceremony that brings a nonshifter into the pack as a full member. Difference here is special and wonderful and it makes the pack better and stronger."

"We view the induction as a way for nonshifters to be fully Dooley," Katie Faith said. "You're already Damon's wife. The pack knows this and I think you can feel that."

Ruby nodded. She truly did. Each day since Halloween, Ruby had woken up with a connection to the pack that seemed to get stronger and clearer. She already wanted to take care of people in Diablo Lake and the imprint with Damon had reinforced that. His wolves were hers too.

But this was saying she was the pack's. Which was a whole new way to view it. Ruby smiled at the other women in the room because they'd helped her understand that too.

"Tomorrow night, you'll take the same oath Katie Faith did and then you'll be taken to the heart of Dooley out in the forest to complete the ceremony. There's a little blood involved and magic I expect you'll connect with right off as Katie Faith did. As I'm sure Aimee will when she and Mac marry and she'll officially join Pembry." Patty patted Ruby's knee. "This is all wonderful. We're absolutely thrilled to have you with us."

"And Damon. Lord knows that boy needs all the people in his corner. People see the looks and forget he's a whole person. You see Damon's heart." Deidre grinned. "I've known him since before he was born and he has such a big, giving heart. You see it. You understand it and value it. That's real love, Ruby."

Love swamped her at the gesture these women, these elders, had brought to Ruby's doorstep.

"I can't thank you enough for this," Ruby told them. She did feel better now that she had a little more information. Less nervous about the unknown. More loved and trusted.

Accepted.

Chapter Twenty-Two

Damon stood at Ruby's side, her hand tucked in his as the entire pack welcomed her into its ranks. She exuded magic. It flowed from her outward, over the assembled shifters. Her scent rose and the loam was more prevalent than it had been even just that morning.

Katie Faith's magic rose as well, swirling with Ruby's. The pack as a whole seemed to breathe in deep, relishing that heady mixture.

And because his hand was in hers, that energy rushed through his body like a caress.

Jace spoke the words in a language older than most others. A language the first wolf shifters spoke before they came to the new world.

A call and response welcoming her, honoring her and making a place just for her shape. The ties between him and Ruby glittered and the joy he tasted was hers thrummed up his spine.

When it was finished, before they took their form as wolf, they turned their faces upward and howled with joy.

And they weren't alone, Ruby too howled.

Shortly after that, she sat astride his back as he ran as wolf. Made sure to take paths to keep her safely in place. Wolf would protect her at all costs, their beautiful, magical mate who brought so much delight to their lives and strength to their pack.

Ruby was drunk on wonder. The entire evening had been fantastic. Full of not just her own magic but awash with pack magic, the energy of the shift between forms and natures.

The melodic and yet sharp-edged language Jace had used and the pack had responded back with had been part of her wonder. A gift to hear something so few ever had before.

When she'd howled with them, they'd responded with joy. Oh, sure, there'd been a few who hadn't been as enamored of Ruby's union with Damon. Some didn't like witches. Those who felt like enough had been lost when Katie Faith joined with Jace. And some, well, those folks didn't like witches too much and they liked Black people who were witches even less.

She'd work to change the minds of the former, but the latter? There were those who would never let go of their ignorance. Ruby didn't bother wasting her time on lost causes, choosing to focus on things worth fighting for.

Damon shifted back to his human and delightfully naked form. Turned out that having grown up in Diablo Lake had left her with a very easygoing attitude about nudity.

"This place is the heart of Dooley. JJ calls it our nature den. Our magic is strong in this spot. The shift is very easy here."

"I will protect the heart of Dooley," she told him and the rest of the wolves. She raised her hands to command attention and remind herself to speak clearly with focus on the elements of the spell.

Fill the space between us all with kindness, compassion and trust.

Skin and fur, finger and claw, nothing malicious to befall.

Protect the heart, feed the head, honor and trust keep this pack in their stead.

Cleanse and purify this pack to dispel any negativity.

Blessings upon you all.

So mote it be.

She put her hands down and the magics that'd been swirling all around them surrounded her, binding her not only to Damon but the pack as well in a way that didn't entirely have to do with him.

Pack magic had let her in, considered her pack as well.

She knew to her bones that they understood she could be trusted with their lives and their well-being. It settled on her shoulders, in her heart and belly. A warm, comfortable weight.

Chapter Twenty-Three

Despite the fact that Scarlett had wasted more time and stalled a full pack vote one last time as predicted, Aimee and Mac's wedding day came and the town seemed ready to celebrate.

"After all these parties and holidays and weddings and stuff, we need to sleep for a week," Ruby told Damon after she put her lipstick on. She'd spent the morning with Aimee and Katie Faith, hanging out, day drinking and mentally getting ready for the wedding. She was very calm and seemed so ready to be finally married to the man she loved.

Ruby had come back home just a little before Damon had returned from working on the new house.

"We get a honeymoon. I say we take our honeymoon somewhere very sunny and warm," he said, getting close enough that the warmth of his body and his scent, sexy werewolf always ready to fuck, hit her and brought a moan to her lips.

Ruby put her palms on his chest, smoothing down the front of his white dress shirt. "Get back or we'll never leave the house."

"That's bad why? I can't remember. Could be because my brain is starved of oxygen since all my blood is currently in my cock."

She laughed, always delighted by her man.

"Because she's one of my closest friends and there'll only be twenty people at the ceremony so people would notice if we weren't there. However." She reached down and squeezed the aforementioned cock. "This will still be available for my enjoyment later tonight after all the festivities."

"Have I told you lately that you're my favorite person?" He flashed that grin that always got her tingly.

"Never hurts to hear such a declaration from a man such as yourself."

He kissed her but once he had two handsful of her ass, she broke things off because she knew how quickly that heated up to the point where all her hard work on hair and makeup would get ruined.

Always enjoyable, but she really didn't want to miss Aimee and Mac's intimate ceremony in the garden at Miz Rose's place and she'd happily get sweaty and naked with him later. It was one of her favorite activities and Damon was an exceptional craftsman when it came to pleasure.

Just two days before they'd been at a massive Thanksgiving dinner. Thornes, Dooleys, Pembrys and all and sundry in between had feasted, visited, gotten to know one another better, reconnected and enjoyed what had turned out to be a clear but crisp late-fall afternoon. She had such a fantastic day around all her favorite people.

Home. Every new day, every sweet moment, each new experience and thing she'd learned about herself or someone else, Ruby was more at ease. Magic, hers and the pack's, seemed to live in her veins.

"Come on then, Ruby darlin', if you won't let me sully you, let's go to a wedding."

Damon was so proud to have Ruby on his arm it wasn't even funny. She looked absolutely gorgeous in a deep blue dress with yellow swirly things at the neck. Whatever jewelry she wore always seemed to complement her outfit. Big and chunky or delicate, she was a beautiful canvas.

She smelled even better than the garden, which had been transformed into an intimate wedding venue for Aimee and Mac.

This, Aimee had told them, was about their closest friends and family. A quiet time to celebrate. In a few hours, the whole town would show up to party on the closed down Diablo Lake Ave to eat, drink and be merry.

As they came around a large fountain, Aimee caught sight of Ruby and came over to hug them.

"You're not supposed to be out here! You're supposed to surprise the groom or whatever," Damon said. "But you sure do look pretty."

She wore a slim, cream-colored dress with lace sleeves. The skirt ended at mid-calf. Her hair had been braided into a crown and red roses were tucked here and there.

Aimee's smile went up a few watts at the compliment. "Thank you, Damon. I'm not surprising Mac. He and I know who the other is. We're walking down the aisle together. But speaking of pretty, you two are just gorgeous. Today is such a happy day and everyone looks lovely." She indicated the small crowd assembled in the garden.

"Can I help with anything?" Ruby asked.

"You just spent hours with me doing things and helping. It's all done. You two sit down. We're starting shortly. Thank you both so much for being here on this best day of my life." Aimee hugged Ruby again.

"Love you so much." They hugged one more time and Aimee scurried away toward where Damon had heard Mac's voice.

And that's when Damon saw Dwayne Pembry seated at the front with Scarlett. Ruby must have as well because she made an unhappy sound but then straightened her back and led him to their seats just across the aisle.

It was Aimee's day and he knew Ruby would never do anything that endangered her friend's happiness.

But he knew Dwayne's attention was on them both so Damon did what werewolves did best. He shined Dwayne on, acting as if the other shifter didn't even exist. There was no moment of detente between two pack leaders. Damon had no respect for Dwayne. He was a poor leader. A poor father. A shitty, selfish person.

Damon on the other hand still ran a pack with his brothers. He was young and strong and smart. So much smarter than a wolf like Dwayne was even capable of understanding.

And because Ruby was so clever, she noted what Damon was up to and mirrored his actions. Neither of them giving one iota of attention to either Scarlett or Dwayne Pembry. Hell, Damon wondered why Dwayne was even there. He'd done damage to Aimee. On purpose.

* * *

Aimee and Mac didn't have any attendants. No fanfare other than the violin and cello playing "Wedding March." They needed none because when Aimee and Mac walked down the aisle together, they practically glowed with love and Ruby was really glad she'd tucked a handkerchief into her purse so her lashes would stay on.

Aimee's dad, the chief of police in town, performed the ceremony but after the necessaries were handled, Aimee and Mac spoke.

"Macrae Pembry came over to my house one evening in April and he looked so serious. For a moment I thought he was going to dump me or that he was sick. But he opened up his palm and on it rested a ring." Aimee held her hand up. "This one. He said his grandmother had given him the ring in February and it had been burning a hole in his pocket until he thought I was finally ready for him to ask me to marry him. He thinks I didn't notice that he'd been patient, waiting for me to be comfortable enough to say yes, even though my heart knew he was it for me long, long before he asked. He even waited for late November to get married so my brother could be here. Mac is my always and forever."

Mac brushed his thumb over Aimee's cheek. "Thank God. You're it for me. I knew it about ten minutes after we shared that first secret kiss. Your heart is bigger than anyone's I know. You're kind of random and don't always pay any mind to making sure your sentences have a point. But I love you like crazy and I will continue to do so until the sun burns out."

There was some pledging and stuff, a kiss, a pronouncement of marriage and several more kisses until they turned to the guests who blew bubbles and threw rose petals over the newlyweds as they walked past.

There was champagne to share so they moved into the garden house, a glass building they often held Consort meetings in.

"I've never been in here," Damon murmured.

"Isn't it beautiful? Miz Rose is a wonder in the garden. This space always soothes me. I used to do my homework in here when it was too noisy or chaotic at home." There were water features in here as well so the sound was merry and the rhythm always wiped away anxiety or hurt feelings.

They visited with Aimee's parents and her brother, who'd come to town from his home in North Carolina, and Katie Faith's parents as well. She accepted their congratulations on her own marriage and promises to be at the church wedding the next month.

"I'm glad we had this private ceremony. Just a quiet celebration that's all me and Mac," Aimee told them. "And I'm so glad you get to be here." She and Ruby hugged.

"Your love for one another shines." Ruby indicated Mac, who stood speaking with his parents.

"He's more than I ever expected." Aimee's goofy smile made Ruby swoon. So beautiful to see her friend blissfully happy.

"Y'all deserve each other. In a good way."

"And now you have Damon and Katie Faith has Jace and it's just, it's a wonderful thing that we all have something this important and full of joy."

"Agreed." Ruby's gaze darted over to where Mac

spoke to Dwayne and Scarlett. "Everything else all right?"

Aimee rolled her eyes. "As all right as it can be."

"All righty then, Ms. Mayor. You let me know if anyone's ass needs kicking, all right?"

Aimee giggled. "Y'all are the best. So far, everyone is behaving as promised. Let's just continue to hope that stays the course."

They stayed until the end of the champagne hour and told Aimee they'd see her on the Ave in less than an hour.

"Are you more excited or less about our wedding?" Damon asked her as they walked back to the car.

"I've been thinking a lot about ceremonies and what they mean. We're already married. I've just felt that to my toes after Halloween night. And after the induction I certainly feel like I'm a member of Dooley and our connection comes via you. I learned a lot from that process. Your grandmother's assistance was so helpful and important in letting me understand why and how things were done. So I do feel like I'll learn things from our second wedding too. It's not about feeling married. Like I said, I already do. It's about ritual. And ceremony. It's all part of making our bond stronger and better. Keeping it healthy."

"I never thought about it like that. I like that you did though." Damon opened her car door and helped her up and once she was in the seat, he leaned in to kiss her slow and very thoroughly.

She held his face in her hands and kissed his nose. "I love you, Damon. I'm so very glad to be yours."

His eyes filled with so much emotion it nearly stole her breath.

"You are the best thing in the world, Ruby darlin'. I love you too. I can't wait to marry you again next month. And then I can't wait to have a few months of quiet after that."

Chapter Twenty-Four

"I lugged those boxes into the spare room like you asked," Damon told her when she got home from work that evening.

"Thank you." He knew she was making a photo book for her family with pictures and things from her aunt, but he didn't know she was doing the same for him and his brothers. He'd gone with her to pick the boxes up from where they'd been stored at her parents' house.

"I need to run." He kissed her quickly. "We're laying floors tonight. I think we'll be ready to move in before Yule. I'll take the boys with me if you like. They always behave and they like being around shifters."

They heard him talking about them and tappy tapped all over the place, vibrating with excitement, trying hard not to bark.

"I think that's an unqualified *Mom can we please hang out with Dad and our uncles* reaction." Ruby bent to give them both some love, pleased with how well they'd all taken to one another.

He left shortly thereafter with a flurry of noise and activity and she was blissfully alone in the quiet. She put on some music and after changing her clothes, she headed into the spare room.

Her aunt Charlene had kept journals since she'd been a teen and when Ruby began to page through them, she found poems, snippets of song lyrics and recipes.

Charli had been a bright, sunny light and the loss of her, Ruby's uncle Chester and her two cousins had been a blow not just to the family, but the town they were such a strong part of. Ruby missed them every day and she knew her family had as well.

Then there were photo albums. Each one she pulled from boxes and opened up had been another step into her past. Another block in the foundation of her family's history. Naturally each photo had been labeled on the back with the people, places and year taken.

Ruby pulled out the photos she needed and marked the pages of poetry and recipes she'd include. A few years back at an art fair, Ruby had seen cutting boards with recipes burned into the wood in the handwriting of the original recipe writer. She'd tucked it aside in her brain, pretty sure she'd use it at some point in the future and here it was, that opportunity. She knew for sure her mom and grandmother would really love it.

She'd save some of the journal stories to give to people individually in private. Ruby wouldn't share anything that was an intimate detail. She made it a point not to read further once she'd discovered an entry that was very personal. She didn't want to embarrass anyone, or betray a confidence. But she knew these pieces of her aunt would be cherished by those who loved her.

It was bittersweet. Ruby's aunt had been the one to teach her how to roller-skate. Ruby learned to make candles at her kitchen counter. Death was another state of existence, but it was so hard for those left behind.

Ruby blew her nose and dried her tears before she

went to grab something for the crying headache she was sure to have later. And opened another several boxes, each full of delightful memories.

And in one of the last boxes, there was a great deal of correspondence. Cards and letters for holidays and birthdays. Her congratulations cards from after the birth of her children. Letters she'd written back and forth with Ruby's mom while her aunt and uncle traveled.

The love letters from her uncle Chester, Ruby placed aside, unlooked at. Those two had a love Ruby had recognized as always and forever. They'd been together and yet wholly themselves. They'd chosen one another and it had shone from them. She'd been lucky to have grown up with so many positive examples of successful, working relationships.

Another bundle, bound with a ratty rubber band, was in the bottom and she pulled it free to see they were all unopened. Five in all. From Mary Rodgers. Scarlett's younger sister.

What the hell?

She got up and went to make a cup of tea. It'd warm her up and give her a task her hands knew well so she could think a bit.

Boxes of effects and many cards and letters and they'd all been opened but the envelopes in her hand. Why? If they hadn't been important in some way, why keep them for over twenty years? And if they had been important why not open them?

Ruby tap, tap, tapped the envelopes against the counter as she thought and fought with herself. Would it be an invasion of privacy if she read them? After all, she'd skipped through anything in the journals that had looked intimate or sex related or anything of the sort. And the envelopes were closed for a reason.

She needed advice, plain and simple, so she grabbed her coat, scribbled a note to Damon that she was going over to her mom's and would be back shortly and headed to the door.

And on her doorstep stood her dad.

"Hey, baby. Did I catch you at a bad time?"

"Not at all. In fact your being here right this moment is absolutely perfect. Come in, I need some advice."

He hugged her on his way past and then hung up both their coats.

"Everything all right?" her dad asked. "Are things okay between you and Damon?"

"Nothing like that, I promise. Things are great between me and Damon. And in general as it happens. It's one of those moral quandary–type situations. Come through to the kitchen for a cup of tea and some cinnamon apple cake and I'll explain."

"Ooh, cake," he said with pleasure and she knew it was the exact right thing that it was him rather than her mom to give her advice.

"I suppose I should have asked you if everything was okay," she called over her shoulder as she got them both big squares of the apple cake. "I wasn't expecting to find you on my doorstep. Though I'm sure glad to see you."

"I just dropped some bags of soil over at Lovie's and when I saw the lights on here, I knew I needed to stop in."

A wave of affection hit her. "Your gut is never wrong, Dad."

When she brought the tea over and settled in once again, she drew out the bundle of letters. "I've been going through some of Auntie Charlene's photos, journals and recipe books. Don't tell anyone but I'm making a present for Mom and Lovie. You know how Charli was, she kept so much. But in these keepsake boxes, everything had some meaning. And then in the bottom of one of them I found these. Unopened. From Mary Rodgers."

Her father gave her a look and then one down to the envelopes. "Back when we were all a lot younger, Mary and your aunt were friends. This was before you were born but we had Greg."

"What happened to end the friendship?"

"I don't know. They were friends and then they weren't. I figured your aunt finally learned Mary was two-faced and got herself free. Charlene always was too nice. But once she was done, she was done. She never brought it up and I never asked. But why not just open the letters and see what they are yourself?"

"That's what I need the advice on. It feels like an invasion of privacy maybe? Aunt Charlene never said anything so that was on purpose. Maybe she doesn't want them to be read. Maybe I'm not the person to open them."

But there was something driving her. Something told her she was supposed to open them but it was hard to know if it was just nosiness or something more.

"Ruby, Charli loved you and all these keepsake boxes of her things would have come to you anyway. You're that person in the family." Her dad shrugged. "If she hadn't wanted those letters opened, why keep them? Why keep them with the pictures and journals and the like? She wanted them found and knowing Charlene, she had a reason for you to be the one to do it. You said yourself everything else in those boxes had a reason.

Why would the letters be any different? Anyway, if it's something you know she wouldn't want anyone to see, you can shred them yourself."

"Will you stay while I read them?"

"Sure will. I bet you have something good to eat in here. Let me call your momma to let her know where I am then I'll make us both a snack." Even though he'd just eaten a giant slice of cake. Goodness she loved her dad.

She wasn't hungry really, but she'd happily have him in her kitchen as she dealt with ghosts of the past.

Thirty minutes later, she'd finished reading the letters twice and she knew why Scarlett and Mary didn't want the ending of the Rule of Silence to be applied retroactively.

"This one," she held it up as she spoke to her father, "isn't from Mary even though it's her return address on the outside. It's from Scarlett."

Charlene,

You have no call to keep upsetting Mary the way you have. If you can't be her friend and protect her, keep your mouth shut and never contact her again.

Let the past go. Mind your business and focus on taking care of your family and your career. Those boys are better off and they aren't worth the damage you'd do to yourself over this.

Protect yours and I'll protect mine, Charlene. Don't be a problem.

Scarlett

"Well now." Her dad plopped down into the seat across from her. "Sounds like a threat. Why don't you fill me in on the rest?"

"Hang on a moment," Ruby told him as she got up from the table. She needed to center herself to process everything she'd just discovered.

She lit a candle and on the way back to the table picked up two shot glasses and pulled vodka from the freezer.

Her dad looked at the booze and back to her. "When does Damon get home? Do you want to wait to talk to him?"

"Well." She poured them both a shot and then took it. "I think this is related to whatever it was that Josiah Dooley did. Which means he's not supposed to talk about it under the Rule of Silence. The same one Mary and Scarlett have been trying to stop."

She took another shot. "For that matter, *I'm* not supposed to I guess, since they inducted me into the pack."

"Bullshit," her dad said, bringing a welcome laugh from her. He pointed at the letters. "Charli kept them for a reason. They came to you because she wanted someone to know at some point. That's a different sort of promise and it weighs more. I do understand your wanting to think awhile on what to tell Damon about all this. So let me be your person to talk to about it all."

"Thank you." Ruby got up to hug him and he did the same. There was nothing in her life like her dad telling her things would be okay and to trust him to help. "Okay so all the letters are dated in the months before Damon's father was sentenced. Which is relevant because apparently Mary and Josiah Dooley had an affair. Looks like it'd been going on for over a year and Charli didn't approve. Mind you this was one-sided so I don't know the whole story. There was something she was covering up, or lying about and I think it has to do with Josiah and whatever he got punished for."

"But no specifics on what?"

Ruby shook her head. "No. Like I said, it's just whatever Mary is reacting to."

"You said you had Charlene's journals here?"

"You're so smart. Yes, in the spare room. She even has the covers dated."

An hour later Ruby once again found her world turned on its head.

"Dad, I think I have to tell Damon about this. There's no way I can keep it from him. He needs to know."

"I think so too. I know you're worried about what to do and say but I'm not. You love him and you'll find a way to protect him. I have every confidence in you. These secrets are poisonous. Enough people have been hurt."

"Damon and his brothers had grown up weighted down by other people's secrets. At the same time, when this comes out there'll be collateral damage. Aimee and Mac will face leadership challenges. And horrible or not, Scarlett is his mother. Mary is his aunt. It's all exhausting. On the other hand, Damon, Major and Jace had lost a parent, the only one they'd had left, and it looked like Scarlett and her sister might be why.

"Most of all though, I know without a doubt that no matter how frustrated Damon is with the speed of this process to get rid of the Rule of Silence, he's dedicated to his pack. He leads by example so if this does come out, I can't let him be responsible for any part of it. The letters and journals aren't wolf business. They're mine to do with what I want."

Her dad patted her shoulder. "I'm going to head home because you need to think a bit on your own before Damon gets back. Just remember the difference between what's legal or fair and what is just. Act accordingly. We both know you were raised right."

Damon came home sometime after eleven, tired and sore but pleased they'd been able to get so much work done. The dogs ran into the house where his beautiful witch sat on the couch with a fire burning merrily.

"Hey, boys. I missed you. All of you. Did you have fun with Daddy?" she asked as K Mags scampered up the ramp to the couch with Biscuit close behind. "So many kisses. Oh my!"

Damon grinned at the sight but something wasn't entirely right with Ruby.

"Have you eaten?" she asked, extricating herself from dogs and the blanket to stand.

He breathed her in as she moved into his arms. "We had a dinner break at eight so I could stand to eat. But first tell me what's wrong." Damon kissed her temple and she snuggled into his arms a moment before she broke free.

"Dinner first. Then I'll tell you. I'm sure the boys are tuckered out after having a fun night with you all but I could be persuaded to provide a bedtime snack for them too."

She put together a meal as he noted the half-empty vodka bottle and two glasses. The only other recent scent he picked up was of her father.

"You and your dad been doing some drinking? Ruby darlin', please share."

"I'm going to share with you but before I do understand I spent a lot of time today working through whether or not I should. And decided I needed to. Just trust me to hit the high notes and then I'll come back to details as needed."

"I do trust you," he told her. And it was surely true but he was not looking forward to whatever she had to say.

"Today I went through my aunt's stuff and I found some letters which led me to some journal entries. Your father and Mary Rodgers had an affair. Lasted a little over a year from what I can tell. During that time she helped him embezzle money from Pembry coffers. There's also evidence he stole from Dooley."

Damon continued to eat as he processed. "No one gets executed and stricken from existence for embezzlement. And since Mary is still around and appears unpunished, I'm guessing she lied in some way to save herself. It's hard to know about what because the charges are sealed as well."

"Damon, are you glad I told you? I wrestled so hard with everything. My dad was such a great sounding board. He said at the end to know the difference between what's legal and what's justice and to choose the right one. I know this knowledge is forbidden to you by pack law, but damn it, I will not have you hurt by these poisonous secrets any longer. And this didn't come from a pack source at all. This came from my aunt's journals and letters from Mary. The one from Scarlett sounds like a threat to me. Charli never even opened them but that's not to say she never felt threat-ened. I don't know why she kept them. It's not like she knew what they said. But like Lovie, she had the gift of seeing. She wanted them to come to light someday."

"Jesus." He ran his hands through his hair. "Yes. I'm glad you told me. Glad you felt I could trust you, because I do. I'm grateful you got such fine advice from your daddy. I can't deny having this information come from an outside source is helpful. I think you're most likely right that Scarlett was part of this and that's why she has, what you so delightfully called, a hate boner for our family. Though why she fuckin' should when the only person responsible for any of this is dead is confusing."

He got up and began to pace.

"I just don't know how to deal with the knowledge."

"Fair enough on an emotional level. But as for the practical issue of how and when to reveal, the actual reveal part will come from me," Ruby said and he heard the steel in her tone.

"That's absolutely not what's going to happen." As it happened, Damon had plenty of his own steel and not putting Ruby in the cross fire of the bomb about to detonate was plenty reason to push back. "These are creatures that tend to throw fists when they get pissed. I'm built for that. Hell, darlin', I excel at that. But you don't."

She huffed out a frustrated breath he found adorable though he had no plans to say so aloud.

"Listen here, Damon Dooley. I don't need to excel at punching or what have you. I have skills of my own and also several large alpha wolf shifters who'll protect me from any danger. You're pack leadership. You're the law. This has to come from me. An outsider. I can act as an advocate for you. And for the pack in general. You let the blame fall on me, do you understand?"

"Do you think I'm so weak I'd let you stand between me and responsibility?"

Ruby waved a hand. "Quit it. That's not what this is and you know it. You're just fighting because you're a control freak and this whole thing has been out of your control your entire life."

All the annoyance ran from him because she was right. Damn it.

"This is a lot. I know it. And I know you've struggled with this way longer than I have. Let me protect you for a change. Let me protect Jace and Major. It's an echo of your job, can't you see that? You and I are both protecting the pack, just differently."

"Why are you being so stubborn?"

"This is nothing. You can't win here. Pretty as you are, sweet as you are. I'm ruthless when it comes to people I love. And that's you. And you know I'm right and you're just arguing for form's sake and that's a waste of time we could be sexing it up."

"Did you just use sex to get me to end an argument?"

She stood with a smirk and headed out of the room toward the bedroom. "I'll just be in here. Naked and lonely."

"You don't fight fair," he told her, following that delicious scent of her arousal.

"Not when it comes to you," she said and a bra landed on his shoulder after she tossed it over her shoulder.

"Holy shit," Katie Faith said after they'd laid out everything they knew so far the following morning. "I didn't have any of this on my bingo card. I admit I wondered if Scarlett and your dad had something but she and Dwayne have always been so solid and I heard they had an imprint."

Ruby and Damon had discussed if they should tell his brothers and in the end, they'd felt it was necessary. *Discussed* was a nice word for the terse argument they'd had, but he'd seen reason.

"We told you because we didn't think it was right that we were making decisions about what to do with this information without your input," Damon said.

"I'm the one breaking the law. If there are consequences I'm going to shoulder them," Ruby announced and Damon sighed deeply.

"How about no?" Jace scoffed. "This is my pack. I'll shoulder responsibility."

"We went over this already," Ruby said. "This needs to be done but if there's blowback, I'm the best person to bear it. You and Katie Faith are Patron. Major and Damon are your seconds. I'm a new member. Easier to forgive. Certainly easier to deal with any punishment because the rules will go lighter on me than any of you. For you it's fatal."

"This isn't political. It's our life," Jace growled and Damon growled back in defense of Ruby.

"Oh you two, stop," Katie Faith said. "It's both. It's political because of who we are in the pack. There's no avoiding that. Ruby's right to understand that and thank goodness for her. And it's personal because you and your brothers have suffered while Scarlett made it worse. When it sure as hell looks like she was part of a lie that caused all this to start with."

Major nodded. "My beautiful sisters-in-law are right. There are some old laws that allow for the appointment of an advocate. Let me read up on that so we have all the info we need going into the next meeting."

"And we'll come up with a few different plans on how to deal with whatever that meeting throws at us," Damon said as he took Ruby's hand.

Chapter Twenty-Five

An all-pack meeting happened twice a year. In the spring and in the fall. Rarely was one as important as this.

After a year of delays and use of governance rules to tie the process into knots to prevent an outcome, it was time for all the wolf shifters in Diablo Lake to cast a vote on whether or not to end the Rule of Silence, applied retroactively.

There were so many shifters in attendance they needed to hold the meeting outside on the football field at the school where the bleachers could take the capacity.

Ruby couldn't tell Aimee and Mac about the letters and journal entries in advance, but she and Katie Faith had agreed that they didn't want their friends to be blindsided by the information when it came out at the meeting. So Ruby made copies of them and dropped them off sealed in an envelope directing Aimee not to open until an hour before the meeting and to make sure she was alone or only with Mac when she did.

They didn't want to tell everything at the meeting. Yes, the truth needed to be figured out and heard but if the packs voted to do the right thing, it could come out later on a smaller scale. Ruby and the others didn't want to create more scandal or potential for pain.

As much as they all wanted to hold Scarlett and her sister to account for whatever had happened, it wasn't necessary to humiliate anyone else to make it happen. Not unless there was no other choice.

"Why hello there, Ruby," Major said with an easy smile when she came into the store looking for Damon.

"Hey, Major. You doing okay?"

"Yeah. Relieved this is finally happening after all these years. It's been a long time coming. You're doing such a good thing for us. For Damon and me and the pack. You're tough enough to do what needs doing. Like an alpha does. My grandparents have had to shoulder a lot of pain over the years because of this. You're freeing them from that. I'll never forget that."

She hugged him.

"We all ready to head over to the meeting now?" Ruby asked. "Where's Damon?"

"He just called before you got here. He's running behind so he'll meet us there."

The crowd milled around chatting as she and Major walked through. "I haven't been here since high school graduation," Ruby said. "Still smells the same. Only with a hundred percent more wolf."

"Let's go find Damon and see where we need to be seated," Major said as he guided them both through the crowd, shielding her with his body.

"You've got to be kidding me," Major said as he pulled her to a halt. "What is he doing here?"

Ruby craned her neck to see what had Major so upset and caught sight of smug fuckface Dwayne Pembry wearing a sticker on his chest that declared him as a visitor.

"Visitor my ass," Major growled. "What the fuck is he doing here? He has no official permission or we'd have known in advance."

"Scarlett. She did this on purpose. It's another delay tactic."

And indeed as more and more people came through the gate and headed to the bleachers, the din got louder. Ruby and Major weren't the only ones pissed off that Dwayne was there.

"Makes Mac look weak. He's spent all his time, blood and effort to rebuild Pembry after years of bad leadership and this? Under his nose?"

His own mother had a part in destabilizing Mac's leadership. Ruby ached for what he had to be feeling. Or would when he showed up.

Ruby looked around and saw Aimee and Mac coming through a different gate. When she saw Ruby, she gave heart hands and mouthed *thank you*. Relief washed through her that their friendship hadn't been hurt by Ruby not telling them until that day.

And then she and Mac jolted to a stop when they too saw who was sitting at Scarlett's side.

Damon made his way over and put his arm around Ruby's shoulder. "That sneaky asshole," he said, tipping his head toward Dwayne, who along with his visitor badge wore a smirk on his face. Like he was still in charge of a pack he'd lost a year before.

The noise level continued to rise, shifters whipping one another up as they reacted with anxiety over tension in the leadership ranks.

Katie Faith yelled at people to calm down and be

quiet so the meeting could start but each time things started to get calm, someone else would start in again and others would follow. Like barking dogs in a neighborhood.

Ruby marched over to the makeshift stage and took the mic from the stand. "Y'all close your mouths and sit down! How many times are you going to let some dramatics get you to take your attention off the purpose of these meetings because some folks don't want to lose, even fairly."

Jace cracked a grin for a millisecond before he took the microphone. "Not that y'all aren't captivating and such, but I'd rather not be out here on a cold December day wasting time. If we're all gonna argue, let's do it the way we're supposed to. This has dragged on long enough."

"I move that we postpone the vote on this incredibly important issue until after the new year when the pack is whole," Scarlett said.

"Second," Mary called out.

Ruby lasered her gaze on Mary Rodgers.

"No need to call for a vote," Mac said. "You don't have the standing to make that motion. The time for that has passed. As we've discussed."

Scarlett wasn't done. "You sent him away from Diablo Lake and want to take a vote like this? How does that reform him? He's doing his sentence but I don't think you have the right to take away his place in this pack."

"As it happens," Mac said through a very tight jaw, "I do have that right. He hasn't completed his sentence and you brought him here. I'll deal with that later. But right now we will not entertain a motion to delay this vote again. Your magic hat is empty. No more tricks."

"A majority of Pembry can vote to overrule you," Scarlett said, turning her appeal to the shifters in the bleachers.

"You'd need to get nine out of ten members to back you." Mac turned to the crowd. "By a show of hands then. Who'd vote with the former Patron?"

A smattering of raised arms, not even five percent much less ninety.

Ruby knew at that point that there was no way Scarlett was going to do the right thing. She'd keep delaying and fucking people over as long as she could to protect herself and her sister. It was time that ended.

Ruby stood, taking the microphone once more. "I move *gravis instans*."

Aimee seconded. Jace was the voice from Dooley agreeing.

Major had spent some time looking through pack law to figure out a way for Ruby to take the floor on business that was of grave, immediate importance to the pack.

"Earlier this week I came upon evidence that a crime happened and though I've been waiting for the parties involved to speak up and do the right thing, it's become clear to me they will not. And so, I will because it's long past time."

"Sit down. This has nothing to do with you," Mary yelled. Scarlett added her agreement, both understanding something was about happen that would end their little fantasy of halting this change forever.

"It has everything to do with you though, Mary. And you, Scarlett. You could use this moment and unburden yourselves. For not just your own good, but the good of the wolves you claim to care so much about. You were Patron, Scarlett, you know what it means to lead. Do it now. It's not too late," Ruby urged.

Suddenly there was an outraged growl and another, far more scary one and a big thump. Damon had been at her side one moment and the next he had Mary Rodgers on the ground, his knees on her arms to hold her in place.

"You can't do that!" Scarlett screamed as Dwayne held her back from the fray.

"He can and he beat me to it," Mac told his mother. "She attacked a nonshifter. A pack member who is under our protection. It was Damon's right to stop that attack not just as the enforcer for Dooley, but as Ruby's husband. Have you lost all your sense?"

"What on earth is happening?" Dwayne asked his wife.

"You've been carrying this weight for decades. How many more people will get hurt before it's over? Tell us what happened with Josiah," Ruby urged.

"Josiah Dooley was found guilty of embezzlement of nearly two hundred thousand dollars from both his own pack and Pembry," Scarlett finally said. "That's what happened."

"And two cases of assault against two different male relatives of a woman he'd been sleeping with," Mary added, the fire still there in her tone but not quite as bright.

"While all those things are bad, none of them would earn not just a death sentence, but a total excision of their existence," Jace said.

"What do you know of any of this?" Mary demanded.

Ruby told the crowd about the letters and journal entries and what they'd been able to piece together regarding Josiah's sentence and crime.

"As you can hear, the information came from outside sources. None of them beholden to pack law," Damon said.

"She is though! As your wife, Ruby is breaking the law just talking about this," Scarlett said.

"I'll compare this to lying to get someone executed to avoid being caught out having an affair. What say you, Mary? You think my speaking of letters and journal entries about something you did is as bad as what you actually did? Let's let the packs decide. Why don't you share what it is you lied about to get a man killed? It's over. The packs are going to vote to end this law and it'll all come out anyway."

"The extenuating charges were drug dealing to minors and sexual coercion," JJ called out. "Mary had toddlers. She claimed Josiah had given them drugs. Drugs she said he'd been dealing to middle and high schoolers. She said he tricked her into helping him steal money from Pembry and that she'd only been with him under duress. They also claimed a niece of theirs had been given heroin by Josiah and he forced her to take it. I'm sorry to say Josiah had enough of a reputation that it really wasn't that hard for people to believe it."

"I put myself in danger to come forward with that information and now you want to make me the bad guy?" Mary asked.

"I knew she was stealing," Scarlett said, defeated but relief also tinged her voice. "But her kids were little. It was a mistake. And he led her into so much trouble.

He was destined for death or prison or whatever. Why should she have to pay for his crimes?"

"She didn't. He could have gone down for the embezzlement. Been banned and sent away from Diablo Lake for good. But you and she made up a plan to make sure he'd die and never expose her complicity. So she could keep on living her life, looking down her nose at Dooleys for years. She learned nothing. And you helped hurt so many people."

"She's my little sister. He was the problem."

"I call for a full vote to end the Rule of Silence, applied retroactively," Aimee called out.

Later that night, after everyone had gone home to process everything that had happened that day, Ruby and Damon lay on an air mattress in the new house. It was chilly but the dogs napped close by and zipped into a sleeping bag with a wolf shifter kept her plenty warm.

"Heat should be up and working by Wednesday," he said, reading her thoughts.

"I love this house already."

"It feels like home already. Sorry you're going to have to move out after moving in just a few months ago," he said, kissing the top of her head.

"Are you all right? It's been a day."

He turned into her body and let her hold him close.

"It's not that I ever thought he was a saint. I guess, well I guess I figured one day I'd find out what happened and it would make sense. It does on some levels. And I expect after some time, most of it will. All of it was just so unnecessary. Scarlett's blaming me and my brothers because she was a horrible person to protect her sister? Who, by the way, is worse than Scarlett and that says a lot. It doesn't change what happened."

"No it doesn't. But it changes how you feel about it. Because it's not some dark secret only hinted at. Not some information that people can use to hurt you and your family because of their own inefficiencies. No one gets to hold this over you again. You're free to process it and learn from it and then to set it aside. It's your truth now. In your hands. Fuck all the people who spent over two decades trying to hurt you with it while denying it to you."

"I love scary Ruby. Today you were fucking magnificent. You were an alpha witch. You showed more compassion than most people deserved. But in doing so, the whole pack could understand you and your motivation."

"I love you. I'm so glad you trusted me with this. And let me be at your side," she told him, kissing his forehead.

"Tomorrow is a new day I get to love you. And I mean that metaphorically as well," he said, making her laugh.

Epilogue

"I'm so glad it's snowing," Damon said to Major. "Ruby's been all wistfully hoping for a snowy wedding day. I'm agnostic on that subject but I'm a fervent believer in anything that'll make my pretty witch happy."

"Oh lord the two of you." Major rolled his eyes.

"I know. We're insufferably in love. I'd be sick of us too." Damon sent his brother a smug smile.

"It's snowing!" Ruby bounded into their new kitchen and headed straight to the windows over the sink.

"Even nature wants to please you, Ruby darlin'," Damon told her.

"Gosh, I sure wish we were getting married today," she teased. "Wait. We are!"

He got up to hug her because what else was there to do with this beautiful creature in his kitchen? "We are at long last."

"Long last." She rolled her eyes. "It really hasn't been that long."

"This is a milestone. It feels like after today our life begins in a new way. Your family will be pleased. My family is already pleased. It's all good."

"You're totally right," she said, kissing him quickly.

"Morning, Major," she called out heading to the coffeepot. "Anyone need a top-up?"

She brought the pot over and warmed his and Major's cups up. "Thank you, Ruby," Major said.

They'd moved into the new house just two weeks before that and it had been Ruby who'd suggested having Major live with them until his house was finished. His brother stayed there a few nights a week but also continued living out of the apartment above the Mercantile to be close to Jace and Katie Faith.

Things were changing. Their family was growing. The future was full of hope and possibility. And Ruby was at the heart of it all. His own personal miracle.

Living with a witch during Yule had been an education. Ruby had included him in as many rituals and ceremonies as he wanted to be part of. The house was already decorated with greens and reds and blues and silvers and golds. Sprigs of holly and other greenery decorated spots the dogs couldn't get to.

The house smelled fucking awesome all the time. Not just her roses and jasmine, but the freshness of the green things she used in her tinctures, the lush, rich scent of the coconut oil she used in her hair.

In short, living with Ruby was the best thing that'd ever happened to him. She looked good, smelled good and threw off magic like catnip. Perfection.

"What are you two up to this fine day? Other than dressing up and being in a wedding in three hours, that is." She grabbed a ham biscuit Major had brought over and hummed after taking a bite. "Nichole is going to be here shortly to pick me up. I'm getting ready at the church so I'll see you both there."

"We're going to check out the reception space, make

sure things are set up on the way over. Jace has been supervising; Greg called earlier when you were in the shower to say all the food was ready and your folks and my grandparents are on that part," Damon assured her.

Ruby said, "My aunts and cousins are at the church dealing with the flowers. They said it was their gift to me to let me have one less thing on my to-do list."

Her family had been such a wonderful addition to his life. Once they'd imprinted, the Thornes had pulled him into their large, loud ranks. Full of love and security. The more time he spent around them, the more he understood Ruby and why she was as wonderful as she was.

That and Arthur, her grandfather, invited Damon and Major to come hang out and drink bourbon laced with coffee while they let him win at dominoes. It had been a great way to get to know one another separate from interactions with Ruby.

When the time came, he knew they'd raise their children knowing how much they were loved and valued for their uniqueness. They'd be shown what it meant to be part of a community that took care of their own.

Nichole showed up as Ruby was rinsing out her coffee cup. The dogs adored Ruby's best friend and sister-in-law. They heard the sound of her voice and came running through the house to her.

"I have the most handsome little tuxedos for you two," Nichole told the dogs as she kissed the tops of their little heads.

Damon cringed inwardly at outfits for dogs, but Ruby loved dressing them up. He knew he'd never deny her the pleasure and the boys always acted so proud and pleased to be wearing this or that shirt or sweater or whatever, he knew there was no reason to say a damned thing about it.

"Can you bring them to the church about twenty minutes before the ceremony starts?" Nichole asked Damon.

"Sure thing."

Ruby came in, dress bag over her arm. He helped her out to Nichole's vehicle, loading a box with cosmetics and what all else she'd need to get ready. He heard the telltale clink of bottles as he put things in her trunk.

"Sounds alcoholic," he murmured.

"Any legitimate excuse for day drinking is one I'm taking, Damon. Like y'all won't be drinking that rotgut shifter booze?" Ruby asked.

"Only once we're at the reception. I can't take the risk of fucking up at the ceremony. Afterward, well, everyone knows how much wolves love a party." He waggled his brows her way. He got close to whisper in her ear. "Don't worry, I'll still be plenty capable to celebrate when we're alone tonight."

Her delighted giggle lightened his entire being. And that's what she did for him. Every day.

"Good. Got to pay your keep. I'll see you in a bit. I love you."

He kissed her. "Love you too. See you at the wedding."

Ruby looked at her reflection in the long mirror on the back of the door. She'd tried on a few white dresses but none of them had been the right one. And on the way out of the last dress shop she saw a sunny yellow dress tucked at the back of a plus-size sale rack.

A-line. Floor length. Long sleeved off the shoulder.

When she walked, the pleating of the skirt swirled all around her legs.

Her hair had been dressed into an updo with braids and pretty little tendrils here and there. Instead of a veil, she chose to have jeweled pins tucked into her hair. Her earrings, gold chandeliers, belonged to Lovie's mother and every bride since then had worn them on her wedding day.

She felt absolutely beautiful. Ethereal as she moved and the dress seemed to caress her legs.

"That yellow makes you look like a gorgeous sunny day," Nichole said as she finished zipping up the back.

Until she'd bought that dress, she'd had an idea to have a Yule theme. Snow and lights and shiny things. But the dress had changed things.

Instead of a winter wonderland, she'd chosen instead to look forward to spring with yellows and lilacs and the occasional splash of pink. And her mother, the queen she was, had managed to track down all the flowers she wanted and had managed to get them with a discount.

She only had one attendant, Nichole. And Major would stand up for Damon. The ceremony itself wasn't as small or intimate as Aimee's was, but they weren't throwing a reception for the whole town either. It just felt like it.

Still, who didn't like a party? And it was even better when it was your party.

Her mom came by with her aunts. They all looked so lovely and tears pricked her eyes.

"You nervous?" Her mom kissed Ruby's cheek.

"Not really. I mean, we're already married. We already live in the same house. This is a happy ritual and after this we'll eat and drink and have a great time. But

I'm already his wife. He's already my husband. I can't wait to see him all gussied up in a tux though."

"Is he still clueless about the dress?" her aunt Rita asked.

"Yup. He's got no idea." He didn't know about the color scheme at the church either. Not that she figured he would be upset in any way. Damon just didn't care. If it made her happy, he supported it.

The dogs showed up and Nichole got them all suited up. Aimee took them out to walk down the aisle with Damon.

"You ready?" her dad asked as he tapped on the door and poked his head in. But when he caught sight of Ruby he sucked in a breath. "Oh my lord, baby, you're perfect."

He came over and hugged her tight.

"Everyone is ready and in place. I can certainly see you are. Your momma and I are so proud. So pleased you found someone like Damon to share your life with. Let's go walk you down the aisle."

Her mom took one arm and her dad the other. Nichole went ahead of them and gave the organist the sign to get things started.

Damon thought he was prepared but nothing could have prepared him for the church full of bright spring flowers and his Ruby darlin', walking down the aisle in a sunflower yellow dress that seemed to float all around her legs.

At Ruby's insistence, they'd removed anything she found objectionable from the ceremony. No one was giving her away as, "I can give my own damned self.

I've not been a kid for years now." There were no sexist, one-sided demands.

"Who stands witness to this union between Ruby and Damon?" the pastor asked when Ruby and her parents finally arrived at the front of the church.

"Her father and I do," Anita said.

"Damon's grandmother and I do," JJ said.

She hadn't told him they'd be doing that and Damon was glad no one could see how choked up he was as he ducked his head.

Damon held a hand out and Ruby placed hers in it. That zing, always there, jumped back and forth between them for a few dizzying moments before calming down.

"You look like a goddess. My goddess," he told her.

She smoothed a hand down his lapels. "You were made for a tuxedo. Is this a rental or did you buy it?" Like they were just hanging out having a chat instead of in front of a hundred people getting married.

"Damn, I love you," he said.

"I love you too. You wanna get married?"

He nodded. "Let's do that. I'm hungry and there's plenty of food waiting at the reception."

They promised to love, honor and cherish. They promised to protect and provide for in good times and bad. Honestly, Damon thought it was all a blur. But what he knew would stay in his memories forever was the way her entire being lit up when he pulled out a ring.

The imprint had been sudden and not expected, so he hadn't had a ring ready. But in the nearly two months since, he'd scoured a few different websites looking for the exact ring. It had been on the day she'd found her wedding dress that he'd found the ring at a little store in Knoxville.

Woven silver and gold band with a simple diamond in the center. He knew she worked with her hands all day long and didn't want anything too big or fragile. She wanted simple and sturdy. But the ring he found was elegant too. Classic.

And her face as she saw it for the first time told him she loved it as much as he hoped she would.

Then there were kisses and proclamations of marriage and after what seemed like ten years to get out of the church, they headed to the reception in the attached multipurpose room. There was a patio just beyond should anyone want to go outside to get air.

The food, provided food truck style, was served by Greg and her cousins so Nichole could do her maid of honor duties better.

He got pulled into dozens of hugs. People kept pressing money into his hands and telling him he married up. He knew that was really true.

There were toasts and the cake was cut after dinner and finally they reached the first dance. He spun her around, their gazes locked. Love flowed from her and he soaked it up like a sponge.

"You're such a badass," he said.

"I am? I mean, I know I am," she teased, "but what do you mean specifically?"

"Years and years chipping away at the Rule of Silence and you come in, kick a door down, shout in Scarlett and Mary's face and send them packing with their tails between their legs."

Mac's reaction to the information had been fairly quick and very decisive. He'd cut Mary and his mother out of the pack. Removed their membership and the protection of the pack. And because Dwayne came back to town without permission, he'd done the same to his father. He even took away the house Scarlett and Dwayne would be living in.

Damon knew that had to have been incredibly difficult. They were still his parents, after all. But they'd damaged Pembry so severely, Mac had no other choice.

And truth be told, Diablo Lake felt a lot less claustrophobic and negative without Scarlett prowling around trying to start a fight.

"I did it because it was the right thing to do. And there's irony in the fact that it was Mary's own words that damned her in the end. They can fuck off a pier, Damon Dooley. Diablo Lake has better things to do."

"You protected me like a warrior."

"That's what people do, Damon."

He shook his head. "It's what people should do. But you know as well as I do, they sometimes don't."

Ruby shook her head then. "I can't erase all the times people failed you and your brothers in the past. But I can do my best to make it better now. I'm your shield. You're mine. You awakened a whole new side to me."

"I love all your sides, Ruby darlin'."

* * * * *